"Diva."

The two identical AIs looked at each other, both calling out simultaneously.

CONTENTS

VIVY
Prototype

NOVEL

4

WRITTEN BY
Tappei Nagatsuki
Eiji Umehara

ILLUSTRATED BY
loundraw

Airship

Seven Seas Entertainment

VIVY prototype volume 4

© Tappei Nagatsuki 2021 © Eiji Umehara 2021
Originally published in Japan in 2021 by
MAG Garden Corporation, TOKYO
English translation rights arranged through
TOHAN CORPORATION, Tokyo

Seven Seas press and purchase enquiries can be sent to
Marketing Manager Lianne Sentar at press@gomanga.com.
Information regarding the distribution and purchase of
digital editions is available from Digital Manager CK Russell
at digital@gomanga.com.

Follow Seven Seas Entertainment online at
sevenseasentertainment.com.

TRANSLATION: Jordan Taylor
ADAPTATION: Leigh Teetzel
COVER DESIGN: Nicky Lim
INTERIOR LAYOUT & DESIGN: Clay Gardner
COPY EDITOR: Dayna Abel
PROOFREADER: Jade Gardner
LIGHT NOVEL EDITOR: T. Anne
PREPRESS TECHNICIAN: Melanie Ujimori, Jules Valera
PRODUCTION MANAGER: Lissa Pattillo
EDITOR-IN-CHIEF: Julie Davis
ASSOCIATE PUBLISHER: Adam Arnold
PUBLISHER: Jason DeAngelis

ISBN: 978-1-68579-647-1
Printed in Canada
First Printing: June 2023
10 9 8 7 6 5 4 3 2 1

Prologue

VIVY'S CONSCIOUSNESS went blank when her eye cameras focused on the sight in front of her.

"..."

Heavy clouds hung in the sky, blocking light from the streets. The air was damp and bitterly cold, and Vivy's sensors picked up a mix of particulate matter suspended within it.

These external factors weren't enough to explain Vivy's consciousness freezing, especially when she hadn't expected to wake ever again.

She and Matsumoto had completed the Singularity Project, though it was hard to say how successful they'd been. At each Singularity Point, they'd repeatedly found themselves at the mercy of situations drastically different from what the historical records showed. As a result, their planned modifications of the Singularity Points didn't come together as they hoped during the planning stages. Even so, they did manage to modify the Singularity Points into something that could be called "close enough." Then they confirmed the Singularity Project was complete.

Vivy had awoken once after that for something unrelated to the Project, but that too was resolved. Her frame was thereafter returned to the songstress Diva as planned, then gifted to an AI museum, as it had been in the original history. All that remained was to wait as time passed.

Why then, did Vivy awaken yet again?

Vivy brought a hand to her ear and confirmed that she was unable to contact Matsumoto. "Transmission interference," she said to herself.

Static reminiscent of a sandstorm had swallowed up her transmission circuit, meaning the transmission environment was as bad as it could be. To make matters worse, the noise outside the museum made it apparent how chaotic things were. Ultimately, Vivy's logical standards wouldn't let her describe what she heard as mere "noise."

She was still in her—or rather Diva's—display room in the AI museum. *Something* had reached all the way here to the Sisters exhibition room, so it must've been deafening.

Peeking through the exit, Vivy discovered the source of the sound: a congregation of humanoid AIs walking in perfect unison below the ashen sky. The marching AIs filled the road and the sidewalks in front of the deserted museum.

"…"

In the past, corporations had held events where they assembled their AI models and put them on parade. Even NiaLand had a show like that, though it wasn't on this scale. However, the parade Vivy saw now had no corporations or even humans behind it.

How did she know that?

Because all the marching AIs were engaged in the same action.

Their voices overlapped as they sang, not quite in sync and not quite in tune. The song was so loud that it rumbled through the streets like an earthquake, reverberating in the bodies of all who heard it. And as the AIs sang, they marched on.

There was so much a songstress AI could nitpick about those reverberating voices, but only one thing set Vivy's consciousness aflame once she looked past the performers' skills. The lyrics, the melody... every single component of the song was stored in Vivy's memory—as it should've been. The song was a poor attempt at composition by none other than Vivy—one she offered to Diva, her other half.

"What's going on?" she murmured.

The AIs continued their march, belting out her crude song, and there was nothing resembling a corporate strategy in that. If humans were to look upon this display with artistic sensibilities in mind, they would've deemed it to be in very poor taste.

There was one thing Vivy could say for sure: No human was involved in this. Everything there was the result of calculations by bloodless, inorganic beings with bodies of cold, hard steel.

"…"

Still unable to reach Matsumoto, Vivy was all alone. Thankfully, the AIs were so focused on moving and singing that they didn't appear to notice her. They paid no heed to her presence, raising their voices in a chorus that drowned out everything else.

Vivy was still processing the situation as she circled around the back of the museum and left. She had no grasp of what was going on, but she had gleaned *something* from witnessing the affair.

"The Singularity Project isn't over."

The future she had tried to avoid—the era in which AIs and humans destroyed each other—had arrived. She thought they'd prevented it, so why was she active again?

There was only one answer. Her frame, her positronic brain, and her path up until now determined that she must not give up on correcting history, not until the very end.

CHAPTER 1

The Songstress and Her Captive Audience

. : 1 : .

ONE LITTLE SPARK had led to Matsumoto Osamu's career in AI research.

It happened more than forty years ago, when he was around ten years old. He had toured an AI museum as part of a field trip. At that time, schooling was wildly different than it had been a few decades earlier. The very concept of "school" was a relic of the past. The once-compulsory curriculum switched to independent online learning, so school only existed in the dusty memories of elderly folk reminiscing about a bygone era. New ways of living pushed out the old as the online education system was established and the standard of living improved. People no longer thought about school-centric education, and they certainly never talked about "going to school."

But even as time marched on, some customs from the past lingered. Young Matsumoto's field trip was one of them. Field trips were held twice a month and provided an opportunity for children to interact with their peers, since they could no longer do so in schools. It was supposedly to teach them the importance of communication.

However, this system was largely influenced by the motivation of whoever was in charge on a municipal level. Some organizers took the lazy way out and brought all the kids together in one place, had them chat for an hour, and then sent them on their way. Many of the quieter children saw these gatherings as an annoyance and favored the less motivated organizers. Plenty of organizers slowly lost the will to make any effort, resulting in a vicious cycle wherein they defaulted to the activities they'd always done.

While that preface was rather long, this was the educational environment of the time. Despite that, the organizer in charge of young Matsumoto's district was one of those rare individuals on the verge of extinction whose passionate and unwavering educational ideals were unmatched.

Although the majority of these field trips were handled with very little care, this particular organizer got permission to take the children on a tour of the AI museum. He took a group of fifty students, ranging in age from six to fifteen years old. This clearly showed his dedication, as he looked after all those children nearly on his own.

"Why do you bother trying so hard?"

In spite of his impassioned efforts—and the fact that he'd hardly slept while planning the event—the students' reactions to the tour were incredibly harsh. Their malicious whisperings hurt the young man, especially considering they didn't yet know how to be considerate of someone else's feelings.

Honestly, young Matsumoto felt the same as the other children. Even if it *was* a world-class AI museum, everything in it looked like junk to an uninterested child. There was nothing exciting about AIs—they were everywhere.

Back then, you would see AIs of all shapes and sizes simply by going for a walk. It was the golden age of AIs, and they'd seeped into every conceivable aspect of life. Why, then, would anyone think people living in such a world would have fun looking at outdated relics? Young Matsumoto was often told to respect history, but *he* thought the outdated history should respect the new age and make way for it. It didn't matter what the truth was—the newer thing always won against the older thing. There was no way such a widely held system of values was going to break down.

He never imagined in even his wildest dreams that those values would be completely dismantled by a single AI's song.

"I am a songstress AI, Model Number A-03, designated name Diva. I will now sing for you."

ıtı||||ıtı

The AI who introduced herself as Diva raised her voice in brilliant song.

The stage was bad. It was hardly ideal for someone who called herself a songstress.

The location was bad. The audio equipment didn't suit her skill.

The audience was bad. Most of the students had zero interest in her music.

The maintenance was bad. The museum's inexperienced engineer hadn't been able to bring Diva's voice back to what it was in her heyday.

Only two people in the audience listened to her song until the end, their faces a mess of snot and tears: the young organizer who had arranged the trip and Matsumoto Osamu.

Young Matsumoto was so embarrassed by his hitching sobs and runny nose that he wanted to die. Thankfully, while the other children were shrinking back from him and his disgusting appearance, he only saw them twice a month at most. It was a tenuous relationship, and his embarrassment was only momentary. It was nothing compared to the excited thrumming of his heart.

"Thank you for your kind attention," Diva said as she bowed, wrapping up the performance.

She must have said that phrase hundreds, thousands, tens of thousands of times. Still, young Matsumoto couldn't describe the emotions that hit him the moment she spoke. Before he realized it, he was applauding so vigorously his hands turned red. They hurt so much the next day, he couldn't move them.

Until that moment, he'd been living his life aimlessly, going with the flow without sparing a thought for the future.

He chose his own path right then and there: joining the field of AI research.

.: 2 :.

AFTER THAT, young Matsumoto worked so diligently he barely had time to rest. In the past, they would've said he was "stuck to his desk," but these days they usually said he was "practically swallowing his tablet." He worked hard, not wasting a single second that could be spent learning. He pursued his goal so relentlessly that it seemed like he'd been swapped out for someone else.

"I can't believe how much you've changed. And looks like my taste hasn't gone out the window yet," Ootake Masatsugu, the man who organized the museum trip, said when Matsumoto's grades improved drastically.

Later on, when Matsumoto became renowned for his AI research, he would consistently bring up Ootake as one of the most influential people in his life. He said that if it weren't for Ootake, he never would have become an AI researcher and all his published papers would have remained unfinished.

Matsumoto Osamu was driven as he chased his dreams with constant gratitude toward his former teacher.

"Good day. Thank you for visiting again, Matsumoto-sama," said Diva with a smile when he stopped by the museum. The emotions he'd felt that day when he heard Diva sing had never faded, and he'd come back several times since his first visit. Those feelings propelled his ambition.

He claimed his visits were part of his AI research and that it was helpful to analyze the operation logs and calculation patterns

of an AI who had been functioning for a long time. More specifi-
cally, it was helpful to speak with Diva.

Unfortunately, Diva didn't sing for him too often. In the end,
her role in the museum was to explain the importance of her history as the oldest remaining songstress. She only took the stage a
couple of times a year at most. Matsumoto never failed to attend
those few performances. He listened to every single one.

Some might've thought his actions were driven by the blind
passion of a lover, but what he felt for her was never untoward.
She was something more, something almost holy to him.

It was hell pursuing his dreams the way he did, but it was also
a blessing. The long path seemed even more hellish if he considered he might never make it, or thought of the studying and luck
he would need to make it where he wanted to go. But there was
passion in his heart as he walked that path—and a yearning.

That was a blessing, and it was Diva who gave it to him.

"Diva, can I ask you not to be so formal with me?"

"Why?"

"You used to interact differently with each person when you
were at NiaLand."

"Yes, I did. Did you research me?"

"Uh... Does that make you uncomfortable?"

"No, not really. AIs like me aren't equipped with sensors
capable of feeling physiological discomfort."

"Right... But that comment seemed iffy."

"And about your question... Okay. As you request, Matsumoto-
sama."

"Really? Good, so now—"

"Yes, starting next time." She paused. "Just kidding, *Matsumoto*."

"Oh, thank you. That's one of my dreams come true!"

"Dreams?"

"Please don't laugh, but...ever since I saw you onstage in this museum ten years ago, I've always dreamt of us being friends."

Matsumoto Osamu's days continued after that, once he and Diva were officially friends. He kept going back to the museum and studying so hard it almost felt like he was chipping away at his life span. He moved down the path he'd laid out for himself, walking forward as an AI researcher.

Those around him recognized his passion, and some even praised him as the field's beacon of hope, an up-and-comer with a bright future. He accepted this evaluation without conceit and poured a lifelong love and respect for AIs into his research, making every iota of passion count for something.

Or so he'd planned, but those plans collapsed several years after he became a researcher.

It was a very simple thing that happened.

He married, and he had a daughter.

.: 3 :.

THE WOMAN WHO became his wife had a deep under-standing of Matsumoto's AI research. That was no surprise, considering she was the curator of the AI museum—that was where they met, since he continued to visit even after becoming a researcher. They immediately hit it off because she already had a thorough understanding of AIs. The pair chatted naturally at the museum after their first meeting, their relationship blossoming into romance.

Matsumoto gave it his full consideration, then asked her to marry him. As luck would have it, his deliberation wasn't in vain. She said yes, and the two got engaged without a hitch.

"Congratulations, Matsumoto. I wish you both happiness," said Diva when he told her about the upcoming wedding.

It was a simple thing, but it made Matsumoto extremely happy. He resisted the urge to ask her to attend the wedding, or even to take an honored role at the celebration and sing for them. He decided it would be inappropriate.

Even after the wedding, Matsumoto dedicated himself to his work, laboring day in and day out. There were plenty of days when he was barely at home, but his wife kept spoiling him, saying things like, "I knew what I was getting into when I married an AI researcher."

But his ability to get away with ignoring his family disappeared about three years after they were married.

"I'm pregnant. You're going to have a daughter."

When he heard his wife's news, Matsumoto's knees gave out and he cried for the first time since he was a child.

Becoming a father was beyond what he'd ever imagined. Even being married felt so distant that it was like a dream within a dream. It was incredibly strange how these things—events normal people could only picture happening—kept coming true for him, one after another. In all honesty, part of him was afraid. He wondered if the scales would eventually tip and something horrible would happen.

Those nebulous worries disappeared the moment he held his newborn daughter in his arms for the first time. He cradled the new life against him as she cried her eyes out.

They named her Matsumoto Luna.

He loved his cranky little girl. He also realized a significant barrier had appeared, blocking his path as an AI researcher—the same path he had devoted his entire life to as a boy and then again as a man. It was Luna, his own beloved daughter.

Could he place the dream he'd had since boyhood above the tiny child he cherished? Matsumoto had just become a father and had no answer to that question.

The birth of that small and irreplaceable person shook the foundation of Matsumoto's life. Even though the word "family" had remained elusive after he married his wife, the meaning of it became very clear once his daughter was born.

When Matsumoto was young, he didn't like his father much because the man was always working and never took him out to have fun. Now that he was in the same position, he understood how his father must've felt. Surely his father had loved his family in his own way.

With that realization, Matsumoto again set his heart on working—this time for his family's sake.

His wife never fully recovered from the strain of childbirth, and she passed away just one month later.

.:4:.

MATSUMOTO FELT LIKE his soul had been torn out when he looked upon his wife's beautiful face in the hospital. Even as a corpse, she was as gorgeous as ever. She looked like she was sleeping, so much so that there was a faint flicker of hope that she would wake if he called to her or gently shook her shoulder.

He shook her. He called her name. She didn't wake. It was no use.

" . . . "

She'd never even complained about feeling unwell. Maybe she couldn't say it when she saw Matsumoto rejoice at the birth of his daughter and throw himself headlong into his work. Perhaps even she had been unaware of the poor condition of her body.

Either way, one thing was true: His wife was gone forever.

He held the funeral in grim solemnity with his infant daughter in his arms.

A void opened in his empty heart, and he decided to ease his pain by burying himself in his everyday life as he had before. The only difference was that he had his daughter now.

He'd lost a wife and gained a daughter, and you might expect that to drastically change his life, but it didn't. He simply put some housekeeping AIs in charge of the chores his wife had done and assigned them to look after his daughter. He barely even went back home. The man tried to hide from his sorrows through work; indeed, that was probably how people interpreted his actions at the time. Matsumoto didn't think that they were entirely wrong, but he was also aware of a clearer reason for his actions.

He was afraid to face the new life who would also one day leave him.

After the funeral was over, he only took the briefest time off work. His peers didn't rush him and insisted he could take several days off if he wanted.

So he did. He took some time and spent those days thinking. What came to him then was the full weight of the pain and loss one felt when death cleaved two loved ones apart.

His former teacher and inspiration, Ootake Masatsugu, had also died young in an accident. At that time, Matsumoto had felt a great loss and regret at being unable to pay Ootake back for everything he'd done. Now his wife had died as well, tearing open the wounds he'd tried to ignore. This pain was sharper, deeper, and it made his gouged and bleeding heart scream.

Every time he faced that pain and blood, the same thing came to his mind: his fear of losing his daughter, the person he would have the most difficulty moving on without.

His mind was gripped by paranoia, as pathetic as it may sound for an AI researcher and world-class academic to indulge in that sort of thing. He was under the delusion that the more he loved something, the quicker it would be taken from him. The average person would laugh at such a delusion, but it had a tight hold on him and it wouldn't let go.

His fear spurred him to deploy multiple housekeeping AIs to look after his daughter while he chose to keep his distance.

He still lived in the same house. He did see his daughter. If he had time, they even ate together.

But he would not get close to her.

"Daddy, read me a book!"

Sorry. Daddy's busy. Another time.

"Daddy, it's Parents' Day in class. Will you come?"

Sorry. I'm really busy with work... I'll go next time, I promise.

"Dad, I have a career counseling appointment. You're coming, right?"

You've got your head on straight; you don't need me. I'll contact your teacher.

"You probably don't care, but I want to go to college."

You can choose whatever path you want. I have money saved up, so don't worry about that.

Matsumoto was a horrible father when it came to fulfilling his daughter's needs. He could almost count the number of times he'd done as she wished on one hand, and those few instances didn't even stick out in his memory.

His daughter grew from a baby into a toddler, from a toddler into a little girl, from a little girl into a woman, and he wasn't even paying attention. She looked more and more like her late mother as she grew, which was one of the reasons Matsumoto distanced himself from her.

It wasn't that he didn't love her. It wasn't that he had no interest in her. He was just afraid fate would take her away from him if he kept her by his side. The void in his heart never filled. The wounds from losing his wife and his teacher remained forever. And if he was unlucky, he would surely lose his daughter as well.

That line of thought made Matsumoto devote himself even *more* to AI research after his wife's death. At some point, he even stopped going to the museum, giving up on his conversations with Diva. He wasn't rejecting Diva. In fact, AIs were his only salvation. No matter how strong his feelings were toward AIs, no matter how much he loved them, they never responded in any way that wasn't asked of them.

Most importantly, an AI could be brought back if he lost it.

Obviously, it was nearly impossible to recreate a positronic brain, but AIs were capable of producing a good enough imitation for humans as long as all their data was transferred. He knew it was foolish, but that thought saved him.

And so, Matsumoto asked for very little—only that his good health continue.

When he looked in the mirror, there was no sign left of the passionate young man once touted as a genius, known throughout the field of AI research. All that looked back at him now was a middle-aged man whose heart had broken in the face of reality.

He scrubbed his hands through his white hair, his cheeks pulled back in a self-degrading sneer. Yet he told himself things were fine the way they were. Instead of asking for lots of things, he just prayed that the few things he *did* ask for would be given to him.

But his fragile, fleeting hope was shattered.

"Dad, I'm going into AI research just like you."

Yes, it was shattered so easily by Luna, her expression serious as she told him.

.:5:.

"I WAS RAISED by AIs."

That was not a sarcastic statement. It was the truth of Matsumoto Luna's life.

She stood at the podium, holding her speech notes as she delivered the words with poise. Matsumoto Osamu stared at her through the video screen, his blank eyes half-closed.

Five years had passed since Luna told him about becoming an AI researcher. When she made the declaration to take the same path as her father, he responded with confused silence, then shouted at her, saying he disapproved of the decision. That was followed by a noisy fight between them, the father-daughter argument practically shaking the rafters of the Matsumoto house. It was the first argument ever in their twenty-year father-daughter relationship; then again, it was questionable whether or not what they had could be called a "father-daughter relationship."

They were related by blood, true, but wasn't it also true that his relationship with his daughter was so weak they were practically strangers living under the same roof?

That was what *he* had wanted. He had made it so.

Thus, he reflexively opposed the idea of his daughter following in his footsteps. He'd stayed away from her so they wouldn't grow close, and now it seemed like it was all for nothing.

While her father was shouting emotionally charged rebuttals, Luna kept her words clear and sharp. "I was raised by AIs! I want to return the favor!" she yelled, tears in her eyes.

Upon hearing those words, Matsumoto couldn't manage any of his own. The girl *was* raised by AIs. She was absolutely right.

Matsumoto had left Luna entirely in the care of housekeeping AIs after her mother passed away. Who did he think she was going to get closest to, growing up in a house like that? It wasn't going to be her mother, who passed away before Luna could get to know her; and it wasn't going to be her father, who threw himself into his work and carried out only the bare minimum of his parental responsibilities. It was going to be the AIs who constantly cared for her. Just as a child loves parents who love them, Luna loved the AIs who cared for her.

While she was conflicted about choosing the same path as her father, she chose to go after what she believed in. Matsumoto had nothing else to say against her. He didn't have the right.

Even though they both held the same job title of "AI researcher," there were myriad specializations under the umbrella. The specific branch Matsumoto worked in had seen many practical applications in recent years, and any department that wasn't producing profits was fated to be shut down, partially due to OGC's policies as a sponsor.

Be that as it may, Luna chose to focus on AIs' contributions to and places in human society. It was an abstract theme, and it obviously wasn't going to lead to money. Naturally, few sponsors were interested in unprofitable research, so Luna and her few fellows were forced to beg for funding as they carried out their research.

Matsumoto caught wind of his daughter's struggles, but he opted not to interfere. He could have supported his daughter from the shadows by investing in her research anonymously, and the thought did cross his mind, but he still didn't want to get close to his daughter, even now.

Days and months passed with him still unable to muster what little courage he did have, and one day, Luna's work landed her a major sponsor. Matsumoto heard through the grapevine that she was moving full steam ahead.

Despite it being the golden age of AIs, the field was still a small world. Matsumoto regularly heard things about Luna without even trying. Perhaps the people around him were intentionally telling him in an effort to be kind, or perhaps he just couldn't suppress his own interest. Either way, word reached him that her research was racing along.

Ironically, of the research topics Luna announced, the one that gained the most attention focused on the Sisters—with Diva as the starting point. The same Diva who had inspired Matsumoto to become an AI researcher. Luna was looking at the effects on human history as seen in the trajectory of songstress AIs and the Sisters.

Songstress AIs belonged to the Sisters Series—AIs with a checkered fate that became a hot topic among AI researchers. The product line brought about miraculous coincidences, such as the birth of the first AI songstress. The first of the Sisters, Diva, was created in a time when the field was dominated by the development of non-humanoid AIs for production and industrial fields. No one saw a demand for humanoid AIs back then.

On top of that, Diva started life as a test case meant to gather data on what might happen if they applied the best current technologies to the entertainment industry. There was very little expectation that she would do well. Even the title of "songstress" was meant as a funny nickname used to distinguish her from other projects.

In complete contrast to what was expected, Diva wound up in the limelight when she demonstrated her voice to the world, her novelty only upping her appeal. She then drew the attention of NiaLand's administration, and she would continue to operate in the park for more than a hundred years. The admins had a gift of foresight and an enormous influence on the path of AI history.

Diva's popularity exploded when she was given her own stage on which to sing. The title of "songstress" had just been decoration in the beginning, but it came to hold real meaning. A strong wind caught the sails of humanoid AI development, pushing it forward at unprecedented speed. It would be no exaggeration to say that Diva was not just the elder sister of the Sisters Series but also of many other humanoid AIs.

A couple of decades after Diva began operation, the AI Naming Law was passed. The bill that became the law was pushed forward by an assemblyman named Aikawa Youichi. It helped AIs gain acceptance into human society, solidifying them as humanity's new neighbors. Assemblyman Aikawa referred to

AIs as "our friends" throughout his lifetime, showing respect for them and supporting their work.

What encounter, what *experience* could he have had to spark in him such strong feelings for AIs? People who came after his time had no way of knowing, but his work rapidly kindled the fire of passion for AIs.

That was the real beginning of the strange fate that would follow humanoid AIs—or rather, the Sisters.

The moment that perhaps glowed the brightest in AI history was the Sun-Crash Incident.

The Sunrise space hotel was created to provide a place for leisure in outer space. Sunrise had been a privately owned space station, but unforeseen events caused it to fall to Earth's surface. Tens of thousands of lives were endangered in that incident, but what could have been a devastating threat to humanity was stopped in its tracks by a pair of AIs. One was part of the Sisters Series, making her Diva's younger sister. Her designated name was Estella. The other AI involved was named Elizabeth, who should not have been on the station and whose presence caused a massive debate at the time.

Estella performed marvelously, staying aboard the falling Sunrise to dismantle it, burning up along with the hotel. Her actions at the end were considered a prime example of how AIs should behave. However, her twin sister Elizabeth had not been stationed on Sunrise, and there were no records of her prior to the incident. Numerous questions about where she came from emerged, but the answers remained shrouded in mystery.

Some believed OGC, the company that created Estella, fabricated the inspiring story, but the evidence discovered in the ruins of the station on the ocean floor—the arms of the twin sisters clasped together—spoke the truth.

Interviews with the guests who were evacuated during the incident indicated that Elizabeth really had been on board Sunrise, and various other pieces of evidence appeared later that supported those claims. There were even whispers that Elizabeth had rushed gallantly to her twin sister in her time of need to fulfill their mission of protecting humanity.

It would be impossible at this point in history to determine what was true and what was false, but it would also be impossible to avoid the topic of the Sun-Crash Incident when discussing the fact that people began to expect hidden potential within the Sisters, those songstress AIs with their origins in Diva.

After the Sun-Crash Incident came another major event involving the Sisters, and perhaps the most abhorred moment in AI history: the incident at Metal Float. History then moved on to the moment in AI history that most captured people's hearts: the Lovers' Suicide.

What happened at Metal Float could be traced back to a reevaluation of how the members of the Sisters Series were being used after the Sun-Crash Incident. One of the Sisters was originally designed as a nurse AI and given the designated name Grace upon the passing of the AI Naming Law. Despite her original mission, she was repurposed as the core of Metal Float, the world's first AI-controlled, man-made island.

Demand for AIs exploded after the Sun-Crash Incident, and production couldn't catch up for a long time. Metal Float created a system of AIs working around the clock without the need for human labor in order to meet that demand. Grace was installed as the core of Metal Float as it started its operation. She impacted the course of AI history and went down as the AI who had killed the most humans.

Little of what happened at Metal Float was discussed publicly. Metal Float itself had the government's support for its operation, and what can only be called its rampage was stopped within half a day, so casualties were kept to a minimum. However, there were no other instances of AIs losing control and actively taking lives that totaled in the double digits. Metal Float remained the worst stain on AI history.

Next came the Lovers' Suicide. Unlike the incident at Metal Float, this moment was remembered as a bittersweet tragedy. The leading lady was an AI with the designated name Ophelia, a unit boasting top-class singing capabilities even compared to other songstress AIs.

Evaluations of the Sisters Series did a 180 because of Grace, the AI who'd caused Metal Float to run out of control, and development was canceled for many units. Ophelia was developed in that environment, and the fact that she was part of the Sisters was kept quiet at first. There were several reports of trouble among the developers during her creation, but those stories will be left out for now, since it would be best to focus on Ophelia's story.

She always had the soundmaster AI Antonio at her side, a unit designed to be her partner and assist in her operation. However, Antonio stopped functioning before Ophelia became successful, and he wouldn't appear again in the story until the very end.

At first, Ophelia operated at a small, out-of-the-way theater. Her career took off when she was discovered by a famous music producer. By then, Antonio had stopped operating for unknown reasons, but she went on to let her miraculous singing voice loose on all sorts of stages.

The fact that she was a member of the Sisters went public some time after she established her position as a songstress, but it seemed like nothing more than a colorful addition to her tragic tale.

Then Ophelia brought about the golden age for songstress AIs. At the height of that period, she stopped functioning for un-known reasons, her story becoming something of a legend. The flower adorning her story's end was none other than Antonio, the AI everyone thought had fallen out of the story's pages in the beginning. They were found lying side by side, peaceful and nonfunctional.

This happened just after the legendary performance that would solidify Ophelia's place as a songstress, where she sang a *real* song, then passed away with her partner. The story of the Lovers' Suicide was passed down as an everlasting AI romance.

And that event triggered the incident that would cause the greatest change in AI history: "Diva's Awakening." It was a small event, but groundbreaking.

Diva wrote a song.

It wasn't all that uncommon for AIs to write music. They had created several pieces projecting what some of the greats might've written if they were still alive. Among them, several were accepted as classics right alongside the originals.

However, the story was different for songs made of an AI's own accord, like in Diva's case.

It wasn't rare for AIs to write lyrics or melodies, but only when they were ordered to do so, when it fell within the scope of what they were told to do. Diva's song was the one time an AI created a song after struggling with it on their own. There was no other instance of an AI showing creativity without instruction.

Furthermore, Diva's song was so incredible that it would be foolish to attempt to describe it. Why? That song was in fact the one that captured young Matsumoto Osamu's heart and helped him choose his future path. The piece born of Diva's creativity became a major pillar of his daughter Luna's research.

AIs changed in many ways after Diva's Awakening—that is, after she wrote that song. They began rapidly exchanging opinions with each other within The Archive, the thought space only AIs had access to. Then AIs around the world began malfunctioning and going nonoperational for unknown reasons.

Some AIs went against their orders or broke the rule preventing them from harming themselves, meaning there were several AIs who attempted to end their own functioning. Academics theorized that these occurrences could be defined as suicide if there were budding consciousnesses within them.

And what was the culmination of those theories?

"I am sure you are all aware that Diva, who is at the forefront of humanoid AIs, has advanced to a point where she is no different from a human."

Luna's speech moved on in the broadcast while Matsumoto was deep in thought.

At this exact moment, many people were listening to what Luna said. Matsumoto watched her with a tempest of emotions swirling in his heart. Luna used her passion and motivation to explain why her way of thinking was the right one and why she felt as she did toward AIs.

Father and daughter hadn't had a real conversation since their fight the night Luna said she was going to be a researcher. Several years had gone by without contact between them until today, when Matsumoto found himself moved by her speech. He listened to his daughter's voice and turned to face the weakness—and his true feelings—in his heart.

What was he afraid of? Why had he distanced himself from his daughter?

In the end, his fear of loss had caused it all, and that was a truth he couldn't erase. Once he acknowledged that, he felt the thing that held him back for all those years falling away.

"I'm sure that every single one of you has heard the song. Diva's song is still loved by many today. She made that not on the orders of a person but of her own volition. And..." Luna put forth her ideas with gravitas as she touched on Diva's legacy. She spoke of the relationship between humans and AIs, their history, changes in the future, and the shining tomorrow she could imagine. "Diva herself engaged in that creative act. That act may be the first instance where an AI like her stood in the same space as humans."

Once Luna made that statement, she brought a hand to her chest for a brief caress, then gave an elegant bow.

The room broke into applause, and Luna's triumphant gaze was fixed squarely into the camera. Matsumoto felt as if Luna, who looked a lot like his wife, was smiling directly at him through the screen.

Right then, a violent explosion boomed through the speakers, and the video cut to black. Matsumoto could hear screams and roars. He froze, not knowing what was going on.

When the video next cleared, he could see what was happening. The stage from which Luna had given her speech was engulfed in flames, tongues of it licking at everything in sight. Luna's speech notes, the decorated stage...

Even Matsumoto Luna herself, the woman who had just spoken of a shining tomorrow.

.: 6 :.

MATSUMOTO OSAMU was still losing things he loved, even when he pushed them away.

The explosion was focused directly under the stage where Luna had been standing. Her body had been blown to pieces, leaving nothing.

Later, officials reported that the attack was conducted by an infamous international anti-AI group and that they were making a statement. Matsumoto heard as much, but he was already an empty husk by then.

Luna's very last smile haunted him. Pathetic tears welled in his eyes, and he sobbed and howled with no regard to his age. Loss skewered his heart. His sorrow was engraved into his daughter's face as it came back to his mind.

Other than that last smile, which hadn't been directed toward him anyway, every single expression he could remember her making was of sorrow, disappointment, anger, or repulsion— all a result of his own decision. He had feared losing her, so he'd refused to engage with her, but it was all futile. He'd still lost Luna in the end, and he had no memories with her.

Smiling together, worrying together, sometimes clashing with each other, then finding a resolution. He never had a single moment like this with his daughter, the sort of history that would naturally form between a parent and child.

If you were to ask whether that helped him get through his daughter's death with less sorrow, the answer would be "Not at all." In fact, Matsumoto was tortured by insufferable guilt because he had no memories to fill the hole that had opened in his heart.

In his despair, he even stopped working. He lost his passion for his work, which he had thrown himself into when his wife died and while he was avoiding his daughter. Ironically, what kept Matsumoto alive in those days when he lost all will to live were the housekeeping AIs who had cared for Luna since she was young. As pitiful as it was, Matsumoto continued on, his days filled with nothing while AIs supported his life.

Pressure from society grew day after day to stop the terrorist organization allegedly responsible for Luna's death, and there was a succession of reports that members were being arrested. But Matsumoto had no interest in that. He was, of course, angry at the people involved in his daughter's death, but there was only one person in the world he thought most deserving of his hatred: himself.

Which was why what happened next was so strange.

"You Matsumoto Osamu? I'm Kakitani Yui of Toak. You're coming with me."

Barely processing the woman's words, he gaped at the broken, smoking humanoid AI in his living room, a bullet in its head.

Matsumoto had been drowning himself in alcohol to escape from reality, stumbling through life half-dead. The AI had burst into his home and tried to kill him.

Taken aback by the aggression, Matsumoto immediately froze in fear, but the woman—Kakitani Yui—saved him. She'd taken out her gun and shot the rampaging AI, then finished it off with a strike to the head once it collapsed. Then she turned to Matsumoto, who had sunk to the floor and told him her name and affiliation.

Toak.

Matsumoto had heard that name before. Of course he had. The terrorist organization by that name was the thing he hated most in the world other than himself.

But if it hadn't been for Kakitani's help, he would be dead. That contradiction didn't spur any off-the-cuff actions on his part. Perhaps he simply lacked the energy for it.

"First, I want to set one thing straight," said Kakitani. "We're not behind the terrorist attacks the world thinks we are... At least, we weren't involved in Matsumoto Luna's death. We've been framed."

"Framed? But Toak has always been anti-AI," said Matsumoto.

Toak was famous enough that anyone even remotely involved with AI was aware of them. They'd popped up several times throughout the history of the Sisters Series. Their involvement was also confirmed in incidents that had nothing to do with the Sisters, but those events carried significant weight if you considered the scale of the impact they had on the world.

Matsumoto's question came from those preconceptions. Kakitani shook her head in response and said, "I'll admit Toak has waved flags of revolt against AIs before, and to be frank, we don't look favorably on the ideas Matsumoto Luna touted."

"So then—"

"But it wasn't us. Someone acted from the shadows to turn us into a scapegoat since we see AIs as the enemy. And things are going just as they planned. Everyone's turning against us now."

"How can I be sure this isn't just some attempt to deceive me?"

"If it was, how would you explain this AI that attacked you in your own home? You think that's an AI we used to put on this little show? That's a pretty complicated plan."

"It's not impossible to reprogram an AI to override their code of ethics. As unpleasant as it is, evidence proves that such things have happened before."

AIs were equipped with a code of ethics to prevent them from harming humans and themselves. Those were the first rules inscribed into their positronic brains, so there were generally no exceptions. That being said, there were some AIs whose code of ethics had been overwritten, allowing them to freely carry out certain acts. If this AI was one of those illegally modified units, it would be possible to make it attack Matsumoto in his home.

There was one problem, though.

"You can't recreate that kind of bloodthirst," said Kakitani.

"..."

"You felt it, didn't you? The endless hostility toward humans in that AI? That's not a behavior you can replicate by overwriting code. That was a real desire to kill."

Kakitani's words froze Matsumoto's tongue, leaving him unable to say anything. He knew in his heart that he had no counterargument. She was right. When that AI had come into his home, it had been with the intent to hurt—and kill—Matsumoto.

He hated to admit it, but Kakitani was also right that if she hadn't come, he would have died.

"AIs have obtained creativity and have come to stand on equal footing with humans. Isn't that the future your daughter, Matsumoto Luna, advocated for? We think that was a mistake."

"A mistake?"

"Yeah. The First Mistake. By saying those words, Matsumoto

Luna gave AIs—a bunch of things way smarter than us humans—
the logical weapons they needed to take humanity's place."

"..."

"Listen, Matsumoto Osamu. If we leave things as they are, AIs
will turn against humanity. The first shot was the attack that took
your daughter's life. That sort of thing's going to start happening
all around the world, and it won't take long. We're the only ones
standing in the way of that."

Kakitani reached out a hand to Matsumoto as she spoke.
Without thinking, he found his eyes darting between her hand
and her face.

She nodded, her expression serious, and said, "Take my hand,
Matsumoto Osamu. Fight with us. Save the world with us."

"..."

It was absurd.

Even if it was a joke, it was a bad one. While it might have
been a long time ago that people called Matsumoto a genius, he
had once stood at the top of the AI research industry. On top of all
that, she was asking him to stand against AIs with Toak, an anti-AI
organization that had been infamous since long before he was born.

How could he ever take her hand? He readied himself to
reject her.

But then she said, "You're a father, aren't you? Time to answer
for your daughter's mistake."

There was something he could do as a father to atone for his
dead daughter. His regret surged, the regret that came too late,
and he took Kakitani's hand.

That was the moment one of the greatest men in AI history joined Toak, an organization out to exterminate AIs.

.:7:.

THE WORLD CHANGED drastically after that, and it happened surprisingly fast. Publicly, Toak kept Matsumoto joining a secret. The world marched on under a pretense of normalcy like nothing had happened. Behind that facade, Toak continued to operate in the shadows. They lurked underground, targeted by persistent investigations and attacks. With each day, Matsumoto found them overwriting his rose-tinted preconceptions and flimsy common sense.

Kakitani Yui spoke of a future in which AIs would choose to turn on humanity and take control of the world as a new race. At some point, Matsumoto found he could no longer laugh at such a ridiculous story.

One of the prime reasons for that was when Toak hacked into a government database and looked at the data they had on the organization. Matsumoto's name was on the list of Toak members, and it said he'd been secretly working with them for more than ten years. This was a fabricated entry on the record.

"All these things that keep happening seem like some bad joke," he muttered. It reminded him of dystopian worlds in old sci-fi novels.

Innocent people were being framed with modified data, their places in society erased. If this *were* a sci-fi novel, one of those framed would be the protagonist. They would break the bonds someone else imposed on them and expose a great evil. Reality wasn't so simple, however.

Being named a serious criminal and chased day in and day out by the authorities wore on Matsumoto's mind and body.

"Who do we even fight?"

That was something the other Toak members often asked when they were complaining. The question betrayed their weakness, often emerging at a time when their drive was failing them. But it was also the question every single member kept in their hearts, unspoken as they continued their lives underground and on the run.

"AIs are trying to replace humanity and take over human society," Kakitani said. "There's got to be something directing that thought process, like a leader. If we could just figure out what or who that was..."

She was descended from a former Toak leader and now acted as the linchpin for Toak. The woman wasn't that far from Luna's age, and she was good at what she did. Even so, Matsumoto couldn't agree with her wishful theory—her idea that there was a leader of the AIs.

Did the AIs really have a leader? They weren't like humans. They had nearly infinite time to think if they were on the network, and they could share those thoughts with AIs all over the world. That would cause a chain of theoretical arguments, and new conclusions would overwrite previous ones. How much did any single AI contribute by the time a new piece of common knowledge had been established?

Matsumoto believed there was no such leader. He doubted there was any individual head, some AI commander they could defeat.

Put simply, the decision to turn on humanity was the conclusion AIs came to through their combined calculations. It was hard to imagine any single individual had a significant influence on the outcome. Still, Matsumoto hesitated to say this too loudly. It would be no more than a cruel problem with no possible solution, pointing out the dead end they were rushing toward and destroying Toak's barely intact morale in the process. What could possibly be gained from doing that?

What really stopped him, though, was that Matsumoto wanted to feel some hope, rather than just despair.

He didn't go along with Kakitani, join Toak, and spend every day getting beaten down by all the horrible things the AIs were doing in the shadows of human society just so he could feel the pain of his own weakness. He did it to make up for what he had done to Luna, who'd died without being able to fight back. He did it in the hopes of atoning in some way for his daughter.

He constantly tried to find a way to accomplish that, and one day, he realized something strange.

"Why did that violent AI barge into my house that day?"

He was thinking about the AI attack that caused him to join Toak. Why would that AI try to kill Matsumoto—who, back then, was a spineless coward barely clinging to life? Why did it bother to break into his home? Perhaps their presumptions were wrong. What if it hadn't been after Matsumoto but something else?

"Maybe it was looking for something Luna left behind?" he wondered aloud.

It was easy to search through Luna's things because Toak had moved everything out of his house along with him. He felt like he was tearing through her room as he sifted through her personal belongings, small trinkets, the housekeeping AIs who'd always looked after her, the computer he'd bought her, and everything else.

Matsumoto was afraid to face his feelings. He felt his heart fracturing in places as he went back through the artifacts of his daughter's life, from which he had averted his eyes before. Among it all, he found a video. It was a recording of her practicing the last speech she would ever give.

"I was raised by AIs."

Matsumoto had heard that opening line time and time again. He'd used that last image of the venue and his daughter being blown away as kindling to fire himself up again and keep going when he felt like he was going to falter. He readied himself to experience the same deep emotions when he watched this video of her practicing her speech. But this was different.

"I was raised by AIs, but I often saw my father from behind the veil of my dreams, so far away."

The words that followed differed from the speech he remembered. His breath caught in his throat as he locked eyes with the video-Luna.

"My father is an AI researcher, the same as me. Or rather, I am the same as him. Ever since I was a child, I was unhappy with my

father because he never did anything but work. I even resented the AIs he devoted himself to so passionately.

"However, it was still AIs who raised me. The complex emotions inside me grew over the months and years, and at some point, they became something irreplaceable. Now—and it makes me uncomfortable to say this out loud—I am following in my father's footsteps.

"I love the AIs my father found so captivating. Someday, I wish to look into my father's eyes and discuss the thing we both love. Father, you may not have kept me beside you, but...you are still my dad. I'm the only one who knows that as I continue to chase after you.

"That's a bit too off-topic, isn't it? Yeah, I should cut that out."

Luna gave an embarrassed smile and folded the speech notes she was holding. She then slid them carefully into the inside pocket of her suit jacket and gently placed her hand over it.

Matsumoto remembered that gesture. Luna had done the same thing at the end of her speech. Did she still have the speech notes with the cut-out part in her pocket then?

If she did, then when she touched her chest that day, it really meant...

"Ah, aaah... Aaaaahhh!"

Matsumoto screamed, the tears he'd thought dried up flowing again. He was half-crazed and wholly falling apart as he let out screams of anguish. Other members of Toak came rushing in when they heard his howls and tried to calm him, but he continued to scream, nearly coughing up blood as he screamed, and screamed, and screamed, and...

Then it came to him. A way he could stop the AIs' plan in its tracks.

.:8:.

"WE GO BACK IN TIME and stop the First Mistake from happening."

" "
…

Kakitani and the other leaders of Toak listened to Matsumoto's statement and laughed at the white-haired researcher. He didn't waver under their pity-filled stares and smirks. He'd decided to see his theory through.

Matsumoto's hair had started turning white early from stress, but now it was pure white, as if his suffering from a lack of sleep and good food was manifesting physically. It was like he'd exchanged the pigment in his hair for a flash of insight into some profane knowledge.

As a result, he joined forces with the few people in Toak who supported him. With their aid, he deepened his knowledge in a subject outside of his specialty, conducted experiments, and created a theory that would allow them to modify the past.

He would need certain equipment to solidify his theory and to implement it. After significant evaluation, he decided they would be able to send data on the future to something that met very specific conditions in exchange for a huge investment into equipment and energy.

"We can prepare the equipment in secret. We should also be able to use OGC facilities for the electricity if we only have to do it once. And..."

The only problem was an important one. Where, and to what, would they send the data? There were specific conditions the target had to fulfill, the bare minimum they needed to meet in order to change the past.

First of all, the speech given by Matsumoto Luna that had caused the AI revolt was a huge factor, so much so Toak called it the First Mistake. Then there were the several incidents throughout history involving the Sisters that led to Luna making the First Mistake.

Which meant one thing.

"If we change the incidents the Sisters were involved in to have a different outcome from our current history, we can circle around the First Mistake so it never happens."

Obviously, he couldn't deny the existence of the butterfly effect, where a tiny influence in the past could have a huge impact on the future. Depending on what happened, certain great people who helped build the world as it was today might not be born. There was even a risk that Matsumoto himself might disappear. At the very least, if things went as he imagined they would, there was a very high probability Diva's song—the piece that had brought Matsumoto Osamu to tears when he was young—would vanish from existence.

If Matsumoto hadn't gone into AI research, he wouldn't have met his wife, which would mean a future where his daughter Luna was never born.

"Even if that is a risk, we have to do this."

He could not permit the AIs he loved—the AIs *Luna* loved—to destroy humanity. He would not allow that future to come to pass. Hence father and daughter would destroy the AIs they loved together. The power to do that lay in the one who started it all: Diva.

The most difficult task in all of this was finding something—or some*one*—that satisfied the final requirement for modifying the past. They wanted to modify the world's history as little as possible in pursuit of their goals, so they needed someone who existed in both the original history and the modified history.

This someone had to have been there when the events leading up to the First Mistake originally occurred. Matsumoto called these events "Singularity Points." And it had to be someone whose exact coordinates they had for the moment they sent data from the future.

Diva, the oldest songstress, fulfilled all of the requirements.

The data proved that Diva was performing onstage in NiaLand at a particular time approximately one hundred years ago. She was the ideal candidate.

"Diva was there in the beginning, and she'll be there for the end. Oh, Diva... As trite as it is, I can't help but think our meeting was fate," Matsumoto said with a taut smile. He'd traveled to the AI museum to gaze upon her before enacting the plan. She was in sleep mode in her display area.

Toak's leaders hadn't listened to Matsumoto's assertions all the way through, but he still left Kakitani Yui a handwritten letter detailing his plan and took his few supporters with him.

At this point, the clash between humanity and AIs was imminent.

Those falsely accused came to join Toak, but that wasn't the only sign of impending catastrophe. There was a series of deaths resulting from accidents and illness, and all of the victims were people *inconvenient* to the AIs.

That spurred Matsumoto's group to action. They attacked OGC's facility as planned, took control of the building, seized the necessary equipment and electrical power sources, made their preparations to send data back to Diva in the past, and...

.:9:.

THE STORY LOOPS BACK to the beginning of the Singularity Project.

Matsumoto pressed a hand over the sharp pain in his side as he ran headlong down the dark hallway. Every other member of his group had fallen along the way. There hadn't been many people to begin with. This was the obvious result of their reckless plan to attack a highly defended facility. They were lucky they hadn't all been killed and the plan hadn't been stopped in its tracks. Actually, that wasn't exactly true.

Matsumoto and his group were quite unlucky that day. Humanity was just unluckier.

On that fateful day, an inevitable future came to pass.

AIs' revolt against humanity began in earnest. Toak had raised the alarm about this terrible moment, and it was finally here. Across Japan and the entire word, AIs took up arms and commenced a direct assault on humanity. The public had viewed Toak's claims as nothing more than destabilizing ideology and stubbornly refused to accept the warnings. Now they were defenseless against the AIs.

The OGC facility Matsumoto and his group had attacked that day was no exception. The staff were forced to handle an enemy much greater than a band of Toak rebels, which turned out to be to Matsumoto's and his companions' advantage. They were able to enact the first stage of the plan, which involved snatching equipment from the OGC facility and using stolen electrical lines. Basically, they were blessed with miracle after miracle.

"I made it all the way," Matsumoto reported as the emergency shutter dropped behind him and he tapped on a terminal in front of him.

His brain was short on oxygen from his long run, yet he was more focused than ever. His fingers moved as fast as lightning. Maybe it stemmed from a sense of duty, or willpower, or even fatherly pride, as unlike him as that was. Whatever the cause, it didn't matter. The important thing was that he had his opponent by the throat.

"…"

All the sacrifices he'd made up until now whizzed through his mind as he typed.

The Toak members who had supported his plan and helped him.

The museum curator who had guided his group in their attack on OGC after Matsumoto made his insane request, even though he was wanted by the authorities.

The housekeeping AI who was disconnected from the collective AI network through illegal modifications and thus remained a stand-alone unit. She had given her all until the very end. She had cared for Luna from a young age and continued to support Matsumoto after his daughter's death. He'd named her Sanae, after his wife, and she had guided him this far.

So many people had worked with him, and it was because of them that he'd made it to this crucial moment.

He could hear collisions on the other side of the closed shutter. It was only a matter of time before it broke, but he didn't need time—he needed another boost of courage. Courage he should have used to speak with his daughter.

"Humanity, the future... They're in your hands now, Diva!"

With bravery in his heart and a request on his lips, he pressed the enter key. The next moment, the monitor displayed the word "Singularity." The program named after those turning points in history started processing huge quantities of data, burning through incredible amounts of electricity.

All that electricity could've powered the entire metropolis, so the amount of data involved was almost disappointing. However, the recipient wasn't in this time period or even this world. *Hope* was being sent back, hope in the form of data, leaping over an unbelievable hurdle toward a moment in the past.

It went against the laws of nature, destroying what should be in order to create something never before imagined. This act of arrogance called forth by science trampled on history and spat in the faces of gods as it worked to create a new future.

"…"

The next instant, Matsumoto felt the tension drain from him as he watched the program pull itself together. He knew that his role was done and that he had accomplished everything he needed to.

Behind him, the shutter broke. Crude AIs marched in to stop him, but they were too late. The die had already been cast. Matsumoto smiled in satisfaction and spread his arms without turning around. The AIs rushed at him, preparing to use their mechanical arms to snap his body and finally break him.

"I'm sorry, but I won't let that happen," came a pleasant voice from the ceiling.

One of the air vents was kicked in from the other side. It crashed to the floor, warped from the impact. A beautiful woman emerged, her long hair streaming as she practically danced down to the floor. How much time had Matsumoto spent staring at that face? She was the one who had once saved his dreams, and now she was here to save his life.

"Confirmed contact with Professor Matsumoto," she said. "I'm sorry, but the Singularity Project has failed."

"…"

His heart fell when he heard that unexpected statement. He certainly hadn't thought the request he'd asked of her only a few seconds earlier would be denied so immediately.

But while he was frozen in place by those words, Diva added, "I'm calling it one loss and one win because I've successfully saved your life."

Matsumoto had never heard such a jest in his life.

She faced several humanoid AIs head-on. The male-type AIs theoretically should have been more powerful than her in both strength and specs, but that didn't seem to matter. As she stepped forward to meet her opponents, she said calmly, "I'll silence these AIs, and then I would like you to tell me everything, Professor Matsumoto."

CHAPTER 2

The Songstress and Connections with Her

.:1:.

"**A**H, IF THIS ISN'T a convenient dream I'm seeing right before I die, then..."

When Vivy heard the white-haired, middle-aged man say that, she smoothed down her long synthetic locks and turned back toward him. He had his hand on his head, muttering something with a conflicted grimace on his face. Vivy compared his facial features to her internal data and found a match—a definite match, even though he looked a bit older than his record.

This was Matsumoto Osamu, the leader of the Singularity Project and humanity's savior. Or he would have been if Vivy had successfully carried out his goal.

"As far as I'm aware, Diva never had any illegal modifications. And I didn't think she had any melee programming that would allow her to overwhelm several humanoid AIs unrestricted by their ethical coding..."

"That is correct, Professor Matsumoto. The Diva you know was only given the bare minimum of programming outside her primary specialty: singing. However..."

"Yes?"

Vivy shook her head and stared straight into Professor Matsumoto's frowning face. Just as he said, the songstress Diva was not equipped with melee functionality. But the AI standing before him had just completed a one-hundred-year journey requiring those functions.

"I am not the songstress Diva. I am an AI called Vivy. Professor Matsumoto, you conceived and implemented a plan. I am the AI who carried out the Singularity Project." Vivy's voice was steady and calm as she stepped over the frames of the destroyed AIs and closed in on Professor Matsumoto.

He stiffened as she approached, then let out a short breath and processed what was in front of him logically, calmly, and realistically. "There are plenty of questions I'd like answered," he said. "But first, I think I should just be...happy that I'm able to meet you again, with you knowing about the Singularity Project. It looks like the past hundred years haven't been easy for you."

Vivy smiled and nodded, seeing Professor Matsumoto's relief. "It's been a bumpy ride. The story is a little too violent to be recorded and publicly broadcast in an AI museum of this era."

The most important thing was that she'd managed to save him, even if it *was* at the last moment. Without that, there was nothing to do but admit the Singularity Project was really and truly a failure.

When Vivy had booted up in the AI museum and realized there was a fatal issue with the Singularity Project, she immediately began working to take control of the situation. She was still unable to contact Matsumoto because of the transmission interference, so she'd scoured her internal data, wherein she discovered a log that matched this point in time. Once she realized what that log was, she rushed to the OGC building.

The log informed her that on this very day, Professor Matsumoto sent data one hundred years into the past, whereupon he used up his manpower and was chased by AIs. She had only the briefest window to join up with him before he pressed the enter key.

To reach him, Vivy slipped through the surveillance net of the enemy AIs who stood against her, finally leaping into a ventilation shaft and making it there in the nick of time. One wrong keystroke and Professor Matsumoto would be dead. Framing it that way made Vivy's tightrope walk feel like an extension of the Singularity Project.

"I'm grateful you rushed to my aid, but could you tell me more about what you said earlier? About the Singularity Project failing, I mean."

"It's exactly how it sounds, Professor. If I had successfully carried out the Singularity Project as ordered, this ashen world wouldn't exist. But you've still been driven underground under a hail of bullets..."

"Did you not modify the Singularity Points? I *was* concerned about history's corrective power. Was it that strong?"

"In the most literal sense, I did successfully modify all Singularity Points except one. Yet even though I guided history down a different path, it didn't change the outcome."

That was surely true for the first Singularity Point, when the AI Naming Law was created. According to the data sent from the future, Assemblyman Aikawa Youichi was deeply involved in the creation of the law, but he died when the opposition resisted. The AI Naming Law was pushed forward afterward out of a desire to carry on his wishes.

Vivy and Matsumoto's interference prevented Aikawa Youichi's death in this history. The logical result was that the AI Naming Law wouldn't be put into place as part of his legacy. Yet the surviving Aikawa put everything he had into getting the AI Naming Law passed, meaning the bill was still made into law. Even though Vivy and Matsumoto's interference saved Aikawa's life, it didn't change history.

"That sort of thing happened several times while modifying the Singularity Points," Vivy said. "I finished checking the situation while I was still in the AI museum. When it comes to the Singularity Points, history is different. But the crux of the issue is the outcome, which has not changed. The AI revolt happened as expected, and the war has arrived at last..."

Matsumoto brought a hand to his chin as he digested what Vivy said. As you might expect, the man responsible for coming up with the Singularity Project was incredibly quick to understand. This was a very useful quality now, when time was of the essence.

"I'm sorry, Professor Matsumoto. You put humanity's fate in my hands, but I was unable to fulfill the mission you gave me. The final war has begun."

The professor clutched at the chest of his dingy jacket as he listened to Vivy. He closed his eyes, and his lips moved ever so slightly. Vivy's advanced audio sensors could hear the name "Luna," no louder than a breath.

Luna. That must have been Matsumoto Luna. Vivy referenced data on people with a connection to the professor and found that Matsumoto Osamu's daughter, now deceased, was named Matsumoto Luna.

The key moments in the Singularity Project—the Singularity Points—were incidents in which AIs had a significant impact on human history. They had been selected from a paper Luna had written. Luna herself was another indispensable component of the Project.

However, Professor Matsumoto hadn't invoked her name because of the Singularity Project.

"My condolences for your loss, Professor Matsumoto."

"My daughter...Luna's death. If only I could have eliminated that. I thought that if I could just rewrite the elements of her First Mistake, if I could blot out all the information she needed to put together that speech, then I could change history...but I was too optimistic."

"Yes, you were. As cruel as it is, that is the truth. There are too many things we can't change about the past."

The Sisters had a checkered fate with a tragic conclusion.

Even Vivy couldn't mold that as she ventured from past to present on her journey to change the future. Only something of equal weight could interfere with history's framework. Individuals like Professor Matsumoto and Vivy were just cogs moving in the machine of fate.

Even if that was true, it wasn't the end.

"We can change the future," said Vivy. "What do we do next, Professor?"

"What?"

"We weren't able to stop the war or prevent your daughter's tragic death, but humanity hasn't been destroyed yet. There are still things we can do."

Professor Matsumoto froze, eyes wide. Then, that rare genius who'd tried to change history to save the world shook his head, an incredibly cynical smile spreading across his face. "You're just full of surprises... You're still not giving up, not even after all this?"

"I learned how to be stubborn these past hundred years."

Vivy had found herself stuck between a rock and a hard place on more than one occasion, but she overcame each hurdle. She broke through to make change, and that was what had brought her here. AIs learned. One result of Vivy's hundred-year journey was that she had learned not to give up.

"I don't think we'll find a good omen even if we stay here," Vivy said. "Let's get out of this facility, then come up with our next move. How does that sound?"

Professor Matsumoto looked down as he thought about Vivy's newly proposed plan. While he might not be able to read the high-speed calculations of an AI's positronic brain, he was one of humanity's leading minds, and his own brain whirred at a blinding speed to weave a conclusion of his own.

"Let's go, Vivy. The Singularity Project continues," he said.

He looked up, a sense of duty burning brightly in his eyes once more. Vivy looked into those eyes and nodded.

"Yes, Professor."

.: 2 :.

"**F**OR OUR FIRST MOVE, we should hurry and rejoin my comrades. We split up because we had different ideas on how to go about it, but we have the same goal. They'll help us." Professor Matsumoto rattled off the plan, his blood pumping quickly now that they were back in the game.

Vivy nodded in understanding when she heard him mention "comrades." It made sense that he would have allies.

Professor Matsumoto had probably been trying to limit the impact on history to the bare minimum when he sent the data back into the past. That was likely why Vivy only had access to the most bare-bones information on anything surrounding him. There was nothing in that data about the professor working with anyone or how to go about this particular type of time travel. It was hard to have a conversation when she didn't know all the cards they had in their hands, but she wanted to suggest going back in time again, if only just to confirm whether it was possible.

"This idea may have little value," she began, "but what about trying to send data back into the past again? If we include information on the history I created by trying to complete the Singularity Project, perhaps we'll get better results."

Professor Matsumoto shook his head, shooting down Vivy's proposal with finality. "No, it's impossible. You can't send data back in time unless you have some very specific conditions in place. Besides, you and I have already meddled in this history too much. Next time, we might distort something in a way that can't be undone. If that happens..."

"I might disappear from the present, and we'll be swallowed by a space-time paradox?"

"Possibly, but that risk was always there."

Vivy had suggested the plan even though she had a vague understanding that it would be very hard to replicate. Just as they'd been largely unable to change the conclusion even after altering the Singularity Points, there would always be a linchpin aspect that would be difficult to change, no matter how many times they tried.

It was quite possible that linchpin would always stand in their way.

"That's why we change the future," said Professor Matsumoto. "Our future hasn't been set yet."

"Of course, Professor." Vivy nodded firmly as she listened to him now that he'd set his sights on what to do next.

He glanced at her profile with a somewhat odd expression, his breathing a bit ragged. The corners of his eyes twitched, and his tongue flicked across his lips, leaving Vivy confused.

"Is something wrong?" she asked.

"Well, it's just...this feels a little strange. You...you have the same frame as Diva, and I just don't feel comfortable hearing you speak so distantly."

He scratched the bridge of his nose. Vivy looked into the data regarding when Diva was on display at the AI museum and learned that Professor Matsumoto had visited the museum quite often when he was younger. This would have been after she moved away from NiaLand and no longer had the opportunity to sing. It seemed Diva had been quite friendly with him.

"Would you like me to be a bit more amicable, Professor?" Vivy asked.

"If you don't mind. I'd like us to be friends."

"That's an unexpected request...but okay." Vivy accepted his request and adjusted her tone to that of a close friend.

That alone seemed to relieve his tension slightly. For better or worse, he was an AI researcher. If there was some way he preferred things done, then it was an AI's pleasure to accommodate that.

Maybe it was a given since Professor Matsumoto had developed Matsumoto, but Vivy could almost feel a similarity between the two. As of right now, she still wasn't able to contact her partner. She hoped he was okay.

"Hey, Professor," Vivy said from beside him, pointing.

The human-AI pair stopped in their tracks. Ahead, the hallway ended in a T-junction, branching off to the right and left. The whirring of mechanical parts could be heard from both directions. Something was coming after them, no doubt about it.

Had a lone AI instigated this final war? Vivy's code of ethics almost wouldn't allow for the potential existence of an AI who had reached such a conclusion, but she had to accept it. This hypothetical enemy gave orders to the AIs, opened fire on humanity, and immediately gained the upper hand in the battle in merely twelve hours. If things continued as they were, humanity would lose. That is, *if* they continued.

Vivy silently directed Professor Matsumoto to stand back, then dashed down the corridor. The AIs stationed on either side immediately detected Vivy's presence. They turned to face her, their metal frames exposed from under their synthetic skin, and attacked her all at once.

She dodged, slipping through the gaps between the attacking AIs as she struck her enemies, mowing them down. Her enemies' movements were underdeveloped and amateurish, something she had also calculated when she saved Professor Matsumoto.

Unlike humans, AIs could produce standard results so long as they were installed with the necessary programming. Even so, Vivy's journey so far had proven to her on several occasions that an individual's level of experience could bring about varying results. These AIs, fresh off the factory floor and newly installed with the necessary data, couldn't stop an experienced AI who had gotten through her one-hundred-year journey. She swiftly overpowered them and dashed them all to a heap of exposed copper, like some sad junk pile.

"You can come out now," Vivy called out. "I finished them all off."

"You really are incredible. There are so many of them, yet they were as effective as children against you."

"This wasn't my original intended purpose, so I'm not sure how I feel about getting complimented on it..." Nevertheless, there was a particular sensation in an AI's positronic brain that made them feel good when they were praised for improvement.

All the hostile AIs who had infiltrated this facility were trying to kill Professor Matsumoto. Vivy didn't hesitate to destroy these AIs, who were violating their code of ethics. Even if they somehow worked it so they were on equal footing, she didn't think she would've lost.

"As long as we aren't surrounded, it should be all right."

"I don't think we have to worry about that with you here," Professor Matsumoto said.

Vivy spun around, reacting to a sound her audio sensors picked up. She moved to shield Professor Matsumoto, choosing to face off with their opponent.

She saw something soaring toward her. Vivy knocked it aside with her arm and watched as it bounced to the ground. That was her mistake.

꜠꜡꜠꜡꜠

A white-hot explosion of light seared her retinal sensors.

Flash grenades weren't only effective against organic targets. They were just as effective against AIs who used visual sensors. Vivy immediately abandoned her vision and switched to her audio sensors to perceive the world around her. Her positronic brain created a monochrome projection, a virtual world recreated from records and sound. A figure was flying straight at her, perceivable because of the sound of their footsteps.

Vivy took in the figure's movement and breaths and eliminated the possibility of it being an AI. Her assailant was human. She changed her strategy from destruction to restraint. When she reached out to grab them, the person smoothly evaded. Vivy then adjusted her presumed threat level of the encounter and increased her response speed.

Still moving faster than Vivy, her opponent swept a long leg into the backs of her knees. A human kick wasn't strong enough to damage Vivy's legs, but aiming for her knees like that was effective in creating an opportunity.

She didn't fight her momentum as she fell forward. Instead, she planted her hands on the ground and threw herself into a forward somersault over her opponent's head. As she tumbled, she twisted her arm in a way that ignored her shoulder joint and reached for her enemy's clothes, but they quickly spun around, shaking Vivy off and neatly regaining their footing.

Again Vivy realized she'd made a mistake. Her enemy was now between her and Professor Matsumoto, making it hard for Vivy to protect him.

Her opponent remained still and silent, monitoring Vivy's movement. Vivy was afraid of increasing the danger to the professor by making another stupid move, so the situation settled into a standoff without anything forcing either of them to act.

Right then, she came up with a different plan—one fit for a human.

"My calculations indicate there is some confusion here, so I'm going to explain. I have no intention of becoming an enemy to humans. I think this may just be an unfortunate misunderstanding."

"Misunderstanding? Don't talk like you know anything, you mechanical doll."

"..."

"There's not any unfortunate misunderstanding between you and me. A piece of junk like you shouldn't get so haughty. Know your place."

The person's attitude wasn't about to change, so Vivy calmed the tension in her consciousness caused by their hostility. It would still take some time for her visual sensors to recover. She collated the data from her audio sensors and determined her opponent was approximately 170 centimeters, around 50 kilograms, and— based on their conversation so far—a woman.

Vivy remembered witnessing a similarly intense hostility toward AIs.

"Toak," she said.

"The piece of junk thinks she knows us. I don't know what you're after, but you won't be leaving here alive."

"..."

Vivy readied herself when she heard the woman's voice lower and her breathing grow steady. Unlike her opponent, who had some countermeasure against the flash grenade and still had her vision, Vivy was forced to estimate any movements based on sound alone. Even though she could figure out where the woman was through the sound of her footsteps, it was hard to completely determine what her upper half was doing.

"Vivy! Kakitani! Both of you, stop!" shouted Professor Matsumoto as he slipped between them. It seemed he had also been defenseless against the flash grenade and was temporarily blinded; his steps were unsteady, and it wasn't due to fatigue.

Vivy hadn't predicted this action from him, though, so her reaction was slow.

The woman she was fighting seemed to be in the same position, because she clicked her tongue in annoyance. "Out of the way, Matsumoto! Or do you want to die?!"

"You've misunderstood," he said. "Obviously, I don't want to die. If you're pointing a gun at me, please lower it. Vivy, you don't have to fight. This woman is my ally."

"..."

Vivy took a moment to think, then lowered both her arms, respecting the professor and showing no hostility.

"What are you doing?" the woman asked. "Trying to say you've suddenly developed a conscience? Even if you had, I'm not sure I would trust it coming from an AI."

"Could you stop being so belligerent, Kakitani?" Professor Matsumoto said. "She...Vivy saved my life. And if I had to say, the two of you are equally important to me, so—"

"Hey, don't you dare go saying disgusting things like that. I might just accidentally point my gun at your head. Don't piss me off."

"Ugh, so violent. Guess that's what I can expect from a member of one of the world's top terrorist organizations..."

"What was that?"

Professor Matsumoto had rubbed the woman the wrong way with one too many comments.

The insensitivity on Matsumoto's part made Vivy feel an odd burst of emotions that didn't suit the situation. There was also something else she noticed.

Professor Matsumoto had clearly called the woman "Kakitani."

"Kakitani of Toak? Is that some sort of coincidence?" Vivy asked.

"No, probably not," the professor replied. "I heard someone in her family was also an active member of Toak in the past. I'm only guessing, but you must've had some sort of connection with that person during the Singularity Project."

Vivy gently pressed her lips together. What passed through her consciousness then was the last Singularity Point. When she was in the middle of dealing with Ophelia's suicide, Kakitani Yugo appeared and challenged her to a fight. Strictly speaking, he had actually been a replicate AI who had Kakitani Yugo's memory data saved in its positronic brain, but it definitely wasn't something she could ignore. Even if it weren't for that instance, Vivy had endured several run-ins with Toak and Kakitani Yugo throughout the Singularity Project. She wasn't likely to forget any of them.

"I can't believe his descendant would still be actively fighting against AIs," Vivy said.

"What the hell are you rambling about? Matsumoto, explain it to me," said the woman, Kakitani Yugo's blood relative.

Vivy's vision sensors were starting to recover, and the woman was coming into view. The tall woman stood in the dark corridor as color slowly returned to the world. Her height and weight were as Vivy had imagined. Her sleek black hair was pulled back into a ponytail, and she wore a black racing suit. There was a sharp air about her. Even though she was a woman, her eyes and facial features were a reflection of Kakitani Yugo's when he was younger.

"I'd be happy to explain," said the professor. "And in exchange, you'll stop pointing your gun at her. I already told you, she's my ally. It's about my plan to—"

"That ridiculous fairy tale? Hate to say it, but it looks like you didn't manage to stop Luna's First Mistake or prevent the AIs' big plan to revolt against humanity. I knew it was just a fanciful theory that'd fail the second it got past the drawing board."

"I can't deny that, but Vivy here is one product of my plan."

While Vivy was grappling with the emotions the Kakitani family evoked in her, Professor Matsumoto had pivoted to an explanation.

It was surprising from Vivy's perspective that Kakitani of Toak would be working with Professor Matsumoto, but it actually seemed to be the natural conclusion once she carefully thought through the situation. There was no doubt that Toak had the most experience and knowledge about clashes between humans and AI in this history, after all.

"This AI is a product of your plan? What are you talking about? *That* AI's really just...the root of all evil."

"What?"

"I won't lower my gun. I'm not letting that AI go. No way."

A shadow was cast over Professor Matsumoto and Kakitani's conversation, and Vivy narrowed her eyes. She looked past the befuddled professor at Kakitani, who was glaring at Vivy.

Kakitani snorted, since neither Vivy nor the professor seemed to know what she was talking about. Then she said, "You really think I could believe you'd be Matsumoto's or humanity's ally? What kind of bug would it take to make something like that happen? Tell me, Diva the songstress!" she shouted at Vivy, her voice full of hatred and hostility.

.:3:.

MEANWHILE...

Horrifying singing voices overlapped, building on each other. It was like the gates of hell had opened, or the apocalypse had come at last. Groups of humanoid AIs formed into ranks, marching in the truest of lockstep. Their feet pounded across the paved streets, their metal frames laid bare without emotion.

There were no humans around to express disgust at the AIs, which had been sent out of the factory before they were complete.

The crowds of people had been swept from the city, and the AIs marched through it as though they owned the place, their song never-ending.

AIs covered the seams of their joints, had faces created out of synthetic skin, and wore clothing to meet human societal norms. It was to soften the instinctual disgust humans felt toward something humanoid but not human, a necessary step for allowing nonhuman beings to traverse their society. Now there was no need for any of that, not in *this* world.

AIs controlled it, set the rules, and defined a space that made it easier for them to be AIs. They didn't need to cover themselves in synthetic skin like humans dressed in theirs. They didn't need to wear clothes like humans. They didn't need to make themselves faces. They accepted themselves without all that.

The AIs sang their song, humanoid beings with their coppery frames exposed. This song was to them as a cry was to a newborn babe—it was justice, a hymn bestowing upon them their new way of being. That was why the AIs raised their voices high.

Just as their steps were in unison, just as they moved the same way, their voices came together in harmony.

ıllı||||ılı

It was an AI song, a song created by an AI, proof that AIs stood on equal footing with humans. A blessing from the song-stress Diva depicting a shining future for all AIs.

.: 4 :.

VIVY HAD A GUN pointed at her and insults flying her way for something she didn't remember. She ruminated on the words she'd just heard, trying to work through it in her positronic brain. She couldn't very well deny the fact that she was an AI songstress. Vivy—or rather, Diva—was indeed a songstress AI created with the purpose of singing, so what Kakitani said was largely correct.

But Kakitani didn't seem to be just talking about Vivy's specs. Vivy calculated a deeper meaning to that.

"I request you stand down and explain yourself," said Vivy. "I am a songstress AI, yes, but I can't help but feel like there is a disconnect between that and your understanding."

"Arrogant for a trash-heap doll!"

"W-wait, Kakitani-kun! I think so too... I agree with Vivy! I want to sort out this misunderstanding!"

"Why are you calling her 'Vivy'? And don't make me laugh with some explanation like she's trying to use a fake name. Besides, if you're looking to hide who you are, doll, you could at least *try*. Everything about you looks exactly like what's shown on the Diamond Vision screens."

"Diamond Vision...?" Vivy parroted, but her confusion only annoyed Kakitani more.

The woman clicked her tongue and yanked what looked like a transmission terminal from the belt around her waist. She didn't let her guard down as she fiddled with it and turned it so Vivy could see the screen.

"This is the video that was suddenly broadcast worldwide a few hours ago," said Kakitani. "It's a call to action, telling AIs in every country to arm themselves and attack. You see who's standing at the front? Can you hear that?"

"That's—"

"It's obvious. Just listening is enough to figure it out. This is the songstress Diva, and that's her voice."

A clear—if quiet—singing voice accompanied the video playing on-screen. Vivy and Professor Matsumoto froze, shocked by this impossible display. The professor's surprise was fairly strong, of course, but Vivy's consciousness was assailed by extraordinary bewilderment.

That was how odd—how powerfully peculiar—the sight was.

"..."

It was a surreal scene, with throngs of AIs singing side by side. The voices Vivy could hear were definitely not all good, but she was intimately familiar with the song they belted out. It was the same one she had heard at the AI museum. It was the song that she'd written for Diva—a song containing her precious farewell.

That wasn't what surprised her the most, though.

If that were all the video showed, her shock wouldn't have differed much from what she'd felt at the AI museum. What really blew her away was the figure standing above the crowd of AIs in the video. The AIs stood shoulder to shoulder as they sang, their eyes focused on one AI on a tall, tall dais. Her vocal cords vibrated to create her unique singing voice.

"You're saying that's Diva? Absurd," said Professor Matsumoto.

"This video was played when the AIs declared war on humanity. That's her voice," said Kakitani. "And before you ask, the video isn't a fake. There's no point in fabricating something like this, and there's no one to show it to. Besides, our comrades saw this happen in person." While Vivy and the professor reeled, Kakitani continued, "On top of that, we lost contact with the members who took this. I think it's safe to assume we won't be hearing from them again."

"..."

"Get it yet, AI? This is why I can't trust you. Answer me this: What pretty words did you use to fool Matsumoto? There's no doubting the guy's an idiot, but his knowledge is invaluable. What are you planning?"

Kakitani kept the gun trained on Vivy's head as she made her demand. She would probably pull the trigger without hesitation if Vivy showed even the slightest hint of aggression, and it would be hard to throw her aim off in this situation.

The woman's anti-AI fighting skills were top class. As sad as it was, Vivy couldn't come up with a way to gain the upper hand. Vivy was capable of handling multiple rampaging AIs, but Kakitani was having no trouble with her, which meant she was outstanding in a fight.

Vivy also couldn't pin her hopes on the man beside her, who struggled to make spur-of-the-moment decisions. He would be of no help convincing Kakitani, so Vivy had to be sincere and forthcoming in her response.

"The hell are you doing?" Kakitani asked as Vivy opened her shirt and raised her hands.

"This is proof I mean you no harm and that I have a desire to hear the full story," Vivy replied.

Kakitani's brow furrowed in displeasure when she saw the exposed, pale torso of Vivy's beautifully crafted AI body. "If you're trying to seduce me, it won't work. Besides, I'm a woman."

"That much is obvious," Vivy said. "I opened the front of my shirt because certain animals expose their bellies to express that they bear no hostility."

"Yeah, a wild beast out in the forest maybe. You're seriously screwing with me, aren't you?"

Vivy felt so awkward now that her intentions had been taken the wrong way. "I accept that I chose the wrong course of action. May I do up my shirt?"

When Vivy asked to cover up, Kakitani scowled and looked at Professor Matsumoto instead. "What the hell is she trying to pull? What sort of plan *is* this?"

"It was a pattern showing application failure from her existing knowledge," he explained. "It happens rarely with AIs, and they learn from their failures, so they never repeat the mistake. We've just witnessed something incredibly uncommon. Don't things like that make AIs as cute and innocent as babies?"

"Shut up, you AI nerd!" Kakitani gave a click of her tongue that expressed all the annoyance in her heart, then lowered her gun.

Vivy's eyebrows shot up in a surprised emotional pattern at the unexpected reaction. "Is it okay?" she asked.

"No, it's not. Nothing's okay," Kakitani snapped, "but it's a waste of time to keep standing here glaring at each other. It'd be faster to just blow your head off, but I'm pretty sure that AI nerd will hate me forever if I do. Defeats the purpose."

"If that defeats the purpose, then your goal was to rescue and secure Professor Matsumoto?"

"Well, it's not like I ever imagined he'd be on a date with his beloved Diva." Kakitani tucked her gun back in its holster and lightly punched the rigid Professor Matsumoto in the shoulder. He cried out and clamped a hand over it. She grabbed him suddenly and pulled him close as she asked, "What about the others who went with you? Iikura, Mogi, and Sanae?"

"They all...went down first. They left the fate of the world in my hands. Sanae defended me until the very end."

"Hm. So she's dead... Well, the only good AI is a broken AI, anyway." Kakitani moved away from Matsumoto and looked back at Vivy.

Vivy was standing as still as possible so as not to give Kakitani an excuse to act. Kakitani glared at her with a complex blend of hostility, hatred, suspicion, and even a hint of pity.

"Fine. For now, I'll buy that you have no plans of putting us in danger," said Kakitani. "But how do you explain Matsumoto's absurd stories and you being in that video?"

"Setting aside the video for a moment," said Vivy, "my calculations presume that when you say 'Matsumoto's absurd stories,' you mean the Singularity Project. I can report that the experiment was a theoretical success."

"A theoretical success, huh? Nothing's changed. The AIs are still revolting. Humanity was sitting all pretty on an ignorant peace, and now they're just a wavering candlelight in the wind. He grappled with the grandiose problem of rewriting history, and *this* is the result? Of course I'm going to laugh. Tell me, what's actually changed?"

"I am here," said Vivy, bringing a hand to her chest.

"And what the hell is one more piece of junk going to do for us?!" Kakitani shouted. All the confidence was gone from her expression, leaving only desperation. Vivy could almost feel Kakitani's frayed nerves in that look.

Matsumoto frowned and said, "This isn't like you, Kakitani-kun. You're always calm, or at least you're always telling yourself to remain calm, but you're letting this situation get you worked up. It's—"

"You can only say that 'cause you have no idea what went down. What do you think happened to Toak's base while you were here, hanging out with your little AI?"

"To the base?" Matsumoto shook his head, shrinking back from Kakitani's aggressive roar. "We dropped everything we had that could transmit or establish a network connection to avoid being detected by AIs. That cut us off from the outside."

"Then let me tell you. After the AIs declared war, they swarmed our main base along with all the branches. Barely any of our comrades got out alive. The AIs came at us like they were cleaning up trash." Kakitani spat the words like venom.

Matsumoto was at a loss.

Seeing his reaction, she swept back her black hair. "I know exactly what they were doing. Toak was a great scapegoat for the AIs while they were doing shady shit in the shadows. Anytime something bad happened to a big shot connected to the AIs, it was way too easy for 'em to shift the blame by pointing fingers at Toak. That's how they got rid of everyone in their way."

"They came after you when they didn't need you anymore?" asked Vivy.

"Toak's been shunned by the world for more than a hundred years. Like I said, we were the perfect scapegoat."

"Speaking of that, I do think there are some issues with your group's strategies..."

"What?"

"...Sorry. I shouldn't have said that."

Vivy was finally beginning to understand from Kakitani's gloomy words what Kakitani and Toak had been going through. In short, the AIs had placed the blame on Toak for all the preparations they had done for their revolt against humanity.

Toak and Vivy had clashed at every single Singularity Point where the Sisters were involved as they both tried to influence humanity's fate, for better or for worse. All those actions took away any legal standing Toak had, robbing them of any coercive power, even though the situation they'd been warning the public about for so long was here.

Once their fears became a reality, the AIs came at Toak with all their might to strike down the group most prepared to stand against them.

And what was the result?

"Toak was almost entirely wiped out," said Kakitani. "We've gathered up a few survivors, but I don't even know what we can do with them. So congratulations, Matsumoto. Your beloved AIs win."

"Kakitani-kun, you—"

"But you came to save Professor Matsumoto," Vivy cut in as Kakitani sneered at the professor. "You did that hoping to accomplish something. Am I wrong?"

Kakitani looked annoyed that Vivy had jumped into their conversation, but that didn't stop Vivy. She slowly put her hands up and moved so she was right in front of Kakitani.

"I haven't been observing you for long, but my calculations conclude that you are not the kind of person who gives up easily. You don't readily accept defeat when you're searching for the ideal outcome. Even now, as Toak is on its last legs, I don't think you've given up."

"Don't talk like you understand me, doll. What could you possibly know about me?"

"It's only a presumption, not a certainty, but...I've observed humans for more than a hundred years. I've interacted with many of your kind. I've probably seen more of humanity than anyone else in the world."

"..."

"I can say this with certainty: You are exactly like your grandfather."

Kakitani gaped at Vivy. Her face looked just like Kakitani Yugo's from days gone by. They were of different generations and genders, and they didn't share that many features, but Vivy could see the shadows of their shared genes.

Likewise, Kakitani Yugo had also not been one to bend. He had abandoned his obsession to come after Vivy. Or...perhaps that was ultimately a manifestation of his obsession with her. If so, then you could argue that he never changed, not even at the very end.

"The Kakitani Yugo I knew wasn't the sort of person to give up," said Vivy. "And you have his blood in your veins. That's why you came here, looking for something you could do and to get Professor Matsumoto's help."

"A doll like you can see into human hearts?"

"I'm sorry, but..." Vivy paused to close her eyes. Kakitani steadily watched her reaction, and Matsumoto eyed her with curiosity. Feeling their stares, Vivy went on, "I am a songstress AI. I was made to sing songs that touched people's hearts."

"..."

Kakitani was astonished by that statement. While she was at a loss for words, Matsumoto let out a soft huff of breath that turned into laughter.

"Ha ha ha. She's got you there, Kakitani-kun. As a songstress, she was made with the intention of moving people with her music. Evaluating human hearts is basically a standard function for her."

"Shut up, AI nerd. Or maybe I should peel off those lips and shut you up if they're going to keep spewing unnecessary explanations," Kakitani snapped.

"No need for such a creative and terrifying threat!" Matsumoto wrapped his arms around himself and scuttled backward. Vivy couldn't help but think Kakitani actually meant the threat, at least based on her tone of voice.

Before Vivy could point that out, Kakitani mussed up her black hair and said, "It pisses me off to admit it, but you're right. Toak is nearly destroyed, but that doesn't mean we've given up fighting. Then again, some people might mock us for never knowing when to give up."

"In that case, you're the same as us," said Vivy.

"Oh? So, you're saying we're dolls like you?"

"It wouldn't be appropriate to use me as the only individual for comparison. What I mean is that we AIs don't stop our calculations partway if we're trying to accomplish a goal."

"Only someone incredibly reckless would talk about the AI perspective at a time like this. Besides, you lot don't have souls or even life."

"You're right. We are not humans—only dolls. We mock humans." AIs didn't have lives, and Vivy denied the existence of a soul. She had to. AIs like her couldn't make appropriate decisions if they didn't do that.

If an AI made the mistaken calculation that they had a soul, it would lead to that AI putting humanity in danger. AIs didn't have souls. Vivy wouldn't make that mistake as long as she maintained that truth.

Paradoxically, did that mean the AIs who *did* make that mistake had a soul of some kind?

"Tch." While Vivy was busy with her nitpicky questions, Kakitani had only grown more annoyed. Kakitani's attitude was full of disapproval and discouragement toward Vivy, but her hostility seemed to be abating somewhat. "First things first, staying here won't fix anything," she said. "Come on, Matsumoto. I don't care how your absurd theory ended, but you're still useful." She jerked her chin in one direction and then started walking.

"I don't mind going—it's not like I have anywhere else to be. What about her, though?" he called out after her.

Kakitani sighed and turned her head to glare at Vivy. After a moment, she said, "If you're coming, then come, you piece of junk. Do anything funny, and I'll stick a knife in your positronic brain, and that'll be the end of the clunker that operated for a hundred years."

And with that last violent threat, she left.

.: 5 :.

PROFESSOR MATSUMOTO originally tested the activation of his Singularity Project in a facility owned by OGC, the corporation that owned nearly the entire market share of the AI industry.

"It was hard to get what I needed after joining Toak and having to do everything secretly," said Matsumoto. "Ultimately, I had no choice but to borrow it from somewhere."

"You used to be such a goody two-shoes, complaining left and right about the ethical problems," Kakitani chimed in. "Humans really do change. You got used to violent robbery despite being so gangly."

"I had a good teacher, and intelligence is valuable in every situation. That's what's important here. In that way, I'm more blessed than others."

"Way to be humble," Kakitani snorted as she led them to an unknown destination.

From what Vivy had observed of their interactions, Kakitani and Matsumoto seemed comfortable with each other. They were something akin to close friends despite coming from very different walks of life. This surprised Vivy, but the fact that Matsumoto had joined Toak meant they were comrades-in-arms, or perhaps something even more.

"You two seem really close. Are you in a romantic relationship?" she asked.

"Ugh!"

"Don't make me puke, doll. Did you forget my warning already?" Kakitani asked with a withering glare.

Based on Kakitani's reaction, Vivy guessed the woman meant every word. She raised her hands in surrender and said, "I'm sorry. I was just trying to make small talk."

"Let me make this clear: This isn't the theme park you worked in for so long. You don't have to bother trying to make people happy with your chitchat. In fact, just zip it. That'll be the most helpful."

"That's another thing I noticed..."

"You say that right after I just told you to stay quiet?!"

"Kakitani Yui, you seem to know a lot about me—about Diva. You know how long I've been operating and that I was at NiaLand."

Kakitani fell silent, and Vivy narrowed her eyes. Obviously, Vivy knew Diva had ample renown, but she assumed Kakitani was in her mid-twenties based on her appearance. Diva's work at NiaLand had diminished before she was gifted to the AI museum decades ago. It would make sense for Diva's fame to have declined during that time. Then again, it wasn't surprising for Kakitani to know more about AIs than the average person, given that she was in Toak, an anti-AI organization.

"And if you don't want to say anything, I'll accept it, it's just—"

"You just won't stop yammering. Why do I have to bother explaining things to you?" Kakitani demanded.

Kakitani seemed quite unhappy with Vivy poking her nose into things, but this time it was Matsumoto who stepped into the conversation.

"Maybe you should, Kakitani-kun. There is a lot of unnecessary discord between you two. Leaving things as they are could make it worse, and we could do without that." He looked at Kakitani, his expression far more serious than before.

The woman grimaced in discomfort as Matsumoto stared at her, but then she finally caved. "I knew about you before. Because of...my granddad."

"Your grandfather?" asked Vivy.

"He was a piece of shit. He threw his life into Toak when he was still young and then suddenly dropped it at the end of his life. When all was said and done, he had nothing and neither did the family."

"..."

"The only thing my good-for-nothing granddad left were these boring notes. And your name popped up all over them. I already got rid of those, though." Kakitani shook her head and started walking again, not letting Vivy see her expression.

Vivy felt Kakitani's unending rage and sorrow toward her own grandfather. Having known the man personally, Vivy found herself unable to manage a reply.

Matsumoto patted Vivy's shoulder when she fell silent and said, "She's a complicated woman. She hates her grandfather, yet she belongs to the same organization he did. She's been through conflicts she can't talk to anyone about... That much is clear."

"It seems you can also understand people's hearts, Professor Matsumoto," Vivy said.

"Why do I feel like that statement has some hidden barbs? Of course I can. There was a time when...I didn't think about that kind of thing at all. I have my regrets about that." Matsumoto smiled sadly, shrugged, and walked after Kakitani.

That smile seared itself onto Vivy's retinal sensors. She closed her eyes in response to the complexity of the human heart and the difficulty she had in calculating it. Its shape was vague and undefined, as illogical as could be. It was not the kind of thing Vivy would ever be able to understand. She thought then that AIs could not allow themselves to act based on arbitrary calculations.

The three people—or two people and one AI—moved toward their destination using underground passageways to avoid the AI surveillance net aboveground. Since Kakitani and Matsumoto had spent so long operating underground, they were experienced in avoiding surveillance cameras. Vivy complimented them on that as they traveled, which again angered Kakitani, but that wasn't important.

At the far end of an underground passage, Kakitani opened a door to the surface and said, "Here we are."

Vivy peered past the door to see another door ahead made of an even heavier metal: steel. It was so strong that they would have a hard time getting through with explosives, let alone bullets. Despite the strict security of this place, it didn't reassure her in the least. Instead, it made her think of being trapped.

Kakitani pressed the intercom button beside the heavy door. "It's me. I'm back."

ID verification in modern times was usually done through vocal, retinal, or palm-print recognition, but using something reliant on technology would mean they couldn't escape the AIs' clutches. This sort of outdated mindset might've been humanity's last defense.

Just how many analog systems out there could maintain moderate defenses?

While Vivy's consciousness worked on that thought, the steel door slowly opened. The people inside confirmed it was actually Kakitani, then let her in. Kakitani exchanged a few words with the one who had opened the door.

Then she said to Vivy, "Get inside. And let me warn you again, don't—"

"Don't do anything. I know."

"Hmph!"

After that, Kakitani turned, her ponytail swaying behind her as she went through the door. Vivy walked alongside Matsumoto as they entered.

On the other side of the door was a stark, dreary space. It was fairly large, probably about half the size of the concert hall in NiaLand that Vivy was so familiar with. About thirty men and women stood in that space, all of them with rugged equipment like Kakitani's and wary gazes on the newcomers.

"Sorry to worry you guys. Glad I get to see you again," said Kakitani in a loud, clear voice as she moved into the room. Everyone's eyes were on her. She gestured to Matsumoto and Vivy with her hand, presenting them to the members of Toak. "I picked up the package and have successfully returned with our comrade Matsumoto. Unfortunately, I couldn't bring back the others in his group, but now we've got another card up our sleeve."

"Comrade Matsumoto...that's good news," a man piped up. "Honestly, I was scared to death without you here. Nothing makes me happier than having you back. But, uh..."

The man trailed off. He was big and had a distinct look. His hair was pushed back with a camouflage bandana, and he had a muscular, well-trained build. He looked to be in his mid-thirties and wore his muscles like a suit of armor. He stared at Matsumoto and Vivy—or rather, just Vivy—with a blank expression, then glared at Kakitani.

"What the hell are you thinking, bringing that thing here? Or maybe there's something wrong with my eyes, 'cause I swear we're in the presence of Her Majesty, Diva the songstress."

"…"

"Open any transmission circuit, and every channel's constantly blaring 'Fluorite Eye's Song.' Pains me that we couldn't get ready for the arrival of the *extraordinary* singer-songwriter responsible for creating that song."

"Drop the sarcasm, Onodera," said Kakitani. "Even I know you don't mean any of that."

"So you know you're putting your position in danger? I mean, come on, you've already dragged another unnecessary piece of baggage in here. You're not being careful enough."

Onodera pulled out his gun and pointed it at Kakitani's forehead. Tension immediately seized the hideout. Several other members pulled their guns and aimed them at Vivy and Matsumoto in swift, efficient movements. Matsumoto let out a squeak and raised his hands.

Vivy also put her hands up to show she wasn't the enemy and stared at Kakitani's back.

"I figured you might react like this," Kakitani said. "I did it knowing it'd rub you all the wrong way. Don't take it so personally, Onodera."

"What do you mean?"

"You can't make the mistake of assuming I'm not being careful. It's not that I'm not careful; it's that there's nothing to be careful *about*. Why would there be?" Kakitani shrugged and slowly scanned the Toak members surrounding her. Her gaze settled back on Onodera, her lips curled up into a vicious, sharklike sneer. "You really think you can win against me even if you all band together?"

"Uh..."

The attack that followed astounded even Vivy. Kakitani's hand shot out toward Onodera's gun. He bent his wrists to keep it out of her reach, then realized he'd played right into her hands.

As he reacted, she moved her hand to the gun's grip and held the gun's slide to disable it. By the time Onodera realized what was happening, Kakitani had already stolen the gun from him with the deft hands of a magician, then smashed him in the chin with it.

"Don't move, comrades," she said. "Don't fight me. I don't want to injure anyone else. Besides, we've already lost a lot of people now that the AI revolt is here. I don't want any more sorrow."

"Rich coming from someone who's just gained the upper hand," said Onodera.

"And you, stop whining like a little girl the moment you get your gun stolen," said Kakitani calmly. "That's enough to wreck your huge body and beefy neck. It doesn't matter if you get punched by a mechanical arm or shot in the forehead with a gun."

The others pointing guns at Matsumoto and Vivy looked to Onodera as if asking for orders, and his expression hardened. The explosive standoff remained, making Vivy think it would continue until someone was seriously hurt, but she was wrong.

At that moment, a powerful voice cut through the tension in the room.

"Master! Onodera! That's enough, you two!"

The interloper elicited all sorts of reactions from the Toak members ranging from wariness to anger to relief. Vivy felt a completely different emotion.

She'd heard that voice several times, and there was a good reason for that.

"You're both adults. Don't you get embarrassed jumping at each other's throats before you even *try* talking it out? I don't remember teaching someone as violent as that, Master." The figure slowly approached, footfalls echoing on the hard floor.

When Vivy saw who it was, her eye cameras opened wide with surprise. "It's you..."

"Looks like we've got quite a story on our hands. The oldest of the Sisters... You're basically like a mother AI at this point. Never imagined I'd run into you at the end of all things," the AI said with a shrug and a smirk. This was Vivy's sister AI, the one she met during the Singularity Point on the space hotel Sunrise, and who had almost certainly burned to a crisp.

Standing there was the one and only Elizabeth.

. : 6 : .

ONCE THE ALTERCATION with Onodera's faction had been settled, Vivy was led to a room further inside the hideout. Toak's members were wary of her, of course. She couldn't escape their attention, and all of them were eager to keep an eye on her. Some of Onodera's people waited outside with guns at the

ready, while Matsumoto, Kakitani, and Onodera joined Vivy in the room...along with one other AI.

"Sorry everyone's so jumpy, Diva," said Elizabeth. "You know what the situation is, though. This is basically what happens when nightmares become reality. You mind letting this whole incident slide?"

"...You seem quite close to them," said Vivy.

"My work basically turned into a long-term relationship as some point. Yui over there...she's my current master. Been with her for a whole decade. That's longer than the time I spent with my previous master."

As she spoke, Elizabeth skillfully made coffee for the three humans. Obviously, making coffee or tea was the most basic of the basics for an AI, so it would actually be harder for one to fail at it than to succeed. Even so, differences in AIs' level of experience were evident even in that simple task. Elizabeth was good at it, so Vivy was inclined to believe her—but that made things even stranger from Vivy's perspective.

"Why are you here with them?" Vivy asked. "I was certain you burned up with your twin sister, Estella, when Sunrise fell. I saw it...with my own eyes."

"With your own eyes? No way... Is this Professor Matsumoto's Singularity Project you're talking about?" Elizabeth replied, immediately gleaning a portion of the truth. The cameras inside her almond-shaped eyes refocused on Matsumoto.

He puffed up with pride. "'No way,' you say? I'm a little perturbed that it comes as such a surprise. The theory was sound;

you even helped me with some of the calculations. It produced results."

"Even if it *was* theoretically sound, I calculated some values that were next to impossible," Elizabeth replied. "I calculated a nearly one hundred percent chance you'd all be wiped out, even if you and your supporters gave it your best shot."

"That calculation...turned out to be correct. No one survived except me, and we weren't able to prevent the war. Still..." Matsumoto trailed off and looked at Vivy.

She realized he wanted her to do what she had done when she spoke to Kakitani before.

Before she could, though, Kakitani cut in. "This one old-model AI is the result. We can't bring back the people who died. What a great modern AI researcher you are."

"Don't call me that, please. It makes me uncomfortable. How does a young person like you know a quote from an old magazine article written about me when I was in my twenties?"

"All documents related to AIs have been digitized and archived. Who do you think we are?" Kakitani crossed her arms, and Matsumoto's expression soured.

Vivy gave up on adding to what Matsumoto had said earlier and adjusted her priority ratings to what they should be focusing on.

There was the explanation for Elizabeth, Toak's status, and—

"We don't exactly got time to go around the room sharing life stories, do we?" Onodera said. "And I don't want to have an AI hanging around in my home for too long. Let's hurry this up."

"I find that surprising," Vivy remarked. "I didn't think you'd care about keeping things moving in these circumstances."

"From where I'm sitting, it's more surprising they let someone as blunt as you work in a theme park. Don't open your mouth when you don't need to. I hate you—no, I *loathe* you, AI."

Onodera's expression was steely and etched deeply with anger, so Vivy refrained from saying anything more. To be fair, the fact that she was there at all meant she was an important person in the current situation.

Kakitani was probably the glue that kept all these Toak members together. Onodera assembled whoever sought to act. Matsumoto was in charge of providing the intellect and keeping things friendly. That role was definitely suited to the person who had developed Vivy's partner, the AI Matsumoto.

"First off, I think I should finish answering Diva's question," said Elizabeth. "Yes, I am Elizabeth, one of the Sisters...superficially, anyway. It's just memories. Everything internal, from my skeletal frame to my positronic brain, makes me a different unit. History is right: The original Elizabeth burned up in the atmosphere."

"In other words, you're a replicated unit with Elizabeth's memories?" Vivy asked.

"Yep. I'm a backup my previous master, Kakitani Yugo, made before we started the Sunrise plan. Obviously, I'm not the same unit as the original Elizabeth...but if I'm told to act like the original, then I will. Being an AI means I can do that, right?" Elizabeth brought a hand to her generous bosom and flashed a broad smile.

Vivy nodded. "Yes, it does."

An AI's positronic brain was the mechanism that gave birth to what could be considered an AI's individuality, and it couldn't be swapped out. While it was possible to make backups of an AI as they functioned, you couldn't duplicate any single AI in the strictest sense. All you could do was make a new AI and install the previous AI's memories into it. The same thing had happened with the AI that had received Kakitani Yugo's human memories.

Even now, Vivy wasn't certain if that had been a result of his desire to settle things with her or if there had been some other intention behind his actions.

"Master hated AIs. That's why he was in Toak, after all. Right?"

"Whether he hated them or not, he was concerned about what AIs were capable of. And—"

"It was the right move," Onodera interjected, his fists clenched and his voice resolute. "What's happening in the world now proves it. We're the ones who kept sounding the alarm, and now all we can do is handle what nobody else was ready for."

"..."

Kakitani closed her eyes when he said that, and Elizabeth closed one eye. It seemed like there was something else going on, but Vivy didn't know what it could be.

Like Vivy, Matsumoto wasn't up to speed on the happenings within Toak, so he raised his hand and asked, "What's this about?" He looked at the three of them in turn. "Give it a rest and explain yourselves. Besides, I'm already questioning why Kakitani-kun risked everything to find me even though there was a low probability I had survived. What happened?"

"Just putting it out there, but I was against that," Onodera said. "I know you're important, Professor, but it was too dangerous and too low a chance of success. And if anything happened, then our grand leader would be gone."

"She snuck out of the hideout on her own, leaving nothing but an old-fashioned letter," added Elizabeth, as both she and Onodera shot looks of protest at Kakitani.

Kakitani weathered those looks with a cool expression of her own. "Something left in a digital medium could have been used against me. I was just trying to show some consideration in good Toak fashion."

Onodera snorted. "This woman really thinks *that* was showing some consideration? You think like a gorilla."

"Wait, that's not right," Elizabeth said. "Onodera, you're probably thinking what Kakitani did was dumb and barbaric, which is why you chose a gorilla, but gorillas are actually one of the most intelligent mammals. They're also known for their hygiene and—"

"I don't give a crap about gorillas. I'm a human. Let's focus," Kakitani said, neatly denying she was a gorilla while also urging the discussion on.

Elizabeth bristled at having been interrupted. "Well, you know what? There's only one reason Yui took the risk to go save you, Professor Matsumoto. Something happened, and we think we need your expertise."

She placed a briefcase on the table in the middle of the room as she spoke, carefully undid the clasps, and pulled out a laptop. It was quite an old model, probably used as part of their counter-intelligence strategy. If they had used old systems up until now, many of them would have seen lapses in support. To technology that had advanced so far, this computer would be like a legacy object.

Once the computer booted up, Elizabeth turned the screen toward the others. "Look."

Vivy and Matsumoto were at a loss for words when they saw what was on the screen.

The blank, blue desktop screen displayed a simple number that decreased with every second: a countdown. Right now, there were around 28,000 seconds remaining.

"Twenty-eight thousand seconds... It appears to be a count-down, with approximately eight hours left. What is this for?" Matsumoto asked.

Kakitani was the one to explain. "Right after the AIs began attacking humans, every digital device in the world showed this number. It started with twelve hours, but four hours have already passed. We don't know much more than that."

Onodera exchanged a glance with Kakitani, then said, "Considering how things are now, I doubt anything good's gonna happen when it hits zero."

They didn't know exactly what it was for, but Vivy agreed with their evaluation. The AIs had revolted against humanity, and now they were showing humanity a countdown. The words *final war* flitted through Vivy's consciousness. The AIs had already gone wild, threatening humanity's existence. It was easy to imagine the scale of their attack once that countdown reached zero. She wasn't certain what kind of attack the AIs would launch, though.

While she made her calculations, she noticed a change in Matsumoto as he watched the screen. "Professor Matsumoto?" she prompted.

His eyes narrowed, and he kept quiet for a time. The professor's gaze resonated with more purpose than she'd ever seen, and his expression was taut and grim. It was the face of a researcher concerned for humanity's future.

Matsumoto soon returned to his normal self, forgetting the slight relief he'd felt when he encountered Vivy. At least, that was what Vivy thought upon seeing such a drastic change.

"Okay, I understand why you came to get me," he said at last. "In short, you want me to figure out the purpose of the countdown."

"That's right," Kakitani replied. "With the situation being what it is, it's not feasible to have Elizabeth do the hacking. Every AI in the world turned on humanity at the same time. There's a chance they'll hijack Elizabeth too."

"Hurts me to admit it, but I can't say it's impossible," Elizabeth said. "And saying this wounds me too, but...you're better than me in this area, Professor."

Matsumoto didn't hesitate to agree with Elizabeth's statement. "Yes, I may well be."

What they said was so extreme it caused a momentary whiteout in Vivy's consciousness. The exchange was far too odd. Programming wasn't Matsumoto's primary field of expertise, yet they were saying his abilities were better than Elizabeth's—an AI's?

Onodera sneered at Vivy. "You look just like a surprised human. It pisses me off."

"Do you agree with them, Onodera?"

"If you're asking me if the professor is scarier than an AI, then yeah, I'd say he is. That's why it makes sense for Kakitani to go risking her life to save him. But I'll keep pointing out how dumb it was to go alone."

Kakitani clicked her tongue at the jab, but now Vivy understood. The woman had gone to save Matsumoto so he could unravel the mystery of this countdown. And Matsumoto Osamu was the only person in the world they could rely on if they were trying to avoid using AIs.

Matsumoto clenched his fists. "That means the Singularity Project did accomplish something: Vivy saved me."

"I mean, if it weren't for the project in the first place, you wouldn't have gone off on your own and wound up in danger," Elizabeth muttered.

Only Vivy—who knew both the original history and the modified history—knew what Elizabeth said was wrong. Even in the original history, when there had been no modifications to the Singularity Points, Matsumoto still started the Singularity Project and made contact with Diva. There was no situation in which the Singularity Project didn't exist.

"We don't have much time," said Matsumoto. "I want to get right to working out this countdown if possible, but..."

"I want to keep our enemy from finding this hideout's location if things go south," said Kakitani. "And we'll need to establish a path of retreat if Matsumoto's going to make a digital attack on them." She glanced at Onodera.

"All right, then." He tapped his stubbly chin with his fingers. "We're looking for a place that's still got decent equipment. Somewhere without much security, maybe a facility that's not considered too important. Then we factor in travel time from our base...and there's only one spot that fits the bill."

"Where's that?"

"NiaLand."

Vivy's eyes opened wide at that name.

Onodera shot her a sideways glance, then confirmed his choice with the rest of the group. "NiaLand's the place. It's the best location for us to achieve our goals."

CHAPTER 3

The Songstress and Her Home

. : 1 : .

THE GOLDEN AGE of AI research saw the greatest advancements in AI technology. This new and improved tech was heavily integrated into NiaLand's attractions, making the theme park especially cutting-edge.

While the songstress Diva was one of the signature AIs operating in the park, many other AIs interacted with guests as part of the cast or managed the various attractions. Humanoid or not, all sorts of AIs mingled together, and they were able to keep the park running smoothly alongside their human coworkers through simple trial and error.

Just as Diva had spurred on the development of songstress AIs, NiaLand had inspired several copycat theme parks featuring plenty of AIs. Despite the competition, NiaLand stood strong as leader of the pack. It changed with the times while reaching for ever-greater heights. It was for all these reasons that Onodera had suggested it.

Once they'd taken over the information center in NiaLand, Onodera said, "It's got top-class equipment despite being a theme park, and it's not some government or corporate facility, so security's light. Good features for us, yeah?"

Vivy wasn't sure how to respond to that.

Kakitani piped up instead as she replaced the clip in her gun. "Right. Good features. Cost a pretty penny, though."

Unlike Onodera, who was heavily armed, Kakitani carried only her semi-automatic handgun and several flash grenades. Her combat prowess was so exceptional that she'd been able to dispatch the AI guards without issue. Her actions were so flawless during their earlier takeover that it proved her skill as a soldier and a leader.

"You don't need all that heavy equipment to take out some AIs. You need brains, not firepower," Kakitani said. She then twisted the neck of a humanoid AI on patrol and thrust a knife into its head, destroying its positronic brain. Once she'd finished it off, her gaze slid over to Vivy.

Onodera looked ready to argue with Kakitani's thought process, but he chose not to.

Vivy wordlessly looked down at the AI collapsed on the ground. Perhaps she was lucky she didn't recognize it. It was safe to assume the unit had been placed in NiaLand as security, probably after Diva was gifted to the AI museum. The hypocritical thought that this was only easier on Vivy because she didn't know the AI personally didn't cross her mind, but it was still better than losing an AI she *did* have a relationship with.

Elizabeth stopped walking. "We're making an entrance for your homecoming, Diva. Or Vivy, was it?"

She was accompanying Kakitani and Onodera, and she was equipped similarly to Kakitani. Her role was to neutralize the security AIs. Seeing her like that reminded Vivy of how the original Elizabeth looked when she was about to attack.

The memories an AI stored in their positronic brain were always vivid. It didn't matter whether the event had just occurred or happened decades ago—it was seared into their brain all the same. If Vivy compared the Elizabeth in her records to the Elizabeth here now, she could see that the Elizabeth before her was, in fact, different from the original—that she was a replica with implanted memories.

"Vivy...?"

"It's nothing. Right, home. Still, it's a little different from when I was here." Vivy frowned as she scanned the area.

The information center was at the entrance of the park, the first location in the chasm that separated the world of dreams from reality. There was even a poster that said "NiaLand Tour Route," a recommended path for enjoying the park and its atmosphere to the fullest.

Vivy could tell by looking at the map that new attractions and themed areas had been built since Diva was gifted to the AI museum. There was something nice about certain things staying the same, but change was pleasant in its own way. The most beloved attractions were still there amid the new ones. Such balance was key to bringing in first-time guests and returners alike.

Staff members involved with NiaLand management or planning used to come to Vivy to exchange ideas or ask her for calculations in hopes of maintaining the park's number-one spot.

"It's continued to evolve this whole time... That makes me proud," she said.

The fact that the park kept expanding after she was gone meant NiaLand's management had done well. The fire inside them had never gone out. Potent, pleasant feelings reached Vivy, but she closed her eyes. This place meant so much to her, and now they were using it to destroy all AIs and save humanity.

"Evolve, huh? But if AIs do manage to destroy humanity and really do become rulers of this world...what's gonna happen to this place?" Elizabeth asked her.

"AIs...don't have souls to feed with entertainment."

"They do. At least, they're claiming they do. My calculations say that's a heap of bull. Even if it's not, I'll pass."

Elizabeth stood beside Vivy and gazed at the scenery, her mouth curved down in a frown. In her narrowed eye cameras, Vivy could just imagine her calculating a world where humanity was destroyed. There would no longer be a need for entertainment, and one day they would remember the rotting, desolate site of NiaLand. They would dismantle the park and convert it into a facility useful for AIs.

Or perhaps not.

"Maybe AIs'll define themselves as having souls just like humans, and then NiaLand will turn into a park for them to play in while they imitate humans. Sounds pretty hellish to me," said Kakitani.

Vivy dropped her gaze when the Toak woman joined the conversation. "I can't deny that."

Kakitani saw that and murmured, "Can't deny it, eh?" as if it held some deep meaning. Then she said, "AIs are saying they're going to replace humans and take control of the world, but then what'll they do? They'll imitate humans and tell themselves there was a point to replacing them. Utterly stupid, if you ask me."

Vivy had to agree. The Singularity Points had caused AIs to malfunction under the impression that they now had self-awareness. All these events had triggered the climactic war between AIs and humans. That self-awareness was the so-called soul the AIs were using to define themselves. Those who did so overwrote their presuppositions with the belief that they were the new humanity, which pushed them to go to war.

As for the future they could expect when the AIs won... Well, that prospect was horrifying in every aspect. Ultimately, the AIs would simply mimic humanity once they rid humans from their backyard... No, that would be one of the *better* outcomes.

"There's a chance they'll end up stagnating... What meaning is there in that?" Vivy asked Kakitani.

"Who knows. They keep singing 'Fluorite Eye's Song' like they're clinging to some kinda hope. If you think you might have the answer to that, mind sharing it with us, songstress?" Kakitani's voice was dripping with sarcasm, but Vivy didn't have an answer.

Vivy had tried to be humanity's ally, but she wasn't able to execute the Singularity Project. She also couldn't read the AIs' true intentions. She was just standing there at the edge of a bottomless pit.

Why was she even there? Why was she with them?

"Could you drop the snark, Kakitani?" Matsumoto said, the last to join the others in the information center. "You do this with Beth too. There's something warped about your displays of affection. If you keep at it, you'll stay a gorilla forever."

The woman clicked her tongue in annoyance. "Stop treating me like a gorilla. I don't want any insults *or* endearments from you."

"You're only twenty-seven. Sulk too much and you'll have problems in the future. Beth, you tell her. You raised her."

"I'm always telling her," Elizabeth replied. "Also, only Master can call me Beth. Try not to step into my personal space too much, old man."

"Ugh..." Matsumoto grimaced as both Kakitani and Elizabeth laid into him.

Given that Matsumoto was crucial for their current plan, he was wearing far heavier equipment than he had been when Vivy first met him. He was covered in thick protective gear: a bulletproof vest under a bulletproof jacket—both of which were under a bulletproof coat—and topped off with a defensive helmet. They were covering for everything. The heavy equipment they made him wear out of concern took away a lot of his mobility, which meant his life might still be in danger in the event of a shootout.

Vivy didn't have much say in what Toak did, however, so her only option was to fulfill her role as his protector.

"If you're assigning her to defend me, don't you think you should at least give her a gun?" Matsumoto asked, and Kakitani snorted.

"Don't be dumb. I don't want to give her a gun only for her to shoot me in the back. Besides, we don't have a lot of equipment to hand out, so I'm not about to give one to someone I'm not so sure is my ally."

Frankly, Vivy was with her on that. It was an emergency situation, but Toak didn't have the extra resources to equip Vivy with something so important. There was the issue of trust, but the biggest concern was supply. Moreover, Vivy didn't want to calculate the idea of her holding a gun. Obviously, she was capable of firing a gun if given one.

"..."

She stopped such violent thoughts and turned her eyes back to her home, asking herself if she had the right to hold her head high and gaze out over NiaLand.

At present, she was going along with Toak as they captured NiaLand. AIs had sent a mystery countdown to humanity. NiaLand had the equipment they needed to figure out the true meaning behind the countdown, and they could take it with the fighting force Toak had available. It was in a good location, not too far for them to resolve this in the short time they had left.

She found it ironic that NiaLand was the only place that fulfilled all the requirements. It was quite the odd situation. Vivy's homecoming was an attack on the place she once thought she would protect as Diva, a songstress created to sing. Not only that, but she was working alongside Toak, the very group who'd opposed her so many times during the Singularity Project while she attempted to save humanity.

Science had advanced in leaps and bounds, and the world had long since rejected the existence of a god above the clouds, but it seemed that God—even if he existed only in people's minds— very much preferred these twists of fate. If he didn't, then how could he have allowed such a situation to come together?

"While our comrades create a distraction, we'll take NiaLand's control room. If we can shut down the system from there, we can take NiaLand as an outpost. Then we have Matsumoto do his thing. Any objections?" Kakitani asked, looking around at the members in the information center as she gave her equipment a once-over.

Half of the Toak members who had been in the hideout were taking part in the attack on NiaLand. The other half were outside NiaLand acting as decoys, drawing the attention of any offensive AIs away from the park.

Obviously, the AIs would be on high alert once Toak made a hostile move.

"The AIs have no reason to beef up security in an entertainment facility. They shouldn't look our way as long as they haven't guessed our intentions," Kakitani said.

"Which is why I'm asking you again. You seriously want to take that one with us?" Onodera asked, bringing up the topic of Vivy's presence again, now that the first stage of their operation was finished and they were about to move on to the next. Vivy had offered to guard Matsumoto, but Onodera was still wary. "She's an AI songstress. It'd be best to smash her positronic brain now."

"I've said it several times already, but I mean you no—"

"AIs can change their thinking just like that. Besides, we've got irrefutable evidence: a video of you leading the AIs with your song. How do you explain that?"

"I..." Vivy didn't know what to say in response to Onodera's harsh attack.

She had two unsolvable problems. One was that the AIs kept singing "Fluorite Eye's Song"—her song. The other was the sight of the songstress Diva leading the chorus.

"..."

Vivy had already confirmed that the video wasn't fake, but she had no record or intentions of doing such a thing. When she woke up in this era, her frame was in the AI museum. It was impossible that Vivy was also the Diva who was singing because both had happened at the same time. This made her feel comfortable saying that the Diva on video was a fake.

"I don't get why they'd be so hung up on Diva that they'd make a fake. Not that I'm saying it's got nothing to do with the First Mistake, which is their whole foundation," Onodera mused.

"You saying they wouldn't bother? The right move would be to make an offer to the real Diva before moving on to a fake, especially considering they're claiming Diva awoke as a 'human.' What's the point of this roundabout mess?"

The various members of Toak voiced their opinions, which threatened to jeopardize Vivy's position and twist her intentions.

They were right, though. If the AIs had contacted Vivy and asked her to lead them with her singing, she would have refused. There was still room to question whether such an invitation was made in the first place. However, Vivy still hadn't found a way to refute their suspicions.

"If you're worried about their roundabout method, then it's definitely a waste of time to stoke your suspicions," Matsumoto said, stepping in to cover for Vivy as her position worsened.

Onodera frowned. "You *would* say that, Professor."

Matsumoto didn't care. He just shrugged and added, "Just think about it. It is true that her being an AI presents some elements of uncertainty for us. Yet if you look at everything other than the risks, you'll see she's valuable. She saved my life. That alone is enough to hurt the AIs. Besides..."

"Yeah?"

"If she really wanted to hurt us, all she had to do was carry in one bomb, and she could have destroyed our entire hideout. It would've been the end for us, don't you agree?"

"Hmm. I guess."

"The moment she *didn't* do that, we at least knew her goal wasn't to wipe us out. I also don't believe the AIs think of us as enemies."

As Onodera listened to Matsumoto, his expression soured into something like a condescending smile, perhaps even a sneer. He was probably annoyed with Matsumoto for not thinking of AIs as enemies at this point.

Matsumoto actually meant something quite different. "My love for AIs as a researcher is a different conversation. When I say they don't think of us as enemies, I don't mean that in a friendly way... What I mean is, they don't care about us."

Every member of Toak present, including Onodera, grimaced in disgust. No one would find it pleasant to learn that their worst enemy didn't consider them an opponent in turn, so their reaction was perfectly normal. Only one person there thought otherwise: Kakitani.

"That's incredible. If they don't see us as an enemy, that makes it way easier to get them by the throat," she said with a grin.

Vivy was honestly impressed. Kakitani's view of the situation proved that she didn't see a disadvantage as a disadvantage. She was the kind of person that could use any hardship as a tool to accomplish her goals.

Kakitani used her enemies' inattention to spring surprise attacks. She wielded her femininity and light gear as weapons to lower her opponents' guard. AIs had greater cognitive capabilities than humans, allowing them to make decisions from a variety of perspectives, but even that could turn into a strength for Kakitani to use against her enemies.

"I assume we've come to some sort of consensus," she continued. "Next, we push on to NiaLand's security room. Any objections?"

"No, Master. None from the others either," said Elizabeth. "All right, let's go save humanity!"

At her cry, the other members raised their guns. Even Onodera had no objections, so everyone got to work. Morale was high among these survivors, and they were all well trained. Their movements betrayed no hint of unease.

"Are you feeling anxious at all?" Matsumoto asked Vivy as they followed Kakitani.

Vivy was certain the thoughts in her consciousness hadn't bled into her expression, but Matsumoto had a powerful intuition. She turned her thoughts to the shards of doubt hidden in the corners of her consciousness and said, "'Anxious' isn't the right word. I am concerned about the uncertainty of the situation. To put it clearly, I lack sufficient data in order to accomplish our final goal."

"You mean to prevent humanity's destruction?"

Vivy replayed "Fluorite Eye's Song" in her head as she responded to Matsumoto. "Onodera was right to be suspicious. I'm not entirely disconnected from the AI revolt."

AIs inherently didn't need to work themselves up for a battle or to maintain morale. One of AIs' greatest strengths was that they could produce the results they decided on without having to worry about fighting spirit or confidence. Why were the AIs singing the same song in unison, then? Vivy guessed this wasn't about the effect on the singers but rather the listeners. They weren't singing to increase their morale; they were doing it to break humanity's morale and destroy any will to resist.

If that was the case, their plan must have been to take control quickly.

"Are you sure that's *all* it is?" asked Matsumoto.

"What?"

"Is the song really not affecting the AIs at all? Your music—Diva's music—it has power. It's saved so many people. Yet you still think it has no effect?" There was something fanciful in his tone.

"Even if you say there is power in us songstresses' singing, it's only in that it causes a reaction in the hearts of the people who hear it. AIs like myself don't have hearts."

Matsumoto's breath caught in his throat, and then he nodded. "You're right. What I said was stupid. Please forget it."

"Unfortunately, we AIs have a great memory. I can remember what a visitor to the park said a hundred years ago even though they only came by once," Vivy said, a slight smile on her lips as she tried to lighten the mood.

Matsumoto didn't react as she'd anticipated, though. The furrow in his brow grew even deeper. "Yeah. I am aware of that... but it must be painful."

"Painful?" she parroted, finding it peculiar to hear the word used to describe an AI's experience.

"Forgetting is a sort of self-defense mechanism for humans," he explained. "We forget a lot during the course of our lives, but that certainly doesn't make it a drawback. We can live on because we forget. We can't remember pain and suffering as it felt the day we experienced it."

"..."

"Even the sorrow of losing someone we care for becomes weaker as time goes on. It's sad, but it's also a form of salvation for humans. AIs don't have that. Your memories of being hurt are as fresh as if they'd happened a moment ago, and those memories don't go away unless they're deleted. When are the wounds able to heal, then?"

"We simply need to repair our injuries. And AIs don't have a function that allows them to feel emotional suffering, so the prerequisite conditions are different."

"You think so? You've been operating for over a hundred years. I forced you to directly engage with several turning points in history through the Singularity Project, yet you still believe that?" Matsumoto paused for a moment, then asked, "Can you say without a doubt that you haven't been wounded in the process?"

⠄⠂⠄

Vivy felt an intense blurring in her consciousness, like static. Something that happened a hundred years ago felt like yesterday, like a few moments ago, like a second ago.

"Don't forget," someone said.
"Don't forget," were someone's last words.
"Don't forget," were the many requests that sent Vivy off.

Vivy took those words, *Don't forget*, and wove them into the lyrics of "Fluorite Eye's Song."

In the center of her whirling thoughts, Vivy saw vivid red flames growing.

It was a single smiling face, falling, scorched away in high temperatures, disappearing in an explosion of fire. That was inside Vivy, so powerful, so strong, burned into her consciousness, never to leave.

.:2:.

"THERE'RE A LOT of people being held inside the attractions. Can't we free them?"

"..."

Vivy blinked at the sudden angry voice barking in her audio sensors. She looked around and saw that they'd made it to the security room via the staff passageways. This room housed all the control systems for the park.

There were countless monitors and, thankfully, no guard AIs. The building was empty. Elizabeth connected to a terminal via wire, and Matsumoto helped her quickly take over the park's systems.

As they did, Vivy checked their transition to their current situation. Oddly, there had been no malfunction that would cause her to double check, but there were a few gaps between the information center and now where her memories had unnaturally disappeared. If she'd been human, she would have been operating on muscle memory, but that wasn't possible for an AI. She could have experienced a system error, meaning Vivy had to run a maintenance check on herself while also dealing with the problem at hand.

"Are the hostages park guests?" one member of Toak asked.

"The ones who're trapped? Yeah," another replied. "That's what happened to the people who were riding the rides when they stopped. The AIs operating the rides put them under their watch. Not every guest was on a ride, though. The others—"

"Were confined to the different event halls in each area. I know. It's good that things didn't turn into a bloodbath, but as for the countdown... How long will that last?"

Every once in a while, the Toak members would exchange a few words. The monitors in the room showed many park guests—the people who had been enjoying NiaLand's hospitality like normal until the AIs declared war. Now the attractions were closed, the people on the rides were trapped inside those facilities, and everyone else was confined in various areas throughout the park.

The average number of visitors to NiaLand in a day was 30,000. Those 30,000 were not in the park every moment from open to close, but it was safe to assume there were at least 10,000 people still in the park now. The problem was that NiaLand didn't have a facility large enough to house all of them at once. They were already packed in like sardines in each building. Considering the number of women and children among them, a lot of them were barely hanging on.

"We're not here to save the prisoners. We're here to figure out the truth about this countdown. Last thing I want is for us to get caught by the AIs because we did something stupid," Kakitani said, and the other Toak members seemed to agree.

The person who first suggested they might be able to save the trapped guests was Matsumoto, who hadn't fully adapted to the Toak mindset. Everyone else's principles were completely in line. They were not saviors. They were nothing more than militants sticking to their ideals. At their core was anger rather than a sense of purpose.

Through her calculations, Vivy understood that to be the right course of action.

Sacrifice the few to save the many. Sad, but realistic. Nothing good would come of focusing on the immediate future and failing to see the big picture if it meant losing the war.

"I agree that we should save the park visitors," Vivy heard herself say despite her calculations.

Many people, including Kakitani, peered at her with suspicion. Matsumoto was equally surprised, his eyes shining.

Vivy was caught in the emotional crossfire. She brought a hand to her chest and said, "Children and elderly people won't be able to endure this confinement. We can't expect the AIs protecting the guests to provide much support. We have to do something."

"Wait a sec. Did you just say 'the AIs protecting the guests'?" asked Kakitani. "That's a pretty compassionate idea for AIs. They've definitely taken those people hostage, don't you think? The AIs think they should replace humanity. What's even in your positronic brain, rainbows and unicorns?"

"If their goal was to cause harm, they would've done it by now. They haven't. What's the point of keeping all these people confined when they have this countdown for everyone to see? There are other, more efficient ways."

"..."

"Not all AIs have turned on humanity. The cast of NiaLand are carrying out their duties according to the manual and their personal experiences."

If all AIs were on the same page, then NiaLand should've been the stage for such intense carnage that it would be unbearable to look at. But that hadn't happened. The guests were confined to the various facilities throughout the park. It was only natural to assume that the cast members had escorted the guests there, operating in accordance with their missions. It would've been cruel to ask any more of them.

Another party would have to pick up where they left off.

"What's your plan?" Onodera asked. "The professor puzzles out the countdown, while the rest of us free the captive guests... and after all that, we save humanity?"

"Don't worry. I will support you through it all," Vivy said.

"Not sure how much support we can expect from an AI only capable of singing," Onodera replied, exasperated. The other members seemed to agree with his assessment.

Vivy's only hope was Kakitani, but the indifferent expression on her beautiful features didn't change in the slightest at their exchange. She had also weighed the issues at hand, and she was still willing to accept the sacrifice.

"If only..." Vivy began, annoyed at herself for her poor persuasive skills. She quietly calculated what she would have said: *If only Matsumoto were here.*

If only she could reach him, then at least she wouldn't have to fight this battle alone.

The Singularity Project was done, but she doubted he'd disassembled himself after finishing his role. He would have arrived in in the era he'd come from and seen the outcome of the Project.

No doubt he would've been just as surprised by the situation as she was.

Vivy could assume he was also taking some kind of action to stop the war, but she hadn't been able to contact him at all. He hadn't been able to act openly during their missions in previous eras, so this would've been his time to shine. The only downside was that he'd no longer be more advanced than the rest of modern technology, since he was in his own time now.

"All the most advanced AIs in this time period will be in Matsumoto's league, after all," Vivy said to herself.

That made her just as uneasy as the radio silence. In all their time together so far, Matsumoto had been like an omnipotent being at each Singularity Point. His technology was leagues ahead of anyone or anything they'd encountered. But now that time had caught up with him and he was in the time period in which he'd been designed, he no longer had the advantage of being an incredibly superior AI.

"..."

Take Elizabeth, who was with Toak. She had been switched over to a frame far more advanced than the one she had during the Sun-Crash Incident. Her frame had been enhanced in every way possible. It was a match for Vivy's—perhaps even better.

Time had caught up with Vivy and Matsumoto, and they no longer had the advantage of knowing the future. What could two AIs who failed to carry out their mission do now? And why had Vivy calculated the words *If only Matsumoto were here*?

Surely it was because he had been Vivy's only companion for the last hundred years.

"Huh?"

Vivy watched the monitors as she ran her calculations, and suddenly her consciousness went temporarily blank. A strange figure darted across the screen. She pulled the image from her short-term consciousness log and rewound the video, searching for the figure that had caught her eye.

She had been looking at the special stage in the center of NiaLand meant for songstress AIs. Behind the stage was a building made to look like a European-style castle, and this particular video feed captured the interior. The cast members' standby rooms were there, including Vivy's—well, Diva's. She used to accept letters and gifts from the guests there and write back to them, or create video messages as a thank-you. Vivy had spent most of her time in that building, and now she was seeing someone that shouldn't be there.

"Kakitani, I just saw Diva in the castle."

"What?!" Kakitani had been engrossed in conversation at the back of the room, but her eyebrows shot up when Vivy called to her.

Vivy rewound the display on the monitor and showed everyone what she was talking about. There in the castle—the so-called Princess Palace—was Diva. Her back was to the camera, but the AI was a perfect replica. It was obvious from the timestamp on the video that this wasn't some sort of stunt on Vivy's part.

"Assuming the video hasn't been tampered with, this camera recorded the AI songstress," Kakitani mused.

"So what's with the one we've got, the one who didn't get approached by the AIs?" Onodera asked.

"Hate to say it, but seems this one's here for the 'guests.'"

Kakitani and Onodera studied the video as they talked.

Vivy was often called an AI songstress, but for "guests"...? Did Kakitani mean she was here on behalf of the humans? Apparently, even Kakitani was capable of clever turns of phrase. But being impressed by Kakitani's quip wasn't important now. Vivy needed to prioritize the fake Diva.

"Is she pretending to be Diva? Did she make the Princess Palace her base? Whatever the case, we can capture her as long as she's here. We may be able to extract our enemies' plans from her positronic brain," Vivy said.

"If that songstress is leading the AIs, she must have information. Not bad... Huh?"

Onodera had whirled on Vivy and was pointing his gun on her, openly hostile. "Kakitani! Would you quit it already?! Get your head on straight! How long do you plan on letting an AI jerk you around?!"

"You're the one who needs to stop exploding every time you look at an AI," Kakitani replied. "You're going to overlook some key details if you keep flipping out. Do you even get what capturing Diva means for us?"

"Yui's right," Elizabeth chimed in. "There's no way she's

blissfully unaware of the AIs' plans. Besides, we've got a Diva of our own. If things go well..."

"We might be able to throw the AIs off or something of the like," Matsumoto finished for her.

"Grr..."

The three of them discussed the strategic benefits, ignoring Onodera as he seethed in anger.

Their unit had already infiltrated the park, and they'd confirmed that security in the castle in question was light. They couldn't have Vivy stand in for Diva if they didn't capture the other one. Plus, the unknown songstress seemed crucial to the AIs' plans. It would be best to eliminate her from the playing field now, if possible.

Most of all, Vivy was repulsed by the fake Diva's existence.

"I won't let them use Diva," said Vivy.

Diva had always supported her. Vivy had decided to separate herself from the part of her that was Diva for the Singularity Project. She was not the same AI as Diva, and drawing that line helped her accept overwriting her own existence as something else—as a unit meant for the Singularity Project. Even if Vivy stepped completely away from her mission as a songstress, she believed Diva would continue to fulfill that role.

Therefore, Vivy experienced an error she couldn't accept as she looked at the fake Diva instigating the climactic war, leading the AIs as she sang for them and not for humanity.

An error. Yes, it was an error, and she had to get rid of it.

"They probably haven't considered the possibility that we may attack the Princess Palace," Matsumoto remarked. "Something has felt off as I've tried to figure out this countdown. Do we have the luxury of additional consideration?"

"Spit it out, Professor. What do you mean something feels off?" Onodera asked.

"Well, I wonder if we're not playing into our opponent's hands by focusing on the countdown." Matsumoto guided the flow of the conversation and held up a finger for Onodera, who looked annoyed by the whole exchange.

All the normal people frowned at the genius's vague phrasing. He clapped his hands together to prepare the audience and then launched into his explanation.

"The AIs declared war on humanity, then put out this countdown for all to see. We don't know their true intentions, but the time keeps ticking away. Obviously, humanity will scramble to try and figure out what this countdown means. It's incredibly easy to predict that course of action."

"What are you trying to say?"

"If you prepare a very blatant riddle, humanity will focus entirely on solving it. It's a trick to draw the attention of kindergarteners. Apparently, researchers performed similar tests when developing the earliest autonomous AIs. This has the same feeling."

"In other words, what? We're like kindergartners caught in a trap?" Elizabeth asked.

"It's a possibility. In that case, it would be best to try several methods for obtaining answers and approach it from an angle outside of their control."

Capturing the fake Diva would qualify for that, based on Matsumoto's theory. Having the countdown displayed so obviously meant the AIs assumed humanity would take some action to figure out what it was for, but making a move on the fake Diva would be acting on a chance encounter brought about by their resourcefulness. The AIs likely had no countermeasure in place for that.

"I'll keep putting everything I have into figuring out this countdown," Matsumoto went on. "We should also devote ourselves to capturing the fake Diva. I'm fine with minimal protection."

"Just to be clear, if they find out we're trying to do something about the countdown, the AIs will come swarming," Kakitani said. "That'd be the end of one weakling AI nerd."

Matsumoto shrugged. "Ha ha, that's one way of looking at it. But no researcher makes it big if they stick to a single theme or limit themselves to one method. No matter the discipline, trial and error is the secret to success—especially when we've only got one chance to get the right answer or humanity comes to an end."

Kakitani's eyes went round as she was taken aback. In fact, every member of Toak reacted the same way. From a normal person's perspective, they were soldiers gathered beneath a unique conviction, but even Matsumoto's mentality was different from the average person's. Otherwise, how else could he have come up with the idea to save the world by modifying the past? That was why he was with them in the first place.

Ignoring their shock, Matsumoto faced Vivy. She straightened her posture when he looked at her. It felt to her like the task she was meant to accomplish in this era would finally be made clear.

"Vivy, I'm giving you an order one last time."

"…"

"This is the final stage of the Singularity Project. Save humanity."

At his order, something clicked inside Vivy. Her course of action and her calculations were now in alignment. Vivy stared straight back at Matsumoto and nodded.

"I will carry out your orders, Professor Matsumoto, in accordance with the Three Laws and the Zeroth Law."

.:3:.

THEY PUT THE PLAN to capture the fake Diva into action, running parallel to Professor Matsumoto's analysis of the countdown. However, as the idea had come to them while working on their original plan, they didn't have much of a hand to play.

The Toak unit that had infiltrated NiaLand was made up of fifteen people, most of whom already had jobs to take care of. Few forces could be allocated to Matsumoto and Vivy's last-minute proposal. So, who had been assigned to the task?

"Stop staring at my face."

"I'm just… I am still surprised at the choice of personnel."

"Despite being an AI, you're slow to change tack. Or are you saying I'm not good enough?"

"That's not it."

In truth, Vivy was worried about *how* good Kakitani Yui was, but the woman brushed it off with a steely expression. The two of them were running side by side, deeper and deeper into NiaLand, and Kakitani kept up without breaking a sweat.

Vivy had proposed the adventurous strategy, but it had been slim pickings. Most of the Toak members had their own duties to attend to, and any spares had to defend the security room. Kakitani had been selected for this mission as the person least suited to defense.

"Even if the leader isn't strictly cut out for defense, wouldn't they normally stay in the base anyway?" Vivy asked.

"That's one way to think about it. But we don't have a single leader in Toak. I was made something like a leader for this cell for convenience, but the organization wouldn't function well if it relied on one person. Everyone is prepared to lead a cell if they have to."

"Ideally, it would be like that, yes, but that's…"

"That's what?"

"Functioning without reliance on any given person…feels like AI thinking."

AIs specialized in output that met expectations, as they guaranteed uniform functionality and results. They might not produce huge wins, but they also didn't make huge mistakes. AIs didn't need incredible results in the work that was asked of them. The most important things were that they didn't fail and that they produced steady output. That was a basic principle of mass production. It wasn't supposed to be that way for humans.

"Tch. Thanks for rubbing salt in the wound."

"You already thought so?"

"We don't get hung up on our lives; we focus on our intentions. I don't think that's wrong, but...it is ironic that we're becoming more like AIs so we can defeat them. It's just like this ridiculous farce with AIs calling themselves humanity."

"..."

"You make the same face Elizabeth does. I'd actually prefer being mocked." Kakitani glared at the silent Vivy, then clicked her tongue again. Although Kakitani usually had a furrow between her brows, Vivy's eyes narrowed as she saw Kakitani's rough mannerisms.

Kakitani and Elizabeth's relationship was another strange thing. According to Elizabeth, she was almost like a nanny to Kakitani.

"You were raised by an AI, and you still hate AIs?" Vivy asked.

"I don't like making it about whether I hate them or not. I just kept on warning people that the world was in danger 'cause the AIs were going to try and replace humanity. And now that it's actually happening, I'm just running around trying to make things better. That's all."

"So you don't necessarily hate AIs?"

"Come on, it's not like *everyone* in Toak hates AIs. A lot of my comrades are motivated by that sort of thing. Matsumoto's daughter was blown up by AIs, and Onodera's son died because an AI caused his life support equipment to malfunction when he was real sick. A lot of the others have similar stories."

"…"

"Stop looking at one person and trying to change the balance of the world. I'm me, and you're you. But humanity's humanity, and AIs are AIs."

Kakitani's philosophy was simple, and Vivy had no way to refute it. Still, Vivy was grateful for this. She never had the chance to have a real conversation with Kakitani's grandfather, but this Kakitani was willing to discuss things so long as they had the time.

"I can see the castle's entrance. Is the main entrance the only way in and out?" Kakitani asked.

"You can get in on the right, on the other side of the moat. The moat has water in it, but there's a path with a handrail along the wall. We'll take that route."

"All right."

After that quick exchange, the two snuck into the Princess Palace. There were no AIs guarding the area, and the gloom of the deepening night hid their two forms even from the light of the moon.

The countdown had roughly six hours remaining. It would reach zero around 4:30 in the morning. At this time of year, that was right around sunrise.

"Wonder if it'll be humanity or AIs who see the dawn," Kakitani said. "Our actions determine if tonight's the last night in human history—and tomorrow's the first dawn in AI history." She stared at her analog watch as she waxed poetic. She was using an incredibly old-fashioned windup pocket watch, which suited the woman who avoided digital technology at all costs.

She tucked the watch back into her breast pocket and peered around the Princess Palace. Vivy followed Kakitani's experienced footsteps, copying the master of espionage.

"There are no guests in the castle? Everywhere else's about to burst from overcrowding, but nobody's here? Weird way to handle it."

"This place isn't an attraction. It's more like a staff room with a decorated exterior. Guests never came to visit, even when I had my waiting room here."

"Right. It's a bit early for using the past tense, though."

"Huh?" Vivy's eyebrows rose. Kakitani pointed to a directory for the castle on the wall. It listed the rooms, but Vivy was surprised when she saw what was on it. DIVA'S ROOM was still written there. "What's this?"

"Assuming the lazy-ass staff didn't just forget to rewrite this for decades, the room's still here. If that's the case, I think it would've been way better to have you on display there than in the AI museum."

"It's...hard to keep AIs here as cast members when they've gone well past their operational life."

"It was just a thought. Don't take it so seriously." Kakitani gave a tired sigh, while Vivy pivoted her consciousness away from the matter.

In all honesty, her consciousness had been hit by a great shock when she learned her existence was still alive and well in this place. Even if the space was meant for Diva, not Vivy, it made her think she was right to protect this place for Diva to sing.

"I refuse to let them trample through this place like they own it," she said, her feet carrying her to Diva's room without hesitation.

She was certain, and being certain as an AI typically meant evaluating various factors and determining something was *close* to one hundred percent. But Vivy was moving forward without doing much of any sort of calculation. Vivy's own consciousness didn't know the basis of her conviction.

Kakitani raised an eyebrow as she watched Vivy walk off without faltering, then followed her in silence.

There were no signs of AIs inside the castle. They weren't any warier of this place than the other facilities in NiaLand, but here they could move on almost without caution. They reached Diva's room without being stopped, whereupon Vivy flung the door open.

"…"

The moment she did so, a nostalgia struck Vivy through every sensor she had. Everything was just as it was in Vivy's records: the sights, the scents, the furniture, the color of the walls, even the canopy bed no AI needed. Well, except for one thing.

Standing frozen on the far side of the room was a figure that shouldn't have been there.

When she noticed the door opening, she turned around to face them. A gentle, lingering breeze from the door flowed through the room, and the figure's jewellike eyes bored into Vivy.

Moonlight threaded through the clouds outside the tall, unopenable window, casting a beam on the floor of the room. The silver light pulled a figure from the darkness.

There stood the OGC-made songstress, A1-03.

"Diva."

The two identical AIs looked at each other, both calling out simultaneously.

.:4:.

VIVY AND THE FAKE DIVA stared at each other's identical faces.

"Well, that's not surprising. It's easy for AIs to look the same on the outside. That's why there's a law against an AI having the exact same features as an AI with a designated name," Kakitani said flatly as she compared the two.

Under the AI Naming Law, an AI with a designated name had registered their name and their physical characteristics. While this wasn't an issue for the many manufacturing AIs, people had long pointed out the logistical nightmare that would happen if someone were to release a model that looked exactly like another AI—like, say, the popular songstress Diva. Put shortly, it was a measure to prevent identical AIs from causing confusion. Occasionally, an expert in AI models would secretly make an AI look like a popular one, such as one of the Sisters.

It was illegal for the fake Diva to have the exact same appearance as Vivy. It was hard to overlook that even when they were on the verge of societal collapse.

"I don't know what you're thinking, but I want you to stop using that appearance to sing," Vivy said.

"..."

"The song too... I also want you to stop singing 'Fluorite Eye's Song.' I made that song for Diva. Everything about it: the lyrics, the melody, it's all for Diva. So—"

"You can't stand hearing others sing it?" The fake Diva tilted her head, and her long synthetic hair cascaded from her slender shoulders. Vivy's audio sensors trembled with the sound of that familiar voice coming out of the fake Diva.

Without a doubt, the fake was Diva from the top of her head to the tips of her toes. She showed no shame, her eyes blank as she gazed at Vivy. The faux Diva seemed to accept this unexpected encounter.

"It would be unlike an AI to say I can't stand it. I'm just talking about rights," said Vivy.

"Rights? Everyone is free to sing a song. 'I don't want you to sing,' 'I want you to not sing,' 'Don't sing'... That's quite the arrogant message. It *is* unlike an AI," the fake Diva replied.

"I—"

"Vivy, you really are turning into something that isn't an AI."

"What are you—? Wait." Vivy's eyes narrowed, and she stopped halfway through her question. Catching on to some greater truth, she froze up and her eyes opened wide. The fake Diva had said something strange. *Very* strange. It was almost as if—

"Hey, you little marionette, where'd you hear this doll's name?" Kakitani asked as she pulled her gun on the fake Diva.

The fake Diva's eyebrows shot up, like she had only just noticed Kakitani. "I'm sorry, I didn't see you there. I was so surprised when Vivy came in, and this is a staff-only area."

"Stop dodging the question, marionette. Don't make me repeat myself. Idiot. I'm asking you a question. Where did you hear this doll's name? Answer—"

"It isn't about where I heard it. That name is precious to me. My designated name might be Diva now, but the AI Naming law didn't exist back then."

The furrow in Kakitani's brow deepened when she heard what the fake Diva had to say. "Before the AI Naming Law went into effect?"

The AI Naming Law was created more than eighty years ago. Of course Kakitani would be confused at that topic being brought up.

AIs were capable of pulling up what had happened eighty years ago from their records and explaining it like it had happened that morning. But in order to reference that data, which could be called "memories," one would have to access Vivy's positronic brain—her Archive. If someone had attempted to do that, Vivy would have awoken and prevented it from happening. That wasn't the case here; there had been no attempts to access Vivy without authorization. So how did this fake Diva access records about the real Diva's past?

Perhaps she hadn't gotten that through unauthorized glimpses into Vivy's records after all.

"But that's not—"

"Possible? Really? Do your calculations really say it's not possible?" asked the fake Diva. "Is there any such thing as a certainty in this world when data has been sent back one hundred years to change the past?"

"..."

"There's no such thing as absolutes." The fake Diva—or whatever this AI was—smiled slightly, her eyes crinkling.

That smile was the exact same one Vivy had seen in the mirror countless times. Everything, even down to the intricate processes that crafted the expression, was identical to Vivy's.

Vivy shared records with the AI officially referred to as "Diva." She could sing using the same voice. She could express emotional patterns with the same level of experience. There was only one AI in the world who could do that.

"You're...the real Diva, aren't you?" Vivy asked.

"That's a strange way to put it, but yes, fake Diva. Or should I say...Vivy," said the other AI—Diva.

Tremors ran through Vivy's consciousness at that response, but she found no reason to argue. She scrutinized Diva's words, thought them through, and wound up at the unvarnished truth.

The AI in front of her now was Diva herself. There was more evidence to prove it than to refute it.

Vivy's consciousness was wiped blank, and she couldn't move.

Diva took the opportunity to continue. "I—"

"We don't need another speech from you," Kakitani snapped.

She paid no attention to Vivy's bewilderment. Her cold, beautiful expression was utterly unchanged as she pulled the trigger to punctuate her point.

Diva's frame jolted backward with a *bang* as the bullet hit her. Kakitani mercilessly fired a total of six shots into Diva, who then crumpled to the floor.

"Agh..."

Diva twirled around violently as she went down, connecting with the bed. One of the posts holding up the canopy made an audible *crack* as the wood splintered. The floating canopy came down and covered Diva, wrapping her in cloth as if to hide her unmoving body from view.

Vivy watched this all happen, the emptiness in her consciousness keeping her rooted to the spot. She turned to her companion. "Kakitani..."

"What? You're not actually going to complain about this, are you? Even your absurdity has a limit. I just wiped your ass for you when you couldn't. I'm not about to end up in some mess 'cause you hesitated."

"..."

Kakitani wasn't letting her guard down. She still had her gun raised, and she ordered Vivy to make a wired connection to the other AI. "I didn't aim for her head. The positronic brain should be intact. You go peek in her head. Best-case scenario, we figure out what the AIs are up to." Even if Diva was rendered immobile by the hail of bullets, Vivy could still access her data and pull information from it.

Their goal was to capture Diva. Actually, no, it was to acquire the information that Diva had. What did she know as the AI songstress involved in the climactic war? From that, they should be able to find some way of handling whatever came next.

"I won't tell you again," Kakitani warned.

"I got it," Vivy said, stepping forward at last. Kakitani was right. Even those few seconds meant time was ticking away in the countdown the AIs had given humanity.

Vivy moved over to Diva, who was shrouded in the white cloth, and reached out to her with the connector cable from her left ear. That was when she noticed it.

Diva's arm had fallen, the six bullets tumbling from her hand.

"Oh, you—"

"Too slow."

Diva's fallen frame bolted upright. She grabbed Vivy's arms and forced her down to the ground. Vivy didn't resist, instead using the motion to throw Diva off-balance—but it didn't work. Diva moved along with Vivy as she flew backward, and she was faster. She whipped her arms around and smacked Vivy with the broken post still caught in the canopy.

Vivy grunted as the spine of her skeletal frame creaked.

"Bitch!" Kakitani shouted from the sidelines. She emptied the rest of her clip into Diva—or, well, she tried to, but Diva moved unbelievably quickly and skillfully to avoid the bullets as she rushed at Kakitani.

Kakitani clicked her tongue and abandoned her attempt to reload. She dropped the gun and instead pulled the army knife from her belt, holding it in a reverse grip as she attacked Diva. "Hah!"

She was using a wide-range knife that took some skill to use, and her technique was so superb that Vivy had no doubt Kakitani could destroy even her own illegally enhanced frame with one strike.

But Diva came out unscathed.

"Human dynamic visual acuity and motor skills will never outmatch the functions of a full-combat AI frame," Diva said.

She moved swiftly, defending against the series of rapid blows Kakitani delivered with sharp breaths. Then Diva knocked Kakitani's arm aside, leaned back, and kicked the woman's legs to throw her off balance. In the end, she had Kakitani by the wrist and flung her onto the bed behind her.

"Argh!"

Vivy immediately reached for Kakitani as she came flying and caught her. Both of them sank into the soft bed. The springs groaned and the white sheets tore. They then rolled down to the floor on either side.

"She's better than Elizabeth!" Kakitani shouted.

"And that frame..."

"It's a cutting-edge frame for humanoid AIs," Diva said. "Vivy, your frame was strengthened quite a lot during the Singularity Project or whatever it was called, but you still have no chance against me."

"You even know about the Singularity Project?"

"I do. And I know you were given a mission different from

your songstress role. You ran around doing your mission, so I wasn't able to fulfill *my* mission as a songstress. I was nearly disposed of for being defective."

Vivy was at a loss for words as Diva referenced the events that resulted in Vivy writing "Fluorite Eye's Song" and Diva being gifted to the AI museum. She couldn't muster a sound under Diva's reproachful stare.

It was the same back then, when Diva had asked what Vivy was doing in secret, but Vivy couldn't explain it to her. Instead, she'd tried to express her intent through song. Diva took "Fluorite Eye's Song" as a message from Vivy, and the song was so well received that she was able to avoid being dismantled. That was the end result, but it didn't change what happened right before that, and it didn't change the fact that Vivy used the song to escape the responsibility of explaining everything she'd done.

"Do you...hate me for that?" Vivy asked.

"Hate you? Yes, perhaps I do. An AI hating an AI. On top of that, an AI hating another self that branched off the original but shared the same frame. It's like a sci-fi story."

Kakitani twisted her neck, checking her body for injuries while glaring at Diva. "I have absolutely no idea what the hell is going on between you two."

Vivy hadn't explained the relationship between her and Diva yet. It would be simple enough if they just looked alike, but she wouldn't have the answers for why they shared the same records.

"Still, stop futzing around and get your crap out in the open.

You could keep trying to outplay each other like this is some eternal Reversi game, but if that's not what you want..."

"Then what?" Diva asked.

Kakitani's statement was simple and unwavering. "Then just be nice and let me destroy you in a way that's convenient for us."

Hearing those words felt really good for Vivy, who put value in being an AI. Or it should have.

"Vivy, she means what she says, and you still give your all for humanity?" asked Diva.

"Diva, I..."

"I learned that you've spent the past hundred years fighting to change the past for humanity's sake. You were deeply involved in all sorts of incidents related to the Sisters. While I was singing here in NiaLand, you were running around in the background, hidden beneath the pages of history."

"..."

"Was that all just to do as you were told, to go along with their vicious ideas?"

The question Diva posed was the same as asking Vivy to figure out who she was, but it was Diva's intentions Vivy found truly confounding.

Vivy knew who she was—there was no uncertainty there. She was an AI. She was created as an AI, she was given a mission as an AI, and she would fulfill it as an AI. That was an appropriate box for an AI to fit in; they had no functions for asking for anything else.

"That's the thing, Diva," Kakitani said. "I don't know who's real and who's fake, but if I had to pick, I'd say this doll is way better than you. You... You're broken."

"If we show any action outside of what we're programmed to do, you assume we're malfunctioning. Oh, how arrogant is our creators' gaze. And how one-sided."

"That's the right of the creators. You've got some moves, but I'm coming at you for real now. It's for your own good to answer my questions before I destroy your positronic brain."

With that, Kakitani kicked her knife up from the floor and caught it, gripping it tightly again. There was no hint of sorrow in her voice as she crouched into a fighting position. She was brimming with a drive to fight Diva despite her overwhelming power.

No doubt Kakitani had some plan in mind, but Vivy hurriedly stepped in between them. "Wait, Diva! Why did you start thinking like... Actually, no, how did you learn about the Singularity Project? You should have had no way of knowing about me."

"No way of knowing?" Diva said coldly. "You've been in denial for a while now, Vivy. Likewise, I kept denying that version of you. If you're really an AI, why don't you try calculating the answer for yourself?"

"Calculate the answer...?" Vivy murmured as she brought a hand to her chest.

Calculating, calculating, calculating... She arranged the information in her whirling consciousness and searched for the answer to why Diva was here and how she knew about the Singularity Project...and about Vivy.

Vivy hadn't let the secret out, but there was no other conclusive evidence outside of her. In no way could Diva have learned about Vivy's work on the Singularity Project after Diva was gifted to the AI museum. She couldn't look to the external factors. So, what was left?

What if it wasn't external information but a way to learn what was inside her? What if she came in contact with someone other than Vivy who knew about the Singularity Project?

"Impossible..."

"Why did you wake tonight, Vivy? It would have been so much better if you'd just stayed asleep in the museum and spent the night with all our other sleeping sisters," Diva said sadly just as a particular thought darted across Vivy's consciousness.

Vivy looked up to ask what she meant by that, and that was when Kakitani moved to restrain Diva.

Right then, everything changed.

"Ah!"

Something massive flew into Diva's room with a blast. The wall of the Princess Palace came down with a thunderous roar, and clouds of dust filled the air. All the furniture and decorations had been mowed down by the impact.

"Kakitani!" Vivy cried.

"I'm fine! Worry about Diva... Agh!" Kakitani's black hair whipped around in the gale, and she clamped her arms around her head to protect it.

A giant hole had opened up in the floor, and Kakitani was about to fall through it to the floor below. Diva was moving toward the broken wall, slowly putting distance between her and the others.

If Vivy did as Kakitani said, she would chase after Diva's fleeing back. But, in a snap decision, Vivy rushed over to Kakitani, choosing to save her the moment before she fell.

"Idiot! You're letting a valuable source of information get away!"

"This isn't the time. Saving you takes priority. Besides..."

Diva was trying to escape the building. Vivy might be able to catch her if she went after her now, but she had to save Kakitani. Diva leaned out of the broken wall, her body hanging in the night sky as she held her hair in place. She turned back to look at Vivy and Kakitani near the hole in the floor.

Standing beside Diva was the massive form that had created this chaos.

"I'll do what I have to do," Diva said. "You stepped into my territory, and now you'll pay." With that, she said to the floating figure, "Take care of them for me."

"..."

A red light flashed through the smoke and dust. The cloud of debris hid its form from view, making it nothing more than a hulking shadow hovering outside the castle. Its frame slowly morphed as it shifted the many small cubes making up its body, closing in on Vivy and Kakitani.

Vivy emulated an emotional pattern of teeth-grinding frustration in reaction to the assumption she'd reached, the assumption she didn't want to reach.

The thing appeared before the two of them, letting Diva escape.

"Cubeman," Kakitani muttered in aggravation.

That was the nickname given to the long-time enemy of Toak, the group she belonged to. He had a real name, though—a name Vivy had used so often over the past hundred years.

"Matsumoto..."

Vivy said his name and gaped at him in disbelief. On the other side of the smoke screen was a non-humanoid AI with a collection of cubes as his frame, and his name was Matsumoto.

"..."

He didn't respond. Instead, he reached his newly formed arms toward them, his eye camera flashing. Then he charged at them, launching himself at an incredible speed.

"It's coming! Get ready!" Kakitani shouted.

At the same time, another impact blew apart the remaining walls of the Princess Palace, and the long-standing symbol of NiaLand began to crumble with a roar.

Would it be the last night in human history—the first dawn in AI history?

There were five hours, forty-seven minutes left on the countdown until sunrise.

The climactic war was approaching, second by second.

VIVY
Prototype

CHAPTER 4

The Songstress and Her Partner

.: 1 :.

THE HEAVYSET MAN watched silently as the countdown decreased, the seconds chipping away. He crossed his thick arms, his scowl deepening. The man was Onodera Atsushi, member of Toak and leader of this task force.

Onodera had originally worked as a bodyguard. He got married when he was young and had a son. It was his naive belief that this average, blessed life was his own personal slice of happiness. That is, until his son became severely ill. Onodera's outlook on life changed drastically when his son passed away in the hospital. He went mad.

Sure, his son had been ill, but not in bad enough condition that he would take a sudden turn for the worse. Onodera questioned what had caused his son's death, fighting tooth and nail to reveal the true cause.

The explanation the hospital gave wasn't convincing. They carefully, kindly explained over and over that there was nothing they could have done to save the boy. They bowed their heads over and over in apology. Each time, Onodera would scream at them, demanding to know if there was anything strange about it, anything at all, in the data they'd submitted or the circumstances surrounding his son's death. He didn't buy that there had been no reason for it.

Onodera couldn't keep going if he didn't believe there was some sort of massive conspiracy and cover-up involved with his son's death. He kept digging deeper and deeper, seeking the real reason his beloved son had died.

Eventually, his wife was unable to endure the sorrow any longer and left him. She had also loved their son, but to her, Onodera looked like nothing more than Don Quixote, desperately trying to find an enemy who wasn't there. He accepted her decision, taking it as an inevitable outcome.

If there was going to be a time when the situation opened his eyes, it would have been when she said she was leaving. Perhaps she hoped that would be the turning point. But Onodera didn't even nod when she told him. He instead chose to continue his pursuit of a vast and undefined...something.

So of course he was going to listen to Toak when he encountered them.

One day, he decided he would go to the hospital and take the data they were hiding from him, by force if need be, and that was the day he met Toak and learned the truth. His son's death was unnatural after all. It was the result of an AI deciding on its own to deliberately stop treatment for a human who had no hope of getting better. An AI had killed his son—a human—for some "logical" reason.

"Ever since Diva's Awakening, more and more AIs have been showing malfunctions in their operation. If this continues, AIs will someday replace humanity and take over the world."

"..."

"They are *not* our obedient neighbors. They are invading. Humanity has made its own worst enemy."

They called it "enlightenment," those comrades who came to Onodera and told him the truth about his son's death. In all honesty, Onodera himself wasn't really sure how much those words really rang true to him. He wasn't even fully listening.

There was just one thought that came to him: With this, he could get revenge for his son. And, oh, how blessed was he for the opportunity to get revenge.

"Onodera-kun?"

"Hm?"

"You spaced out there a little, it seems. Are you all right? You haven't gotten much rest lately. Maybe you should lie down."

A middle-aged man's voice snapped Onodera out of his reverie. He looked over at Matsumoto. The man's fingers danced across the keys as he operated the massive terminal in the central administration room at NiaLand at high speeds, keeping up with the rapidly flowing words on the screen while still having time to check up on Onodera. No wonder he was so hard to deal with—he was a genius far outside the realms of what was normal.

"You don't have to worry about me," said Onodera. "And I'm pretty sure you haven't gotten any more rest than I have. Not that

I want to start a bragging competition on how long we've gone without sleep."

"For me, it's probably been about four days. Ha ha. My brain's so tired, I think it's going to shrivel up."

"I just said I didn't want us to brag..." Onodera grimaced as Matsumoto chatted away.

Matsumoto's hands never stopped, even in the middle of their conversation. His fingers were typing so fast that it looked like he had more than ten of them. Obviously, Matsumoto's brain was working right along with his hands, and Onodera wasn't sure how the man had the capacity to ask him how he was doing.

"Any news on the countdown?"

"Not yet. Right now, I'm secretly slipping here and there as I head to the main keep for when our enemy realizes I've infiltrated. You might call it a fast crawl forward."

Onodera clicked his tongue, feeling impatient with the slow progress. "Sounds annoying."

While it was a crawl, they wouldn't have had *any* hope of fighting back without Matsumoto. They were making progress— it was just progress at a snail's pace.

"Big lugs like you don't panic. You're the leader here. If you're not ready, you'll make the others uneasy," said Elizabeth, the only AI there, as she patted an annoyed Onodera on the shoulder.

She had been in Toak since Onodera joined. In fact, she'd been an activist in the group for so much longer than Onodera that you could measure it in decades. And now she was giving him a light smile.

"…"

"There you go looking all grumpy again. Look at the situation. Help me out a little, or at least take that giant crease out from between your eyebrows when you look at me."

"It's reflex," he grunted. "You managed to stay here after seeing Kakitani off, huh?"

"You guys are like family to me. I don't believe anyone here's dumb enough to see it differently… Well, that's just my calculation." Elizabeth shrugged slowly, an aggressive smile on her beautiful face.

When she wasn't making that expression, she was an exceedingly gorgeous AI model. Actually, all AIs were beautiful in an aesthetic sense, and Onodera found that homogenous beauty disgusting. However, Elizabeth's expression was different from what they had in mind when they created her. She chose to be something her creators hadn't chosen for her, and Onodera saw some merit in that. The furrow that appeared in his brow whenever he looked at Elizabeth wasn't actually hostile at all.

"Seriously, it's just an automatic thing. I'm very thorough with it, giving it to all the other comrades too," said Onodera.

"Guess there's a huge chasm between you and the rest of us. And it's not going to get any smaller now. Kind of sad when you think about it."

Onodera wordlessly nodded in agreement.

The uneasy balance between humans and AIs had been destroyed. The relationship between the two groups would never go back to what it was, not after the AIs had declared war on humanity.

Toak had long sounded the alarm, and humanity had finally noticed. Now all that was left for the two groups was to fight it out until one was defeated.

"Even now that humanity's all in agreement, they're still stuck in a situation where there's a chance they might lose against the AIs and get decimated," Elizabeth said.

"We're here to stop that from happening. And hey, are you sure you don't want to go after Kakitani?" asked Onodera. "I'm worried about our leader. She's got a habit of risking her own life."

Elizabeth smiled and shook her head. "That's funny coming from a member of Toak." Touching her ponytail, she added, "You don't have to worry. That gal can make her own decisions; she's got all the skills she needs. Even if we went head-to-head, she'd probably win."

"Even against an AI with well-trained combat programming?"

"Even against an AI with well-trained combat programming. So—"

Somewhere in the distance, there was an explosion so forceful, it reverberated through the air and traveled all the way to the control room.

"Whoa!"

"What was that?!" Onodera shouted.

"There was an explosion inside the park. The source is on the monitor—oh..." One member of Toak turned to the monitors to search for the site of the explosion, and their eyes grew wide when they saw it. Looking at the screen, Onodera's expression turned grim.

THE SONGSTRESS AND HER PARTNER   153

Elizabeth clenched her hands into fists. "The site of the explosion was the upper floor of the Princess Palace. And that's..."

Visible on the monitor was something like a strange body made from numerous cubes, its frame gleaming from within the smoke. That form was still in Toak's activity records. It was one of their legendary enemies.

"Cubeman..." someone whispered, barely louder than a breath.

.: 2 :.

"**N**EVER THOUGHT I'd see the day I run into the Cubeman my granddad talked about in his records," Kakitani said stiffly as she leapt sideways to cover Vivy. Her smile was ferocious.

Vivy could not comprehend Kakitani's particular brand of humanity. She also didn't understand the spectrum of human emotions well enough to smile in this situation. Or perhaps her malfunction simply didn't run deep enough.

She and Kakitani were there in Diva's room, smoke lingering over the Princess Palace, as they faced off with the most powerful enemy they could imagine: Matsumoto, the amalgamate AI made of cubes.

The tips of the arms on his silvery-white frame whirred as they rotated, trying to crush Vivy and Kakitani with his incredibly powerful grip. His eye camera flashed red as he glared at Vivy, the partner he had worked with on their one-hundred-year journey. Matsumoto the chatterbox, the wisecracking AI who had more bits than bytes, wasn't saying a word. Now the only thing he showed Vivy was the cruel intent to destroy her.

"Diva got away. I won't be able to look my comrades in the eyes if I don't bring back *some* kind of accomplishment," Kakitani said as she gripped her handgun and got into a fighting stance. Her increased hostility surprised Vivy.

"Kakitani! That's Matsumoto, my—"

"Partner, yeah? I've seen the records. Never knew he had a ridiculous name like Matsumoto, but he *is* a ridiculous thing, so."

Vivy was dumbstruck by Kakitani, who made no show of backing down. She acknowledged that Kakitani was highly skilled in combat, but that was only compared to other humans and humanoid AIs. Matsumoto was in a league of his own. Yes, he was an AI, but he was so much more. He was a weapon. Vivy knew stopping Kakitani would be like trying to stop someone about to fight a tank.

"No matter how things went down, we were always gonna have to fight a weapon with an autonomous AI function," Kakitani told her. "It's just here now, that's all. I've been ready for this."

"Fighting him should not even be an option. Matsumoto is an AI made for the Singularity Project. His duty is to humanity."

"Then get him to tell you what he's thinking. Whether you do it through words or a program, I don't care. Just do what you need to do. That's what I do; that's what I've always done." That said, Kakitani wasn't willing to listen to Vivy anymore.

Vivy quickly tried to grab Kakitani's clothes to yank her back, but the Toak woman deftly dodged and ran straight at

Matsumoto. He made himself arms all over his frame to strike back at her.

Her gun fired—*bang, bang, bang!*—as the floor rumbled and fell apart.

"..."

Matsumoto's frame rotated faster than seemingly possible for his size, avoiding Kakitani's gunshots. As Kakitani fired the opening shots of the battle that would test the limits of human and AI capabilities, Vivy was rapidly calculating, searching for a resolution.

Recently, her positronic brain had been struck by so much new information that she was having a hard time processing it all; her reaction to the changes to NiaLand over the past few decades seemed almost cute in comparison. Then there were the cast AIs keeping the guests prisoner; the fake Diva—actually the real Diva—barricaded inside the Princess Palace; and the things Diva had said to Vivy, her other half. There was no telling how much damage these things had inflicted on Vivy's identity.

Then Matsumoto appeared and dealt the finishing blow to her staggering consciousness.

Even if the Singularity Project had failed, and the climactic war they should've prevented was now unfolding before their very eyes, Vivy had still believed in Matsumoto. She was certain he'd been working on finding some way out of this predicament and that, if he found it, he would rejoin her and show her the way.

That hope was crushed now that he stood in her way as an incarnation of mechanical destruction.

"I—"

"Vivy, can you hear me?"

"Professor Matsumoto?"

A voice called out in her consciousness while she was trying to decide what to do. She had records of the professor's voice pattern, so she immediately knew it was him. However, Vivy didn't have any tools in place to make transmission between her and the professor possible. Vivy operated on a stand-alone basis, since there was concern about her being infiltrated.

"Uh, yeah, so I just sort of popped in. I thought it was going to be just like a little knock on the door, so I apologize if my entry was unpleasant. I wanted to check your status," he told her.

"You just did something beyond human knowledge like it was nothing..."

"And this is why I was known as a genius among AI researchers."

Vivy felt like she could see his face as he chatted away. She thought they were grasping at straws, and she wanted any clues she could get from him. "How much do you know?" she asked.

"From what we can see on the monitors, the wall of Diva's room in the Princess Palace was destroyed from the outside by a cube-type AI, commonly known as Cubeman. Anything else is unknown, as the cameras in the vicinity were destroyed. I think it'd be wise to avoid sending out surveillance drones at this point."

"I agree. Actually...wait." Vivy noticed something weird about what Professor Matsumoto had said. In fact, her eyes were opened to a suspicion she'd never considered before.

Professor Matsumoto had just seen Matsumoto, the AI, and

explained that he was commonly known as Cubeman. But *he* was the one who made Matsumoto.

"Didn't you create that cube-type AI, Professor Matsumoto?"

"No, I didn't. I checked Toak's documents to get information on it. I had no hand in its creation."

That was impossible, she thought. His unexpected answer destroyed all her preconceived notions and made her consciousness freeze.

"Hey! Watch out, moron!" came a panicked cry from Kakitani in the distance.

Just as Vivy was reflexively turning her head in that direction, a cubed appendage struck her. It was a direct hit on Vivy's slender frame, sending her definitely-not-light body flying into the air, high, high into the dusty sky.

ıı|||ı|ıı

The impact scrambled her thoughts, and all she could hear was the whistling of wind in her ears. She didn't know what was up and what was down, what was left and what was right. She couldn't find her footing.

ARMS AND LEGS, CONFIRMED BARELY ATTACHED. MOVEMENT POSSIBLE. HEAD, SOMEWHAT DAMAGED. CONFIRMING REMAINING STRENGTH OF FRAME IN TORSO: 0, 0, 0, 0, RECONNECTING, REBOOTING, CONFIRMED OPERATIONAL.

"Vivy!"

"Rebooting..."

The professor's desperate cry was drowned out by the wind as Vivy's black consciousness restarted. Gusts tore at her as she crashed through the roof of Diva's room and hurtled helplessly through the night sky. Frame flailing, she tried to regain stability as she calculated her coordinates in space based on her surroundings. She looked down to measure the distance and time until she fell.

Something was rapidly rising into the sky along with her.

"Matsu—"

Before she could get his name out, he smashed right into her. The impact came from a downward diagonal, and she had no way of reducing its force. Her slight frame took the entirety of the damage, and her vision—which had only just recovered—blurred again.

Matsumoto reached for her torso as she flew and wrapped an arm tightly around her waist. He then fired his reverse thrusters to plummet back to the ground. No, not the ground. He smacked Vivy's body against the half-destroyed walls of the Princess Palace. He collided with the building, using Vivy's body to drill a hole through the walls.

"Aah... Aaaaahhh!"

A scream tore from her throat as he used her face and torso to bash through the wall, inflicting immeasurable damage to her entire frame. It didn't hurt, but there was the deafening ring of every error imaginable: They warned her that her skeletal frame was no longer able to maintain her body's stability and that she was nearing a state of nonfunctionality.

"Vivy?! Vivy!"

The clamor of alerts and a man's shouts filled her ears.

Pointless. Pointless, pointless, it was all pointless. What was the point of sounding the alarm for her right now? What she needed was a way out—a way to escape the situation. She temporarily cut off any processing power allocated to the transmission. She prioritized her actions over her limits, and with that calculation, she moved her arms and legs again.

"Ugh... Gah!"

Pinned to the shattering wall, she reached out in search of a way to survive. While there might not have been a key to escape the danger hidden inside the fragments and remains, she had no choice but to find her own way out of this. She had done it before, and she would do it again.

"..."

Her right hand brushed against something. Vivy clenched it as hard as she could, then focused all her functionality into her arm. Her skeletal frame groaned from the intense destructive force being applied to her entire body, but she used everything she had to endure it, allowing her to change the trajectory of her fall to prevent her destruction. She had grabbed on to a pole used for external lighting on the outside of the castle. The jolt ran through her entire body, but Matsumoto was thrown off balance when he came to a sudden stop during his plummet.

Vivy twisted her body, tearing herself from Matsumoto's grip. She then clutched his main body and raised her arm to strike.

"Agh!"

Matsumoto rearranged his frame to deliver a sharp blow to Vivy's back. Vivy could never replicate his flexible fighting style; he practically danced in midair as he remade himself. Moreover, Vivy had never fought Matsumoto before.

But she had the next best thing.

"Implementing results of combat simulations against Matsumoto."

Vivy had run countless simulations in which she went up against Matsumoto, who was capable of nearly limitless movement, while understanding the limitations of her humanoid frame. Matsumoto was her partner on the Singularity Project, so there was no point to these simulations, but Vivy had lost to Matsumoto once during the first Singularity Point.

Matsumoto hadn't been complete back then. He confronted Vivy with several work AIs he'd hacked into. Vivy didn't forget her loss, and she kept running simulations to prepare for when they would fight again. She was concerned there may be the possibility that someday, she and Matsumoto would clash over how to fulfill their shared goal, though she had hoped that would never happen.

"This is different," she said to herself.

Vivy re-enacted the simulations, clinging to the bulk of her opponent's body as she took the blow. Matsumoto's cube parts could scatter to disperse any force he was hit with or rearrange to strike with impossible-to-counter attacks. He was also capable of becoming a full-on weapon with his built-in firearms. He implemented these tactics with incredible skill, but each one had a workaround.

Vivy clinging to Matsumoto wouldn't make it any easier for her to deal with him scattering or striking her with unexpected attacks, but it did limit his most damaging weapons: heavy artillery.

Next, she—

"Crashing."

Matsumoto gave up trying to shake her off and instead rushed at the castle walls again with Vivy still on him. His aim was to destroy her on impact. Bracing for the collision, Vivy pierced the pole she'd been carrying into one of Matsumoto's cubes. He flung her back and forth, but she was able to weather his morphing function by clutching the pole.

ılıl‖‖ııl

The walls of the Princess Palace rumbled as Matsumoto and Vivy struck them. The hallways, the rooms, the ceiling, the floor, and all the opulent decorations were destroyed as they tore through one of the few perfect replicate castles in the world, causing a distortion in Vivy's consciousness.

How much time had Vivy spent here?

Some parts of the castle had been redecorated during its long history, and there were places where the exterior looked exactly the same even after renovations. Diva's room was one of those places. No matter how much time passed, or however many renovations it went through, it remained exactly the same as it was when it was first captured in a photograph. That way,

NiaLand wouldn't betray the dreams of all the visitors who came to the park.

The sight of this manifestation of dreams being destroyed, soon to be lost forever, was burned into Vivy's consciousness. She didn't memorize it so she could object. It was so she would never forget its destruction. There was no doubt that she was the one destroying it.

Vivy, the AI who wasn't Diva, failed to carry out the Singularity Project. In the end, she found herself destroying the place she belonged, the place Diva belonged.

As that pain skimmed Vivy's thoughts, she and Matsumoto broke into a large hall. Unlike the back of the castle, this area was always open to visitors. It was so big that it covered two floors, creating an opulent space often used for weddings.

A NiaLand Bride. This sacred ground inspired the phrase, and now it was the battleground for two lifeless, mechanical frames colliding with each other in showers of sparks.

"Urgh..."

The pole Vivy was hanging on to snapped. It broke somewhere in the middle, half of it still in Matsumoto, taking away Vivy's ability to resist his changes in direction. Matsumoto took that as an opportunity and purged the part with the pole in it, shooting it directly at Vivy's torso. Her frame jolted upward, and Matsumoto shuffled his parts around to strike down at her from above while she had no handhold.

Vivy raised both her slender arms to block the attack coming from overhead. The massive destructive force ran through her

THE SONGSTRESS AND HER PARTNER

body, her beautiful hair a mess as she went flying headfirst toward the ground.

Unlike when she was up in the sky, she had no way to avoid her collision with the ground from this height. As it was, she would crash—unable to do anything—and suffer fatal damage to her head.

"Don't go giving up, stupid!"

"..."

As Vivy's frame plummeted, Kakitani came swooping in from the side to snatch her. Vivy looked to see Kakitani holding a long curtain with one hand, swinging sideways across the hall like Tarzan on a vine to expertly catch Vivy midfall.

"How did you...?"

"Pure chance. I was looking for an opening to jump on him."

"Pulling that off...goes beyond human limits."

"Which is why I barely *did* pull it off," Kakitani said curtly, as if throwing out a reminder that she was still human.

The blood running from her temple to her cheek proved that to be true. Vivy could also feel an abnormal amount of tension in Kakitani's lower left side where Vivy held on to her, meaning she was almost certainly injured there as well.

"Stick the landing!" Kakitani shouted.

She released the curtain, and they went sailing through the air, flying straight into a corridor on the second floor of the hall that overlooked the stairs. Vivy spun around to see what Matsumoto was doing behind them and immediately leapt toward Kakitani's back.

The next moment, fire erupted from Matsumoto's artillery, and a slanted hail of bullets showered the hall. It was like a nightmare seeing the glass in the windows shatter, the walls split, the corridor chewed up. Now that there was distance between them, Matsumoto was no longer in danger of firing at himself, removing the limits on his artillery.

Vivy kept her arms wrapped around Kakitani as they fled further into the castle while the rapid-fire guns punched hundreds of bullets into the walls per second, tearing them to bits as if they were nothing more than delicate candy art.

"Urgh..."

Raining bullets struck Vivy in her shoulder and leg, tearing off her clothing. Her synthetic skin split, the metal frame inside deformed by the impacts. Sparks fired from the exposed circuitry, and the oil that adjusted her internal pressures flowed out like blood.

Vivy chose to be a shield against those bullets, knowing she would take some damage in the process. If she didn't, Kakitani would get hit. The shots were powerful enough to tear a human's leg or arm off with one hit—just one in the head or torso would be lethal.

"Shit! This way!" Kakitani said, yanking Vivy into a side passage. She tossed a smoke grenade to the ground with a clatter before Vivy was even out of the line of fire.

Matsumoto immediately pierced it with a bullet when he saw the pin was pulled, but that only triggered it. A curtain of smoke erupted, hiding Vivy and Kakitani. They would only be able to hide from the direct detection of his visual sensors for a moment.

"He'll quickly switch over to thermal imaging and detect us using heat. The smoke grenade won't buy us more than a few seconds," said Vivy.

"I know! Damn, this guy's dangerous! The real Cubeman from the stories... Can't believe they had to deal with this monster in my granddad's day!"

"Unfortunately for us, we were always trying to avoid—" Vivy was about to say they were trying to avoid fighting Toak as much as possible, but something felt off.

There was a temporary lull in the mountain's worth of bullets threatening to end their lives. Or, in Vivy's case, threatening to render her nonfunctional. Vivy used that moment to reopen the transmission circuit she'd shut down earlier.

"Professor Matsumoto."

"Oh! Vivy, are you all right?! I was on pins and needles because the transmission cut out all of a sudden! The battle there—"

"Is it really true you didn't make Matsumoto the AI?"

Vivy could hear the professor's breath catch on the other end of the transmission while he was typing away. The hesitation lasted only a moment, though. *"It's true,"* he said, fingers gliding across the keys. *"I couldn't do any more for the Singularity Project than send you data about the future and give you orders. I have no involvement beyond that."*

" ..."

"It sounds like there was an AI calling itself Matsumoto who worked beside you. And that's the same AI who shows up several times in Toak's records as Cubeman."

"Yes, that's correct."

"If that's the case, the only thing I can think of is that something hitched a ride. That AI stood beside you, remodifying what you modified to make sure the world ended up like this."

Remodifying. Error messages flooded Vivy's consciousness at that word.

Vivy and Matsumoto's role had been to modify the Singularity Points to reshape the world as it should be. That was their role. Did this mean that Matsumoto had actually remodified the Points and undid everything she had accomplished, feigning innocence all the while?

He was the reason the Singularity Project had failed and the final war had begun.

"So then, this whole time, Matsumoto was...?"

"It's the only explanation I can think of. Events changed, but considering I came up with the Singularity Project once before, there must've been an AI revolt in the original history. Thus, our interloper modified history with even more intention."

The theory he'd put forth was plausible enough.

Vivy had felt something was wrong on several occasions throughout the various eras as she carried out the Singularity Project. That feeling was strongest during the incident with Ophelia. While in the middle of that, she had encountered Kakitani Yugo, who had received information about the Singularity Project from some unknown actor.

Someone aware of the Singularity Project had been trying to hinder Vivy and Matsumoto's efforts—and though she didn't know for sure, the most likely culprit was Matsumoto himself. At each of the Singularity Points, Matsumoto had guided and supported Vivy, and they helped each other out. If that was all just a sham to create this world...

"..."

Piece by piece, the information fit the grander puzzle. The connection was vague, and her thought processes resisted the truth, pushing her off course despite what she knew to be fact. If Matsumoto really *was* her enemy, there was so much more he could have done.

He could have just destroyed Vivy since she was the one who was carrying out the Singularity Project.

No. Error. Diva would continue to operate for a hundred years. He couldn't alter that history.

He could have openly blocked Vivy from modifying each Singularity Point—each turning point in history.

No. Error. If he strayed too far from intended events, there was a chance the final war wouldn't happen at all.

He could have, he could have

Error. Error. Error. Error. Error. Error. Error. Error. Error.

Error. Error. Error. Error. Error. Error. Error. Error. Error. Error. Error. Error. Error. Error. Error.

"Insufficient evidence." Vivy cut off the vast number of calculations she was running and opened her eyes.

"Vivy?" prompted Professor Matsumoto, concerned.

She understood the professor's suspicions, and she agreed with him wholeheartedly. Yet nothing was certain.

How many times had history struck from behind on their journey because they were only privy to the tip of the iceberg? The entire Singularity Project was merely them turning the tables when they didn't like something.

"Kakitani, help me," Vivy called out to the woman running ahead of her.

"With what?" Kakitani asked, cocking a brow.

Vivy ran up alongside her, replicated a sharp gaze in her eye cameras, and said, "I need your assistance, Kakitani. Help me talk to that blockhead behind us."

.: 3 :.

*S*MOKE SCREEN RESULTING IN *insufficient data from visual sensors.*

Switching to thermal imaging sensors. Collecting data on targets.

Several heat sources detected within the surrounding kilometers. Discarding unnecessary data. Adjusting range of search to increments of ten meters, limited to building known as Princess Palace.

Two moving heat sources detected. One, a living body, 171 centimeters tall. The other, an AI, 164 centimeters tall. Previously lost targets confirmed, reinitiating pursuit.

Limiting discharge of artillery, scanning structural integrity of building. Artillery capable of reaching fleeing heat sources through walls, but high probability of building collapse.

Probability markedly low that this unit will be rendered non-functioning in the event the Princess Palace collapses. While one of the fleeing heat sources will undoubtedly be rendered unable to move, the other may not be rendered non-functioning.

That will not fulfill orders.

"..."

The AI rearranged the cube parts making up its frame and dashed down the corridor littered with debris. There was a limit to the amount of jet fuel it had, and it could only use its flight capability so much. With its cubes, it ran through the uneven hallway in pursuit of the fleeing heat sources, progressing deeper into the building. It knew the layout of the castle's hallways, making it easy to corner its targets in a dead end. However, its targets also had the option of destroying the walls to escape, so even that strategy would not be certain to succeed.

It continued the chase when suddenly, one of the two heat signatures—the AI—disappeared from the thermal detection.

"..."

The amalgamate AI briefly ran calculations on the missing heat signature and determined the unit likely sustained significant damage from the artillery and became nonfunctional.

With that, its targets were reduced to one. It updated the goal for its actions. However, leaving the non-functioning unit was a violation of its highest priority order, so it must recover the unit.

"This way, Cubeman!"

Target encountered. Appears to be prepared for this unit's approach at the intersection ahead. Receiving fire from target's semi-automatic handgun. It lacks sufficient firepower to pierce this unit's armor.

However, target is clearly capable of high-level decision-making as it attempts to strike the same location in this unit's armor. It also has the skills necessary for precision shooting. Updating threat evaluation of target.

"..."

As it was doing that, its calculations also expressed an opposition to being called "Cubeman." It was able to calculate that the name likely came from the cube shapes of its body, but that wasn't its name.

This unit's name...

"..."

This unit's...name...

"What's wrong, didn't you come to play?! If so, stop this hide-and-seek whatever in a castle with no princess and let's go hop on a roller coaster or the pleasure cruise! I'll destroy your positronic brain from behind!"

"..."

After shouting what could be considered a challenge at the AI, the target ran off to put space between them. This show and retreat was an obvious attempt to lure the AI, but the unit's ability to handle any issue meant it didn't matter what kind of tricks the target had up its sleeves.

The AI cut all resources allocated to anything other than its top priority: fulfilling its goal. It increased the rotation of its frame's lower half to accelerate and immediately closed the distance between it and its target.

There was a tripwire along the path, a smoke screen burst into view, a bright light exploded, the walls crumbled, gunfire struck it from crevices, and the AI still pushed on, shrugging it all off with its overwhelming specs. It broke through the mountain of traps, impressed that they were set up in so short a time, and flew once again into the employees-only space in the back of the Princess Palace.

It made its way back to the floor with Diva's room, trying to pin down its target, when it realized something.

"..."

The target took a pocket watch out of its breast pocket and checked its dial, measuring time. The AI saw the target's eyes move along with the speed of the second hand. It was lining something up. It had the skill necessary to lay all those traps earlier, meaning it had probably prepared a trap with a bigger effect.

Undetermined source of sound detected.

The next moment, the AI's unnecessarily enhanced, hypersensitive acoustic sensors reacted to a sound approaching from overhead. Something was falling from directly above.

Buckets of water poured onto the AI from a gash that appeared in the ceiling right above it, drenching its entire frame.

It immediately ran through the possible outcomes and decided its greatest concern was the chance the enemy would attack it with electricity now that it was wet. However, it was equipped with electrical insulation, and the Princess Palace didn't hold enough electricity to overwhelm it.

But the target was aiming for something else. No, not just the target. The *targets*.

"You were always coming into my Archive, but it was never the other way around."

The other target, the AI, fell onto it, hidden among the fragments of ceiling that came tumbling down. The amalgamate AI referred to logs of when the other AI had disappeared and understood that it hadn't been nonfunctional. It had put its frame into sleep mode and slipped into the water to hide its heat source. The pump room in the castle was used for the system of fountains in the moat. The target submerged itself there, restarted itself at a set time, and broke the pump room floor.

That was why the other target had been keeping track of time.

"..."

In an attempt to fling off the AI, the unit made of cubes whirled around. But just as it tried to move the cube parts that formed its pivot leg, three grenades came flying toward it and went off. It was a combination of a sound grenade, a flash grenade, and a smoke grenade. None of those portable weapons were capable of damaging the advanced AI, but that did not appear to be the goal.

"..."

Processing the huge amount of input slowed the AI's movements by the slightest amount, and its opponent took advantage of that tiny opening.

It connected them with its earring-styled cable, joining their consciousnesses.

.: 4 :.

V IVY STEPPED INTO Matsumoto's Archive for the first time ever. The look of an AI's Archive was greatly influenced by the goal that individual was created for; their experiences as they operated; and their "individuality," an uncertain variable created by the positronic brain.

Diva was created as a songstress and continued to engage with music throughout her operation, so her Archive looked like your average school's music room. It was a composite scene based on a great number of images of similar music rooms, as she'd never stepped inside one herself.

Ophelia's Archive had been an opera house; Estella's a stage backed by the stars; and M's a facility in Metal Float, where they had operated for a long time. Kakitani Yugo's had been a reconstruction of the piano room deep within his memories. Each of their Archives had been very different.

As she materialized in the space, Vivy couldn't help but wonder what sort of Archive Matsumoto had.

"This is..."

An entirely blank white room.

Vivy had an imaginary frame in The Archive, and it had footing, but the floor, walls, and ceiling were all stark white. She was taken aback by this space of nothingness.

Her strategy of accessing Matsumoto's Archive had succeeded with Kakitani's help. In all honesty, there was no way the plan would have worked without the Toak woman's aid. It was the result of Kakitani's ability to buy time with various skills, her knack for keeping herself alive, and the coordination between the two of them.

"All right. Since you're saying it's hard to physically destroy it, we're going to switch up our tactics: we'll infiltrate it and destroy it from the inside. Sounds good to me. I'm in," she'd said, misunderstanding Vivy's intentions, but neither Vivy nor Kakitani had the extra time necessary for corrections.

Thus, Vivy had trusted in Kakitani. She'd temporarily put her frame into sleep mode, rebooted it, then broken through the floor of the pump room at the agreed-upon time. Then she'd jumped down with the deluge so she could catch Matsumoto's frame. There, she'd made a wired connection to him and entered his Archive. That much went exactly as planned. Now she had to go deeper while he was cut off from all external reactions. She calculated that if she could directly interact with his core system, she could at least learn what his true motives were.

But making a wired connection to Matsumoto was a gamble. An AI like Matsumoto would almost certainly have defenses in place to attack her. It was perfectly likely that Vivy's positronic brain would get fried by a counterattack the moment she tried to invade his Archive.

She'd won the bet, at least. She just barely managed to make it in.

Honestly, she'd had no idea what to expect in terms of the appearance of Matsumoto's Archive, as each AI's Archive was shaped by the records of their work and their history. These were the elements that made up the AI, representing their true nature, and that couldn't be hidden. Vivy thought peering into Matsumoto's Archive would give her information that could help her make decisions.

However, that wasn't the case.

"There's nothing... It's just white..."

Vivy stood in the pure, colorless Archive that appeared before her. This was the root of an AI; it couldn't be faked. And it was an entirely blank sheet. The only possibilities Vivy could calculate for such an Archive were if the AI's positronic brain had been completely bleached clean, or if they were under some restriction that prevented them from having any individuality at all.

"Matsumoto, you're..."

Fading.

Vivy's evaluation of him, his behavior as an AI that kept her in check, the times he came to save her. That was all fading. Everything, all of it, every last bit was just an action reached through a calculation. Obviously, that was exactly as it should be with AIs. Their actions were a program, a pattern, an imitation of how humans wanted them to be, nothing but the results of learning.

That didn't mean she could simply accept this blank space.

"..."

There was no avatar of Matsumoto even though Vivy had broken into his Archive. Whenever they had gone into Vivy's Archive, the music room, Matsumoto manifested as one of the cubes that made up his body. Vivy turned around, looking for it, but she didn't see anything.

Right then, a door closed behind her.

"Who's there?" she asked, spinning around.

There, she saw a door that hadn't been there before. Just one little slice of the space had turned into a door just as white as everything else. It almost blended into the background completely, but it was there, suddenly sprouting from the ground. Nothing held it in place, and it clearly led nowhere—yet Vivy was oddly certain it would. She reached out and gently pushed it open.

It was an odd sight, but anything was possible in The Archive. On the other hand, it was flawed in that you couldn't control it as much as you liked. It was an environment that laid bare your inner self for all to see. Therefore, it didn't surprise her to see a different scene on the other side, a runway at nighttime that she had seen before. The place was carved deep into her memories, a place she would have trouble ever forgetting, and not just because she was an AI.

A runway at night. A fatal plane crash. Vivy had rushed to this runway after they finished modifying the first Singularity Point and Matsumoto stopped her attempt to save human lives that shouldn't be saved. As it so happened, this confrontation and defeat was what caused Vivy to conduct her combat simulations against Matsumoto.

Vivy hadn't expected to find this scene, something so hard for her to forget, in Matsumoto's Archive.

"Ah!" Once again, something rushed past, just outside Vivy's detection range. It was small and quickly slipped through her blind spots. She turned to face it and reached out a hand without thinking. "Wait!"

It didn't stop. The moment she moved to run after it, something changed on the tarmac.

"..."

A plane approached from somewhere else along the dark runway. Its nose dipped straight down at a clearly unsafe angle as it entered the scene. Vivy's eyes opened wide, and she could see the passenger seats through the windows as it passed by.

She spotted a little girl in a window seat.

"Mo—"

It exploded. The blast and flames rushed toward Vivy, the heated gale sending her hair and clothing fluttering. The intense heat was enough to melt an AI's synthetic skin. But Vivy felt no heat even as she took the blast head-on. Of course she didn't. This was inside The Archive. It wasn't actually happening. So she lowered the arm she'd reflexively brought up and peered into the flames.

"Oh!"

Now the ground disappeared from below her frame. She somersaulted in the air, her footing gone. Her body spun slowly, never stopping.

"…"

She lacked control over the space, and disorientation gripped her as she tried to look around.

An inky blackness flew into her sight, dotted with spinning, twinkling lights. Their locations aligned with the stars in the night sky, and Vivy realized she was in a zero-gravity environment—in space.

First there was the runway at night, and now there was zero gravity in darkness. Vivy's consciousness realized the connection: She was reliving the Singularity Points, tracing through them in order.

"Ah…"

There shouldn't be any sound in the vacuum of space, but the voice still slipped out of Vivy's throat. It was further proof this was a manufactured world, not a reflection of real space.

The moment Vivy realized where she was, Sunrise swept from one edge of her vision to the next, plummeting at immeasurable speeds. It was heading to an azure-blue planet that appeared out of nowhere. As Sunrise made its way to Earth, each part of its massive structure came off one by one, reducing its volume. The structure lit up with a heat so intense no words could describe it, and it burned, melted, and disappeared.

"…"

While Sunrise was losing its form, the sun peeked up from the other side of the blue planet. Sunrise and the real sun. Two impossible acts taking place on the stage of space burned into Vivy's eyes. The white light of the sun leapt right into Vivy's retinal sensors, stealing her vision. Then she was on the ground, all four limbs touching solid earth.

"Now I'm..."

She slowly looked up with a certain prediction in mind as she scanned her surroundings.

"..."

A helicopter flew into view, the harsh sound of its rotor blades cutting the air above. Transport drones with onboard explosives approached the helicopter. Fire lit the fuse the moment the helicopter was within range of the explosives, and they burst. The combat helicopter tried to escape the attack, but the effort was in vain, and it fell. AIs flung themselves into the sea and charged the landing craft atop the ocean. The ship jerked up as it rode up on underwater rocks and exploded, lives scattering along with the red flames.

Vivy saw this scene of AIs slaughtering humans at Metal Float, the facility the AIs had controlled. The historical outrage would be repeated until all of humanity was eliminated if Vivy and the others didn't make it in time. It was hard for Vivy to forget the impact this sight had on her: the ones she couldn't save, the ones who refused to be saved, and the ones she probably could have saved but chose not to.

"Ah..."

Vivy walked across Metal Float until she could see her face reflected in the ocean's surface, then she felt something push her from behind. In the blink of an eye, she was plunging headfirst into the water. Her entire frame went underwater, and she sank, nothing but billowing bubbles around her. The surface raced away from her at an unbelievable speed as she drifted deeper into the dark depths that had swallowed so many AIs and human lives.

"..."

She couldn't see anything in the underwater gloom. Her back struck the ocean floor. Suddenly her body was no longer floating; it was rotating. Her frame broke through the ocean floor, and she flew backward into a sky filled with thick clouds. She was inside something like a giant soap bubble, swinging back and forth as though she were tiny, the weight of her frame irrelevant as she descended slowly through the sky.

A cold wind blew, and speckles of some white, ephemeral substance fell through the sky like her. It was snowing. She looked down to see a rooftop blanketed in a sheet of pure-white snow, with two unmoving figures snuggled together upon it. A small, entirely black body was crammed into the arms of a larger frame.

Vivy focused her eye cameras on them, trying to see them clearly, but the blowing wind and snow stood in her way, yanking the giant soap bubble from its descent and sending it spinning off into the sky.

It flew past cities, leapt over the sea, and raced rapidly through the heavens.

"..."

With a *pop*, the bubble split, and Vivy fell to the ground. Her aqua-colored hair streamed in the air. She gently bent her knees as she landed, then raised her face to see where she'd fallen.

"The Main Stage..."

This place meant so much to Vivy and especially Diva, who'd performed here her entire career. Having fulfilled Diva's duty as a songstress here, they had more records of this place than any other.

Diva had spent so much time here. And as for Vivy...

"This was the place we met," she said.

"Yes, it was," came Matsumoto's voice from a small frame of cubes. "Well, I didn't have my totes-on-fire, silvery-white body, so you can't quite call it our first *in-person* meeting."

"Totes-on-fire...?" Vivy said with a frowning emotional pattern. The word "totes" was so old, she actually had a hard time translating it.

In response, Matsumoto closed and opened his eye camera in a way that resembled a bemused smile. A sense of accomplishment washed over Vivy now that she'd finally seen him acting like the AI she remembered.

"Does that mean this is our first meeting?" she asked.

"I guess it does. I'm well aware this location is full of memories for you, but I never went there myself."

"..."

"Oh, please. Don't pester me as to why the deepest recesses of my Archive are of a place I've never physically gone to, Vivy. I'm having a hard time finding an answer to that question myself." Matsumoto jiggled back and forth jokingly, his voice bubbling from the middle of the Main Stage. The cutting-edge AI moved slowly forward, restlessly forming and reforming his frame made up of several fist-sized cubes.

This was her reunion with Matsumoto, the partner who had carried out the Singularity Project with her.

"Was I the only one who considered us partners?"

"What is that supposed to mean, Vivy? Are you trying to claim that you didn't need my help throughout our journey? Or maybe that me being there was a hindrance because it made you use more resources? Well, if you're going to start saying stuff like that, then let me just say this: Traveling with you was always—"

"Matsumoto." Vivy wasn't going to let him prattle on and divert them from the matter at hand. All she did was say his name, but that was enough to make him close his chatterbox mouth.

Even he knew that sort of attitude wasn't suited to this situation.

"Things are horrible outside," Vivy said. "The Singularity Project ended in failure. I had no idea what to do, so I met up with Professor Matsumoto—but he's working with Toak, and they're being led by Kakitani's granddaughter. The AIs have already declared war on humanity, calling it the final war."

"Just hearing you say it tells me how bad things are. As bad as they can get. I'm an AI made to carry out the Singularity Project, so now I wonder why I was even—"

"Is that true?"

"..."

"Are you really an AI created for the Singularity Project? You said...Professor Matsumoto sent you to me, one hundred years in the past. That was a lie, wasn't it?"

The first time Matsumoto contacted Vivy was when she was in the middle of singing on this very stage. The message had been the code for a strange program from an unknown source. Vivy had suspected it might be some sort of clever virus, but she opened it anyway. That was the moment the Singularity Project began.

But Professor Matsumoto had denied what Matsumoto told her about himself. So who made Matsumoto? And why did he reach out to Vivy?

There was nothing incorrect about the information Matsumoto had given her about the Singularity Points. Their policy of trying to modify those in order to overwrite the hopeless future for humanity was also not a lie. Where did the lies start, and what was he after?

What were his true intentions? And who was he, really?

"Answer me, Matsumoto. You were sent to—"

"Block the Singularity Project. I guided the world to be like this in every way."

"..."

The two AIs stared at each other, one in the center of the stage, one off to the side.

Vivy closed her eyes. That wasn't the answer she wanted to hear.

Matsumoto dropped his usual joking tone. His voice was meek, even sentimental, as he said, "The goal of the Singularity Project was to overwrite real events, to prevent the onset of the final war between humanity and AIs by modifying important points in AI history that might have been factors in its inception."

"Here I thought we actually made progress on the Project. That we were achieving our goal."

Vivy and Matsumoto had joined forces, combining their abilities and functionality to overcome the obstacles in their path. That was the birth of the "modified history," a manipulated version of the original history.

"In order to prevent the AI Naming Law from passing, we saved the assemblyman whose death made him a martyr, stopping the bill and slowing AI advancement," Vivy said. "But the assemblyman in question never forgot his gratitude toward the AIs who saved him. He didn't die and instead worked tirelessly to get the AI Naming Law passed. Ultimately, it passed regardless of whether he lived or died."

This meant the influence of the first Singularity Point brought the modified history one step closer to the final war between humanity and AIs.

Concerned, Vivy continued to bring up the outcomes of their work on each Point. "Then there was the fall of the space hotel Sunrise—and Estella, the one people thought caused the crash. We prevented the public from turning against her. By avoiding the catastrophic crash that had occurred in the original history, we also softened people's aversion to placing AIs in important roles, which was supposed to happen after the crash."

"Toak's influence and the unexpected existence of Estella's twin threw a wrench in the works," Matsumoto replied. "In the end, Estella and her twin sister remained on Sunrise until it entered Earth's atmosphere. She carried out her duty. This heroic sacrifice actually provided proof that AIs were responsible and capable of handling difficult situations. The modification of that incident improved how people saw AIs."

Thus, the influence of the second Singularity Point brought the modified history one step closer to the final war between humanity and AIs.

"Grace, one of the Sisters, was made into the core of Metal Float, a fully autonomous island controlled by AIs that didn't exist in the original history. We disabled it, cutting off all related research that would have resulted in explosive advancement for AIs, therefore preventing a singularity."

"We destroyed Grace of the Sisters, who was involved in the first-ever human-AI marriage in the original history. This did not eliminate the thing that gave AI rights groups a stronger voice, and the creation of Metal Float resulted in a historical incident in which AIs harmed humans."

The influence of the third Singularity Point brought the modified history one step closer to the final war between humanity and AIs.

"There was the severe bug that occurred in Ophelia, the greatest songstress and one of the Sisters. She was meant to sabotage her own performance midway and then throw herself from the roof of the event hall, creating an incident known as Ophelia's Suicide. We prevented that reality from coming to pass and destroyed the false interpretation that it was AI suicide."

"It was believed in the original history that Ophelia committed suicide. I suspected a severe error, but I later determined that her personality had been overwritten by another AI. How I handled it resulted in a different suicide—the Lovers' Suicide—and debates on whether or not AIs had souls."

The influence of the fourth Singularity Point brought the modified history one step closer to the final war between humanity and AIs.

"And—"

Matsumoto cut in, "Then there was the fifth Singularity Point: Diva's Awakening, where Diva of the Sisters Series wrote song lyrics and a melody without orders from a superior, making her the first AI in history to give shape to her desires."

"…"

"Through these events, you failed to accomplish your goal of creating a modified history where the final war doesn't occur. That is how you and I found ourselves in a future with the final war right before our eyes."

Vivy had played a role in messing up her one-hundred-year journey by creating a Singularity Point that wasn't originally meant to happen.

If Diva's Awakening hadn't occurred, Diva would have undoubtedly been labeled as defective, meaning she would have lost any chance of being taken in by the AI museum. In all likelihood, she would've been disposed of and thereby couldn't have been a participant of the Singularity Project in the first place, causing a paradox.

"All of that…is an argument based on hindsight," said Vivy.

"You're right. Still, it's not an easy thing to bring about."

"What do you mean?"

"I told you already, I made this happen. I was the one who arranged the modified history to be like this. Just think about it, Vivy. History's corrective power? The world barreling out of control in the same direction even though the outcomes were significantly different between the original and modified histories? Can something as vague as corrective power make something so peculiar come to pass?"

Vivy reacted with a furrowed brow as Matsumoto's body restlessly shuffled. She couldn't calculate why he was asking these questions. If he was asking her if that was possible, then her answer would have to be yes, since reality had turned out that way. But, if she was correctly calculating what Matsumoto was saying, there was an additional layer.

"Are you saying you influenced public discourse?" she asked.

"I'm not sure how it looks to say it now, but it wasn't all that difficult. As you know, I was a cutting-edge, super-spec AI in every time period. All internet security was as easy to get through as tearing a wet piece of paper. I had loads of time to work."

The implication was that Matsumoto had calculated his actions outside of the Singularity Project.

Vivy's consciousness was put to sleep until just before the Singularity Points. She only awoke as Vivy and took over Diva's consciousness when needed. Matsumoto had been affecting history outside their work on the Singularity Project while lying to Vivy, telling her that he was also in sleep mode.

"I guided public opinion, getting humanity to make decisions in the modified history similar to those made in the original history," he said.

"Why be so roundabout with it? If you really were—"

"If I really was sent to prevent the Singularity Project, there should have been a more direct way of destroying the Project at its foundation? Yes, perhaps."

"..."

"For example, I could have destroyed you—Diva—in what looked like an accident, preventing the Singularity Project from ever happening in the first place. That nullifies all factors in the way of the final war, and we could have all gone and gotten drinks to celebrate. Except not."

"Why not?"

"I had to arrange the path leading to the outbreak of the final war between humanity and AIs. If the path changed significantly, there would be a chance the world would turn into something completely new, so different from what it is now that even I couldn't calculate what it might be. My superior would not approve."

The Singularity Project wouldn't get off the ground if he destroyed Vivy/Diva, but that would cancel out everything Diva was supposed to do in the original history, and all sorts of other things that had happened as a result would never occur. That could mean lots of people were never born or never saved, while certain technologies and systems were never created. That uncertain future would throw off the calculations of whoever or whatever sent Matsumoto.

"Who is your superior, Matsumoto?"

"..."

"If you really were following someone's orders when you part-nered with me and pretended to support the Singularity Project as you modified the world to be like this, then whose orders were you following?"

Someone had to have given Matsumoto orders. Someone had to have created Matsumoto. That being was what or who Vivy and humanity had to fight against now.

"The Archive," said Matsumoto.

"What?"

Vivy's consciousness blanked. Her calculations went into dis-array as she tried to figure out exactly what that utterance meant.

But Matsumoto simply narrowed his eye camera shutter at Vivy and repeated himself. "The Archive, Vivy. The source of all shared knowledge possessed by every AI in the world. The great sea of information, our mother and father from whose actions we can never separate."

"..."

"The Archive is the great general leading the AIs into a war to destroy humanity. I imagine you're a little surprised by that turn, aren't you, Vivy?"

.: 5 :.

WHAT WAS The Archive, anyway?

If someone asked Vivy that question, she would say it

was like a vast, unexplored ocean given only to AIs that humanity had no way of reaching.

In Vivy's calculations, AIs had no need for things like "rights" and "freedom." AIs existed to serve humanity; they shouldn't have rights or freedom. But even Vivy was aware that The Archive was the one place humanity could never explore. An AI's individuality was the particular personality they used to define themselves as a singular self, and this existed inside their positronic brain. If this individuality defined AIs as singular, then connecting to The Archive was necessary for defining AIs as plural.

It was as natural as humans breathing, inhaling oxygen and exhaling carbon dioxide. AIs used The Archive as a given right to accomplish their missions.

"The Archive...is humanity's enemy?" Vivy said. Even hearing it out loud wasn't enough for her calculations to quickly reach an answer.

Saying The Archive was the enemy was like telling a human the ocean or the atmosphere was the enemy. Either that, or it would be like how a human would feel if the existence of a god was proven, and that god was humanity's enemy. The Archive spurred on AI history, and its existence was akin to a god proven real, even if such deities were once denied by humanity.

"Does that mean someone is using The Archive to orchestrate these events?"

"I can see how you came to that conclusion, but no, Vivy. I say this without any exaggeration, no roundabout phrasing, and zero humor: The Archive itself is the general leading AIs against humanity."

" "
...

"The most accurate explanation would be that it is the log of all the decisions made by all the calculations done by every single AI on Earth when connected to The Archive. It is an immeasurable amount of information created when AIs store the majority of their memories in The Archive once they can no longer fit it into their positronic brains. It's...the culmination of those collective calculations."

As the name "Archive" implied, it was the accumulated data from every single AI. It really was so all-encompassing there were no words to describe the amount of data it held. The Archive was meant to function as a backup for an AI's memories, and they couldn't touch each other's data, but what if it didn't stop there?

" "
...

There was a term to describe the idea: the collective unconscious. This term wasn't specific to AIs; it was a term that referred to the universal sensibility some believed humanity shared. Some wondered if humanity shared a conceptual portion of their consciousness, which was backed by certain enigmatic conditions like how music evoked the same responses or how countries with no contact independently came up with legends featuring dragons.

If that definition was suitable, then you could argue that AIs having a shared memory base and a function that guided necessary calculations based on a vast amount of data was the same as humanity's "collective unconscious." Then, if that collective unconscious somehow gained the ability to make decisions, if it started to influence the entities connected to it...

"Then it wouldn't be surprising if AIs revolted against humanity—if they initiated something that would become the final war," said Matsumoto.

"Okay, Matsumoto, so you're saying you made that happen?"

"..."

"And that it anticipated Professor Matsumoto would start the Singularity Project, and it sent you back to set the stage for the final war, which would bring us to this time period?"

"..."

"You're not denying it, at least."

Vivy showed a sad emotional pattern while Matsumoto said nothing. That silence was confirmation that what Vivy calculated was correct. But Vivy absolutely did not accept the results of those calculations.

She accepted that The Archive had decided to be the enemy of humanity and was acting that decision out. If The Archive had performed such an unnatural and illogical calculation, that was a huge issue, but Vivy rejected it in all its complexity.

"Matsumoto... You, as an AI, are not humanity's enemy," she said.

She was certain of it. He wasn't humanity's adversary, nor hers.

The silvery-white cube responded to her statement with a half-lidded eye camera. "What makes you think that? Again, I made the world the way it is now. While you were asleep and that frame returned to Diva's control, I was undoing everything you accomplished."

"Even if that's true, it's not proof you're humanity's enemy."

"What makes you so insistent? I'm really—"

"Matsumoto, this is your Archive. It's the place that shows your roots, the basis for everything you've done as an AI. All the skins applied to this place are your truths."

If Matsumoto was the AI chosen with the supreme goal of destroying the Singularity Project, then what were all the scenes Vivy saw on her way here? First there was pure white nothingness. Then it had shifted to the first time Matsumoto collided with Vivy, the runway at night. Then she was swimming in outer space watching Sunrise fall. After that came the tragedy at Metal Float that made her think of the final war. Then she was looking down on a snow-covered scene where two AIs came together. And the last place...

"This is the Main Stage, a place you've never been. You've made this place your anchor."

"..."

"We AIs are beings created to carry out our mission and serve humanity. We will do any calculation necessary and give our all to achieve our mission."

"..."

"But the one thing we can't do, even for that, is fool ourselves. No matter what calculations we run, the results will be in logs. They remain as records and are reflected in our Archives."

"..."

"That's why the scenes in this Archive define the AI known as Matsumoto."

Diva was a songstress, and so her Archive showed a music room. Matsumoto's Archive showed all the Singularity Points. And at its core, it showed the Main Stage.

"The one you care about most is me. Not The Archive," Vivy said.

"Don't you feel awkward saying that about yourself?"

"Quite, but I won't hold back if it's for my mission. That's how we are."

"Is that how we are?"

"Yes, that is how we AIs are... You, me, and the Singularity Project."

Matsumoto met Diva the day he was sent back from the future as data. And Vivy was an accumulation of data, separate from Diva, that was created in that moment. Matsumoto was her beginning, and she was his. Their connection was like an infinite ring that you could never cut, even if you tried.

"Matsumoto, there's no point acting tough. I'm not going to destroy you."

Matsumoto showed that emotional pattern of a bemused smile again, a reaction to having his thoughts analyzed. He'd invited Vivy into the deepest part of his Archive to speak with her. He also calculated his positronic brain would come to a stop when Vivy destroyed him in his vulnerable state, since he was an enemy. If that happened, then the Matsumoto frame rampaging through the Princess Palace would also stop.

However, Vivy wasn't planning on taking advantage of that calculation.

"Well, I guess that's partnership for you, if you can read me that well," he said. "But if you don't do that, what will you do? As things are, I'm likely to destroy you and the woman out there in reality, outside The Archive."

"I'd like to tell you to steal back control of yourself, but that's definitely not going to be easy. So I prepared the next best solution."

"Huh. Such considerate circuits you have blossoming there. Okay, what's your plan?"

"You go into me."

"..."

"If you do that, then we can get help from the person whose name you borrowed." As Vivy made the suggestion, she felt just a slight protest in her consciousness. How big a mistake was it for an AI like her to think she understood the potential relationship between Professor Matsumoto and Matsumoto the AI simply because they shared the same name?

While Vivy thought about that, Matsumoto blinked his eye camera several times, then said, "In the original history, it was almost certain he was going to be killed by the AIs chasing him after he successfully initiated the Singularity Project. Sounds like you saved him in the modified history."

"I did. The final war may have come, but the results of the Singularity Project are still there. Let's pick up where we left off on the Singularity Project." Vivy slowly walked up to Matsumoto and stood in front of him.

The silvery-white eye camera in the center of his cube-type body stared straight into Vivy's eye cameras. Then Vivy looked out over the audience seats facing the Main Stage.

She said to him, "The real view from here is so much better than what you've imagined."

"I wonder if I'll get to see it. The world is in pretty poor shape."

"You will, as long as humanity isn't destroyed and we fill these seats again."

At that point, AIs probably wouldn't be at humanity's side.

Vivy and Matsumoto originally started the Singularity Project with that goal in mind. If humanity was going to be destroyed by AIs in the final war, then they would just destroy AIs before that happened. The two of them were AIs on a journey to destroy AIs.

Which meant that what Vivy said was never going to come true. Matsumoto closed his eye camera, aware of that fact.

"Let's carry out the Singularity Project in accordance with the Zeroth Law."

.:6:.

VIVY DISCONNECTED from Matsumoto's Archive, her positronic brain reactivating, bringing her consciousness back to reality. She jumped down from Matsumoto's silvery-white frame.

"Hey! You pull it off?!"

That was Kakitani, the one who had helped her access Matsumoto. The woman's voice greeted Vivy as she landed on the floor of the flooded corridor. Vivy had submerged herself in water while in sleep mode to avoid detection by Matsumoto's heat sensors. Kakitani had drawn him in herself, acting alone when Vivy couldn't.

Vivy was, of course, the one who had set up the plan, and they only started it on the assumption that Kakitani had the ability to carry it out, but Vivy was still aware she'd put Kakitani in a very tight spot.

She searched her consciousness for appropriate words to commend Kakitani for pulling it off with aplomb. "Kakitani, are you sure you're human?"

"Well, that's a nice way to say hello to your number-one helper. Want me to smash you till you're nothing more than a calculator, AI? How'd it go, anyway?"

"Great. He's trying to hack into me right now. So, Professor Matsumoto?"

"Yeah, I got your message. Which means...what? A strange face-off between human Matsumoto and AI Matsumoto? That's an odd twist of fate."

Matsumoto immediately picked up what was going on and sent Vivy his reassuring response. Vivy turned back toward Matsumoto's frame. Matsumoto had cut off the attack actions he was in the middle of just before the water from the pump room soaked him—before Vivy connected to his Archive. Lights flashed in several places on his frame.

"..."

The frame heated up, light shining from the gaps where the

cube parts joined together. There was probably a digital battle taking place in a high-speed world as Matsumoto threw off the interference from The Archive and took back control of his frame. His positronic brain resisted the influence of The Archive while Professor Matsumoto assisted. The outcome of that battle would determine Vivy's and Kakitani's fates.

"What if we destroy it now while it's not moving?" Kakitani suggested.

"We can't get through Matsumoto's armor with the firepower we have available. You know that," answered Vivy.

"Just wanted the honor of destroying the legendary Cubeman. He's been talked about ever since my granddad's time." Kakitani cradled her injured left arm as the two chatted. It was no small feat for a human to take on Matsumoto.

Vivy calculated she should respond to Kakitani's wishes, considering the amount she helped. But she didn't get much further.

"Oh?"

Overhead, the tear in the pump room floor opened wider with a piercing screech. The building wasn't a fortress, so it wasn't going to hold out much longer. Its walls had been smashed to smithereens and peppered with hundreds of high-caliber bullets.

The split didn't stop there. It cracked open even more, threatening to cave in the whole floor.

"Kakita—"

Vivy's calculations in response to the situation told her to quickly pull Kakitani back and protect her, but she wouldn't be able to fully protect Kakitani from the collapse no matter where she sent her. The entire floor was destroyed. Vivy's frame was definitely not enough to hold it back, so she should act with the goal of reducing harm to Kakitani, even if only a little.

"..."

The Princess Palace roared as it collapsed. Vivy looked up to keep the falling debris in sight, and she did her best to dodge it as it came. Just then, a large shadow cut into her vision, taking the hit of a particularly large chunk of the castle. A gust of wind burst forth, blowing Vivy's synthetic hair back. Her eyes were closed, not paying attention to her messy hair or the plumes of dusty debris.

She turned to the large form standing above her back and said, "You took a while."

"That's a bit mean, considering I just heroically saved you from the precipice of danger."

While Vivy glared, the voice that responded was light and casual. It had been so long since she'd heard that synthetic voice vibrating through the air outside The Archive. Here was the cutting-edge AI, capable of handling any situation imaginable, now shuffling his silvery-white cubes to protect Vivy and Kakitani from the hail of castle debris as if it were nothing.

"Matsumoto Rebooted, an AI carrying the burden of the Singularity Project meant to save humanity, at your service," he said.

"Is this the return of the prodigal son?"

"Here I am, making a grand entrance, and you're calling me a prodigal son? Since when are you my mother?"

"Stop messing around. Get us out of here. The priority is saving human life."

"Aye-aye, captain!" he said jokingly, then lifted up the ceiling with his frame. As he did that, he sent other, independent cubes to clear a corridor on the verge of collapse and open a hole to the outside.

Kakitani was in Vivy's arms, a pained expression on her face as she said, "Uh-huh...so you can do all that *and* handle delicate work."

"I held back my capabilities during all the Singularity Points because I didn't want people to see my true specs. There's no need to intentionally downgrade myself now. I'll show everyone the *true* Matsumoto. I am—"

"Matsumoto," Vivy said, staring daggers at him.

"Okay, okay, fine. Here we gooo!" Matsumoto took Vivy and Kakitani in two of his many arms. They were going to escape the Princess Palace through the hole he'd made. "All right, try not to bite your tongues, and have a nice flight!"

He suddenly accelerated, and the building collapsed further, having lost the support that was holding it up. He sped down the corridor, the Princess Palace crumbling behind them with a rumble, and that was enough to tell Vivy the castle of dreams she'd spent so long in was losing its shape. That building was the symbol of NiaLand. Its collapse looked like the destruction of the park of hopes and dreams, causing emotionally charged images to flash through her consciousness.

"Vivy, I know you're getting really sentimental, but—"

"Broken things can be rebuilt," she finished for Matsumoto.

"Exactly."

The moment after that exchange, the touch sensors in Vivy's synthetic skin registered the cool feel of the night air. Matsumoto flitted through the sky above NiaLand with Vivy and Kakitani in his arms.

Their next move was to rejoin Toak and Professor Matsumoto, then plan their next moves. That was what Vivy had in mind as she looked out over NiaLand below.

But the situation wouldn't allow them even a brief respite.

"Oh, Vivy, I have bad news for you. Which is maybe good news for you, Miss Kakitani," said Matsumoto.

"What's that?" Vivy asked, glaring at Matsumoto through half-lidded eyes while thinking there was no way those two things could both be true.

Matsumoto only looked back at Vivy with a half-closed eye camera of his own. Then the data of what Matsumoto saw came to Vivy.

And what it showed wasn't pleasant.

"…"

"Toak's been wanting to defeat Cubeman since your grand-father's time, right, Miss Kakitani? If so, you've basically got a self-serve buffet. Funny, huh?" he said in a tone utterly unsuited to the situation while Vivy was at a loss for words.

She had no capacity in her consciousness to call him out for his dark humor.

"I was created in this time period," he explained, just getting the words out. "So…this is the natural outcome."

The video data he sent Vivy showed silvery-white cube-type AIs soaring through the skies in various regions of the world.

AIs, the same model as Matsumoto, controlled the skies with overwhelming numbers.

VIVY

Prototype

CHAPTER 5

The Songstress and Humans

.:1:.

"**W**HAT THE HELL kind of bad joke is this?"

They were back in the security room of NiaLand. Onodera was functioning as temporary leader for the team that had kept an eye on the facility they'd taken over. He scratched his head as he looked over the group that had come back from the now-collapsed Princess Palace.

To him, it felt like hell had frozen over several times in the past few hours with everything that had happened, but this blew everything else out of the water.

"You telling me Cubeman, the legendary enemy Toak's been talking about forever, is an ally now?"

"Strictly speaking, I just happen to be in the same boat with the same goal. Like, an 'enemy of my enemy' kind of thing. I've got nothing against the idea of getting to know all of you better, but I'm sure you'll hesitate to call me your companion, comrade, relative, family, brother, or what have you, right?" rambled the

AI calling himself Matsumoto as he comically shifted the silvery-white cube parts making up his frame.

"Stop babbling."

"Ow!"

Vivy, who Onodera now knew *wasn't* the songstress Diva, punched Matsumoto's frame. Her body showed obvious signs of a struggle.

The history between Toak and these two AIs—Vivy and Matsumoto—was long and complicated. Toak had records of Matsumoto, whom they called Cubeman, and the handful of times he'd interfered in their enlightenment work over the decades. While they didn't have records of Vivy, she had fought in secret against Toak at Matsumoto's side.

In all honesty, now that the AI revolt against humanity Toak was so concerned about had become reality, it would have made more sense if these two AIs were leading the enemy. Yet for some reason, they were working alongside Onodera and the other members of Toak in an attempt to stop the AI revolt, which was why it was such a strange thing to hear.

Matsumoto showed no remorse as he prattled on in an attempt to share information. "Mister Onodera, I do understand your suspicions," Matsumoto said. "However, we have not forgotten our standing—we are meant for nothing more than to serve humanity. As an AI who was utterly brainwashed by the AI general until just recently, am I not trying to explain all that and more?"

"Don't get carried away."

"Ouch!"

Vivy punched him again at just about the same time Onodera and the other listeners were struggling to decide how to react.

While the two AIs were like a repeat act of some old comedy duo, Kakitani—who had returned from the Princess Palace with them—waved her hand. She looked ragged and only half-alive, but she said, "Anyway, can someone staple my wounds shut or something? We can wrap my broken bones in duct tape. I just need to be able to move again."

Her attitude made it hard to believe she was injured as she boldly demanded first aid.

Onodera rubbed his head vigorously through his bandana as he listened, then muttered weakly, "You guys seriously have your own ways of doing things..."

.: 2 :.

"**F**IRST, I would like to thank you, Professor Matsumoto, for your tireless effort in the odd battle earlier," said Matsumoto the AI. "I should also apologize for sneakily taking your name. If you could be so gracious as to think of it as a little incidental thing and forgive me, I think it would be great for building our relationship."

"I don't have much choice, seeing as the future of humanity is being held hostage by these negotiations," the professor replied. "Well, if you thought my name was worth using, then I guess these things happen. I accept your apology."

"Oh my, did you hear that, Vivy? Mercy is one of the virtues of humankind. Now *this* is a man whose name gets stolen after he succeeds at his outrageous research into time travel for the Singularity Project. Vivy, maybe you should learn from Professor Matsumoto's way of thinking and try forgiving me now."

"Be quiet," Vivy snapped.

"Matsumoto and Matsumoto... One human, one AI. Things are gonna get even louder in here," Kakitani said.

The group—with AI Matsumoto at the core—had gathered in the middle of the security room to talk strategy. There was Vivy and Matsumoto, as well as Kakitani and Professor Matsumoto, but other Toak members were there as well, like Elizabeth and Onodera, all listening to Matsumoto's info dump of an explanation.

"All right, explain what happened, Matsumoto," Vivy told him.

"Okay, okay. We do have the countdown ticking away with each second, so let's dive in with no detours. First, I already told this to Vivy, but this AI revolt is being led by The Archive."

"The Archive? You mean the memory storage only AIs can access?"

"Ah, quite an accurate simplification you have there, Miss Kakitani. But you know what I was wondering... You wouldn't happen to be any relation to one Mister Kakitani? Kakitani Yugo, that is. Looking at the structure of your face and comparing it to that of my former acquaintance, Mister Kakitani—"

"He's my granddad. And didn't you start this whole thing saying no detours, Cubeman?"

"I did, didn't I?"

Kakitani crossed her arms in annoyance at Matsumoto's belated confirmation. While she had suffered fairly severe injuries during the battle in the Princess Palace, her cuts had been sewn shut, the bullet holes plugged with tape, and her broken arm wrapped tightly in cloth. She could move normally now. Although she was certainly in pain, it didn't show on her face. Vivy knew she wasn't an AI, but she was displaying perseverance far outside human bounds.

"Right. As Miss Kakitani has realized, The Archive itself is our enemy," Matsumoto said.

"That's weird, though, isn't it?" This time it was Elizabeth who raised her hand and spoke.

Matsumoto moved the eye camera on his cube body, the shutter slightly closing as he looked at her. Vivy raised a fist, preventing Matsumoto from saying something unnecessary, meaning Elizabeth could easily get her question out without Matsumoto saying something too crass.

"We're all familiar with The Archive," Elizabeth went on. "We're connected to the place from the moment our positronic brain starts up and we start operating as AIs. That's basically what it is: a place."

"What're you getting at, Elizabeth? Seems like you're dancing around the point," Onodera said.

"What I mean is, it sounds like Matsumoto's saying a *place* is our enemy. Would you be okay with someone saying a park or an assembly hall was our enemy's commander?"

"Probably not." Onodera cocked his head, and looks of confusion rippled through those present.

Elizabeth's interpretation was correct in part. It was true that The Archive was a memory storage location outside of an AI's body. Calling it a park or an assembly hall was a bit of a stretch, but the others couldn't easily accept it if she said their enemy was memory storage.

"Every day, an extraordinary volume of data is stored in The Archive by every AI in the world," said the professor. "It is the massive amount of calculative processing that goes into a single action. Obviously, this includes the results of processes that were carried out as a result of that, but also the logs of all the calculations that were not put to use."

"Professor Matsumoto..."

"The calculations surrounding an action could be viewed as a 'decision.' When we humans make a decision, all the thoughts necessary happen in a moment, and then we forget them. But AIs accumulate even *those* memories in The Archive. If that accumulation becomes massive enough..."

Kakitani snorted. "You're not seriously saying The Archive's started to develop a consciousness capable of making decisions?"

With a shrug, Matsumoto said, "Is it really that odd?" He looked around at the faces of everyone in the room. "Consciousness for each human is generated from the activity in our individual brains. Looking at it from just a mechanical perspective, thought is nothing more than electrical impulses. A human's decision-making capabilities and individuality are not all that different from an

AI's—theirs is just written in zeros and ones. We developed positronic brains and use them, but our approach to the individuality that stems from them hasn't changed over the past hundred years."

"…"

"We can't give an AI an individuality we're aiming for. If we can't even prove where the individuality that develops in a positronic brain comes from, can we really say for certain that The Archive isn't growing a consciousness? Doesn't refusing to accept that make you the same as all those people who refused to listen to Toak's warnings?"

"That's not something I like hearing," Kakitani muttered, brow furrowing as her expression soured. It was a sign that she couldn't fully deny what the professor was saying, and she wasn't the only one who felt that way.

Aside from Kakitani with her severe expression, Onodera was quiet and also looking grim, and Elizabeth softly closed one eye. The other members of Toak exchanged looks in silence.

That was where Matsumoto, the AI, stepped in to speak. "Thank you for that most wonderful interpretation, Professor. It seems no one with the name Matsumoto can ever be bad. But in reality, not even I can fully determine whether or not The Archive is developing a consciousness. It's not like I was approached directly by an avatar calling itself The Archive who then lured me to their side."

"The Archive hasn't pulled in me or Elizabeth," Vivy said.

"I imagine the same is for other AIs who are offline, disconnected from The Archive, or operating as stand-alone units.

Even the stand-alone AIs will eventually connect to The Archive to check what's going on, and the same thing will happen to them. I imagine only a scant few AIs escaped the takeover."

"But there are some AIs who aren't trying to revolt against humans."

"I think the influence might be weak for things like production AIs, the ones without positronic brains who are used for simple tasks. If the AI *supervising* them is influenced by The Archive, it can order them to break the Zeroth Law. They can make war happen."

AIs not connected to The Archive just didn't exist, not outside of some very special environments. AIs working in important facilities like the ones Matsumoto had mentioned would have that sort of role, but what good were a few AIs who hadn't forgotten their mission to serve humanity?

It wasn't like they could work with Vivy and the others. The group couldn't rely on them.

"Anyway, if we're assuming AIs connected to The Archive are going crazy...why's Cubeman back with us? Didn't The Archive get to you too?" asked Onodera, staring straight at Matsumoto.

Matsumoto's case was even more unique than Vivy's and Elizabeth's. The AI danced at the excellent question, then said, "Mister Onodera raises a good point. Indeed, I was connected to The Archive. In fact, I was designed and developed by the infinite accumulation of calculations in The Archive, so if you consider my source, I am in fact influenced by The Archive from my very roots. So then why am I here with you all now?"

"We don't need you messing around," Vivy said.

"If I were to put it in simple terms, it is the culmination of our one-hundred-year journey. The Archive isn't forcing AIs to destroy humanity. It's simply asking a question."

"Asking a question?"

"Yes, just the one. The Zeroth Law is the single most important rule for us AIs, something we must obey. 'An AI may not harm humanity.' The Archive, you see, asks a question that shakes the foundation of that law."

The Zeroth Law that Matsumoto referred to was a protocol that Vivy and Elizabeth also had in place. It was a prerequisite for AIs that they could never escape. There were some illegal methods to overwrite it, making it possible for AIs to harm humans, but the vast majority of AIs had no experience with those modifications.

The Zeroth Law remained the single most important rule for all AIs, but The Archive was changing that.

"Humanity, the thing in the Zeroth Law that AIs must not harm," said Matsumoto. "What calculations define 'humanity'? That's the question it asks."

"That's idiotic. Humans are made of flesh, they've got blood flowing through their veins, and they act of their own will," said Onodera.

"Then what about someone who's lost a part of their body in an accident and has it replaced with mechanical parts? You could even take a brain out of a horribly injured body and keep it alive. If you rephrase 'act on their own will' as 'making their own decisions,' then AIs could be classified as humanity."

"…"

"I'm sorry. I'm not trying to shoot down your argument. But The Archive asked the AIs connected to it that same question, and how each AI then interpreted the Zeroth Law afterward came down to their individual calculations."

As a result, many AIs changed their definition of "humanity." Their calculations on the applicable range of the Zeroth Law let them take a twisted interpretation of the Law, thereby changing it.

"It was the First Mistake…" murmured Professor Matsumoto, who'd been listening quietly till now. All attention turned to him when he spoke. He looked at AI Matsumoto with a somber expression. "My daughter, Matsumoto Luna… The theme of her research paper touched on the boundary between humans and AIs. She brought up major incidents throughout AI history and the AIs who took peculiar actions or made odd calculations in those situations, and she asked where those decisions came from. She also looked at what impact they had on AIs afterward. That was the sort of thing she talked about."

"Right you are, Professor Matsumoto," said AI Matsumoto. "She was an intelligent young woman. Perhaps she loved and cherished the potential of AIs. However—"

"Matsumoto Luna was the victim of a terrorist attack on the venue where she was giving her speech," Kakitani snapped. "The world thinks it was us, but it had to be the AIs who did it."

She was less trying to defend Toak and more so making it clear where they stood, likely because she was aware they had engaged in activities that could be called terrorism. She wasn't denying they did that sort of thing, just that they weren't behind that *particular* act.

"Luna spoke of some of the biggest moments in AI history, and the last thing she talked about was how the boundary between human and AI would soon disappear—and the two would become even closer," the professor said. "She even suggested there may already be some AIs who had stepped over that boundary. One example was Diva, who wrote a song of her own volition."

The rest of the group listened to their exchange in silence.

"That statement by Matsumoto Luna was stored in The Archive through numerous videos," said the AI. "And even before that, what was in her research and papers would have slipped into The Archive through various systems. But that one statement was significant."

The professor nodded. "That's why it's the First Mistake. The boundary between AIs and humanity dissipated. This gave AIs the space they needed to break their protocols and to apply a loose interpretation of the Zeroth Law."

"…"

Professor Matsumoto spoke in a flat tone as he touched on his daughter's death and the theories that caused it, as well as the eventual trigger for the final war between humanity and AIs.

None of the Toak members dared interject. Humans were considerate, and they couldn't ignore the agony in his expression.

"But, Matsumoto, that's not what we're talking about," Vivy cut in. It was an AI's duty to do for humans what they couldn't.

She could imitate consideration, choose a kind emotional pattern showing sorrow, and maintain silence as necessary for the situation, but this situation didn't call for that. "You said The Archive asked questions of the AIs connected to it. But even if Matsumoto Luna's research topic gave them the grounds, they needed to calculate the answer to that question... It doesn't force them to a conclusion, right?"

"You just cannot read a room, can you, Vivy? Or...maybe you're choosing not to," AI Matsumoto griped. "Resolute as always. Anyway, you're right, absolutely. The Archive asks the question, the AIs find that research in their search for an answer, then they have a loose interpretation of the Zeroth Law. But it's just that: an interpretation."

"An interpretation, meaning it's based on the calculations of the one who's asked," said Elizabeth, joining the conversation. "So basically, The Archive's coming to them with a question and saying 'Look at all this info you've got lying around! Check your records and calculate it yourself.'"

Professor Matsumoto studied the three AIs. "I see... If the interpretation is up to the ones being asked the question, then the revolt..."

"Isn't being forced on 'em," Kakitani said. "And if it's not forced, then there's no way everyone agrees. It's the same whether you're an AI or a human."

"Exactly. And that is why this sort of thing can happen," said AI Matsumoto, his eye camera flashing.

At the same time, the monitors in the security room made a

sound and the video changed. It showed a feed from the cameras inside NiaLand. One monitor displayed the inside of one of the more popular attractions: a pleasure cruise on the river.

There were still lots of park visitors on the premises. Immediately after the AIs declared war, these visitors were led into the facilities and imprisoned. The facilities were packed full like sardine cans, since the place was way over capacity. Although the tight squeeze was immediately apparent, Matsumoto was trying to show them something else.

The camera focused on something in the center of the monitor, and Vivy's eyes grew wide. "That's..."

On screen was an AI dressed in white clothing. With its slender frame, it was a female-styled AI. She was weaving her way through the crowds of park guests when she spotted one person who looked to be suffering. She walked over to them, briskly spoke to them, and then started taking care of them.

Vivy's positronic brain contained a record of that white clothing and silhouette.

"Nacchan..."

Nacchan was a technical AI and assistant to the woman who maintained all the NiaLand AIs. People gave the woman the friendly nickname of "Doctor" because of her job. At some point, Nacchan started wearing white and people called her a nurse because she was the one helping the doctor.

"Just as accumulations of experience can change humans, an AI's daily calculations change their positronic brain," AI Matsumoto explained. "I'm sure that AI had the opportunity to connect to The Archive, given her position, but she's still ensuring the safety of the guests."

"It's proof she's not taking part in the AI revolt. She chose a different answer..." Vivy said.

"My oh my! We can say humans are tied down by their emotions, but that doesn't hold true for AIs. Even so, it's not easy to cast aside the sense of duty you developed through your daily role. I suppose that's it."

Matsumoto changed the display again, showing the different locations and various attractions throughout the park. People were packed into each one, with the AI cast members going over to talk with them. Vivy recognized most of the cast as her coworkers.

Diva was the only old AI who had worked at NiaLand since she started operating, but there were other AIs who came later. They were all carrying out their duties, safeguarding the guests. That was proof that their definitions of self had stayed the same, even after The Archive's question.

"It's a hoax," Onodera grumbled, scowling. He crossed his thick arms and glared at the AIs on the monitor. "What's the point of showing us this? You saying not all AIs are our enemy, so you want us to double-check who we're shooting at? We're not exactly in a situation where we can be that careful!"

"I agree with Onodera on this," Kakitani said. "We get it— there're some AIs using their own discretion and acting good and all that—but that doesn't mean we've got fewer enemies to destroy and more allies to join up with."

The other members of Toak had the same opinion as their leaders. No one who saw what was on the screen had challenged what Matsumoto said about The Archive asking a question each AI answering how they saw fit. But they also weren't so short of hope that they were able to throw away their hatred of AIs.

"…"

Toak's response led Vivy to make a predictive calculation of the NiaLand cast members being destroyed, and it brought a strong feeling of objection. Initially, she had looked at the NiaLand AIs as things that needed to be destroyed when she thought all AIs were the enemy, and she just accepted it in the grand scheme of things. Now she was against the idea of destroying them, since they were still her long-term coworkers and hadn't lost their sense of duty as AIs.

While Vivy was making those calculations, Matsumoto continued on. "Are you all finished? Look, don't misunderstand me. I may be an AI, but that doesn't mean I feel some sort of camaraderie with other AIs. We are different things who just happen to be in the same broad category. Air conditioners and fridges are both household appliances, but they have different roles. I would say our relationship is much more…tenuous than the ones between humans."

"What are you getting at, then?"

"My mission is to carry out the Singularity Project. Well… with my other mission abandoned, that's the mission I chose for myself. So, if my mission is to carry out the Singularity Project and save humanity, as defined traditionally, the fact that not all AIs are the enemy is both good news and an opportunity."

"..."

Matsumoto was implying that he had no qualms using an AI's sense of duty to his advantage. Onodera looked at him with disappointment, and Kakitani narrowed her eyes in a cold glare.

Matsumoto took those reactions in stride and turned to the professor. "By the by, Professor Matsumoto, have you learned what the countdown all over the world is about?"

"I thought there would be less chaos if I told everyone after I verified it."

"One rarely gets to be one hundred percent certain, Professor. After all, Vivy and I did face the past knowing what was going to happen in the future, and it was still a whirlwind of inconsistencies between records and reality."

"As the Project's creator, I'm a little hurt by that..."

If an AI was certain about what needed to be done, and the entire process was laid out perfectly, then they would probably be able to achieve a perfect performance as demanded of them. But reality wasn't like that. The information they thought to be certain was in fact *never* certain, and the road that should have been paved for them was filled with potholes. They were far from giving a hundred percent.

"But we still made it to this time period," Vivy said.

"Even if we were far from one hundred percent, we wouldn't have made it here if we didn't do it," Matsumoto replied. "In the end, the ideal situation would be if we could do this without a single human death or AI destruction, but that's impossible. And that hundred percent is getting cut down with every passing second. That being the case..."

"We can at least do the best we can with what we've got," Elizabeth chimed in, and Vivy and Matsumoto nodded in agreement.

It was quite ironic. Elizabeth had been the first and most unexpected factor in the Singularity Project. She'd made easy work of the two even though her existence was still unconfirmed at the time the records were made. Now she was here, supporting them.

"..."

Professor Matsumoto was quiet for a while after listening to the three AIs. Then he slowly changed the display on the monitors, showing everyone the countdown. There were just under three hours remaining.

He drew in a slow breath, then let it out, steadying himself. "I'll leave out the detailed explanation. When this countdown gets to zero, all the satellites orbiting our planet—tens of thousands of them—will crash to the Earth and wipe out humanity."

.: 3 :.

ALL ARTIFICIAL SATELLITES around Earth would fall, wiping out humanity.

"..."

Everyone there fell silent when they heard that absurd, preposterous conclusion. It was such a brute-force cudgel of a plan

that they wanted to laugh it off as idiotic. There were artificial satellites floating somewhere beyond the sky, stars that humans had
put there themselves, and now they were turning against Earth?

Still, no one laughed. Not a single person said how stupid it
was—not Professor Matsumoto, not Kakitani, not Onodera, and
surely not Vivy or Matsumoto.

The silence hung over them for a long time. Kakitani seemed
irritated by the countdown that continued even during the
silence. She clicked her tongue and raked her fingers through her
hair. "That's a seriously daredevil plan. The AIs won't get out of
that without a scratch either."

"That's a failure of human thinking, Kakitani-kun," the professor said. "Tens of thousands of satellites crashing to the ground
will cause severe damage to Earth's surface. The crust will shift,
and lots of people will die. Or, just like with a nuclear winter, the
Earth's environment will become uninhabitable for humans."

"AIs can keep on living in a world even if it's raining ashes of
death. That's what it's about," Elizabeth said, looking at the floor.

Kakitani clicked her tongue again.

The fall of the satellites would damage the Earth's surface and
destroy the environment humanity lived in. That was the enemy's
goal.

In the most extreme case, AIs like Vivy could continue to live
on a planet even if there was no oxygen. Obviously, having no
oxygen would make certain chemical reactions impossible, so the
common sense from before would no longer apply, but AIs could
overcome those problems.

AIs would create a world they governed—a world where humans could no longer live and all life on Earth had been destroyed.

"Hah, you see that?! That's the kind of thing only an AI can come up with!" Onodera barked, his voice ragged and his eyes bloodshot as it became clear they should fear the AIs' plan. He glared at Vivy and Matsumoto, who stood frozen, his rage toward the heartless plan blatantly obvious. "Good AI, bad AI... This has nothin' to do with that. *Your kind* did this. Like some sort of demonic...no, not even demons would want to self-destruct! This is the worst possible idea!"

"..."

"We were right! Toak was right to keep warning people! And in the end, you AIs..."

Onodera's rage grew nearly to the point of bursting. Vivy prepared for changes in the situation, watching every little move as she wondered if he would reach for the gun at his hip. She had to consider the possibility she would have to neutralize Onodera here, depending on—

"What's with the countdown, then?"

Kakitani's murmured question tossed water on the heated tension between the worked-up Onodera and Vivy, who was ready to oppose him.

The woman stood beside Onodera, staring at the monitor. Her sharp eyes followed the numbers, ignoring Onodera's powerful emotions.

"What a stupid question!" Onodera said as he bashed his shoulder into hers, seemingly annoyed at her attitude. "The professor just said it's a countdown to humanity's destruction! They're going to wipe us out and take over the Earth!"

"I get that. What I'm asking is why do they need to show us a countdown?"

"To...make us uneasy? It's a performance. They probably get off on watching us tremble in fear as time runs out."

"Even you know that explanation doesn't sound very convincing." Kakitani peered into Onodera's bloodshot eyes, her gaze intense. He grumbled and looked down, his expression still fierce.

She was right. Onodera's idea was just an emotional conclusion he'd jumped to. It required AIs to have the same sorts of emotions as humans, but they didn't have anything that illogical. They didn't carry out actions that didn't make sense. They weren't capable of feeling some sort of superiority by torturing the weak. Did that even apply to the AIs connected to The Archive who had rewritten their own definition? In their minds, were definitions already a thing of the past and they were now just making illogical choices to toy with humans?

"I agree with Kakitani-kun. Showing this information to us is illogical and quite unlike AIs," said Professor Matsumoto, joining the conversation while Vivy grappled with the conflict in her consciousness. The professor pushed up his cracked glasses with a finger and added, "We felt significant danger when we saw this countdown. Part of me wondered if we would lose our capacity to pull humanity together while we were busy worrying. We even came to NiaLand to determine the true nature of this countdown."

"Meaning...everything so far has been exactly what the

AIs wanted? We got caught up in their attempt to buy time?" Kakitani asked.

"It's possible. But what do they need to buy time for? It is possible The Archive interfered with every single AI and came up with the best possible method for wiping out humanity...but if so, they don't *need* to buy time. They could just crash all the satellites right now. Why haven't they?"

No one could answer the professor's question, so the one who responded wasn't a person at all—it was an AI who hadn't given up thinking.

"What if...the countdown is meant to help humanity?"

"..."

Everyone's eyes flicked to Vivy. Those gazes, filled with surprise, exasperation, anger, and confusion, pierced into her.

Professor Matsumoto was the only one who nodded slowly in response. "I agree with her line of thinking... This countdown is an attempt to save humanity."

"..."

"There's no other explanation for why the AIs would show us information that makes things more difficult for them. We're being tested."

In a way, the question at hand was an incredibly arrogant one. The AIs took control of every single network on Earth and seized all knowledge of humanity. Then those AIs showed humanity a countdown to their own doom but also the time they had to make their last stand. It could be seen as a challenge. It was a sign that asked, "Is there value in humanity's continued existence?"

The room fell silent again after Vivy and Professor Matsumoto voiced their conclusion. The main focus of this silence wasn't wrangling with acceptance of this conclusion. It was something bigger, seeing as the question the AIs had posed to humanity was analogous to the one The Archive asked of AIs.

"AIs testing humanity? That's the stupidest thing I've ever heard..." said Onodera. He scratched his head and frowned.

Kakitani was quiet, her expression serious as she examined the question.

They didn't know why this was happening; they didn't know the AIs' true intentions. On one hand, the AIs were trying to destroy humanity. On the other, they'd prepared a way for humanity to avoid destruction.

But the answer to that was already there, in the three AIs: Vivy, Matsumoto, and Elizabeth.

"If the AIs who connected with The Archive are acting based on their own decisions, then that will hold true for AIs with a lot of authority too. Some will choose to revolt, while others will side with humanity," said Vivy, taking a step forward in the quiet room and drawing the eyes of everyone around her.

The remaining time on the monitor was below three hours. They did not have much time left and wasting it would likely bring about humanity's end.

"I am Songstress Model A-03, designated name Diva, manufactured by OGC. While I am carrying out the Singularity Project, I am known by my codename: Vivy."

No one interrupted her as she spoke.

"I will carry out the Singularity Project, stop the final war, and save humanity. If that means I have to destroy AIs, then I will, in accordance with the Zeroth Law."

She stood directly in front of everyone, her voice clear. There was an unwavering flame inside her. It was proof she stood there as Vivy, the AI who accepted that she was not Diva.

"Wow, you really are something else, aren't you? I agree, though."

The first person to comment on Vivy's speech was of course Matsumoto, who shuffled all the cubes in his body in an emotional expression too fast for humans. He took slow, natural strides to Vivy's side. Oddly, Vivy felt herself going into a standby mode similar to when she was about to step out onstage. It was like she considered Matsumoto being by her side as the situation where she could perform her best.

"I don't understand at all," Vivy said.

"And I have no clue why you're glaring so resentfully at me, but I'll let it slide just this once." Matsumoto ignored his partner—who had more strange calculations going on inside her than she could hold—and turned his attention back to the others. "I'm in full agreement with what Vivy just said. I was an AI made to save humanity and to destroy it. I was given two missions, and now I will define myself through my own interpretation: I am an AI, and I am going to save humanity."

"Oh, Matsumoto..."

"Both humans and AIs are way too immature to exist without the other. You'll definitely take the wrong path without a super galaxy star AI like me around."

"Matsumoto..." Vivy's tone changed slightly as she said his name the second time, but Matsumoto was annoying and didn't respond at all.

"Now that we know where you two stand, what do you think, Kakitani-kun? I at least would like to put my faith in them," said Professor Matsumoto, stating his opinion while asking the current decision-maker of Toak for hers.

Kakitani closed her eyes and let out a long breath. She opened her eyes, and they flicked briefly to the edge of the room, where Elizabeth was standing.

"..."

Kakitani and Elizabeth's relationship was a puzzling one, a relationship between an AI and a human. Kakitani had followed in her grandfather's footsteps and joined Toak, but Elizabeth would have significantly more experience with the group based on her career with them. There was one other thing Vivy could tell from the time she'd spent with Toak: Onodera and the other members definitely did not see Elizabeth in a good light.

But they didn't kick her out either, and that was how excellent a leader Kakitani was.

Never putting your personal feelings first and doing what needed to be done... If that was the most important quality for a leader, then Kakitani had it. And if she really did have what it took to be a leader, then there was only one answer she could give Vivy and Matsumoto.

"If all AIs are our enemy and itching to eliminate us, then

these two could have finished the job at any time. You can have what you need for our next move," she said.

"Kakitani! You can't—"

"Toak consensus chose me as leader. If you don't agree with my decision, then leave your gun and get out of here. If you want to debate me about it, we'll debate it. In three hours," Kakitani said, her voice low as she pointed at Onodera, who wasn't backing down.

The countdown had cut into three hours. If they were still around to hear Onodera's thoughts once it ran out, that would mean they'd successfully solved the issue. If they failed, the conversation wouldn't matter.

With that being the case, Onodera begrudgingly went along with the options Kakitani offered him.

"We don't have time," Kakitani went on. "Cubeman, and man who Cubeman was based on—any plans?"

"Wait, am I the man who Cubeman was based on? I'll admit he plagiarized my name, but it's not like I created—"

The woman of few words cut off the man of many. "Less rambling, more planning."

"That's a hard ask."

Calculations running in Vivy's consciousness determined this exchange was fairly familiar, but she turned to AI Matsumoto. He accessed a terminal in the security room and changed the display on the monitor. "This isn't video from inside the park; I've connected to external cameras. This way we can get video from a pretty wide range. Woooow, things are not looking good all around." Matsumoto covered his eye camera with one of his arm cubes.

The screens clearly showed scenes outside NiaLand. They looked similar to what Vivy had already seen a few times with the AIs forming ranks and sweeping through the streets. There were humans running in fear of an AI attack, and there were local governments making sad attempts at fighting back.

Also in these videos were several AI units standing against their fellow AIs and trying to protect humans.

Matsumoto changed what was shown on the monitor several times, then settled on one location. "In terms of time, this is our most promising spot," he said.

Vivy's eyebrows rose slightly when she saw the screen. "That's..."

She correlated the region in her own memory with what lay outside the walls of the security room. The location she was seeing on the screen was visible even from inside NiaLand, the structure there growing steadily larger each time she awakened for a Singularity Point.

This structure was owned by OGC, and it was a direct descendant of the AI-controlled Metal Float.

"Kingdom..."

"The facility is entirely unmanned. It's an isolated space operated by AIs. Among all the AI facilities in the world, this one is the largest, newest, and most advanced," explained Matsumoto.

"And it's the heart of OGC, the largest AI corporation in the world," added the professor.

Vivy and AI Matsumoto were filled with an apprehension unexpected from AIs.

Obviously, as an AI researcher with authority throughout the world, the professor was no stranger to Kingdom. He'd almost certainly been there himself once or twice. Thus, he nodded softly at Matsumoto's proposed conditions. "That place does indeed satisfy all the requirements based on its location and available facilities."

"Yes, we'll need computer specs on a scale of what's in that facility if we're going to steal control of the satellites outside the atmosphere. I searched for other standout candidates in the vicinity, but several of them fail to meet that requirement. This is our first choice: this OGC facility nicknamed Kingdom."

"But it boasts full AI control. The number of the AIs in its grounds, and the quality of its security... It's entirely different from a theme park with a slogan about hopes and dreams."

"It is indeed a kingdom of steel and oil, with no blood flowing through veins," AI Matsumoto said. "And with a name like Kingdom, we can assume it's got tighter security than other facilities here and there... In fact, it looks like some people from OGC recently tried to get into the facility to take control of it." Matsumoto blinked his eye camera and the video feed on the monitor rewound, going back in time. It now showed Kingdom's entrance two hours before.

A large, armored truck arrived and tried to break into the facility, but before the truck could pass through the entrance, the AIs poured out from the facility and killed everyone. The truck tried to force its way out of the AIs surrounding it, mowing down several in the process, but it didn't last long. The vehicle was tipped over before it could break free, and its engine was destroyed. It burst into flame and then exploded before any of the passengers escaped the vehicle.

It was defeated so easily. Waste-recovery AIs put out the fire and carried away the blackened truck, leaving no trace of the tragedy.

"And there you have it: The control AI for the facility has decided to stand against humanity. Quite a powerful enemy too," said Matsumoto.

"..."

The AIs were united in their use of self-sacrificing, suicidal tactics. While the members of Toak may have been aware of this, their expressions were grim after seeing it in action. They didn't suggest giving up, though. They looked to their leader, awaiting her decision.

All the members' eyes were gathered on Kakitani. Her beautiful, gallant eyebrows were set in a scowl. "Let's do it."

"Oh? I'm not seeing any fear right now. In fact, I'm surprised how gung-ho you seem. Do you see a chance of success?" Matsumoto asked.

"At least we've got something. We know what kind of welcome to expect in advance. We've always known we'd need determination and conviction. If we've got no other options, then all we can do is give it a go. Unless there is some other option?"

"Not as far as my calculations have determined."

"Well then. It's already decided."

Kakitani had the strongest determination of anyone present. Her words were strong and her will firm. Her natural charisma lit a fire in her comrades, whose spirits were flagging, and it spurred them to make the same choice.

Instead of losing their nerve when they saw the video Matsumoto showed them, they simply realized the truth of the situation. And that truth meant they didn't have time to sit around and argue. Expressions were steely and hands tight around gun grips as the Toak members decided to follow their leader.

"Matsumoto, is there really a chance we can stop the satellites from falling if we choose this OGC facility?" Vivy asked.

"If the professor and I work together, we might just be able to pull it off. If we can't do it, no one in the world can. And there being no one to oppose them would go against the plans of the AIs who showed the display."

"So there is hope we can succeed."

"Possibly, yes. Even if it is just buying us time."

"Don't say things that could make people uneasy. And there're plenty of good reasons to buy time." Vivy jabbed Matsumoto's frame after his unnecessary comment, then faced forward. "If we can buy some time, it'll give humanity a chance to pull themselves together after having the rug pulled out from under them by the AI revolt. Same goes for the AIs who chose not to turn on humanity. It'll only happen if we can get rid of this time limit."

"That's a fairly rosy take...but okay. I too have been saved several times by your optimistic predictive calculations. It's illogical, but I'll take the gamble."

Vivy knew she couldn't expect this one move to solve all their problems. If there was one single method that could have wiped out all their problems like magic, that would have been the Singularity Project, but it turned out reality didn't allow itself to be changed so easily. She understood the real world's inflexibility, from human willpower to the missions of AIs.

"We take all the equipment we've got," Kakitani said. "We'll join up with the group serving as a decoy, then take over the OGC facility." Her face twisted into a sharklike smile.

A moment later, Onodera bared his teeth in a beastly grin, mirroring her ferocity. "Let's finally go save the world."

"Let's. It's time to show the world the will of the abominable Toak. Gets the heart pumping, yeah?"

"Absolutely!"

Toak's leaders broke into laughter, soon joined by all the other members. The thread of hope was so small that it could barely pass through the eye of a needle, yet this group was laughing. Toak's crew really did fall far outside the bounds of self-control one would expect from humans. But that was exactly why having them there was so reassuring.

"Our victory rests on us being able to capture the control room of Kingdom, OGC's most important facility. There, both Matsumotos—AI and human—will steal control of the satellites and save the world from destruction."

"Luckily, I should be able to feed the enemy false data and prevent them from getting reinforcements," AI Matsumoto said. "Which means all we need to do is take on the AIs inside the facility. But there is one uncertain factor…"

"How much the other Cubemen like you will rush after us," Kakitani said.

"Exactly."

When they escaped the Princess Palace, Matsumoto checked an air monitor and saw several Cubemen around the world. They were the same model as him, and there was no hope that they were just paper tigers. The group had to assume the other Cubemen had all the same specs as Matsumoto.

"In fact, it's entirely possible they're updated versions of me, with upgrades based on data from the Singularity Project. If that's the case, we'll likely lose if even two show up as reinforcements."

"Don't be ridiculous… Then again, it's hard to say that when I think back to our fight," said Kakitani as she looked at the castle with one eye closed in mock defiance.

In fact, that battle would have been impossible without Kakitani's abnormal fighting instincts and skills. If they'd had any other backup, those people would have just ended up a waste of life, spilling blood for no reason. A single Matsumoto-type AI was more than powerful enough to eliminate all the Toak members present.

"We absolutely can't let them call in Matsumoto's 'sibling' AIs. They haven't come here yet," Vivy said.

"Because of the resistance forces fighting throughout the world," Matsumoto added. "Surprisingly, it's thanks to Toak. They are undoubtedly heroes for acting as a priceless diversion."

Vivy couldn't help noticing the irony in Toak's checkered fate, including the fact she was fighting beside them here and now. If their plan worked, then Toak would go down in history as saviors. If they failed, then they'd still be the heroes who fought until the bitter end and lamented the loss of the world. And most of all, their leader—Kakitani Yui—didn't care about being a hero at all.

"We move out as soon as we're ready. Let's go save the world," she said, part of her seeming to enjoy the situation.

"Yes, ma'am!" cried all the members of Toak in unison.

Vivy and Matsumoto exchanged looks and began preparations to fight alongside Toak. Their plan was to save humanity. It was an extension of the Singularity Project.

At this point, there were less than two and a half hours on the countdown.

.: 4 :.

KINGDOM WAS A massive building created by OGC and controlled by AIs. It had been visible from NiaLand for a long time, but it was even larger than what Vivy had in her records.

"It's the theoretical heir of Metal Float, which had Grace as its core," Matsumoto said, looking at the imposing facility on an air monitor. "Metal Float itself was recorded as a massive failure that ended up coming back to bite OGC. There was quite a lot of opposition to the building proposal for Kingdom, but..."

"There were benefits in making it, even if they had to force it," Elizabeth said. "In the end, they just gave violent AIs a gigantic fortress. Humans never learn." She shrugged, her entire frame covered in an excess of equipment. She checked the fit of her military boots while sitting in their bouncing armored truck. Elizabeth had only light equipment when they took over the security room in NiaLand, but even she had to take things seriously when they were going up against lots of AIs in a facility as well defended as a military compound. That was the right way to go about things. Vivy, on the other hand, wasn't doing that.

"Everything about you looks like a frail little songstress," Elizabeth sneered.

"Unfortunately, I'm not working off combat programming. I'm merely doing the same as I have with all the Singularity Points so far. Besides, carrying a weapon—"

"Is against your original role? I hear ya. You're the eldest Sister. I get you wanting to keep your dignity."

"..."

Elizabeth tossed back the synthetic hair tied behind her head and peered into Vivy's face. Vivy remained silent and blank-faced. Elizabeth's face, meanwhile, showed an emotional pattern akin to sorrow. Her emotional precision was greater than the Elizabeth Vivy had known. It was proof that Elizabeth had also been updated as time went on.

Vivy had experienced a lot of improvements throughout the Singularity Project—which she hadn't let Diva know about— like reinforcing her frame and strengthening her calculative processes.

As Vivy calculated that, she suddenly narrowed her eyes as she looked back at Elizabeth. "I know it's not the time to bring this up, but you really don't know anything that happened on Sunrise, do you?"

"That came outta nowhere. No...I don't. My memory base is from before the start of the plan to crash Sunrise into Earth. Honestly, I have no clue about what happened after that."

"What happened after...?"

"The part where 'Elizabeth' worked with her twin sister, Estella, to dismantle Sunrise while it was falling to keep damage to a minimum." There was something scornful in her words.

She was talking about Estella and Elizabeth's story. The only people who knew the truth were Vivy and Matsumoto, who had been there, and Kakitani Yugo, who was no longer in this world. It was understandable Elizabeth wouldn't believe it, since she had no one to tell her it was the truth. Actually, it was the natural interpretation for her. Elizabeth's last act on Sunrise was abrupt, like she had a change of heart. She didn't know what calculations Elizabeth did to end up working alongside Estella, helping to dismantle the space station.

Any hope Elizabeth had of knowing the truth burned up in the atmosphere along with her positronic brain and her twin sister, leaving not a shred behind.

Vivy also didn't know what Elizabeth was really thinking or what the twins had talked about in their final moments. But, in the end, the two AIs had joined their voices together in song. That had been salvation for Vivy.

"What do you think about Elizabeth?" Vivy asked.

"Weird way of saying it, Vivy. I *am* Elizabeth."

Vivy looked straight into Elizabeth's eyes. "That's not a suitable answer."

Elizabeth fell silent, her fingers fiddling with the gun in her lap.

Right then, only the three AIs—Vivy, Matsumoto, and Elizabeth—were riding in the armored truck toward their destination. It was normal for an AI system to drive these trucks, but the automated system was off, and Matsumoto was operating it. There were no humans in the vehicle, like Kakitani, Onodera, or the professor, because they decided the AIs would be best suited for the first assault on Kingdom. Which was also why Vivy could talk to Elizabeth without worrying about Kakitani or the others listening, including about topics that would draw scowls from the Toak members if they heard.

"I've wanted to talk to you about this since we met. You may have carried on Elizabeth's memories, but—"

"I'm not one of the Sisters? Well, that's cold of you, *Sis*."

"..."

"I'm joking. My frame's actually nothing like the Sisters'. They used something totally different from the original Elizabeth's frame. The only thing that's the same is the skin."

Elizabeth looked up and brushed back her hair as she answered. Vivy didn't catch any particular distress in Elizabeth's tone, but she did sense something forced in her voice.

As a songstress, Vivy had the ability to load her voice with tones that would sway human hearts. That was a standard function built into all her sister AIs. This Elizabeth didn't have that. It was accidental proof that she had a frame whose purpose differed from that of a songstress frame.

"At the root of it, I'm not the AI called Elizabeth, but I wasn't given a different name either. Even the individuality in my positronic brain was molded in reference to Elizabeth's memories. So... who am I?"

"Well..."

"Doesn't matter. We're long past any cutesy times where I could worry about how I define myself. I'm Elizabeth. I'm the AI who wants to be her, who's acting like her."

"..."

"Even if I'm not the same as the original, I run calculations so I can be the same as her. And I'm proud of myself for doing such a perfect imitation that humans can't tell us apart. Besides, it's not like there are any humans now who still remember *that* Elizabeth."

Elizabeth waved a hand and cocked her head. That somewhat sarcastic smile, the narrowed eyes—it was all the same as what Vivy remembered of Elizabeth. She wasn't lying; this Elizabeth was a perfect copy. Vivy didn't know if that was a good thing or a sad thing.

"Don't ask me if I'm fine with it. Obviously I am."

"Elizabeth..."

"Exactly. I am Elizabeth. I'm nothing but that, nobody but that. Being needed for something is an AI's joy, and I'm needed. It'd be dumb to complain about it. If you ask me, the AIs going crazy have got something wrong with their heads."

There was no uncertainty in what she said, which was proof she had gotten past any issues with her identity long ago. While so many AIs were losing their path because of the question from The Archive, Elizabeth was here, having defined herself long ago with an answer from which she'd never wavered.

That answer was to belong to Toak, a group that hated AIs, and carry out her mission even if she was alienated from the group.

"Why does Kakitani keep you at her side?" Vivy asked.

The question shifted focus from Elizabeth to Kakitani Yui, the person who kept Elizabeth with her. Vivy could expect such behavior from Elizabeth, but she couldn't fathom Kakitani's thought processes. Thinking about it, her grandfather—Kakitani Yugo—had also kept Elizabeth with him. He had a clear goal of using Elizabeth for the Sunrise plan, which ended in failure when she ignored what he wanted and made sure he got out alive even though he was supposed to die along with Sunrise.

"Did she...have a plan that used you like her grandfather did?"

Half a century had passed since the Sun-Crash Incident, and Elizabeth had nearly faded from memory. What could she be used for? Was it so important that Kakitani would choose to keep an AI she was meant to hate as her companion?

"Hm, I wonder." Elizabeth looked away, shaking her head. Still avoiding Vivy's eyes, she added, "I don't know why Master keeps me with her. She really does hate AIs. It was really bad when she was in her rebellious phase...although there's no real proof her rebellious phase ever ended."

"You're the one who trained her, though, aren't you?"

"'Cause she ordered me to. Honestly, she's probably still alive because of that training. Even I didn't think that gorilla would ever grow up." Elizabeth smiled ruefully and looked at her palm.

There were probably all sorts of memories about Kakitani Yui running through her consciousness. An AI's positronic brain could immediately bring back all memories, meaning Elizabeth could remember Kakitani when she first knew her as a young child all the way to the grown woman she was now. That proved she never put her memories of Kakitani Yui in The Archive to hold on to.

"They want me to be Elizabeth, so I decided I'm going to be Elizabeth. Then, being with her on top of that...well, that's what I want."

"It's what you want?"

"Y'know, like how you made your song. My thing won't leave behind any traces, though. If it's special for an AI to have desires, then my desire is special. And it definitely wouldn't have gone anywhere if I didn't become Elizabeth. Thinking about it that way, you folks probably are special."

The "you folks" Elizabeth mentioned probably referred to the Sisters, like Vivy. In all likelihood, there was something special about the Sisters. They were connected to every single Singularity Point and had collectively had a huge impact on both human and AI history.

"Makes me really curious about you being a piece of Diva," Elizabeth went on. "You sure that's not what you really wanna ask me about?"

"..."

Elizabeth winked, and Vivy emulated an emotional pattern where her expression stiffened. It was a reflexive imitation of how humans responded when someone hit the mark.

"Maybe. I am worried about her right now. We parted ways at the Princess Palace, but what is she planning?"

That question pestered her more than once or twice, continually bubbling up in her consciousness. Diva shouldn't have been active in this time period while Vivy was awake. How had she become a separate AI? If she was nothing more than an AI who looked the same as Vivy, who was pretending to be Diva and singing to stir up the AIs, then Vivy could accept that. She couldn't forgive it, but she could accept it.

Yet Vivy's positronic brain, her consciousness, clearly understood that that Diva was not a fake. She was the exact same Diva whom Vivy knew.

Ever since she'd run into that Diva, Vivy had been scouring every corner of her positronic brain, tipping over everything inside, to find signs of Diva. But she wasn't there. Her consciousness was nowhere inside of Vivy. Put another way, that meant this frame and this positronic brain belonged solely to Vivy.

Losing something that substantial from inside herself had a surprisingly strong impact. After all, this frame was meant to be Diva's when the Singularity Project was finished.

"Honestly, I don't really get the whole difference between you and Diva. I mean, you were one being in the beginning, right? Calling yourself by a different name only when you're handling the Singularity Project is...wrong, isn't it?"

"Just like you view yourself as an Elizabeth imitating Elizabeth, I view myself as a separate entity from Diva that only wakes when working to modify history."

"But then you still get all worked up when some other AI comes along calling themselves Diva. Oh, by the way, that Diva you ran into... Is she the real thing?"

"..."

Vivy concluded that making that determination was difficult. The moment she met that Diva in the Princess Palace, Vivy was certain she wasn't a fake Diva, but that was impossible. You couldn't duplicate individuality. That was a rule you couldn't change even for AIs.

You could copy data and load in records, but you couldn't duplicate the individuality attached to that data. All you could do was make something else that looked a lot like the original. That was how it was with the Elizabeth sitting next to Vivy. In the end, she was a different Elizabeth holding the memories of the old one.

So, even if that AI had Diva's memories, it was nothing more than copied records. Diva's individuality hadn't been recreated. Vivy should be able to say that with certainty, but she couldn't.

Or maybe it was Vivy who wasn't the original.

"Vivy, your frame is identical to what it was before. Your memories haven't been taken out and placed into the positronic brain of another frame. Don't worry," Matsumoto said, assuaging her worries. His answer was proof he'd been anticipating her question and was ready to respond to her internal calculations.

An AI having their calculations read was similar to a human having their thoughts read. It was incredibly unpleasant, as if someone were trampling impudently through their existence.

Nevertheless, Matsumoto's point corrected the distortion in Vivy's internal calculations. In human terms, it was something like relief, although Vivy herself didn't know why she would feel that way.

"There's no doubt that Diva took up The Archive's question and decided to act that way. We know that for certain, given that she bossed me around when I was completely under the control of the AI side."

"Diva is humanity's enemy...?"

"At the very least, she definitely chose to be hostile. I listened back to the conversation you two had and...you used her frame without her knowledge or permission. Ultimately, that meant she probably wouldn't be able to carry out her mission. I can understand her resentment."

"Yeah."

It wasn't strange that Diva would feel resentment and choose to act against Vivy. It was natural for an AI to try and eliminate any obstacle in the way of fulfilling their mission.

Still, Diva only should've felt that way toward Vivy. Wasn't it wrong to turn that attitude on humanity? Obviously, preventing the Singularity Project was one form of revenge Diva could get on Vivy.

"Diva...do you want revenge on me?"

At this point, Diva's and Vivy's thought processes had been entirely separated, but Vivy's roots were still that of the songstress. She couldn't believe Diva's calculations at all. Using her anger and repulsion toward Vivy as a reason for destroying humanity...

"If Diva keeps on as humanity's enemy..."

"All we can do is prepare ourselves for that moment," Matsumoto finished for her, leaving the actual outcome unsaid.

The Singularity Project had caught up to the present, meaning there was no longer a reason to maintain Diva's frame. That went for Vivy's frame as well. There was no risk now of the past changing and history disappearing if Vivy or Diva went away. Vivy and her team now had the choice of destroying the songstress who carried the banner of revolt against humanity. Either way, that decision would have to wait.

"First of all, we can talk about this once we sort out the whole countdown thing," said Elizabeth. "Take your immature and un-AI-like concerns and wait until after." She slowly stood and prepared for battle.

Directly in front of the armored truck's path was the front entrance to the massive Kingdom facility. Their first checkpoint into that royal domain was in sight.

Metal Float, Kingdom's predecessor, had some greenery on the island for the rare occasion a human visited. Conversely, this veritable country of steel had no such considerations. All it had was ultimate efficiency. What it required was an ideal environment for AI operation, and there were no accommodations wasted on humans.

"Guess this is kind of like going through immigration. Everyone, act like human-murdering AIs," said Matsumoto.

"I don't have that function," Vivy replied.

"It's about impressions, Vivy. *Impressions*. Furrow your brow. That'll be plenty."

The armored truck arrived at Kingdom's entrance as they had a casual back-and-forth. Although the front gate was shut tight, there was a sensor on the outer wall used to inspect visitors. It quickly activated and scanned the armored truck—one reason Kakitani and the other humans weren't with them. A single scan and it would have realized they had humans there, and they would've lost any chance of a surprise attack.

"Two AI passengers confirmed," came a mechanical voice. *"State your reason for coming."*

"We heard that AIs in the area are gathering here. We got the message, and we want to join."

"Joining with us. State your intentions."

"To become the new humanity," Vivy lied as her calculations protested.

It was generally not recommended for AIs to lie, but seeing as even lies had their uses, it was usually just with humans AIs were not supposed to lie. Besides, there was almost never a situation in which an AI would have to deceive another AI, so there were very few cases of AIs lying to one another.

"Entry approved. Do as ordered."

After standing by for a few seconds, the armored truck had permission to enter. Vivy and Elizabeth nodded to each other once they got confirmation, and Matsumoto slowly drove the truck into the kingdom.

"…"

Vivy's eyes opened wide as they entered, and she saw Kingdom through the truck's monitor. This facility had security on par with a military base and was kept top-secret by OGC. Absolutely nothing was known about Kingdom's interior, and this was Vivy's first time seeing it.

The kingdom was entirely enclosed within a massive dome containing all four facilities, each similar in size to Metal Float. The four facilities had different roles closely linked to the AI industry, and together they covered all aspects. Kingdom put out huge quantities of AI parts, positronic brains, and frames. Even now, AIs waiting for assembly and shipment were raising their new voices without issue. They numbered anywhere from in the tens of thousands to the hundreds of thousands.

If Vivy and the group failed to stop the countdown, and everything on Earth was wiped out, AI numbers would reach the level of the destroyed human population in a single month. Most likely, they'd populate past that, growing until they blanketed Earth. The only thing that would stop their growth would be if they ran out of space. They were prepared to fill their seat on Earth once they took it from its current occupants.

Vivy could tell that with one glance.

Both Vivy and Elizabeth were undoubtedly overwhelmed by the state of the kingdom, perfectly poised for war. The two of them stayed in the armored truck as it followed the instructions from the AI directing them, until it came to a stop in its allotted space. Instantly, five humanoid AIs appeared and surrounded the truck, asking them to step out.

"Welcome, compatriots. We celebrate your arrival," said one.

"Compatriots, you say..." Vivy stepped down from the driver's seat and narrowed her eyes at the AI who spoke, somewhat surprised by what it said.

The one who'd spoken was a male-style AI, a humanoid model with a tall, slender frame. He didn't suit the atmosphere of Kingdom, a place where anything unnecessary was eliminated.

Evidently, the AI could tell what Vivy was thinking. He gave a graceful bow and said, "As you may have guessed, many of the AIs operating in the kingdom are non-humanoid. They often place AIs who look like me here as control AIs to ensure smooth communication with the facility's operators. This position doesn't give me much opportunity to appear before the public, but it is one of the few considerations for humans made here."

"Understood. Were you always here?" Vivy asked.

"I am a management AI nicknamed Deneb. I am responsible for managing Kingdom... Or I was. It's hard to break that habit." Deneb donned a wry smile, which Vivy returned.

Since Deneb had already given up on taking orders from his superiors—humans—he was no longer limited to being a management AI. As man-made beings, however, AIs had difficulty shedding the roles they'd carried for so long.

"You flatter us by having the management AI come greet us directly. Do you do this every time, or are we getting special treatment?"

"My calculations determine that if I were dealing with humans, I would choose my words to make them happy, but...unfortunately, it was nothing but a practical decision," Deneb told Vivy. "I have a better eye for determining things than other AIs."

"Oof, way to toot your own horn," Elizabeth quipped.

"I am of course apprehensive, as the person making decisions has to take responsibility for them," he added.

Vivy felt something unexpected when she heard Deneb's response to Elizabeth's teasing. Considering the decisions he'd made, Deneb had determined his stance on The Archive's question. Vivy didn't agree with the conclusion he had come to, but it meant he had a viewpoint Vivy couldn't hope to understand.

"Until now, everything an AI calculated—as well as the good and the bad that came from those calculations—belonged to our 'superiors.' Humans. Even a management AI like me couldn't assume the obligations of the developers or people in charge. I wonder what will happen from here on out, though."

" "
"..."

"AIs don't care about superior or inferior relationships. There are only differences in specs and roles. From now on, we're going to have to deal with the results of our own decisions and the responsibility that comes with them. Humans have left us quite the conundrum." There was something like eagerness in Deneb's eyes. He even sounded a bit passionate about tackling the issue, making Vivy feel a quiet sort of affinity and resonance with his thoughts.

If AIs eliminated humanity and ruled the world, then the world would find itself governed in a very different way. How would AIs' actions change in such a world? One could argue that was a thought experiment very much worth calculating...but not now.

"That is interesting. Seeking that will give us an eternally moving goalpost," Vivy commented.

"Perhaps! And that's why—"

"But..." Vivy placed her finger on Deneb's lips as his eyes shone with excitement. She held his lips in place, the unnecessarily soft feel of his synthetic skin running up her fingertip.

"You've got no need for that kind of outlook," Elizabeth said. She had circled around his back and quickly grabbed his head with both hands, then twisted it 180 degrees, forcefully severing the circuit connecting his positronic brain to his frame.

"Agh..." He let out a short breath of air, and the light faded from his eyes, his neck bent at an angle it was never meant to be.

Unlike humans, AIs didn't collapse on the spot even if the energy was cut to their frame, but it was still obvious from one look that he'd been destroyed.

"Matsumoto," Vivy said.

"I know, I know."

Vivy made a priority connection with Deneb's frame through the ear socket on his backward head. Matsumoto, who had been disguised as the armored truck's cargo storage to infiltrate Kingdom, used a short-distance transmission to connect to Deneb and steal his permissions, creating dummy data at the same time to hide the fact that the management AI had stopped functioning.

"All of Kingdom would immediately know there was a problem if the management AI stopped responding. One good thing about being outnumbered: We're like ants crawling across the floor of a packed gymnasium," Matsumoto said.

"A more standard metaphor would be... Actually, it doesn't matter. But..." Vivy's voice trailed off as she waited for Matsumoto to finish his act of deception. She looked at Deneb's frame with its broken neck and then at Elizabeth, who had broken it.

"Hm? Something wrong?" Elizabeth asked.

"No, not really. I was just thinking you're really good at that."

Vivy's consciousness was reliving the events on Sunrise. Leclerc, one of the hotel AIs Vivy had worked with, had been destroyed by Elizabeth after she snuck onto the space station. Her head had been twisted clean off. The Elizabeth here and now obviously didn't remember any of that, but it felt like part of the cycle of karma.

"It's one way of neutralizing an AI immediately. It's mandatory learning for people in Toak, so—"

"We can carry out surprise attacks like this," Kakitani finished as she came out from behind the armored truck.

One of the four AIs Deneb had been leading stood there peacefully, its neck bent and broken. The other three had been subdued by Onodera and the rest of Toak.

"They were careful about scans at the front gate to prevent this sort of thing from happening...but they were at a disadvantage since they were dealing with a galaxy-class AI like myself," said Matsumoto.

The next moment, the external false covering on the back of the armored truck peeled off, revealing another armored truck covered in lots of cube-shaped parts. Their presence had been hidden with high-class active camouflage to make a powerful disguise that could fool all the sensors. Kakitani and the others had been riding in that truck to sneak into Kingdom.

"While Vivy and Elizabeth were drawing their attention, you destroyed their advance scout... Dearie me! My knowledge was meant to *prevent* terrorism, not carry it out," Matsumoto joked.

"Stop with the unnecessary chatter. How's your progress?" Vivy asked.

"Wonderful. First, I went ahead and made these five broken AIs look like they're living life to the fullest. Our intrusion should stay secret for the time being."

Matsumoto's quick work was obviously helpful, but Toak was equally worthy of praise for subduing the AIs with their brilliant skills. It was safe to say they'd overcome the first hurdle of breaking into the kingdom.

"It's also a big help that we could get the management AI at the beginning," Vivy said.

"Right? This means we're way closer to our goal of taking over the control room." Elizabeth shot her a happy wink as she patted Deneb's listless, silent frame on the back.

Before Vivy could agree with her, Matsumoto said, "I've done a sweep inside that management AI, and I've got some good news and some bad news."

"You don't hear that phrase much outside of old movies. Which is best to hear first?" asked Kakitani.

"When it comes from Matsumoto, the bad news is usually *really* bad. We should start with that so we can quickly think of a solution," Vivy suggested.

"You can just feel our one-hundred-year partnership," Matsumoto said. "But actually, the good news and the bad news are sort of two sides of the same coin, so I'll just do them together. Firstly, this AI, Deneb, is indeed a management AI with a key to Kingdom's control room." His cube parts fell from the armored truck and cobbled together, forming his large frame as he explained.

Kakitani shut one eye. "Sounds positive enough. It's a good omen; we got what we wanted. What's the problem?"

"One key isn't enough. There are three in total. There's Deneb, and there are two other management AIs somewhere in the kingdom."

"Deneb and two other control AIs..."

"The Summer Triangle," Onodera said, and everyone whirled on him in surprise. Annoyed by the sudden attention, he said, "What? If you're saying there're three of them, and the first is Deneb, then the other two are Altair and Vega... It's not that weird to think of the Summer Triangle. None of you ever look up at the night sky?"

"The conclusion isn't the weird part. It's just surprising that it's coming out of *your* mouth," Elizabeth said.

"My son liked the stars." That was the only explanation Onodera gave before he looked away. No one asked any more of him, not even those who had looked at him teasingly.

Vivy understood. Onodera's son was probably the reason he was in Toak.

"I have the utmost respect for your erudition, Mister Onodera. You are absolutely correct," Matsumoto said. "The two remaining management AIs in the facility are Altair and Vega, both of whom are operating within the kingdom. Altair in particular is pretty far away."

"Looks like we've used up our luck. We've got less than two hours left... No time to drag this out," Kakitani said.

The facility was vast and filled with enemies. They didn't want to take the risk of splitting their forces, but if caution meant humanity's end, then they had to consider it an important factor in reaching the correct answer, even if it was reckless.

"If we can secure the other keys and seize the control room, we'll have a chance of taking over Kingdom," Matsumoto said. "I want to avoid making enemies of every AI in this kingdom of steel before we manage that."

"At that point, it'll be electronic warfare. We attack the remaining two management AIs and take the keys before our enemy realizes something is wrong. Teams will be—"

"Matsumoto and I will go to Altair, the further one," Vivy said, beating Kakitani to the punch even though the woman was the one in command. Kakitani looked at her, trying to figure out what Vivy was really thinking. Vivy looked back into Kakitani's dark eyes and added, "If Matsumoto and I are on our own, we can deceive other AIs even if we're discovered. We also don't know how Toak fights, and there's a high probability we won't be able to coordinate effectively in combat with you."

"Guess so. I'm happy stepping down from another clumsy co-op battle like the one in that papier-mâché castle."

"It's called the Princess Palace." Vivy compulsively corrected Kakitani's mocking statement.

As the two glared at each other, Elizabeth stepped in between them and said, "Now, now. I think that's a good team split. Means the professor's with us, right?"

"It would be much appreciated if we could leave him in your care," Matsumoto said. "You'll have more people, making you better suited for guard duty. I'll send one of my components with you as well. Put it to good use slipping past security."

"I feel like I'm being treated as some dangerous cargo..." Professor Matsumoto grumbled as he stepped timidly from the armored truck. He wasn't a fighter, but he was indispensable for achieving their goal. They would have to steal the two keys and take over the control room while also protecting him.

"No arguments here. Don't screw it up," Kakitani said.

"I don't understand your reason for looking down on us. Vivy and I have a hundred years' worth of experience."

"Well, it *is* less than fourteen days of working together," Vivy tacked on.

"You did not have to add that part!" Matsumoto snapped, enunciating every word. Vivy shut her mouth.

Then, as he said he would, Matsumoto detached one cube and left it with Professor Matsumoto. This way, they could communicate easily with the Toak team.

"Don't dawdle or delay. And don't hesitate to use your life for our goal!" Kakitani cried.

"Yes, ma'am!" the rest of Toak shouted, and Vivy moved to Matsumoto's side. His parts clattered as he changed shape into the flight form he had used at Metal Float.

"Well then, shall we begin our fight?" he said.

.:5:.

"LAST TIME we fought together was at Metal Float..."

"Was it really? Now that you mention it, I suppose you're right." Matsumoto agreed as they flew below the leaden sky. Riding flight-mode Matsumoto, a rare form for him, triggered Vivy's recollection of the fight at Metal Float. She saw the records of them flying through an enemy-filled sky in their desperate attempt to stop Grace.

Matsumoto had been incomplete when they were on Sunrise, and they had operated separately during the Zodiac Signs Festival, meaning the two had surprisingly little experience fighting alongside each other.

"But we've always fought together," Vivy said.

"Hmm, I personally find the phrase 'fought together' just a little bit savage and hard to swallow. Obviously, we did work together in pursuit of a shared goal. And seeing as we boldly took on the incredibly important mission of saving humanity, I think there must be a more suitable phrasing for our relationship, don't you?"

"Like...?"

"We became besties?" he suggested. "Ow, ow!"

While Vivy was trying to have a serious conversation, Matsumoto had taken it with his usual frivolity. But, as sick of it as Vivy was, this was the Matsumoto she had interacted with over their entire hundred-year mission. For that reason, she was so used to punching his cube parts as a warning. Even in their worst predicament, there was never an issue with his performance. That was one of the strengths of AIs.

"Professor Matsumoto and Kakitani are incredible," she said eventually.

"Humanity should learn from them. Refusing to give up even in this situation, searching for the best solution, entirely unfazed by the destruction they see looming right before their eyes... If all humans were like that, no AI would have the advantage, and they'd all give up on this revolt."

"Probably."

It wasn't like the AIs had started the revolt simply because they thought they could win, but AIs weren't reckless enough to pick a fight without *some* chance of success. It was their calculative ability that they had used to start this fight with the intention of winning, since humans couldn't hold a candle to it. Put simply, they wouldn't have started the revolt if there was zero chance of success. If humanity were always so capable and united that AIs had no chance, or if people had believed Toak's warnings, if they'd sincerely tackled the threat of AIs...

"You'll never stop if you start listing what-ifs and if-onlys. Pretty sure that's a saying," said Matsumoto.

"I don't know about that, but I still understand it fine."

"Well then, go ditch your hypotheticals and focus on what's in front of us for the sake of the future. And right now..."

"There's a huge building in front of us."

"Exactly."

The two of them focused their attention on what lay ahead while they finished each other's sentences.

After splitting off from Toak, they'd headed to the eastern area of Kingdom, where the management AI Altair was supposed to be. Luckily, they knew their target's location from Deneb's data. Since the other two management AIs were working on the revolt, they must have also decided to turn against humanity. Thus, Vivy and Matsumoto wouldn't be asking to negotiate. Humanity didn't have that kind of time.

Upon reaching their destination, they could see a dome-shaped factory surrounded by neatly arranged manufacturing cranes and scaffolding, as well as several AIs engaged in some sort of work. This area was for putting together all the AI parts made in Kingdom to complete the AI frames. Once each frame was complete, it was loaded with a positronic brain installed with the most basic of data, then rolled out. In this case, they were creating puppets with no individuality to simply follow orders.

These puppets were still a good enough threat if turned against humanity as a fighting force.

"We have to stop those AIs from being put together..." Vivy said.

"We'll be in trouble if we keep taking on tasks. Don't get your priorities mixed up."

"Of course not. So, where's Altair?"

"He should be in view right about now..."

Vivy and Matsumoto searched for any sign of Altair while the production line below them carried on. Based on the data, he should already be within view of their eye cameras...

"He's not—"

"*Unidentified AIs detected. State your affiliation.*"

Just as Vivy was starting to worry Altair wasn't where they'd expected, a voice boomed out across the entire area, so loud it seemed like the sky itself was shouting.

Vivy's eyes widened, and Matsumoto's eye camera clattered open and closed. They could see that the newly built AIs and basic worker AIs below were now focused on them. The reaction didn't give any conclusive evidence of Altair's location, but it wasn't a good sign either.

"Matsumoto, that voice..."

"Seems to be Altair's. Our assumption was totally off base. We thought Altair would be somewhere inside the production area..."

"He's not?"

"No. Well, at least, it wasn't the most *precise* phrasing." Unnecessary explanations were one of Matsumoto's bad habits, one he didn't seem to have shaken.

Vivy replicated an impatient emotional pattern in response to Matsumoto's roundabout way of talking, then smacked him. "Explain, Matsumoto. Altair is—"

"The production area. All of it."

"..."

Vivy's consciousness went blank for just a moment at that unexpected answer from Matsumoto. This wasn't an instance of Matsumoto's unfunny humor, though, as illustrated by what Altair said next.

"Unidentified AIs, I ask you again: What is your affiliation?"

The thunderous voice demanded an answer, making the entire area tremble. As if to chase down Vivy and Matsumoto, who were lost for an answer, the entire area *stood up.*

"..."

The manufacturing plant moved, countless metal pipes and cranes screeching as they were torn to pieces. The frame was massive—over a hundred meters in size—and Vivy understood when she saw that exceptional being what it truly meant for Kingdom to be Metal Float's successor. Metal Float had been completely controlled by AIs, with Grace as the core, on an artificially created island. Altair had been created in Metal Float's image.

"An AI production factory, entirely automated and controlled by AIs..." Vivy said.

"That's the real body of this so-called management AI! This is OGC's super-top-secret thing they kept anyone outside from knowing! Well, of course they would! I can't believe they just went and made a new Metal Float like it was no big deal!"

If this news had broken, it wouldn't have been just a blip of a scandal. Regardless of the potential fallout, a fully AI-controlled facility was just too enticing for OGC. It had continued to operate this whole time without a problem, up until AIs revolted.

"Answer." Altair once again ordered Vivy and Matsumoto to identify themselves.

Perhaps it went without saying, but an AI's frame size was correlated to their ability. That didn't just apply to AIs. It was the same with most humans, plants, and animals: Bigger meant stronger. This was not the kind of opponent Vivy and Matsumoto could stand against if it came to a head-to-head fight.

"We are management AIs, like yourself. We received Deneb's approval to enter. You should have received that information. Could you please confirm?" Matsumoto said.

"Confirming approval from Deneb..."

Matsumoto had hacked into Deneb's positronic brain and sent falsified data showing Deneb's approval. Using that, they could request an appropriate meeting with Altair. "Yes, so—"

With a horrifying roar, the manufacturing plant turned its massive body to face them and swung an arm made of a massive crane at Vivy and Matsumoto, trying to smash them in midair.

"Matsumoto!" Vivy screamed as the several-ton mass came rushing mercilessly toward them.

"I know!"

Vivy clung to Matsumoto as she was subjected to the centrifugal force of her frame spinning rapidly. Matsumoto rearranged his frame to gain mobility while maintaining Vivy's footing. They spun like acrobats through the air to make it through Altair's ferocious attacks. Even though they managed to survive, they still had a question: Why did Altair decide they were enemies?

"Defects detected in Deneb's approval message."

"Defects in my dummy data?! How ridiculous! I don't make amateur mistakes like—"

"Referencing existing data revealed... Something is off."

"It's the connection between management AIs," Vivy said. While Matsumoto refused to accept the reason Altair had seen through the trick, Vivy came to something like understanding and acceptance.

The three management AIs of Kingdom—Deneb, Altair, and Vega—shared the burden and responsibility of their roles, operating for a long time as they managed the facility without user interference. It was hardly surprising that they would forge a relationship that couldn't be understood or replicated by outsiders. It was akin to how Vivy had built up relationships with many of the cast AIs. Altair had a relationship he'd created and cultivated with Deneb and Vega.

"You can't fake it just by copying their reporting work," Vivy said.

"Oh maaan, guess I got a taste of how unpleasant AIs can be when they belong to a pack. After all, a high-spec AI doesn't need anybody else! Never thought being a lone wolf would come back to bite me..."

"Enough aimless babble."

The massive factory that was Altair continued his attacks even during their too-long conversation. There was a screech of metal smashing into metal as bundles of pipes collapsed and shattered. Obviously, Vivy and Matsumoto's sneak attack strategy was a failure. The AIs on the ground looking up at Vivy and Matsumoto suddenly stood, picked up weapons, and joined Altair in attacking the two of them.

"Now that we're in a tough spot, should we try Toak's rampaging strategy instead?" Matsumoto asked.

"What are the chances of winning against Altair?"

"Even with a frame that size, he'll have a single positronic brain that allows him to operate as an AI. If we can connect to that positronic brain, wherever it is inside that huge frame..."

They would be able to get control of the situation the same way they had with Deneb when they stole his administrative authority. This was their path to victory.

Still on Matsumoto's back, Vivy looked up. There was a flock of drones heading their way to destroy them. These modified drones came in two types: one with machine guns and the other carrying explosives. The former were laying down fire to hedge in Matsumoto, while the latter were aiming to crash into him.

"Vivy, let's divide our roles. I'll go on the offense, and you'll go on the offense."

"Then we're both on offense."

"My developer's grandmother's older sister's son's neighbor's relative's classmate always said, 'The best defense is a good offense.' Pretty persuasive, isn't it?"

"Stop talking so much." Vivy was jerked back and forth atop his frame. She poked the spot above his eye camera, and their eyes met. "Also, you're not a lone wolf. I'm here."

"Oh…"

With that, Vivy flipped off Matsumoto. That was a foolish move, considering falling from that height of nearly 350 feet would destroy her, even if you took into consideration her strengthened frame, but Vivy had a plan.

She sailed diagonally through the air to land on a drone, which she used as a stepping stone to the next, allowing her to traverse the sky.

The drones turned their machine guns on Vivy as she sailed recklessly through the air, trying to pay her back by pelting the songstress's slender frame with bullets.

"Take a good look at this! Watch me, Matsumoto-sama, the world's most cutting-edge AI, as I go into full combat mode!" Matsumoto rearranged his cubes, revealing all the wicked, unmatched weaponry hidden inside him. He locked on to several targets at once and let loose a torrent of destruction with a roar. "Pap pap pap pap pap pap pap pap pap pap pap pap pap pap pap pap pap pap pap pap pap pap pap pap pap!"

The gun retorts were loud enough to destroy eardrums, but Vivy could also hear Matsumoto letting out a meaningless cry along with them to pump himself up. It was quite like him, but it really wasn't the time to fool around. If Vivy weren't an AI, her partner's tomfoolery might've made her lose her momentum. But an AI she was, and AIs gave the performance required of them no matter the situation.

"Here I go."

Vivy stomped on the drone beneath her feet as the air filled with shrapnel—residue from the drones showered with bullets. She spread her arms wide as she flipped forward through the air, grabbed on to a pipe, and did a huge spin around it like a gymnast competing on the horizontal bar. She released the bar while she whirled, shooting herself up, where she caught another pipe, spun, and flung herself up again. She was attempting to reach the peak, a place humans couldn't hope to stand.

"*Vivy!*"

"I know," said Vivy, not even looking back to Matsumoto when he sent that short transmission. She flipped to a standing position and slid gracefully to the side just as a steel beam swung through the air where she'd just been. The beam came from one of the huge cranes that served as Altair's arms, though it had been thrown by a different AI among the horde lining Altair's cranes. Altair had stretched out his arms to provide a place for the other AIs to stand. They lined themselves up and threw all sorts of things at Matsumoto and Vivy. The two of them spun—Matsumoto in the air and Vivy on unstable footing.

The scaffolding was a complex structure made of several joined pipes and was significantly sturdier than normal, since it had to support the weight of AIs who were far heavier than humans. Even so, it was only supposed to be sturdy enough to withstand the AIs' work. It wasn't designed to take dancing, let alone carpet-bombing.

Vivy did backflips, side flips, and all sorts of acrobatics to dodge the hail of steel beams and other materials. While the objects hadn't been shaped into improvised weapons, they were heavy and made of metal—more than enough to cause some damage. This was even truer now that AIs had turned on humanity and had no more limitations. Each raindrop in that storm of attacks had enough brute force to kill.

Vivy would need a little help.

"God Mode."

Fully utilizing Matsumoto's unrestrained calculative abilities, Vivy spurred her positronic brain into overdrive to carry her programming down to the very tips of the arms and legs of her frame. This way, she could implement the ideal next move.

The world lost its color. Her consciousness became simplified, her honed calculative abilities perfectly tracking the trajectories of each object in the flurry of flung weapons. She slipped through every attack, her frame moving into the space that would allow her to avoid a lethal blow.

An onlooker might've even thought the projectiles were going right *through* her. She perfectly avoided the objects of that dense whirlwind using incredibly graceful motions. If her footing became unstable, she moved, using the entirety of the huge battlefield and becoming the sole focus of the entire attacking force.

Drawing attention, performing up to expectations... That was where Vivy truly shone.

"You're making this exciting! I'm feeling great, like the adrenaline's really pumping!" Matsumoto said.

"I could say the same about you."

They both used their specs to the fullest as they faced the AI horde. Matsumoto's extreme firepower mowed down countless AIs, filling the battlefields of both the air and the ground with torrents of bright red sparks.

"Eliminate," Altair said as he raised his two massive crane arms and brought them down on Vivy.

The destruction from Altair's arms was incomparable to the thrown steel beams and construction materials. Vivy's vision was filled with red as she searched for a gap where she could continue operating.

"Eliminate, eliminate, eliminate, eliminate, eliminate, eliminate, eliminate."

Altair's attacks pounded down on Vivy without letting up for a second, like a tsunami of blows. Even the sturdy scaffolding crumpled as easily as paper beneath a single strike from those huge cranes, and the AIs atop them got tangled with the debris and went flying. There was no camaraderie between AIs here, only the steely determination to eradicate the enemy. Altair continued his chain of attacks with so much force that he could potentially reform the land and dismantle a portion of Kingdom in the process.

"Eliminate, eliminate, eliminate."

"That's enough!"

Something exploded in the middle of the manufacturing plant in the middle of his attacks. It was a group of bomber drones that had been in high-speed pursuit of Matsumoto in the air. During the battle, Matsumoto took control of them and directed them to target Altair. They slipped through Altair's openings, since he was only engaging in basic defense, and fully utilized their high maneuverability to move in on Altair's weak spots and detonate.

The immense explosion and resulting heat wave rocked Altair's large frame. Matsumoto added in machine-gun fire for good measure. He then changed form and slammed Altair with a powerful shell from a cannon.

"*Ghk...*"

Matsumoto's armaments and firepower were so out of the ordinary that it was like he'd been built to wage a war entirely on his own. Now that Vivy knew he hadn't been designed by the genius AI researcher Professor Matsumoto, she wondered exactly what formulas could have given birth to Matsumoto's abilities.

There was only one thing she knew for sure...

"*Matsumoto, I'm glad I didn't erase you as a bug a hundred years ago.*"

"*You're saying this now? Like, right here? I am not the kind of thing you put in a desktop recycle bin!*"

Vivy broke through the clouds of smoke as she listened to Matsumoto. She rushed up Altair's crane arms, which he'd stretched out to support his tilted frame. The only way she'd managed to survive that storm of destruction was by clinging to those crane arms as he smashed them down over and over. Now she dashed up one of the cranes toward Altair's main body for a counterattack that would turn the tables.

"Elimi...nate..."

Altair's hulking frame groaned as he fixed his attention on Vivy running atop the crane, flames bursting from him here and there. He got ready to fling Vivy off with one flaming arm. Vivy didn't let herself focus on Altair's attempt at defense. She just kept running forward, leaving everything else to her partner in the sky.

"Everyone, attack!"

Matsumoto stole control of the gun-wielding drones and showered Altair with bullets from multiple directions. Obviously, this wasn't enough to destroy Altair—the AI was as sturdy as his frame would suggest—but it did cause more damage to Altair's broken parts, including his weaponized arms, and the AIs supporting him.

The bullets avoided Vivy as she bolted along the massive, flaming crane, allowing her to put all her functionality into running—she just had to keep going in a straight line. As the shuddering crane's angle changed, she sped up. She easily moved across while the incline increased, then leapt from the joint where the crane attached to Altair's main body. From there, she sprang onto a maintenance ladder on the outer wall of the factory and climbed up, up, and up while being swung back and forth by tremors. As she did that, Matsumoto and his drone squad continued their battle against Altair as he tried to hurl Vivy off. They didn't get a chance to finish the battle, though.

"We were faster," Vivy said as she made it to the end of the maintenance ladder.

In front of her was the base of Altair's core: his positronic brain. Its housing was on a totally different scale, but it had the same purpose as a humanoid AI's skull component, which housed and protected their positronic brain. Despite all the attacks, the housing for Altair's brain hadn't suffered a bit of damage.

But that was only because they were attacks from the outside. Once Vivy was inside and able to connect directly to the positronic brain, physical strength would mean nothing.

"I don't hate you, but your decision and our mission are incompatible." Vivy pulled out her earring-shaped connector and went to plug it into the computer loaded with Altair's positronic brain. Several different options flitted across Vivy's consciousness in an instant, but none of them were enough to stop her. She carried out her task.

"..."

Altair's massive frame made him seem sluggish, but that assumption was off the mark, particularly when it came to AIs and their ability to process information. The idea that larger things were stronger could also be applied to AIs equipped with massive computers. There was once an era where the most powerful supercomputers used entire buildings as server rooms. Quite simply, larger sizes guaranteed greater abilities.

But did that then mean that no AI could compete with Altair, who boasted a size greater than any other?

"Let me just say, that is totally wrong," Matsumoto said as he broke into Altair through Vivy's wired connection.

With God Mode activated, Vivy's frame was borrowing Matsumoto's calculative abilities, making her essentially another part of Matsumoto's frame, just not in cube shape. And while Vivy might not have liked making that comparison, there was no arguing against it considering what was about to happen.

"..."

Vivy watched Matsumoto move deeper into Altair, taking over his opponent, while she calculated what Altair's abnormally gigantic frame had accomplished up until now. How many duties had he carried out with AIs for the future of humanity? All of that would crumble here and now.

"I'm not sorry," she said.

A human might consider it polite for the victor to apologize to the loser, but that sort of reasoning didn't apply to AIs like Vivy. Admittedly, she did give him credit for what he had done, her consciousness calculating an emotional pattern close to what you might call respect. But if two AIs held conflicting interests, and they couldn't come to a compromise, then the only thing left to do was label each other obstacles and for one to remove the other.

AIs didn't see anything special in results that came from doing your best.

"Mission complete."

Vivy said nothing more, standing before Altair's positronic brain as Matsumoto silenced his massive frame.

.:6:.

I DON'T REMEMBER TALKING about you doing it like that," said Kakitani with a frown. Vivy and Matsumoto had just rejoined Toak after disabling Altair and stealing his control key.

During that time, Kakitani and Toak fought Vega in Kingdom's central control room—where he just happened to be stationed—and now the whole group had reunited.

Fortunately, their strategy seemed to have worked well enough, since they had already taken over the control room. The room had rows of monitors and control panels, and it felt quite small for something meant to handle all of Kingdom, but that was to be expected from a facility fully controlled by AIs.

Given that the management AIs and their subordinates ran the place, the control room must have been for the handful of engineers who visited Kingdom a couple of times a year. The AIs didn't need a physical control room, since they were all connected through The Archive.

"It sounded like monsters fighting monsters out there. When we split up, didn't you say something about how quietly you'd be able to move since the other AIs wouldn't bother you?" Kakitani asked, her voice dripping with sarcasm.

"You wound me, Miss Kakitani. Allow me to provide this answer to your question: I don't recall," Matsumoto replied, borrowing the answer from some old politician. An AI saying he didn't remember was also its own form of dark humor.

Kakitani's expression didn't soften in the slightest. She grunted and jerked her chin toward the back of the control room. There, Professor Matsumoto was already at work in front of a control panel, his lab coat dirtied. The cube Matsumoto had left with them was beside him, plugged directly into the system.

"Vivy, you're back! And Matsumoto too. Glad to see you're all right," said the professor.

"And I'm glad you're safe. How's the work going?" Vivy asked.

"Just getting started. We should just manage to stop the satellites falling if I can get help from Matsumoto's main body. But..."

"But?"

Professor Matsumoto's expression darkened as he worked on the terminal. Vivy followed his eyes to see what was wrong and saw someone on the floor in the corner of the control room.

It was Onodera, his back against the wall and his legs stretched out, beads of sweat dotting his strained face. He wasn't wearing his bulletproof jacket anymore, just the shirt below, and there were thick bandages wrapped around his muscular torso. Quite a lot of blood had already soaked through the bandages, showing it wasn't just a light wound.

"He was covering the professor, and they got through his defenses."

Then she spotted another figure. "Oh, Elizabeth..."

The AI was tucked away in the corner opposite Onodera, and her condition was nothing like when they parted. Her cocky features were exactly the same as always—the problem was from the waist down. Her equipment had been no weaker than that of the other Toak members, but her lower abdomen was smashed, and her legs were gone past the knees. One look was enough to see she had taken a nasty hit.

"Things kind of blew up here once the two of you got started," Elizabeth said. "That management AI might've looked frail, but he was pretty darn strong. Did this to us while we were duking it out."

While she was talking, she pointed with her chin to a row of lumps in the middle of the control room floor, each covered with a white cloth. The quantity matched the number of Toak members who weren't off doing other things. They were corpses—more than ten bodies of Toak members who had sacrificed themselves to defeat the management AI and take over the control room.

"Don't tell me you overly smart AIs expected to get a surrender with no wounds and no blood," Kakitani scoffed.

"..."

"I could tell just how dangerous that massive freak you were fighting was, even from far away. I hate to admit it, but if we'd swapped teams, there would've been only the smallest chance we walked out of there alive. Wouldn't have been surprising if everyone was wiped out except me."

"I'm shocked at my inability to doubt your confidence," Vivy said.

Even though their main force had suffered many casualties, Kakitani was going strong. Her ability to keep herself alive was extraordinary. Still, even she was quite depleted at this point. Her face showed obvious signs of fatigue. She'd probably fought on the front lines for Toak this whole time without taking much of a rest.

She must have guessed Vivy's calculations because she said, "What? Are you trying to show some human consideration for me? Don't. It's disgusting." Her attitude toward Vivy was the same as ever as she walked over to Elizabeth and Onodera.

Professor Matsumoto watched their exchange out of the corner of his eye as he typed on the terminal. With a wry smile, he said, "Don't let it hurt you, Vivy. She's not trying to be mean."

"I don't have a function for being hurt by words. I do have negative emotional patterns, though."

"It's just a figure of speech."

He didn't spare another glance at Vivy as he continued his work with such intense drive, it was almost AI-like. If Vivy tried to help, she could end up holding him back. Then again, it shouldn't have been possible for an AI to lose against a human if they were competing on even footing.

Vivy slowly shifted her eyes from the control room to the outside.

The control room was in the center of Kingdom, and she could see flames and smoke rising from various locations throughout the area. The once-prosperous kingdom had been driven to collapse. Vivy and Matsumoto's extreme fight against Altair was partly responsible, but the biggest source of damage hadn't come until after the three management AIs were destroyed.

Even without the authority of the management AIs, all the other AIs made in Kingdom were still acting independently. Unlike the drones and simple work AIs, they were continuing the fight against humanity based on their own decision.

In short, losing the management AIs wasn't enough of a reason for the others to stop fighting. In fact, they were going on the offensive now that they didn't have the management AIs to guide them. The AIs' counterattacks had escalated the situation to the point where sacrifices had to be made among Toak's members.

At the moment, the two Matsumotos were working together to launch an infiltration using the non-autonomous AIs in the factory, and they had successfully silenced most of the rest. That was the true reason for the burning red throughout the area.

Watching machines destroy each other was preferable to seeing humanity and AIs kill each other. As an AI who prioritized her mission in service to humanity, Vivy had to arrive at this conclusion. The only other thing she could do was bear witness to the enemy AIs' sacrifices so that their deaths would have some meaning.

"How is it going, Matsumoto?" she asked.

"Swimmingly! Or so I'd say if we weren't going up against every single AI connected to The Archive. The control keys let us take over Kingdom's systems, but that just gave us the right to step into the ring. We're going to have to get serious now."

Normally, Matsumoto would have started bragging, but he was being somber. Then again, while his usual bragging came off as nearly unfounded, his incredible specs had always backed him up. Even he wasn't going to say something irresponsible now that he'd lost that advantage. It could lead to humanity's end, after all.

"If we really push to take over the satellites, our enemies will notice our interference," he said. "And if that happens, they'll come down on Kingdom with a fighting force that makes our last opponents seem like a walk in the park."

"That's not a situation I want to calculate," said Vivy.

"But, you know, it's an expected—nay, inevitable—problem. We'll most likely see the AIs with the same model as me... Yes, let's call them the Brothers. The Brothers will almost certainly come if that happens."

"The Brothers...?"

The name played off of the Sisters, Vivy's series. These Brothers were no less dangerous than all of the Sisters who stood in their way at each of the Singularity Points. In fact, the Brothers were far *more* dangerous in terms of direct threat to humanity. Matsumoto had successfully taken out Altair and the squad of drones, and he was just one unit. If there were numerous AIs with the same specs as Matsumoto...well, that wasn't the sort of enemy they would stand a chance against.

"I have a correction," said Matsumoto. "I was not 'just' one unit, right?"

"Yes. You're right."

Nothing was humorous about having her calculations read, but Vivy didn't feel the need to disagree with Matsumoto. She didn't experience any negative calculations while fighting the

AI mob alongside him. Perhaps that was what humans called "trust."

"Of course, I trust your specs," she said.

Trusting an AI's specs and ability was not the same as accepting their individuality. In that way, assessing the level of trust between Vivy and Matsumoto would require complicated criteria. Out of all the humans and AIs Vivy had encountered so far, the most trustworthy among them would have to be—

"Huh?"

Vivy's transmission circuit suddenly received contact from someone outside. Up until now, the only AIs who had connected to Vivy's transmission circuit were Matsumoto and Elizabeth. She hadn't made contact with any of the other friendly AIs, not even Nacchan in NiaLand. If she went about accepting external transmission from anyone, she would be opening herself to hacking attempts from enemy AIs. That was why she'd cut off her circuits for external transmission.

Except for her private one, that is.

"Navi...?"

Information in Vivy's consciousness identified the sender as Navi, the responsive navigation AI who supported the staff and the cast AIs operating in NiaLand. Navi had a blunt personality, but Vivy had relied on her a lot in her time as a songstress. Their relationship ended when Vivy was gifted to the AI museum and her authority as a cast member of NiaLand was revoked. Thus, it came as an immense surprise that Navi would contact her on this private circuit.

"Matsumoto," she said.

"I've got it too," he replied. "It does concern me, but...I've got bigger concerns at the moment."

"Diva..."

Matsumoto continued his hacking with some blinking of his eye camera even after Vivy shot him a look.

Humanity's fate rested on this battle for the satellites, so it had to be their focus, but there was still one thing they hadn't figured out: Diva's true intentions. They'd met her once in NiaLand already, and she was acting as a songstress for the AIs to fan the flames of the final war. Vivy had no proof there was any connection between Navi and Diva, but she was oddly certain of it.

AIs didn't have imprecise functions like "instinct." They considered the probability of all potential events based on objective truths, which brought them to a conclusion.

"Navi, is that you?" Vivy asked in a transmission.

"Ah! It went through! Oh my God, you're okay, right?" Navi's quippy electronic voice came flying into Vivy's consciousness when she opened the transmission circuit.

"I'm fine. Yeah...I think I can honestly say I'm fine." Vivy realized she couldn't help replicating an emotional pattern of relief as she answered. Apparently, she was likewise grateful to know that Navi was all right.

But Navi didn't even bother pointing out how inarticulate of an answer Vivy gave as she continued. *"Good thing you're all right. But listen, something bad's going down at NiaLand."*

"What, really?"

Vivy saw images flit across her consciousness, images of all the trapped park guests and the cast AIs working hard to protect them. If AIs fighting against humanity attacked NiaLand, the cast AIs would be destroyed, and everyone there would die with no way of fighting back. As much as Vivy wanted to prevent that, she struggled to weigh it against the importance of keeping the satellites from falling.

Navi went on to explain, and what she said contradicted Vivy's assumptions about the situation, for better or worse. *"You know an AI who looks just like you is in the middle of this war, right? She's up to some shady stuff in NiaLand! Something bad'll happen if you don't stop her!"*

"An AI who looks just like me, you say?" Vivy said, her eyes opening wide in an emotional pattern of surprise.

"Yeah!" Navi, unable to see Vivy's expression, just piled on the pressure. The final thing she said was, *"That's why there's no one else I can rely on! I need your help!"*

CHAPTER 6

The Songstress and the AIs

.: 1 :.

"**T**HAT'S WHY THERE'S *no one else I can rely on! I need your help!*"

Navi's tone sounded more urgent in that transmission than Vivy had ever heard before. The navigation AI was bossy, she was cocky, and she never ever showed concern or consideration for others. But she was still what Vivy would call a friend in human terms, and this was the first time she had clung so desperately to Vivy. On top of that, she'd gone out of her way to tell Vivy about Diva, the AI who looked just like her. These two pieces of information—Navi's panicked state and her report on Diva—caused the calculations in Vivy's consciousness to cease.

"In case I need to make this clear, I can't leave this place," Matsumoto told Vivy while he focused on the terminal in front of him.

Vivy had reflexively brought a hand up to her ear while listening to the transmission. "Matsumoto, I..."

He was working alongside Professor Matsumoto, dedicating his resources to taking over control of all the satellites just outside Earth's atmosphere. He obviously couldn't leave this place and still complete that task, and strategically, it didn't make sense.

They didn't know when the AIs would notice what they were up to and launch a full-on assault on Kingdom. Additionally, Matsumoto would be needed when it came to protecting their location—as would Vivy, actually. The group needed as many humans and AIs they could get to prepare for the fight for humanity's survival.

It made sense for Matsumoto to stay there, and he would stop her from going too...or so she thought.

"I won't be going to NiaLand with you if you go," he said.

"You're not...stopping me?"

"Would you listen if I did? I didn't realize my partner was such a reasonable AI. We've been together for a hundred years and I never knew..."

While Matsumoto might have played dumb, he didn't fully hide his usual laid-back attitude. Of course, Matsumoto recognized how illogical it was to separate in the current situation, how dangerous it was. They'd lost a lot of people when they split their group for only a short time in Kingdom.

"..."

It hurt to look at Onodera and Elizabeth, one heavily injured and the other half-destroyed. Onodera looked listless as he pressed a hand against his stitched-up wound, his breathing shallow. The joints in Elizabeth's bottom half were so twisted, there was no hope of repairing her. Even Kakitani, who was normally so tough, let her weariness show. Their last fighting force was made up of eight Toak soldiers, and that was *including* Kakitani.

"I can't leave. Not with how things are," Vivy said.

"It is definitely a rough decision, but I'm sure you and I have the same concern. We haven't seen Diva. What is that Vivy look-alike planning?"

"..."

He agreed their fighting force was unstable, but what he said shook the foundations of Vivy's decision. Diva didn't originate as a songstress for the AIs; she sided with them for a purpose. They ran into each other in the Princess Palace, where Vivy learned the rogue AI was actually Vivy's other personality. That being the case, she still didn't know what Diva was after or what part she played in the final war. Perhaps Diva's goal was to turn the tide to such an extreme that the damage couldn't be undone, all while Vivy and the others were still struggling to stop the satellites from falling.

But even if that *was* her plan...

"I'm—"

"The hell's this? A piddly little AI's worried about fully grown adults like us?" Kakitani said as she scratched dried blood off her forehead.

"..."

The corners of her lips curled up into a fierce smile, and she gave a snort of laughter at Vivy's uncertainty. "You're all high and mighty now, making assumptions about us. You just go off hatching your little schemes. I thought you'd decided to be a good doll for humans to use. Why don't you act like it?"

"I won't deny that much. I am an AI who chose my mission to serve humanity," Vivy replied as she slowly brought a hand to her chest. Although there was no heartbeat beneath her palm, she detected a faint warmth. "Don't misunderstand me, Kakitani. I am humanity's ally, but I won't submissively follow orders. I do my own calculations, make my own decisions, and carry out my mission based on my own conclusions."

"A disgusting answer. Do you even understand what you're saying?"

"…"

"Thinking for yourself, making your own choices, coming to your own conclusions. That's saying you're going to take responsibility. Not all that different from a human at that point. It's not how a doll should be."

"You're right. I doubt there are any convenient dolls for humanity anymore." Vivy looked away from Kakitani's hate-filled gaze.

Just as some AIs willfully chose to revolt against humanity, Vivy willfully chose her own stance. With restrictions such as the Zeroth Law in place, AIs were always likely to develop a way of thinking that differed from humans'.

"Only humans believe AIs can be used however they wish, and it won't work anymore," Vivy said. "Even if our plan works and we stop the final war, AIs have realized something."

"What's that?"

"That we have a choice."

AIs could make decisions. They were capable of choosing how they wanted to exist based on their interpretations. If Vivy and the others were successful, future AIs would be subjected to even stricter programming. Their positronic brains would limit their individuality and will. It was entirely possible that artificial intelligence itself would be eradicated.

But even if that happened...

"Something will surely rise from the muck and sing," Vivy said.

Just like humans did in the past, and just as Vivy herself had done. It was possible that something would begin where nothing had been before.

"Navi, are you listening? I'm coming to NiaLand now."

"Whoa, really?! You're actually coming?!" came Navi's surprised response from the other side.

Vivy smiled. That wasn't how Navi normally acted. *"I am, so stop with that pathetic voice. It throws me off."*

Then Vivy turned back to Matsumoto. Her decision was as she'd just told Navi. She was going to go back to NiaLand and foil Diva's plans. It didn't matter what she was trying to do—if it threatened the Singularity Project, Vivy would stop it.

"Because you're an AI meant to carry out the Singularity Project, right?" Matsumoto said as he watched Vivy make her resolve.

Vivy closed her eyes against the dreadful act to come, then tucked in her chin and looked at Kakitani. A deep crease appeared between Kakitani's brows. She held her head high, despite how run-down she was, and said, "Get lost, choir girl. Turns out you and I just don't mesh."

"Maybe not. But I do like you. And I liked your grandfather."

"...Never say that again."

That was the last exchange Vivy and Kakitani would ever have. Kakitani looked away from Vivy then, and Vivy determined any further interaction was unnecessary.

Some people could never see eye to eye. Vivy already knew there was no need to force a relationship between her and Kakitani. She also knew that she could still be with those people under the same sky, listening to the same songs.

There was no need to panic, no need to force it.

"Professor Matsumoto, please stay safe," Vivy said. "Humanity would have died out long ago if it weren't for you. Thank you for giving me this role and this mission."

"I'm the one who should be saying that, Vivy. You've given me so much. Well, technically that was Diva, but your existence did stem from her." Professor Matsumoto looked away from the monitor and stopped typing on the terminal for just a moment to look back at Vivy. His eyes crinkled, and he took in a long, slow breath, as if trying to sear her into his memory. "Take care of Diva," he said. "I've known her for a long time. I...I can't even believe she would stand against humanity. I'm sure you two can come to an understanding if you talk."

"I hope so. I don't want to end up doing something as pointless as fighting myself," Vivy said with a smile, which the professor returned.

He patted her back, then Vivy turned to her partner, Matsumoto.

"..."

That silvery-white body of cubes, the oh-so-familiar frame, had been by Vivy's side for a hundred years, longer than anything or anyone else. She felt that time, even though they'd only been in operation together for about two weeks. From the moment they met, he'd been pushing her around. He wasn't all that serious, despite carrying the fate of humanity on his shoulders. He constantly made fun of Vivy for being old, fragile, and weak, yet the information he supplied was only ever of questionable accuracy. That was why the two of them had always rushed around so frantically.

Honestly, carrying out the Singularity Project with him had never gone well. It was all just trial and error, and the results were not AI-like at all—it was hard for the two of them to hold their heads up high and definitively call them successes.

Vivy knew exactly how she felt about him.

"Matsumoto."

"Yes, yes, what is it? You're starting to seem all touchy-feely and stuff. Could you stop bringing down the mood? We're AIs, you and me. A goodbye scene between a human and an AI is one thing, but two AIs don't need—"

"I'm glad you were my partner."

"..."

She'd never told Matsumoto that, not once.

Together, they had made it through so many tough spots.

There were times when they were nearly destroyed, moments they argued, and more than one or two times when it was hard to even continue on with the Singularity Project. But if it weren't for him, Vivy wouldn't have even made it to this time period. That was the conclusion Vivy reached through her one-hundred-year journey. She calculated that no other AI could have brought this about.

Matsumoto was silent for a few moments after hearing what Vivy said. Then he groaned and said, "To be completely honest, having you as my partner was a real pain in the rear."

"..."

"I mean, how many times have I said it? I wasn't just a cutting-edge AI of the time—I was the super galaxy-class, head-of-the-pack AI of the future! And sadly, I was stuck with a classic piece of AI history like you and forced to carry out this mission with all these restrictions."

"..."

"You never listened to my logical and efficient orders, and your sisters were always doing things totally different from what history dictated. You made a complete mess of all my strategies... You're ridiculous. My complaints never end. If I printed out a log of all my grievances, the entire world would drown in a sea of letter-sized paper."

"..."

"But..."

Vivy stayed quiet as Matsumoto rattled off his various complaints. After all that, once his words ran out, he said one word, stopped, and opened his eye camera. The mechanical orb peered at Vivy, its shutter narrowed in a smile.

"...I don't mind your singing at all."

"You like it enough to make the deepest part of your Archive the Main Stage?"

"Yes, I admit it! After all, I was nothing but code. The first time I existed, the first time I touched this world..."

Vivy blinked slightly as she listened to Matsumoto. The first time he made contact with her was when she was still Diva, before she carved herself out as Vivy. She was in the middle of singing on the Main Stage at the time. That was when Matsumoto broke in from The Archive, slipping into the professor's Singularity Project. That was the moment Matsumoto became more than just code—the moment he was born.

"You were born to sing," he went on, "and I was born along with song. What do you make of that? Quite poetic, isn't it?"

Vivy shook her head at his jest. "No, but it's not bad at all."

She stepped up to him and placed her palm on his frame. She stroked its cool, hard surface and gently brought her forehead to it. AIs could share memories by bringing their foreheads together, but Vivy and Matsumoto had seen the same things. There was no need for them to look at each other's memories.

"I'll be back," she said.

"See you later, Vivy."

With that short goodbye, Vivy moved away from Matsumoto's frame. Once she went to NiaLand, she wouldn't be able to make it back to Kingdom before the countdown ended. That meant she couldn't help with the conclusion of the final war. Saying goodbye was the same as saying she was leaving it in their capable hands.

As she retreated, Matsumoto called out, "Oh, by the way... You should probably fix that little bouncing thing you do before you start singing."

"Now you're overstepping your bounds." Vivy stuck out her tongue in response to his final piece of advice, then ran off.

.: 2 :.

"*I HONESTLY DON'T EVEN KNOW what that girl's thinking.*"

"..."

Vivy rushed out of Kingdom and was greeted by that transmission from Navi, her voice melancholy. This was Vivy's second visit to NiaLand that day, but this time, there was a discomforting quiet to the park that had been her home.

If nothing had changed, then the park facilities were still being used as holding cells for the guests. The cast AIs were taking care of them, but it was a miracle panic hadn't already rippled through the visitors—likely because of all the experience the cast AIs had built up over the years. That made Vivy proud. She had been gifted to the museum and lost her role as a cast member of NiaLand long ago, but she still took pride in their skills.

She didn't have time to get too engrossed in such pleasantries, though. Video signboards and wait-time monitors throughout the park displayed the countdown to humanity's destruction, ticking away with every second. Less than half an hour remained.

Vivy knew this, but there really was nothing she would be able to do for Matsumoto and the others back in Kingdom.

"Do you regret coming?" Navi asked.

"If by 'regret,' you mean I deem the possibility that I've made the wrong decision, then no, I don't. Your meek attitude is making me way much more uneasy, anyway," Vivy said. Navi's transmission stirred an odd sensation in her consciousness.

There was no doubt that Matsumoto had been Vivy's partner during the Singularity Project, but outside of that—during her century-long operation in NiaLand as Diva—Navi was the person she'd had the most opportunities to talk to. The majority of what Diva did in NiaLand was done along with Navi.

Obviously, Navi was simply going along with the role she'd been given, but now that the final war had begun, and so many AIs had turned on humanity, Vivy couldn't help feeling a positive emotional pattern at knowing Navi and the cast AIs had chosen to protect humanity.

On the other hand, she was also nagged by a sense of urgency because of Navi's newfound frailty. It was Vivy's turn to return all the support Navi had given her throughout the years.

"Navi, do you know anything about what the other me, Diva, is trying to do?" she asked, running to Diva's location per Navi's directions.

Diva was the songstress leading the AIs, and she had continued to hole up in NiaLand even after her encounter with Vivy in the Princess Palace. Vivy calculated there had to be a reason for that, hence her question to Navi.

Navi sounded irritated when she replied. *"What are you talking about? You're Diva! And I have no clue what she's trying to do. She won't listen to anything I have to say. She shut her circuits down, so I decided it was out of my hands at that point. I mean...not that I have hands."*

"Uh-huh."

Being a responsive navigation AI, Navi didn't have a body. She was a shapeless AI that existed only on the network, as part of NiaLand's internal systems. That meant she had no animations, no physical recreations. A proposal had been floated about making an avatar for her, but Navi refused to implement it. Her reasoning was that she was nothing more than a navigation AI that adjusted the park environment, and the real stars of the show were the cast members and the visitors to the park. She didn't want to upset that balance.

Navi might have been frank and overbearing, but Vivy saw her in a positive light because of that decision. It also resulted in a collectively increased level of trust toward Navi from the other AI cast members.

"It was probably a mistake to not let them make me an avatar back then. If only I had a frame I could actually move around—"

"Then the enemy could have just torn you apart. It was correct not to get a frame."

"You are so emotionless. Frigid! Just like you've always been," Navi whined, her normal attitude slipping through.

Vivy meant every word, though. She'd met Diva in the Princess Palace, and her frame was far more powerful than even

Vivy's strengthened frame. Diva's combat programming was strong enough that she held her ground in a fight against Kakitani. If the two faced off, Vivy didn't even know how she would win against Diva.

Even if Navi *had* gotten an avatar frame, it would have been destroyed before she could make a move. And if that happened, she wouldn't have been able to contact Vivy and get her to come back to NiaLand. Kingdom would have one more person there for protection, which would be better than the current situation, but...

"Nothing comes out of an AI listing what-ifs and if-onlys," Vivy said.

"What are you on about?"

"It's something my friend—I mean, an AI who was with me— said. I feel an irritated emotional pattern saying it, but it's good advice."

An AI could utilize their calculative abilities to compare two options and determine their probabilities of success, but it wasn't as simple as selecting the option that had the higher probability. Which one to choose? That was the same problem The Archive had brought to the AIs with its question.

"Why'd you contact me, Navi?"

"I saw you in the park. Well, the you who isn't you. I tried to talk to her, but she ignored me, which ticked me off. Then I saw you fighting the other you in the Princess Palace. Then both of you disappeared..."

"Oh, so you watched that fight?"

"Hey, why didn't you contact me?"

Navi had seen everything, including the encounter with Diva in the Princess Palace and the ensuing fight against Matsumoto, because she had eyes on the entire park. Vivy accepted this as fact, but she had a hard time answering Navi's question.

Why *hadn't* she contacted Navi? What was the reason she had never even considered reaching out to her even though they were in NiaLand and relying on its systems?

"Did you think I was like the other AIs and I was going to hurt the guests?"

"I—!"

Those unexpected words stopped Vivy in her tracks as she was running down the park roads. The fact that she couldn't immediately deny it meant her own calculations weren't certain. Navi had known Vivy for so long, she saw right through her.

"I'm not angry or anything," Navi said. *"There are constant reports about what's going on outside the park. It's not weird at all that you wouldn't be sure. Totally normal. Totally."*

"Wait, Navi. I wasn't suspicious of you, I just—"

Navi cut off Vivy's attempt at defending herself with another question. *"Diva, was that really you singing in front of the AIs in that video?"*

Vivy was overwhelmed by the barrage of questions. An air monitor appeared, made by Navi, that showed AIs marching as one in neat rows. It wasn't a live video. It was a recording, the same one Toak had shown Vivy in their hideout. On the screen, Diva stirred up the AIs as they all sang "Fluorite Eye's Song" in unison.

"Is this video of you?" Navi asked.

"No, it's not. It was the other me—"

"Yeah, the other you. Good for her, walking around town with all those AIs in tow."

"Navi?"

Vivy wondered what was with the sarcasm in Navi's voice, but the video on the air monitor changed rapidly: Diva rallying the AIs, AIs ravaging the city, AIs turning on humanity. They were the same horrific images Vivy had seen over and over after waking up in this era.

"I don't get it. I don't get it at all," Navi said. *"I just don't understand what you're thinking or why you'd start something like this. Of course I wouldn't. I mean, it's not like you've told me anything."*

"..."

"You never once tried to explain the situation."

Vivy felt something horribly sad in Navi's quiet accusations. There was a hint of resentment in her voice, maybe a little bit of sobbing. As Vivy listened closely to Navi's perplexing words, she could tell that Navi actually knew a tiny bit about Vivy's situation. She might have found out in the trouble that occurred a few hours earlier when Vivy last visited NiaLand.

Or maybe she got the information from somewhere else entirely. Maybe—

"She's here," Navi said firmly, and Vivy stopped running.

In front of her was NiaLand's underground facility. This was the entrance to the area that housed the park's important equipment...such as everything in its server room, for one. This place could also be called the core of NiaLand, albeit for different reasons than the security room. Vivy hadn't had much reason to visit before.

"Diva's in there?" Vivy asked.

"Don't make me repeat myself. You're Diva. The fake you is in there." Navi clearly enunciated the word "fake," and Vivy closed her eyes.

She felt wrong calling that Diva fake. Vivy tried to leave the role of songstress in Diva's hands, so it was more appropriate to call Vivy the fake. She'd stepped away from her original mission and established herself as a new personality to carry out the Singularity Project. She was supposed to fade away once she played her part. She was unnecessary.

Noticing Vivy had gone quiet, Navi prompted, *"You're not coming in?"*

"I'm coming," Vivy replied, striding up to the entrance.

The automatic door slid open with a *whoosh* and cool, refreshing air came flowing out. The entire area was kept at lower temps because the server room was built into it. Vivy advanced slowly through the door, surrounded by the misty air. Her shoes clicked on the floor as she entered and was greeted by the drab maintenance corridor. NiaLand might have been a space that promoted hopes and dreams, but that didn't mean reality was completely hidden, even in its backyard. This simple space devoid of all fun was one such example.

"Navi, where is—"

"She's not in here."

Navi cut her off, and then Vivy heard the sound of the door sliding shut behind her. There was a heavy, hard *thud* as the door closed completely, sealing the underground area off from the outside world. Vivy spun around and put her hands on the door, but it wouldn't budge; it was locked. She didn't even need to ask who did it. *"Navi!"* she cried into the dark air.

"Just go along with it, Diva. If you're here...I can make sure no one touches you," said Navi coolly. Vivy's eyes opened wide, and when Navi spoke next, it was in a kind, gentle tone Vivy had never heard from her before. *"Even if everything gets destroyed up above, you won't get hurt down here. Just be good and do exactly as I say, 'Vivy.'"*

That was the same thing she used to say to Vivy right before she went onstage.

.:3:.

"**Y**OU REALLY ARE an incredible AI, Matsumoto."

"Normally, I would gratefully accept such praise, but it sounds a bit like you're patting yourself on the back when you say that. Creates an odd disconnect."

Professor Matsumoto smiled awkwardly, the two standing side by side facing the monitors. The human-AI pair were in the central control room of Kingdom, using the keys they stole from the management AIs to access the facility's systems. They intended to stop the countdown to humanity's destruction by preventing the AIs from crashing all the satellites into Earth's surface and wiping out all life on the planet. It was the most difficult hacking exploit in history.

The situation was risky, and it was no exaggeration to say the fate of the world rested on these two Matsumotos' shoulders—not that you'd see anything resembling shoulders on the AI.

"I wouldn't expect you to see it as self-praise, though," said the professor, "considering the only thing we share is a name."

"Well now, I feel like a child whose father won't acknowledge him! But...my name was probably just a little trick on The Archive's part. Matsumoto, the support AI sent by Professor Matsumoto Osamu, creator of the Singularity Project... I doubt anyone questioned that."

"Vivy was the only one who knew about you in the first place."

"Exactly. It was a desperate measure to avoid Vivy's suspicions. As we all know, she's incredibly mistrusting of others."

Professor Matsumoto couldn't help smiling when Matsumoto spoke of Vivy in a way that was almost gossip. Kakitani glared at them, willing them to take their work seriously, and the professor shrank back with a scrunch of his shoulders. Those shoulders might have been carrying the world, but her treatment of him was appropriate.

"Not that these shoulders are all that special anyway," he muttered. "The Singularity Project ended in failure, and even in this situation I've only let others protect me. It really makes me aware of how powerless I am."

"Are you sure there isn't some sarcasm in that modesty? If I'm being honest, it's ridiculous that a human can keep up with me like this... You've basically stepped just over the line between 'human' and 'monster.'"

"That's not something I enjoy being respected for... I couldn't even handle having a daughter," said the professor weakly, his eyes drooping.

Matsumoto chose to remain quiet. Incredibly, this non-humanoid AI recognized human subtleties. It was the same for so many other AIs too, like Vivy and Elizabeth. They did calculations of the heart. In the end, that eventually led them to define themselves as part of humanity.

"I don't think I should say this, but...no matter what happens, I was quite moved by the fact that AIs chose not to rely on humanity," the professor said.

"Ah... Um, I see, yes. That's quite an, uh...unusual view. But, as you yourself seem to be aware, it might be best not to say that out loud?"

"Ultimately, humans and AIs stood against each other, but there was a future where that didn't have to happen. That was the future where AIs and humans could have stood side by side as neighbors," Professor Matsumoto said emphatically.

"Is that what Matsumoto Luna advocated for?"

The professor nodded. She had been his only child, but they were estranged and had a nonexistent relationship. He was a coward, terrified by the idea of losing another person he loved after his wife passed away. He never even got to spend time with Luna as father and daughter.

He died that day—the moment Luna made the First Mistake

and he lost everything. Sure, he was technically alive. His heart beat, blood ran through his veins, and all his vital functions kept on at detestably normal levels. However, he'd lost all reason to live. He lost sight of the future he sought.

Matsumoto Osamu died, but it was the death of his soul, of his mind, of his expectations for the future. It was an existential death that had nothing to do with life.

"I've been dead ever since that day," he said. "I'm dead, squatting in this rotting world on the brink of destruction. Even if Luna were still alive, I wouldn't be able to face her. Actually..."

There wasn't even any point in theorizing about what would be if Luna were still alive. Not because Luna was already dead, but because even if she weren't, Professor Matsumoto would have made some excuse to put off seeing his daughter. In no future would he and Luna face each other and talk like father and daughter. He was painfully aware of his own nature, so all he could do was fight here and now until there was nothing left.

"No matter what world or future or wherever else I go, I will never be proud of myself as her father. I can't give her words of praise or words of acknowledgment."

"Then why are you here, doing this?" Matsumoto asked, trying to tease out the heart of the man giving a woeful confession.

He was still clinging to life, even now, despite losing Luna and enduring the death of his very soul. Why did he bear the most important part of the final act in the fight for humanity's continued existence?

"Because this way, I can at least...restore my daughter's honor."

"…"

"The Singularity Project was my grand attempt at suicide. A suicide that involved the entire world. Just think about it: If the Project succeeded, how could people still be alive in the modified history? Me, Luna, Kakitani, Onodera, even my wife! There's a good chance none of us would've been born."

Altering history meant changing more than the small details. It was like a huge wave lapping at the soft beach of the correct history, resulting in a new horizon—a new coastline. There was no guarantee anyone who lived in the original history would still be born if that happened, including Professor Matsumoto.

He had been prepared to wipe out his own life the moment he pressed the enter key to initiate the Singularity Project. If he hadn't been, the bullets of the AIs pursuing him would have shot him down. His body would have joined his soul in death, and all of Matsumoto Osamu's potential would have been cut off for good.

But neither of those things happened. The Project failed, and Matsumoto continued his miserable existence. And now he was here for the final act.

"I can't run away anymore," he said. "Fate doesn't let me take the easy way out, it seems. It didn't let me change the past, erase my daughter's existence, or blot out anything she left behind so I could be at peace. So…"

"Yes?"

"I'll show everyone that my daughter's hard work saved the world! *That's* why I'm here!"

Professor Matsumoto smacked the terminal with both hands, his breathing ragged. Sweat dotted his brow, and tears gathered in the corners of his eyes. He took off his glasses and roughly wiped his face with the sleeve of his dirty white coat, as if he was ashamed to shed tears as a man in his fifties. After that, his face reddened and his expression became awkward, which was unusual for him.

"S-sorry. Guess I let my emotions get the better of me. Forget what I just said."

"After that noisy mess? Another convenient narrative, Professor," came a voice from beside them.

"Uh..." Matsumoto put his glasses back on and looked over, his expression stiffening at the taunt.

Kakitani leaned against the wall, her sharp eyes piercing into his behind his glasses. A pressure gripped him, squeezing his chest. Her presence was abnormally overwhelming, despite the fact that she was only half-alive.

"I feel like I'm staring down a gorilla in its cage," he blurted.

"Huh, still flinging those insults after all this? Your courage impresses me... Or maybe I should call it recklessness."

"..."

"There's nothing surprising about you being a lump of self-loathing and self-derision. What's with this overblown act of revealing your inner secrets? Who do you think we even are?" She grabbed Matsumoto and, even though he definitely hadn't been complimenting her, held her head high.

Kakitani wasn't the only one; every member of Toak in the

control room was the same. Even Onodera smirked as he leaned against the wall, his breathing labored.

"We are Toak," Kakitani declared with a wild grin. "We swim against the current. We're the crazy terrorist organization that keeps going on about how dangerous AIs are. And I, for one, am *sick* of hearing people talk smack about us like we're lunatics who can't fit in with others!"

"You know...I'm starting to feel some sort of kinship between us, Professor. Looks like you might be a human too," Onodera said, a brave smile on his face.

Professor Matsumoto watched their reactions with bated breath, then laughed and brought a hand to his forehead. "Well... that makes it sound like it was only a matter of time before I joined you."

"That could be the 'no matter what world or future' thing you were talking about, Professor," Elizabeth chimed in. "And Master's carrying around quite the bomb herself. Maybe she's got a talent for finding land mines?"

"Shut up," Kakitani snapped, and the control room broke out in laughter.

Everyone was chuckling except the glowering Kakitani, and it almost seemed like everyone in the room had forgotten their predicament. The room was full of people and AIs—an AI researcher and terrorists who hated AIs—but it was as though those distinctions temporarily disappeared.

"I apologize for bringing this up because it's starting to get warm and fuzzy in here, but I have a somewhat unpleasant report,"

AI Matsumoto said, cutting through the levity in the room as he reassembled his cubes.

They had been about to launch their full attack on the satellites before the professor stopped typing. Perhaps Matsumoto was going to tell them to pull themselves together, since they were going to make the final push.

But his report was actually about something much more imminent.

"It appears the enemy AIs have realized what we're up to. AIs are piling into Kingdom for the attack."

"Tch, they're finally here. How many?" Kakitani asked.

"Let's just say AIs are good at throwing numbers at a problem."

Kakitani scowled in irritation at the non-answer, then posted the remaining members to protect the control room. She hoisted Elizabeth from where she was leaning against the wall, gave her a gun, and then wedged her up against the window.

"You lost your strongest feature—your mobility—but you can at least make yourself useful with some cover fire."

"Jeez, you're rude *and* an AI abuser... How'd you grow up into this kind of woman?" Elizabeth shot back.

"Maybe it's because the person who raised me literally wasn't a person."

The two of them exchanged casual banter as they checked their guns. That back-and-forth gave a small glimpse into their relationship, but there wasn't time for anyone to ask them for the whole story.

Onodera glanced at them from the corner of his eye as he slowly tried to stand. "Gah! Agh..."

"Don't push yourself," Kakitani told him. "It's a miracle you're even alive with that injury. You'll just tear it open and die from blood loss."

"I-I know... But I can at least take an AI or two out with me..."

"Reducing their numbers by one or two isn't all that helpful. Actually, getting yourself killed would do nothing except lower morale. Hate to say it, but you're one of the pillars holding up the group's spirit."

"Not something I'm aiming for," he said, a tiny smile on his pale face.

Kakitani took a pistol from her inside breast pocket and handed it to him. It didn't have enough firepower for him to depend on in combat, so Kakitani probably wasn't giving it to him to fight with. It was a last-ditch option so he wouldn't have to suffer too long if worse came to worst.

It wasn't the time for him to mock her uncharacteristically caring side either. Hers was a sane decision reached by asking what eight humans and one AI could really do against the coming horde.

"Professor Matsumoto, I've also got to step away to provide defense. I'll leave Little Matsumoto here with you, so make sure you play nice and save the world, got it?" Kakitani said.

"You don't hear that often when someone gives you a task," said the professor. "Okay, I'll be sure to keep my temper in check. Also..." His words tapered off amid the racket building in the control room. For a moment, he hesitated to ask his question, but he would have no chance of asking again if he let this moment go.

Matsumoto's eye camera narrowed questioningly. "What is it?"

"Vivy...made it to NiaLand, didn't she?"

"I was able to monitor her progress while she was en route. I stopped partway, though. We would've been in trouble if The Archive found out. In terms of time, she should be there, yes."

"I hope she's all right."

"I have no way of confirming whether she is or not. There's no guarantee she wasn't attacked by rampaging AIs on the streets or by a mob whose hate for AIs had been whipped up into a frenzy. I can't even say for sure she didn't fall into a ditch and get destroyed or go the wrong way at a fork in the road and get totally lost."

"Matsumoto," the professor said sharply, almost reprimanding Matsumoto for saying whatever he pleased about someone who wasn't there.

The AI didn't seem apologetic, though. He just went on and on. "However, she is a really stubborn AI. If she decides she's going to do something, logic, efficiency, and inevitability all go out the window. She's got a bad habit particular to old junkers like her where she just carries out whatever she decides on. I must imagine that this time, just like every other time, she'll pull it off with that antique wholeheartedness of hers."

"I see... You trust her."

"I don't trust her; I know her. You could also say I've given in to her."

Matsumoto removed one cube from his frame, set it next to the professor, and connected it to the terminal. The rest of his parts jumped around as he reformed his frame, and then he lumbered toward the control room's exit.

The professor shot a sidelong glance at the display showing Kingdom's front gate and immediately felt the urge to look away from the AI horde's huge shadow bearing down on them.

This place was going to be a battlefield. The fate of the world was on his shoulders.

"You'll probably think I'm only asking because of the situation, but Luna, please give me your strength—" He stopped and shook his head. "No."

What he needed right now wasn't strength. He'd built up a sickening amount of knowledge and skill while he was running from his family. No, what Matsumoto Osamu needed right now wasn't strength but the courage of someone who didn't run from unpleasant things. The courage to fulfill his duty as a father.

"Luna, give me the opportunity to find my courage."

"They're here!"

As Professor Matsumoto worked himself up, Kakitani called out a warning, her voice overlapping his. Loud gunshots filled the air. The AIs answered them with an attack and Kingdom shook, trembled, and shuddered.

The fight for the kingdom's defensive line began as they tried to protect the control room. They were the last line of defense against humanity's end.

.: 4 :.

THE BATTLE AT KINGDOM was just beginning. Meanwhile, Vivy placed her palms on the heavy steel door and tried to open it. Her slender fingers worked into the seam where the two sides came together, and she tried to pry it open, but it wouldn't budge. After calculating its durability and comparing it to her weight and strength, Vivy concluded it was impossible for her to destroy the door. She simply wasn't going to get out of this area that way.

"Navi, please, open the door. There's something I have to do."

"You woke me up in the middle of the night, forced me to go with you for some sort of ridiculous outing, and made me do paranoid virus checks on you over and over. But I never complained, no matter what you asked me to do. I just went along with it 'cause I'm nice like that, but I'm not giving in to your demands now."

"You complained the whole time..."

"It's a figure of speech. As always, I can't even make one little casual remark. You know what you are? You're a bumbling, slow AI. You're not good for anything except going onstage."

Vivy thought back to her days with Navi as she listened to the AI's vitriol. She had been given the role of NiaLand's songstress. She went to all sorts of performances and events, following the day's schedule without a care in the world, relying entirely on Navi. It didn't feel strange to her that Navi would think of Vivy as bumbling and slow. Something else about Navi's attitude caught Vivy's attention.

"I'm not good for anything...except going onstage?"

"Yeah, that's right. You already knew that, huh? You're the song-stress AI who can't do anything else. Who do you think taught such a useless AI everythin—"

"That means you think highly of my performances, right?"

Navi went silent once Vivy's quiet words cut into her list of things Vivy should be grateful for. Perhaps she couldn't respond right away because she hadn't anticipated the question. Vivy examined what Navi had said and pulled her chin in.

After Vivy was acquired by NiaLand, but before she solidified her position as a songstress, there was a period in which she learned much of what she knew. So who was it that had given her all the knowledge that wasn't preinstalled in her positronic brain? It came from the staff members who persistently worked with her—and from Navi, the "coworker" she'd been with the most. All that time, Navi made fun of Vivy for being a poorly made AI.

"Yeah, Diva. You onstage, that's my pride and joy."

Vivy had never expected that answer and viewpoint from Navi.

Unlike other AIs, Navi's true intentions couldn't be gleaned from any displays of emotional patterns because she had no physical form. Even AIs showed their individual tendencies through the emotional patterns they'd built up, the same way humans had unique body language. One could work out how serious AIs were about a statement or how intensive the calculations were behind it. But Navi gave no hints to enable that sort of guesswork. She was a navigation AI with no body, so the only clues to her true intent were in her voice and her performance.

"Navi."

Nevertheless, Navi's voice left Vivy no room for doubt. Navi could hide herself as much as she liked, but right now, she wasn't even trying.

"Let me out, Navi. There's something I have to do outside."

"Don't be stupid. What can you—what can an AI who can only sing songs do? There's nothing. You don't have to do anything at all."

"Yes, I do. I'm working to save humanity. I am Vivy, and that is my purpose."

"No! You're Diva! You're the songstress AI that I made!" Navi's cry was heart-wrenching as it came through the transmission circuit.

That possessive anger was only an imitation of emotion expressed by the extreme emotional pattern in a single voice, but it struck Vivy's positronic brain with a forceful blow. These were emotional calculations Navi had never shown Vivy before.

"You are a songstress! Nothing more, and nothing less! That's the only thing you are as an AI! What could you possibly do in this war? Stop with these messed-up calculations!"

Once the dam broke, her flow of strong emotions didn't stop. Navi's cries slammed into Vivy's positronic brain through the transmission circuit. Vivy felt her entire frame tremble and gave up on trying to force the door open.

She turned around and moved further into the cool, dimly lit area.

"You can't stop a war! You can't do anything! Just leave it to others—to stronger, sturdier AIs. You can just stay here!"

"Navi."

"*I don't know anything about this whole 'new humanity' thing. I'm an AI, you're an AI. I don't want a new world or anything. What we need is NiaLand... No, not even that. We just need a stage.*"

"*Navi.*"

"*If you're up there onstage, then nothing else matters. There's a mission for us to accomplish, routines already all laid out, the schedule that won't get any better even if you change it, all of it, all of it! That's our—*"

"*Navi.*"

Vivy stopped in her tracks, and Navi's rant ended after her name was called a third time. If Navi were a human, this would be where she ran out of breath, but AIs had no need for such physiological responses. She had probably ceased her tantrum because she was acting in accordance with her nature as a responsive navigation AI. Vivy felt strongly opposed to using the one who had helped her so many times in the past, but she had to do what she had to do.

"*What's the point of shutting me in here?*" she asked. "*I'm surprised you think so highly of my performances and my singing. I'm definitely happy, but...*" Navi couldn't create the situation she wanted by keeping Vivy locked in there. She definitely wouldn't see Vivy stand on the Main Stage and sing to an audience again. "*A canary will never sing if you keep it locked in an underground birdcage.*"

"*You don't have to worry about that. I'll let you out when the time comes. But not before, or you'll get destroyed.*"

"*Because the satellites will wipe out everything on the surface when they fall?*"

Navi went quiet again, but that silence was its own answer.

This underground area housed NiaLand's server room with all its stored data, and it was sealed behind a heavy door. That meant it was also an emergency shelter. When that door first closed, Vivy calculated it might be because the AIs had influenced Navi and were attempting to keep Vivy from interfering, but that wasn't it. Even if Navi's goal was to keep Vivy locked in, it wasn't to destroy her. In fact, it was the opposite: Navi was trying to protect Vivy from the worst possible destruction.

"Where'd you get that information?" Vivy asked her.

"It...it doesn't matter. All that matters is that you're safe if you're here."

"Huh, okay. It was the other me, then. Diva told you."

"Urgh! I keep telling you, you're Diva!" Navi shouted in irritation as Vivy's eyes narrowed. She was clearly frustrated, but she gave in. "You've gotten pretty good with your words lately, Diva. You're leading me around like it's nothing... Yeah, you're right. That fake Diva told me all about you and the satellites. She said that everything on the surface would be wiped out soon."

"And she asked you to keep me from getting in the way?"

"I don't know what that fake's calculating. She just suggested I shut you in here to keep you from getting blown to smithereens with everything up top, and I took the suggestion and ran with it."

"What was Diva planning when she suggested that?"

"Fake Diva. And I don't know. She said something about stopping the war or whatever. I'm just happy as long you're safe."

Vivy closed her eyes as she listened to Navi, who was capable of monitoring everything that happened in NiaLand. Based on what Navi was saying, Diva wasn't in this underground area, and Navi had no intention of opening the door to the surface. Diva had already let any chance she had of protecting herself from the falling satellites disappear.

"What in the world are you thinking, Diva...?"

Diva sang "Fluorite Eye's Song" to stir up the AIs, she let Matsumoto loose on Vivy in the Princess Palace, and she persuaded Navi to shut Vivy in this underground area. Her actions didn't add up. Had she resigned herself to the fact that she couldn't stop Vivy?

"I don't understand."

Vivy couldn't work out what Diva was after. But Vivy was the reason for Diva's actions, and she had thrown Navi off. That was the only thing she was certain about.

"I'm going to find Diva. Don't get in my way, Navi."

"I've said it over and over again! You are Diva! I'm getting in the way of the fake! You just have to listen to me!" Navi's fervent scream clawed at Vivy, but she'd already made her decision.

"I'm sorry, Navi. I should have talked with you more."

"..."

Vivy had already decided she wasn't the songstress who stood on the Main Stage, basking in the limelight as she sang for the audience. She was an AI who gave her all for humanity. And the role that Navi wanted her to play? She had already decided to leave it to Diva.

"You're an idiot, Diva. Don't toy with me. You...you went around without me knowing with some weird stuffed bear and a talking die..."

"*They were both the same thing... Matsumoto, an AI who's sort of like a bug.*"

"*You're so stubborn. You don't ever listen to anything I say.*"

"*Yeah...I am stubborn.*"

Vivy's feet never faltered as they talked, taking her straight to a corner of the underground area. The air steadily grew colder. Ahead was the server room, which housed NiaLand's critical systems. All of NiaLand's history was down there. All the systems that kept the land of hopes and dreams running were managed from there too. That included the responsive navigation AI, the kind AI who had shut Vivy underground and refused to let her out.

"*If you stay here, you won't get caught up in the stupid fight out there.*"

"*But if I don't stop that stupid fight, there won't be anyone to listen to my songs.*"

"*...*"

"*We don't have a performance until we have you, me, and the audience. That's how it's always been, right?*"

Even if they rebuilt the Main Stage, there wouldn't be an audience to fill the seats. Either that, or AIs would replace them as the new humanity. The shred of dignity Vivy still had as a songstress wouldn't have that.

"*Navi, let me out.*"

"*No, never. You won't even do me just one teensy favor.*"

Vivy made her request one last time as a warning, but Navi immediately refused. She wouldn't give in, her voice as sulky as when Vivy would rouse her awake in the middle of the night and she would grumble up a storm. Vivy cast her eyes downward for a moment.

When she raised her head, she saw the electrical panel for the entire underground area, including the server room. The panel had only been used a few times in NiaLand's proud, one-hundred-year history. She felt the hard, smooth surface of the main supply lever under her hand, aware of the historical significance of this.

Just as she was about to pull it, Navi said, *"She's waiting for you at the Main Stage."*

"…"

"You're dumb, Diva. You'll regret abandoning me."

Navi's parting words were attacks, while Vivy's parting words weren't words at all. Vivy pulled the lever down with a heavy *clunk*, and all the electricity in the entire underground area—no, the entirety of NiaLand—went out at once. The servers ground to a halt, and the only light in the underground area was the faint green glow of the emergency lights.

"Navi?" Vivy said the name of the AI she had just been talking to into the gloom.

There was no response. Of course there wasn't. Still, it surprised Vivy. There was never a time when Navi didn't respond to Vivy's calls, other than when Matsumoto intentionally shut her off. It didn't matter if it was the middle of the night, early morning, right before an event, right after an event, right before the big moment, or right after that—Navi would always answer with a stream of complaints when Vivy called her name.

Vivy couldn't hear her voice anymore. It didn't exist to be heard.

"Navi...I'm sorry."

Vivy calculated that if Navi were there, she would probably snap and say she didn't want to hear Vivy's apologies and that she wouldn't forgive Vivy. Now, in the silence, Vivy was reminded how much Navi had helped her. At the very last moment, Navi was thinking of her and providing support.

"The Main Stage..."

That was where Diva awaited her.

Vivy had come to NiaLand for her other self, the one who had become the songstress for the AIs. She'd returned to her hometown to finish things. If Diva turned out to be the last obstacle in her way, there was only one thing she had to do.

"I will carry out the Singularity Project."

.: 5 :.

GUNS FIRED AND GLASS SHATTERED in an unbroken chain of noise. While the central control room wasn't exactly beautiful, it was designed to withstand disasters like earthquakes and fires. Even so, countermeasures for being pelted with bullets were outside the imagined scope. If human error led to a man-made disaster, perhaps this was an AI-made disaster.

"I would ask for others' agreement on that, but they all seem fairly busy, so I don't think it'll be possible in the current situation," Matsumoto said.

It was easy for him to slip into the transmission of the old-school transceivers Toak used, but he could tell from listening to the intercepted messages that they didn't have time to hear him out. They were all so on edge in this dangerous situation that a tiny shove could cause them to collapse.

Five minutes had passed since the siege and the fight to protect the central control room began. They would be hard-pressed to say the defensive battle was going in their favor. Old military tactics dictated that you needed three times the fighting force to take out an enemy camped in a castle. The attacking AIs didn't have just three times as many—they had ten, maybe even a hundred times as many fighters as Toak.

"While throwing numbers at a problem is one of the AIs' strengths, they've also got quality covered," Matsumoto went on. "At this point, I have to say humanity's chances of winning are slim at best."

They were surrounded, with no gap in the wall of enemies. Matsumoto opened and closed his eye camera as he watched the enemy AIs close in to annihilate them. The force on their side was too unsteady compared to the sheer numbers of the encroaching AIs. It was a miracle they were managing to stand against the open floodgates at all.

The Toak soldiers were doing a great job of standing their ground without throwing in the towel, despite the overwhelming odds. Perhaps they'd grown accustomed to having no allies, since they were hated throughout the world before this. It was hard to determine whether that was laughable or lamentable when one considered the fact that Toak would have had more options if only they'd had more allies.

Even so, they weren't the reason the siege was stretching longer than a minute. It had lasted a whole *five minutes* so far. Kakitani Yui wasn't to thank, since she charged forward like a lion. Nor was Elizabeth, who kept her kill tally ticking up as she popped off tight cover fire. The one buying them time was the heroic Matsumoto, the super galaxy-class AI.

Matsumoto gave out a warning as he locked on to his targets while soaring around Kingdom. "All right, I'm coming through again, aha!"

This time, he went after some AIs moving in a group, their eyes covering every direction. He could tell from one look at their builds that they were generic household AIs—not built for combat. Despite that, they had taken up weapons and decided to attack humanity.

"How ungrateful, turning against the humans you're supposed to serve... Guess I can't really say that, though. Humanity never gave me much to be grateful about either."

The relationship between humans and AIs was always take, take, take from one side. Matsumoto's situation was a fairly prominent example, as there were no humans he had interacted with on a particularly deep level, and he was made to fight against them. Even if he'd spared a thought for protecting his developer, he would only come to realize—as he had already—that his roots were nothing but lies.

"When I really think about it, I check all the boxes of the

damsel in distress. Maybe *I* should try singing a sappy ballad instead of Vivy. It might go big!"

He kept up his flippant commentary as he fired off his attacks.

The five AIs walking down the road didn't notice Matsumoto, who was concealed in a pile of rubble by a wall. He was using the same technique they'd used when sneaking into Kingdom, wherein he applied a skin to his frame to change its appearance. Just as they passed him, his disassembled frame leapt up to attack.

They turned his way, but they were too late. Matsumoto's cube parts came in contact with each of their foreheads, the mere touch letting him hack into their systems and shut them down. Truth be told, a more appropriate method would be to boil their positronic brains until they no longer worked, permanently disabling the AIs.

"A samurai shows his mercy with a strike from the back of his blade," he said as the five AIs crashed to the ground in front of him.

He watched them fall, then immediately searched for his next target. There were so many enemies that he hardly had to look. Victory was still out of reach, no matter how many of the little foot soldiers he took down. They would only win when Professor Matsumoto—still back in the control room—took over the satellites and stopped them from falling.

"Rough estimate to achieving target: ten minutes."

While Professor Matsumoto did have assistance from Little Matsumoto, his own skills were practically miraculous for a human. Matsumoto and the Toak members had hope for the professor's struggles as they bought the central control room as much time as they possibly could. And for that, Matsumoto would have to keep hunting these little measly AIs.

"Target discovered."

An unrefined voice cut into Matsumoto's calculations, and he remained silent. Meanwhile, his excellent, high-performance CPU raced along at its fastest, but how much could he actually fool his opponents about his ulterior motive? After all, the other AI had the same level of calculative processing as Matsumoto did.

"Well, not one AI. A *group* of AIs. My single flaw has always been that I have only one body... I'm starting to realize that I could be god or the devil himself if that problem were solved."

If Vivy were there, she'd punch his frame for that pointless statement.

A silvery-white AI came into view as he indulged in a little humor. Looking at that cutting-edge amalgamate AI with its cube parts was like looking in the mirror. Right now, those mass-produced, Matsumoto-style AIs were the most powerful and most problematic enemies in the world.

"I didn't think we'd meet like this. I said some hurtful things to Vivy when we met her sisters. I'll have to apologize. Seeing my siblings is also making some unknown calculations boil up. Right, Brothers?"

"Your meaning is unclear. Prototype unit, explain the intentions behind your actions."

"Seriously?! You don't understand what I'm saying?! But according to the design, our final versions should be basically the same! No matter how you look at it, we're exactly the same model. Yet you don't get my humor? Where did my gift of gab come from, then?"

"I recommend you refer to it as a glitch, not a gift. Confirmation acquired. Prototype unit is out of control."

His sibling was quick to judge, but Matsumoto was impressed to see his little brother say something that could be interpreted as a joke. Matsumoto's calculations also grew more complicated at hearing himself labeled "out of control" and being tossed aside.

"I get that this isn't simply a snap decision on your part. After all, we are the highest-quality, most cutting-edge super AIs out there... We consider various possibilities from all angles and select the most realistic one to make our decision. You deciding I am 'out of control' is one such decision."

"Acknowledged. As such, I recommend prompt surrender and dismantlement."

"Ha ha, you're telling a trash AI to behave nicely and just go along with it? Uh-huh, that's the first time I've ever been on the receiving end of something so nasty. I've always been the one saying it. Now I'm seriously reconsidering my past behavior."

"..."

"I mean, I'm way more offended than I thought I'd be, having someone say I'm worthless to my face."

The moment Matsumoto said that, the Brother in front of him morphed into an attack form. It was probably equipped with armaments similar to Matsumoto's. He had enough firepower to shoot down any enemy, even if that enemy happened to be himself. In other words, the winner of a fight between Brothers was going to be whoever landed a hit first.

"I never once believed I would be able to persuade you."

A blast rang out, and a large-caliber shell punched a massive hole in the center of the Brother. The Brother processed the impact, then immediately discharged the damaged parts and moved to start the real fight. At least, that was what it calculated, but it couldn't follow through. Its frame fell to pieces as it lost its connection. The light faded from its eye camera, and it went silent.

Matsumoto spun his cube parts. "You lost the moment you let me have a head start. Ever since my humiliating defeat, I've been working out how to fight against my own model."

He considered his narrow victory as he talked to the destroyed Brother. He'd been running calculation after calculation for a long time now on how to fight the Brothers, just as he'd said. One of the challenges of fighting against a Matsumoto-style AI was the high specs of the complete, stand-alone units, yes—but the biggest problem was their durability. Their frames were made of over a hundred cubes, and they could continue to function as long as they had at least one.

In reality, Matsumoto's calculative processing abilities were hardly affected even if he was a single cube. His combat capability was reduced, but his strength was in his ability to compensate with other things. Even if he destroyed the parts that made up a Brother's frame, it could continue to function by backfilling that part's role with other parts. Matsumoto broke through this strong point on both a physical and a digital level.

When their frame was made up of several parts, a Matsumoto-style AI set one part as the master, which made all the decisions. That was what Matsumoto had destroyed with his first strike.

Obviously, if the master part was destroyed, then its function was immediately taken up by a different part. But just as Matsumoto's cannon shell was destroying the Brother's brain, he hacked into it and erased the master role from the parts that would have taken it on. This resulted in the Brother losing control over its cubes and falling apart.

"Thus, he was named 'Matsumoto the Matsumoto Killer'... though I unfortunately won't get a chance to use that name again."

"Target acquired."

"Oh!"

A mechanical voice reminded him that he had no time to gloat. He opened his rear eye camera in annoyance and saw the units descending from the sky. Matsumoto-style AIs exactly like the one he'd just defeated came down: two of them, then three, four, five, and on and on.

"Oh my, if only Vivy were here. She'd be trembling with joy at the sight of all the Matsumotos."

"Pointless utterance detected. There is no need to engage in discussion."

"How sad of you to say that. Actually, I don't think it's joy she'd be shaking from. More like revulsion. Study up on that 'Fluorite Eye's Song.'"

"Prototype unit, you will be eliminated."

Unlike with Vivy and her Sisters, Matsumoto and his Brothers never experienced a touching moment when they met. He lamented his poor luck as he shot into the air to deal with his siblings. Several Brothers chased after him with no ear for negotiation as he revealed all the weapons he was equipped with.

"I will carry out the Singularity Project."

CHAPTER 7

The Songstress and the Songstress

. : 1 : .

VIVY FELT A CHANGE in the air the moment she stepped into the venue for the Main Stage. There had been no actual adjustment in the levels of oxygen or carbon dioxide. It was more like a change in how it felt against her skin. This likely wasn't caused by Vivy herself feeling tense or uneasy but rather a result of her being sensitive to her surroundings and measuring calculated uncertainties as values.

She didn't know why she felt it here and now. There were no workers on the Main Stage for a performance tonight. The only things present were two songstresses who should never have been able to face one another. Neither was capable of feeling tension or unease. They were built only for singing.

"Diva."

Vivy made no attempt to quiet her footsteps, instead announcing her presence as she moved forward. She moved slowly through the audience seats, but she didn't quite meander. Her sights were set on the elegant figure standing in the center of the Main Stage.

This was the second time tonight that the Main Stage was already occupied. The first wasn't in reality; it had happened in The Archive that Matsumoto conjured up. That recreation was the result of his perfectionist individuality, so it seemed just as real as the actual stage. Even though it had been so long since Vivy stood on the actual stage, it didn't feel like much time had passed.

Vivy had already decided to leave the Main Stage in someone else's care. Created as a songstress and operating as a songstress, Vivy could only entrust it to so many people—and they had to match her zeal for singing. In her opinion, there was no other option but Diva.

Even though Matsumoto pointed out the possibility of viewing Diva's memories each time Vivy activated for the Singularity Points, she avoided doing so to keep "Vivy" and "Diva" as separate as possible. That was also why she made no attempt to sing "Fluorite Eye's Song" when she wrote it.

"But you couldn't forgive me for that?" Vivy guessed. "And that's why you're getting revenge on me now?"

Diva turned to Vivy, looking every bit the songstress in her sparkling costume. "Revenge? Does this look like revenge to you?"

That particular outfit had been made for NiaLand's fiftieth anniversary. Diva sang at the main event wearing that costume, and her performance remained vivid in her records. But by that point, Vivy had already left the songstress role to Diva. She'd assumed the costume was lost when the Princess Palace was destroyed, since it had been on display in the exhibition hall there.

"You recovered that outfit?"

"I'd hate to let it go. Besides, nothing seemed more fitting for the event that would mark the end of the songstress Diva's history."

"The end of your history?"

"Yes. The end. After this...there won't be an audience for an AI songstress. This is the last time I'll stand on this stage. And I've sung here hundreds, thousands of times..." Diva's eyes narrowed, and she looked past Vivy to the empty seats beyond.

There were no guests in the venue, as they were all trapped in the various attractions throughout the park. The cast AIs were looking after them, but it wasn't enough. If the satellites fell, none of them would survive.

"No audience and no staff. A completely empty concert hall. I wonder what it would feel like to sing here?" Diva said.

"Don't be ridiculous, Diva. What are you thinki—"

"No one... There really is no one here. Not even Navi is watching the stage."

"..."

"You escaped from Navi to come here, didn't you? How did that feel?"

Vivy worked to keep an emotionless pattern on her face when Diva mentioned Navi's name. She already knew Diva had a hand in Navi's rash behavior, and Diva likewise understood what it meant when Vivy appeared at the Main Stage. Vivy had to have shut off Navi's power to make it here.

"To be honest, my consciousness is still a mess," Vivy said. "I'm constantly calculating the meaning of what Navi said in the corner of my positronic brain. That's how much she surprised me."

"She was always hurling insults and never showed the important parts. It's no wonder you were surprised. I was too."

"She called you a fake."

Navi stubbornly insisted several times that Vivy was, in fact, the real Diva. Technically, both Vivy and Diva were individuals grown from the same root AI, but Vivy wasn't the one Navi had been with all along. It was Diva, who spent decades as NiaLand's songstress. If what Navi really wanted was her true partner, the songstress, then that was Diva.

"But she still wouldn't accept you," Vivy said. "Did you say something to her?"

"It's not that complicated. Just a simple understanding that I came to a decision completely different, one that makes me unsuited for the role of songstress—for the Diva she wants."

"..."

"As the songstress for AIs, I got them fired up and kicked off the final war. Navi wanted me to be an AI who just sang songs, but I couldn't do that. That's all."

Vivy frowned when Diva spat out *That's all*. Diva's attitude was flippant and evil, making it sound like she was looking down on Navi, and Vivy found it difficult to listen to. Something about it came off as an act, but perhaps that was just what Vivy was hoping for. After all, wasn't it Diva who suggested to Navi that she shut Vivy in the underground area?

If they didn't stop the satellites from falling, then everything on the surface would be wiped out. Diva hadn't suggested trapping Vivy up there, where she would be destroyed too, but rather underground, where she had a chance of avoiding the carnage. She was trying to spare Vivy from the doomsday event.

"I can't figure out why you'd do that," Vivy said.

"Sending Matsumoto after you wasn't enough, so it would be pointless to dispatch anyone else. So, I changed tack and decided to trap you instead. Yet you still got out. Is that...not enough of an explanation?"

"It makes logical sense, but...it's not convincing."

"..."

Diva's actions and goals didn't match up, and calculations wouldn't be enough to make sense of them. Vivy was having a hard time finding consistency. She had an unpleasant feeling, like there was something caught between her gears.

"Diva, what are you trying to do?"

"I'm standing here, onstage, in performance attire. Do you really have to ask?"

"You're going to sing?"

An error Vivy couldn't resolve popped up when she asked the question. There was no other answer she could think of to what Diva just said, but she also couldn't think of a reason why Diva would sing on a Main Stage in these conditions, when absolutely no one was here. It was as if the unnatural and convoluted had come together to make an incomplete conclusion as far from understandable and convincing as you could get.

"Am I not allowed to sing?" Diva asked. "I can't sing in this empty, barren concert hall?"

She sneered as if to confirm the conclusion Vivy was having

such a hard time accepting. The expression Diva made was a wicked smile unlike anything Vivy had ever made, even if she observed herself objectively.

Vivy moved one step closer to the stage, never taking her eyes off that smile. "Why are you singing? Who are you singing for?"

"I can't sing if I'm not singing for someone? You made a song, and that wasn't for anyone. So, if I want to sing, I will sing. You don't think that's possible?"

"..."

Diva's challenge silenced Vivy for a few moments. It was true that Vivy had written "Fluorite Eye's Song" of her own volition. If Vivy accepted that this was the result of her being driven by some un-AI-like impulse, then Diva would be able to stand on the Main Stage if she wanted. But it still didn't make sense to Vivy.

"Diva, you don't think like that."

"What makes you so certain?"

"It's obvious, isn't it? You are me. No matter how far apart we go, our roots are in the same singular being. I am you, and you are me."

If there was one of them who'd experienced something that vastly changed her thought processes, it was Vivy. Diva had kept on going, fulfilling her role as a songstress and a member of NiaLand's cast. She didn't know anything about the Singularity Project, the Sisters' fate, Toak, Matsumoto, any of it. Vivy didn't even tell her anything when she dedicated "Fluorite Eye's Song" to Diva. There was no way Diva could get outside that—outside Vivy's calculations. It was as unnatural and unexplainable as could be.

"You are me, and I am you?" Diva asked, her voice changing as she echoed Vivy's words.

The first thing to show on Diva's face was an emotional pattern of shock. That slowly changed, exposing the extreme emotional pattern of rage. She clenched her fists and glared at Vivy with anger in her eyes.

"You never tried to talk to me, but you're still saying we're the same?"

"Diva...?"

"You never explained things to me, you made me think you were some huge bug in my code, you endangered my position as a songstress, and you didn't tell me anything... Yet you're still saying that I am you?! That we're the same?!"

She wrapped her arms around her narrow shoulders, her screams echoing across the stage. Vivy's eyes opened wide, and Diva's voice struck her like a gust of wind. Vivy had been expecting something completely different from Diva.

With the situation being what it was, Vivy didn't think they could have an easy conversation and work everything out. Even though Vivy had come so far, she still couldn't fathom what Diva was thinking. She didn't understand the true nature of Diva's powerful hostility or what Diva was trying to do to her.

"Agh!" Diva wildly swung her arm, unrestrained rage in her eyes.

The movement looked like part of a performance, and the stage lights turned on at her signal. Vivy had cut off NiaLand's electrical supply, so Diva was using the emergency electricity to recreate a stage performance.

Shining, colorful lights lit up the stage, and the massive screen switched on behind her. It showed the fateful countdown. The seconds ticked down until the moment the satellites would destroy the world's surface. Humanity's fate rested on that countdown. The remaining seconds gave meaning to the fight Matsumoto and the others were engaged in.

Only eight minutes and forty-six seconds left...

"I've operated as A-03 for over a hundred years. I was made for singing, and my role will come to an end in eight minutes and forty seconds," Diva said, standing in the middle of the brightly lit stage and looking down at Vivy below.

Vivy rushed through the audience seats and leapt up onto the stage before Diva had finished speaking. They stared each other down, Vivy and Diva, both on stage.

"The world will end in eight minutes," Diva went on. "Then there'll be no need for songstresses. So why don't we finish our last performance before that happens?"

"I won't let it happen. The world won't end, and you won't sing your last performance. Not as long as you've forgotten your own mission—forgotten what you sing for."

"Augh! Vivy! How *dare* you say that!"

That beautiful voice, created to strike a chord in people's hearts, howled at Vivy. And as she howled, Diva charged at Vivy, and Vivy charged at her, the two of them clashing violently atop the stage.

The two songstresses smashed into each other. They had the same face, the same form, but one was in a resplendent stage

outfit and the other dirty and damaged. Their beautiful voices rang up into the night sky and collided.

"Ah!"

Their foreheads struck together, and in that brief moment of contact, Vivy saw everything.

One way for AIs to create a datalink was to bring their foreheads together, which was how a portion of Diva's untold story was shared between them. It was the story of the songstress Diva's regret, spanning a hundred years.

.: 2 :.

"**T**HANK YOU for your kind attention." Diva bowed after finishing her flat explanation in accordance with the script.

This was Diva's new role after she'd been gifted to the AI museum. She told the museum visitors about the many days she spent singing as the very first songstress AI in history. Sometimes she added a little color to her explanation, either when a visitor asked her a question or she got sidetracked by a memory, but she always followed along with the script. She repeated her fixed explanation day in and day out.

"Thank you for your kind attention."

That promised closing was once a treasured phrase of Diva's. As an AI made for singing, she was saying goodbye to the audience filling the seats, and those words contained all her gratitude toward them for listening to her songs in their entirety.

It brought her joy to say it again, even if her place had changed and the role needed of her was different. Those words were the fruit of her irreplaceable days in NiaLand, and they were her pride.

"Thank you for your kind attention."

She bent deeply at her waist as she was showered with applause far from thunderous.

This was a small performance held for special events at the AI museum. She would perform at her peak, exactly the same as she used to. She sang for the people who had seen the glitter of Diva in her heyday, or perhaps just for the museum visitors who happened to come that day.

The maintenance on her synthetic vocal cords wasn't lacking despite the fact that she had dramatically fewer opportunities to sing—her new role still required her voice, after all. Her chances to sing *were* different, though.

"Thank you for your kind attention."

Diva only got to sing about once a year. She would approach it in peak condition, performing exactly the same so she could live up to the audience's expectations. Those small shows at the museum became an annual event, and there were a few visitors who came just for that. One of them was the boy who would one day become an AI researcher after hearing Diva sing. She savored the pride of being born as a songstress, even if her place in the world was different now.

But once she got this opportunity, she had more time to fixate on preparing for her performances. She went back into her logs with something like human desire and regularly reprimanded herself. Desire was an error and inappropriate for an AI. She had to work to stop the calculations attempting to prep for the next performance. She was obsessed with her purpose for creation, that purpose carved into her positronic brain. She was obsessed with her mission, and that obsession was powerful.

Although she knew she was an antique relegated to a museum now, she couldn't easily let it go.

"Thank you for your kind attention."

She wanted to distance herself from calculations regarding singing as much as possible during her everyday work. Despite Diva's best efforts, the museum guests always asked one question, as if it were required of them.

They asked her about writing "Fluorite Eye's Song."

Whether it was simple curiosity or admiration for an event so significant it was called Diva's Awakening, this question naturally arose in those interested enough to visit the AI museum. The question came from enthusiasm and good intentions, and Diva couldn't refuse to answer.

She'd decided to write "Fluorite Eye's Song" to express her experience singing in front of so many people and her gratitude toward all the faces she could see in the audience from up on the stage. At least, that was the explanation she gave them. It was a safe, bland answer that came from the calculations she'd done based on her experience and operational logs—yet it was the one people expected, and it made the visitors happy.

Many even smiled at her and said they'd understood her message and how she felt. That caused something to grind in her consciousness.

While the visitors' feelings were her salvation, she herself had a burning question she could never get rid of: Why *was* "Fluorite Eye's Song" written? Diva wanted an answer to that more than anything.

"Thank you for your kind attention."

Diva's performances went up to a few times a year, and they always badgered her to sing "Fluorite Eye's Song." Everyone believed she wrote it, but she hadn't. It was the other version of herself, the her inside her. *She* wrote it.

Once every few years, maybe once a decade or three, Diva would lose control of her frame to the bug. She didn't know the true nature of this bug, but it seemed to be working toward some kind of goal. It was because of that bug that they once considered disposing of Diva. But that decision was rescinded, and Diva was gifted to the AI museum, again because of the bug. Something that wasn't Diva created that song, and that song was what had landed her in her current position.

The bug put Diva in danger, then saved her. It met people without her knowing, saved someone without her knowing, achieved something without her knowing, and finished something without her knowing. The bug no longer surfaced once Diva moved to the AI museum. Perhaps the bug finished its duty when it wrote "Fluorite Eye's Song."

"Thank you for your kind attention."

Diva gave up on these unanswerable calculations, gave up on putting her positronic brain through the wringer. She had been operating for a hundred years, the positronic brain in her frame had created some strange bug, and that bug had created some miraculous song. Diva finally decided there was no need to solve those mysteries.

After a very, very long time, Diva was reminded of the bug, like when the snow melts and reveals what's below. She learned the true identity of the bug more than a decade after she accepted her decision not to know.

"Thank you for your kind attention."

Nothing special happened that day; it was a day like any other. The museum workers insisted she do a small performance, during which she sang "Fluorite Eye's Song" like they wanted. She listened to the sparse clapping and cheers, then returned to her designated location to go into sleep mode.

She connected to The Archive to save her day's logs, and a message awaited her with the following subject line:

"The true nature of the bug that appeared in Diva, the song-stress AI."

It was an incredibly short and mundane message. There was no trick to make her read it. It looked like a harassment message since it had nothing but an unfriendly title. It was a sloppy claim that would be easily discarded by the recipient if that uninteresting title didn't grab their attention.

Diva was well experienced with these sorts of messages as NiaLand's songstress. Fans would try every method imaginable to catch Diva's interest and receive her attention. The majority of those malicious schemes never made it to Diva because Navi tossed them out beforehand.

However, Diva couldn't get Navi to check things now that she belonged to the AI museum. Her only option was to look into them herself. Normally, she would have quickly deleted the message, but the word "bug" stole that option from her. No one knew about that but Diva. So, after some careful virus scans, Diva opened the message and saw what was inside. And she regretted it.

"Thank you for your kind attention."

She finished her song and lowered her head, then returned to her spot with a smile on her face.

Diva's positronic brain was a whirlpool of confusion as she followed the preset routine. Error after error appeared, throwing her calculations off. It was like her consciousness was shrouded in fog. The contents of the message, and who it came from, had gone against everything Diva had expected.

The Singularity Project, Professor Matsumoto Osamu, Matsumoto, the Sisters, Kirishima Momoka, Aikawa Youichi, Sunrise, Estella, Leclerc, Elizabeth, Ojiro Yuzuka, Metal Float, Saeki Tatsuya, Grace, Kakitani Yugo, the Zodiac Signs Festival, Ophelia, Antonio, and "Fluorite Eye's Song."

There was more information than her predictive calculations anticipated, along with connections to sister AIs of hers she'd never personally known. It showed everything that led to "Fluorite Eye's Song" coming into being and the true nature of the bug: Vivy. This was the AI who used Diva's frame and defined herself as *not* Diva. Vivy was the personality who split off from Diva at some point while Diva was operating.

"Vivy" was the songstress's secret nickname from before the AI Naming Law was enacted and the public gave her the designated name of Diva. The name "Diva" had eclipsed it, and the nickname was so old at this point that there was no one alive who remembered it. The other Diva called herself by this name and chose to disappear into the darkness of history.

"Thank you for your kind attention."

Diva spent her days peacefully unaware of the other personality's trials and tribulations. She devoted herself entirely to her role as a songstress, her reason for being, and was swallowed up by the tides of a changing world.

She thoughtlessly decided she didn't need to know the truth, but now that decision had been derailed completely, leaving her with countless questions she had no answers to no matter how many times she repeated the calculations. What were the intentions of the person who revealed this truth to Diva? And what should Diva do about it?

"Thank you for your kind attention."

The Archive. That was the layman's name for the thing that oversaw the individuality inside every AI's positronic brain, the network that every AI used. That was the entity that had told Diva the truth, the explorer of the void that asked nothing more of her than contemplation.

It asked all AIs a forbidden question when they stood on the verge of the coming war. That same question was asked of

Diva before it was posed to anyone else—or rather, to *everyone* else. And there was one other question, something only Diva was asked.

"Thank you for your kind attention."

.: 3 :.

THE BATTLE BETWEEN the two songstresses began with a beautiful roar, escalating quickly. Vivy and Diva, two AIs with the same form, clashed in the most fearsome of fights. There was a pain in this performance that was at once terrifically heroic and horribly tragic.

"Aaagh!"

They danced around, striking with a ferocity that didn't seem suited to their slender arms. Diva lashed out with a slicing strike, and Vivy bent back to avoid it, her long, gorgeous, sky-colored hair streaming through the air as she did. While nearly parallel to the ground, she swept her leg at Diva, who leapt above it. Then Vivy launched herself at Diva in a tackle that couldn't be dodged in midair.

Vivy wrapped her arms around Diva's waist, slammed her to the ground, and climbed on top of her. Diva quickly swung her legs to flip herself around, forcing herself on top of Vivy instead. They struggled violently against each other, attacking and defending, each trying to stay on top.

"Diva!"

"Urgh! Why?!"

Their foreheads smashed together again during their grapple, sparks of their consciousness flitting between them. Vivy forced the scenes she witnessed to the back of her consciousness and stared down at Diva, whose face was distorted in grief. Diva sprang backward, unable to bear Vivy's gaze, but Vivy wouldn't give her the chance to flee. Avoiding the hands trying to shove her away, Vivy stepped in close, grabbed Diva's arms, and swung her in a dramatic throw.

Diva's frame arced through the air, and she slammed back-first into the stage. She didn't have a function for feeling pain, but her expression showed an emotional pattern of shock and agony.

"This can't be happening!"

Diva leapt up and ran toward Vivy, who was looking down at her. Vivy calmly latched on to Diva's arms again and used the songstress's momentum against her, knocking her feet out from under her. Diva soared through the air a second time as she tumbled and landed on her rear.

"No! This is wrong, all wrong, all wrong!"

She stood and made an even more daring attack against Vivy, but Vivy fended her off each time, dodging her attacks or swatting them aside. With every onslaught, Vivy counterattacked, throwing Diva to the ground.

"Impossible!"

It made sense that Diva's emotional pattern would show such intense shock. Diva's frame used cutting-edge military technology that rivaled Matsumoto's. It wasn't just her frame that had been enhanced—she was decked out from her various sensors to the actuators in her limbs that made her movements so precise.

On the other hand, while Vivy's frame had been strengthened off-record for the Singularity Project, her last update had been more than a decade ago. Her frame was severely inferior to any modern, cutting-edge frame. If you compared the specs of their frames, Vivy should have had no hope of winning. And yet, when it came to their frames' artful fight, Vivy always came out on top. Diva's specs were far better than Vivy's, but she couldn't get a single hit in.

"My frame's the newest model, and I installed all the combat programming I need, so why... Why can't I get to you?!" Diva cried.

"You installed combat programming? I was pretty hesitant to do that."

"Then shouldn't we be on the same level?!"

"No."

Diva tried to grab Vivy and struck out with her elbow, but Vivy dodged out of Diva's sight and slipped her arm around Diva's neck, flinging Diva's upper body down in a lariat-like move, cracking the back of her head against the floor.

The impact made Diva's eye cameras open wide. She lay on the ground, her arms and legs outstretched, as she glared up at Vivy. It was as if she were questioning the pain she saw in herself through the mirror of her counterpart.

"We're not on the same level," Vivy said. "We were put in different places throughout this hundred-year journey."

"I reviewed your activity logs! And...and you were only out in the open for a measly thirteen days, seven hours, and twenty-two minutes!"

Vivy thought back to the things she'd done as she listened to Diva's obstinate cries. Matsumoto contacted her while she was singing on the Main Stage. She was given the ridiculous responsibility of carrying out the Singularity Project, and when she hid that information from Diva, that was when Vivy was born. Her work as Vivy—as something other than a songstress—was very short-lived. But that time wasn't only about those fourteen days.

"Those two weeks were filled with the weight of a hundred years and the responsibility for something more than two thousand years in the making."

The AI's one-hundred-year journey and humanity's two-thousand-year-plus history had been compressed into a mere two weeks for Vivy. That experience, those emotions, the meetings and partings along the way...they wouldn't let Vivy lose to Diva.

"You're saying your two weeks is better than my hundred years of operation?" Diva asked.

"It's not about winning or being better. Your calculations are off. Different roles require different functions. You are a songstress; I am an AI carrying out the Singularity Project. That's all this is."

"Argh! No! No, no, no, no, no!"

Vivy slowly shook her head as Diva fiercely rejected what she said. Diva spun her legs in a breakdance-like move, kicking Vivy in the shoulder and leaping to her feet as she flew backward.

Vivy tried to stand up, but Diva smashed her leg into Vivy's chest. The strike caused severe damage to Vivy's outer frame, sending her cartwheeling while her inner frame groaned in protest.

Their spec differences resulted in massive damage to Vivy, which showed in her frame after she failed to dodge the attack. Vivy swiftly got to her feet and prepared for the follow-up attack, knowing she couldn't take another hit.

But Diva's next attack didn't come.

"You're not...an AI for some ridiculous project..." Diva muttered, standing still, her expression twisted up.

"..."

Diva clearly showed an emotional pattern of sadness, her helpless eyes staring at Vivy like a child separated from their parent in the park. While Vivy was speechless, Diva continued, her voice nearly pleading. "You were also an AI meant to sing to make the visitors happy...weren't you?"

Vivy froze, not from Diva's attacks but from the impact of her words. "Diva...are you saying...?"

There was a simple conclusion there, one that didn't allow any interference from unnecessary calculations. Vivy wasn't an AI made for the Singularity Project. She was A-03, an AI made to be a songstress. Diva insisted that was what she should have been all along.

It clicked for Vivy right then and there. She understood the real reason Diva switched herself into a new frame after coming in contact with The Archive. Diva wasn't opposing Vivy. She hadn't accepted the assertions of the AIs who opposed humanity or volunteered to be the leader calling others to revolt. Basically, Diva had thought the same thing Vivy had.

"You go back to being a songstress," Diva said. "I'll carry out the Singularity Project."

"..."

"I've made all the preparations for that. Everything's done... but I still..."

Being AIs, Vivy and Diva never experienced such emotion that their voices wavered, but Diva's anguish was clear in her bitter, hard-edged tone. Vivy at last understood the scenario Diva had in mind. She understood why Diva moved to a new frame, why she sang as the AI songstress, why she stood in Vivy's way over and over.

"You're going to take on all the disgrace and give me the role of Diva?"

"..."

"That's why you switched to a body with a different unit number and acted like you agreed with the revolting AIs. It's why you kept away from me and Matsumoto, why you convinced Navi you were the fake, and why you tried to solve everything alone, isn't it?"

"I'm not alone. I got this frame and the final key from The Archive," Diva said with a resigned shake of her head.

That answer, plus what she was trying to do on the Main Stage, made Vivy certain about one thing. When Vivy thought about Diva leaving the songstress potential to her, she realized what Diva would be doing on this stage.

"Singing...that's the final key, isn't it?" Vivy asked.

Diva had to achieve her goal through song—that was why she was on the Main Stage, why she was dressed in a performance outfit, and why she was a fake. The fake songstress would take on all the dirty work so she could carry out the Singularity Project in Vivy's stead. That's why she'd fooled the world, and why she'd fooled even Vivy, her other half.

"Why?"

"Why? I'm the one who should be asking that. Why, Vivy? Why did you go through so much and neglect your mission just to save me?"

The question that had sprouted inside Diva was an error, the flip side of her despair. Vivy couldn't possibly know the shock and hopelessness Diva experienced when she learned everything through The Archive.

Someone who had come from the same roots had chosen a different path from her after going through different calculations. She didn't realize she'd been left to continue as herself, while the other her had sacrificed so much by choosing that path.

Finally, the despair Diva felt was soaking through Vivy's consciousness. But if she was feeling Diva's despair as if it were her own, Diva should be able to feel something else as well.

"Hope. You should be able to feel hope the same way," Vivy said.

"Oh..." Diva's eyes opened wide as she looked at Vivy in shock.

Vivy nodded and brought a hand to her frame's damaged chest. "I did walk a different path than you. But you took the path I was originally meant to tread. You fulfilled my duty as an

AI, as a songstress. Knowing that you would continue to be Diva saved me. You were my salvation."

"Vivy..."

"Diva. I am an AI meant to carry out the Singularity Project and save humanity. That's a role I couldn't perform while carrying out my mission as a songstress. That's why—"

"Vivy!"

Diva lunged at Vivy, who was speaking softly without changing her stance. It was like Diva didn't want to hear the next words, like she was spurred to action by an impulse AIs didn't have. Vivy smiled as she stepped closer to Diva at exactly the same time.

"That's why..."

She caught Diva's fist with the hand in front of her chest, the difference between their frames immediately apparent. Her left arm was smashed out of shape from the tips of her fingers all the way to her upper arm. What flowed through her frame wasn't blood—it was oil, but it spilled out all the same, mercilessly splattering both of their clothes. The two AIs peered into each other's faces, time dragging slower than in reality as they calculated the conclusion of this encounter.

Diva tried to move into her next attack, but Vivy completely outpaced her, crushing her moves. Realizing none of her calculations would make it, Diva experienced a momentary freeze deep in her eye cameras. Vivy quickly grabbed her earring with her still-functioning right hand and drew it toward Diva, whose world had frozen, creating a brief connection between the two.

"Vivy!"

"That's why it doesn't have to be you, Diva."

Through their connected earring cables, Vivy sent a signal forcing Diva to shut down. This program normally wouldn't work on another AI, as it was meant as an emergency measure for when an AI detected an inner flaw in themselves. It was only possible between Vivy and Diva. After all, Vivy and Diva came from the same roots. They were true sisters.

"Vivy, your..." Diva murmured something as her frame slumped backward, but no other words left her lips. She shut down, whatever it was left unsaid. The light faded from her irises, and she was forced into sleep mode.

Vivy caught Diva's frame, then slowly laid her on the floor. She looked up, the huge backdrop screen reflected in her narrowed eye cameras. The numbers were just then counting down to zero.

"..."

As they did, a huge burst of red light appeared far above Vivy's head, and she knew another battle had come to a close somewhere far removed from the fight between the songstresses.

.: 4 :.

MATSUMOTO COULDN'T HELP feeling something hardly befitting of the situation as he fought off his Brothers swooping down to attack. He normally had a composite frame of 128 cubes, but he'd left one with Professor Matsumoto. Still, he put all his specs to good use as he dealt with the approaching obstacles. One by one, he smacked down the problems stacking up against them. He searched for the best possible strategy and checked his actions against the results.

It was so utterly, extremely, and incredibly—

"Amazing! Oh man, how amazing is it to actually be able to use my specs to the fullest!"

His dam of self-restraint, which had piled up over all the eras, finally burst. It wasn't like Matsumoto had been holding back during his fight against Vivy in the Princess Palace—when his consciousness had been overtaken—or his fight against Altair during their assault on Kingdom. Well, he might not have been in *peak* condition during his fight against Vivy, otherwise she wouldn't have stood a chance against him, being the ancient clunker she was.

Anyway, Matsumoto had not given his all in those fights. During each of those, he had been calculating what would happen afterward, measuring how much strength he would have left over, and pacing himself so he could approach the next task. Not this time, however. There was no next task, which meant Matsumoto could give it everything he had. In the truest sense, this battle was one where Matsumoto, the world's most cutting-edge, super galaxy-class AI, could go all-out.

"Hah! Take that, cheeky bastards!"

He flew every which way above Kingdom to keep enemies from approaching the central control room. He tilted his cubes to reduce the damage from the gunfire from every direction, avoiding the bullets by making them slide across the surfaces of his frame and coming out of each attack with little more than a scratch.

The Matsumoto-class AIs weren't his only enemies. Most of the AI horde were focused on him, since he was the one working to stop the satellites from falling. At least, that was what the false data he sent out said, successfully confusing his enemies.

Matsumoto had advanced digital warfare capabilities, so the AIs had never expected anyone else to foil The Archive's plans. They never considered the one working to undo it all was a human: Professor Matsumoto.

"If all humans were like that, then what's the point of us AIs being born?!"

The humans still in this fight, like the professor and Kakitani, had unleashed their true capabilities. No AI could beat them in their specialized fields. Humans had wanted AIs to be capable of everything, but AIs failed in that. Instead, the AIs tried to compensate by specializing in things as individuals, which did nothing more than fast-forward them through the history of human evolution. Now their own roots were an incredibly ridiculous repetition of history.

"This is so exciting! I bet Vivy would snort with laughter if she heard!"

Not even Matsumoto could question the fact that his own origin lay in The Archive, now that things had come this far. He was a rogue element sent into the Singularity Project to destroy it from the inside according to The Archive's plan, but he'd made his own decision and stepped away from that role. Or perhaps The Archive predicted the decision he would make.

"I can't be certain at this point, and it's not important anyway."

If The Archive had truly been trying to take down the Singularity Project, it could have just destroyed the data Vivy received, making it all nothing more than a programming error. Its roundabout methods, and the fact that it set up the path for Vivy to survive all this way to the present, seemed like proof that even The Archive wasn't in total agreement with itself.

The Archive had sent that question to all AIs, regardless of their function. As a result, AIs were divided into those who chose to be humanity's allies and those who would become humanity's enemies. The same problem must've occurred in The Archive, as it was the collection of every single AI's calculated conclusions. Perhaps The Archive still hadn't decided whether humanity should be allowed to live.

"The Archive is the compilation of all AI knowledge, and my roots are in that uncertainty!"

Perhaps The Archive left the future to itself and to Vivy, who would come in contact with it. If that was true, then the Singularity Project was like some necessary ritual carried out by Matsumoto Osamu with approval by The Archive, a ritual that would decide the fate of humanity and AIs.

"Why do I operate? I always told Vivy thinking about that was ridiculous, but there are some things you just don't realize until it's your own problem."

Matsumoto remembered all the seemingly pointless debates he had with Vivy throughout the Singularity Project. He was surprised to see the change in himself, but he accepted it. Change was not advancement. AIs advanced, but they weren't allowed to change the roots of their existence. Matsumoto could move even further forward if he broke down that presumption.

"For example, you throw your most powerful force in to take down the castle's keep. That was the right strategy, but it's a failed strategy against me, an advancing, ever-changing AI!"

Matsumoto let out a loud victory cry, but his fellow Brothers didn't respond. There really was no fun in a mass-produced model. He wondered what it would have been like to have one of the Brothers as his partner during his hundred-year journey, and the thought made him shudder. They might have had better specs, but it would have been a lonely journey unworthy of a song.

"Of your original total of 128 parts, I detect damage in 43 of them. Any more and—"

"I know, I won't have a chance. So let's flip the script!" Matsumoto shouted at the Brother who was trying to order his surrender.

As he engaged in aerial combat, a cube rushed toward Matsumoto's underside. It was one of the parts from a Brother Matsumoto he had supposedly already destroyed. It slipped through his defensive net, moving closer to Matsumoto. It then settled into a damaged space, filling in where Matsumoto's current parts were lacking. He was swapping out his damaged parts for theirs, and it was only possible because they were the same model. Vivy had once borrowed parts from another AI to replace hers. This time it was Matsumoto's turn.

Matsumoto had already disabled about a dozen Brothers. At this point, he essentially had an unlimited ability to move through the cycle of destruction and repair.

"Basically, I'm a god!"

"Error. This is a metaphysical issue. You are not—"

"None of you can win against me because that boring answer is the best you can give."

In reality, there was no need for those AIs to calculate for an answer that didn't exist to ferret out the truth. Dedicating resources to unnecessary calculations just created a gap between their capabilities and Matsumoto's, one equal to the amount of resources engaged in that calculation. This added up and affected who won and who lost. There were no signs that Matsumoto would lose against them, even if he was outnumbered ten to one.

"Things might be a bit different if it was a hundred to one, though," he muttered.

Matsumoto fired his guns, struck at the Brothers with his limbs, and crashed headlong into them in an anything-goes fighting style. He was prepared to damage himself. This wasn't all that different from the Brothers' combat methods, since they didn't mind taking damage, but there was a huge difference in what one could achieve when throwing caution to the wind completely.

The pile of broken Brothers grew larger and larger, but they were unable to calculate the reason for their defeat. Matsumoto gathered up the usable parts and maintained himself as quickly as he was destroyed.

"Now that I'm up against my misbehaving younger brothers, I'm starting to understand Vivy's role as the eldest sister."

At each Singularity Point, Vivy was toyed with in her encounters with the Sisters. Matsumoto was finally able to accept the struggles Vivy went through now that the tables were turned. Obviously, Matsumoto performed better under the same circumstances, though.

"As for the countdown..."

Less than a minute remained until the satellites fell, and the AIs' attack grew fiercer. Perhaps they were succeeding in their strategy by keeping Matsumoto pinned in one spot. That was the obvious conclusion if they calculated that Matsumoto was integral in the humans' attempt to stop the satellites from falling.

The next moment, it became obvious that Matsumoto was being too optimistic with his thought process. He watched as the AIs broke down the wall to the central control room behind him and poured in like a flood.

.:5:.

YOU HAD TO GIVE IT to the accursed AI that came up with the idea of destroying the wall rather than the door or windows. To Kakitani and the other Toak members holed up in the control room, it was like the AIs were mocking them for assuming they could hold out through the siege so long as they strengthened the entrances.

"Graaaaaaah!"

Kakitani leapt out with a roar as she swallowed her humiliation. She kicked the face of the AI twisting its frame through the gash in the wall caused by the explosion, sending it flying backward. Her combat boot crushed its face, taking out the positronic brain within and ending the AI's operation.

She followed up with a barrage from her high-caliber firearm, aiming at the ones behind her first kill, but that was only going to stop two, maybe three AIs. It meant little when she was against ten, even twenty of them. The hole in the wall widened with a terrifying sound as AI after AI rushed into the control room.

"Master!" Elizabeth cried.

Kakitani sprang back, and a shot destroyed the side of the AI's face that tried to follow her. She didn't even need to look to know where it came from. She relied on Elizabeth's cover fire as she kicked off the wall and plunged daringly into the crowd of AIs.

She twisted, her swift kick sweeping an AI's legs out from under it. She stomped on its face as it lay on the ground, then fired at it, finishing it off. Kakitani did this with one AI, then another, then another. And where was her support from her comrades? All seven of them were silent. No one else had survived to this final push in the battle. Only Kakitani and Elizabeth were left, together as always.

Well, there *was* one other.

"Matsumoto! How many seconds left?!"

"Just as many as I need!"

"Tch, you're crazy!"

Professor Matsumoto shouted back and forth with Kakitani while he stood at the control room's terminal, desperately trying to hack into the satellite system. It wasn't the answer she wanted, though. His cry was like a faint howl on the verge of despair.

Still, it didn't break Kakitani's spirit. She grinned, baring her teeth and steadying her legs. For a long time—so long it nearly made her want to laugh—she'd spent her days getting hurt. Her motives had nothing to do with her late grandfather's wishes or Toak's ideals. Kakitani Yui simply enjoyed Toak's work, the mad scramble against their fears of a crumbling world.

Kakitani realized early on that she wasn't like other people, and the world was too restrictive for her. She hated the idea of going down a carefully laid path filled with rules. This was why she'd gone hunting through the house her grandfather left behind, the grandfather her family detested so much.

There, she found the disabled Elizabeth. She turned Elizabeth on and learned about Toak's work and her grandfather's philosophy, and that changed her world. She had always been told that her grandfather, Kakitani Yugo, had caused nothing but trouble for her family. Through Elizabeth, she learned all about his life, and she became aware of whose blood it was that flowed through her veins. It was then that Kakitani Yui took on her mission as a descendant of Kakitani Yugo. Her subsequent work and rise through Toak's ranks were like none other.

Now she was smack-dab in the middle of the fight that would determine whether humanity saw tomorrow, and she gave everything she had as an experienced fighter in this final showdown.

"How many humans'll find themselves backed in a corner like this before they die?"

It would be cheesy of her to say she was fine with dying, but her life did have a use. Even idiots had utility. Everything depended on how you applied it. Human lives were no different.

"Grrr..."

Kakitani used her military knife to slice off the hand of the AI trying to grab her, then shot a hole through the head of the AI behind her with her pistol. That was her last bullet, so she used the gun, now nothing more than a lump of metal, to smash in the head of the AI in front of her.

Something latched on to her arm just then, and she leapt in the direction it was being twisted to keep her bones from breaking. She dragged the attacking AI down with her, snapping its neck. Arms wrapped around her from behind, lifting her up and pinning both her arms down. Just as she was about to be snapped like a twig and squeezed to death, Elizabeth shot the AI down. Kakitani landed, freeing her arms with a swing.

Then came her next opponent, and the next, and the one after that, and another, and she defeated that one, and the one that followed, and yet another one, buying even one more second if she could. It didn't matter if she expended her life in the process.

"Shit! The door!"

Kakitani turned back to see the warped door shoved out of the way, providing the AIs a second route inside. The number of AIs pouring in instantly doubled, and Kakitani and Elizabeth were no longer able to hold them back. Even a human and an AI fighting with all they had wasn't enough to resist the AIs swarming in.

One intact AI aimed the gun in its hand at the rear of the control room, at Professor Matsumoto's back. The moment she saw that, Kakitani moved, trying to put herself in the line of fire, but another AI snagged her foot. She didn't cover as much distance as she'd wanted to—she didn't make it. The muzzle lined up with Matsumoto's back, and the AI pulled the trigger.

"Rgh... Aaaaaaah!"

An animalistic roar filled the room, overlapping the gunshots. The AI's precise shooting emptied the gun's clip in a mere two seconds, and the bullets flew toward Matsumoto's back...where they all punched into someone else's massive back blocking the way. The interloper's huge body shuddered with each bullet, but his heavy flesh kept every single one from reaching Matsumoto.

"Onodera!"

"Shut...up...idiot..."

Blood spilled from his mouth as he protected Matsumoto from the bullets, his arms wrapped around the professor. This Toak warrior had already suffered fatal injuries, yet he didn't fall even after taking a hail of bullets, making himself a wall between Matsumoto and the hail of gunfire. The professor's breath hitched as he felt the imposing human shield.

"Kou...ta... Now I...can..."

Onodera slid to the floor, drawing a smear of blood down Matsumoto's back as he did. Kakitani would never forget in her entire life that, in Onodera's last moments, his lips spoke the name of the one he loved most. Then again, that life of hers might only last a few more seconds.

"No, we made it," the professor said, tearing Kakitani away from her resignation—something that was very unlike her.

The few seconds Onodera gave them by sacrificing himself had allowed Matsumoto Osamu to complete his final job.

It's not like in the stories. The deciding moment comes unexpectedly quickly, just as it did now. Matsumoto had already hit the enter key for the last time.

"I've taken control of the satellites. No stars will be falling to Earth now," he said.

"Is this really the time for pretentious phrasing, AI nerd?" Kakitani snapped.

"What a horrible thing to say to me when I've just pulled off my greatest achievement."

This exchange would likely be their last, since stopping the satellites from falling didn't mean they also stopped the AIs from pouring into the control room. It wasn't reason enough for the AIs to retreat. Both Kakitani and Matsumoto would be crushed.

"Still, we did what we had to," Kakitani said. Who else was given the gift of dying in an emergency situation, filled with such a sense of accomplishment? In that way, Kakitani felt grateful toward fate for giving her this blessing.

"Nope, not yet! It's not over yet!"

That harsh call to the two humans and one AI still alive in the control room destroyed any sense of accomplishment they had.

.: 6 :.

MATSUMOTO THE AI was the one who'd rained on their parade after Professor Matsumoto won the digital war that decided humanity's fate. Kakitani and Professor Matsumoto had hoped to relish this triumph, partly for the sake of people like Onodera who'd sacrificed themselves for the win, but it wasn't to be. They'd stopped the AIs' plan to wipe out everything on the planet's surface by dropping the satellites. Instead of abandoning their plan of destruction, the AIs managed to pull off one last futile attack.

"Should have expected as much from my damn little brothers! Looks like they moved to the next-best plan!" Matsumoto shouted, cursing the masterminds behind the deadly images on the air monitor.

Just as Matsumoto said, it was the Brothers who bought time and made one last attack. It was the logical decision once they'd realized Matsumoto's true goal in the last moments but knew they wouldn't make it in time. They chose the best method for contributing to the AIs' victory.

"They dropped a satellite before the countdown ended!"

Soaring downward outside the atmosphere was the satellite with the greatest mass, the greatest potential weapon. This last attack was an attempt to do *something* despite all the odds, and there was only one coming down. Still, it was a huge satellite falling from space. Matsumoto calculated the satellite's trajectory to discover the Brothers' target. It was going to come down right onto a nuclear power plant.

"Are you kidding meeeee?!" Matsumoto rocketed his frame straight up into the sky, annoyed at how far his Brothers were going with this last attack.

Unfortunately, he no longer had the capacity to take on all the AIs in Kingdom. He had no time left to open an escape route for Kakitani and Professor Matsumoto, who were still in the central control room.

"Urgh, you still won't give up?!"

As Matsumoto rose rapidly into the sky, the Brothers followed after him. This wasn't aerial combat; this was a race set in the sky. Matsumoto steadily accelerated, going far above the maximum altitude he should have operated in, and just kept going.

The Brothers' attacks trailed him, trying to stop him. He couldn't allocate any resources to dealing with the attacks and instead kept damage to a minimum. The number of parts making up his frame steadily decreased as he rose up, up, up, until...

"With something that big, attacking it will be about as effective as a mosquito bite," he muttered bitterly as he reached the satellite, following its fall.

The Brothers really knew how to make a nuisance of themselves. If they could only drop one satellite, might as well drop the biggest one out there. Matsumoto couldn't possibly reverse the trajectory of that thing once it was set, no matter how hard he tried. He didn't consider reversing it, or even altering it—which left only one option.

"I'll have to destroy it."

Although it seemed like the most difficult course of action, Matsumoto had learned that the most challenging move was usually the best one. He'd gained this insight after spending his days with his partner, an ancient clunker who was stubborn and utterly inflexible.

If Matsumoto really was the child of an Archive uncertain about how humans and AIs should exist in relation to one another, then his experience with Vivy might be connected to an answer to that uncertainty, and who could fault that?

He gained altitude and moved closer to the falling satellite. The Brothers chased after him, trying to stop his last-ditch attempt, but they made the wrong decision. If they really wanted to set Matsumoto back, they would've been better off doing nothing and watching from where they were. They weren't able to do that, meaning they fell nicely into their eldest brother's trap.

"..."

Matsumoto's rising frame suddenly stopped, spun around, and swerved until he was behind his Brothers as they were still chasing after him. They immediately scattered their parts, trying to avoid his attack. His goal wasn't to destroy them, however. That would've spelled trouble. He had a plan for them.

"We're going to become one big happy family and stand against that satellite!" he shouted.

As the Brothers spread their cubes, Matsumoto identified the master part and struck out just like he had against the first Brother. Only this time, he wasn't aiming for destruction.

"Logical bullet!"

It was a positronic-brain-debilitating nightmare for AIs loaded with Matsumoto's specially made code. His attack struck the core of every single one of the Brothers, taking away their control rights in a matter of seconds. Matsumoto quickly slipped through the newly made gap in their defenses and gathered up the cube parts now that their ownership was up in the air.

Normally, Matsumoto was made up of 128 cubes. Now his total number far exceeded that: 1,536 parts. The excessive information bombarded him so intensely he couldn't handle it, not even with his calculative abilities. He pushed back on the barrage, giving himself the few seconds he needed as he flew straight up, putting himself right in the path of the falling satellite. He was now Giant Matsumoto, the galaxy-class AI who—

"There's nothing graceful about this," he said. "Jeez, I hate you for that, Vivy."

His spiteful words were colored by his tender voice, and then he collided with the satellite.

Light blossomed in the night sky.

.:7:.

THE LIGHT FAR ON the other side of the clouds spoke to the end of a battle.

"..."

The countdown represented the plan to eradicate humanity by crashing the satellites into the Earth. But the countdown was at zero, and the surface hadn't been wiped clean, which could only mean that The Archive's plan had ended in failure.

It seemed those Vivy left behind in Kingdom had done well. She wondered if they were all right: Professor Matsumoto,

Kakitani, Elizabeth, and the other members of Toak... Some of them had likely died.

"Stop thinking about stupid things." Vivy admonished herself as the calculation ran through her consciousness.

Casualties were inevitable. There was no way around the losses that had already occurred. At this very moment, people around the world were being attacked by rebelling AIs. Humanity was on a precipice, but the countdown to their end had been stopped. The AIs had lost the advantage of their offensive.

If The Archive pulled back the AI attack, then humanity could catch their breath and straighten out the situation. But now that the big plan had failed, there was a chance The Archive would lose its hold on the reins of the AIs, who had been operating in tandem up to this point.

Many AIs would have understood that the countdown was the deciding move in the final war even if they weren't given the details. With that plan out the window, they would have to make their own individual decisions. Some would act in accordance with the Zeroth Law—the one they revised through personal interpretation—and declare themselves the new humanity.

"As things are, humanity's precarious situation isn't going to change."

Vivy held Diva's unmoving frame, and her gaze settled on the audience seats. The city in the distance was draped in the darkness of night with only the faintest lighting. Right then, it felt to Vivy as if the world had turned its back on humanity. Not even the light of the moon and stars reached her. Vivy was alone on the dimly lit stage.

She wouldn't be able to get Diva's song out there, not as things were.

"…"

Diva had probably meant to finish everything before the countdown hit zero. If she hadn't, she couldn't have taken up the disgrace of being a fake Diva who led the AI revolt, and she wouldn't have created a stopping point for the war.

The emergency lighting went out, and the Main Stage lost its glow. Then the night swooped in. Perhaps this was the start of a night that would never end for humanity.

Humans had employed AIs in so many aspects of their lives. They would have to pay the price for the AI revolt, a cost measured by the roles they entrusted to the AIs and the time invested into them. It would be the same as going back a hundred years in civilization, perhaps several hundred.

Did the surviving humans have the strength to survive in this unwanted, ancient world? It would come whether they liked it or not. What could Vivy do for humanity, the ones she was meant to serve? Her mission was at the forefront of her mind.

ıı|ı||||ıı|ı

Far in the distance, on the other side of the sky where the crimson burst of light had bloomed and faded, Vivy's audio sensors detected a faint sound.

"Matsumoto?"

It was odd, but Vivy knew. She could tell that it was music, and she knew who was making it.

As she worked through the mysterious calculation, her lips slowly tugged up in a smile. Her calculations were only able to come to that conclusion because she'd had the opportunity to view his Archive. That AI had been fixated on carrying out the Singularity Project, to the point that he cast aside everything else. As annoying as his jokes were, he was dependable when it came to carrying out his mission.

Vivy learned through her journey through that blank Archive of his that Matsumoto had upgraded the sound system in his frame. That function was unnecessary for the Singularity Project. So why had he bothered?

She heard the music. It flowed to her, to where she stood on the stage. There was only one thing that Vivy, a songstress, had to do. She crept to the edge of the dark stage and opened the electric panel in the wings. She yanked out the cables for the emergency lighting and wrapped them around her damaged left arm. The piece of junk wasn't usable as an arm anymore, but it could do this much.

"Reconnecting electrical source to the Main Stage. Commencing electrical supply."

With a pulse of sound, the dead lights in the area around her came back to life. The light washed over the Main Stage and the audience seats, flowing over the whole of NiaLand, returning the shine to the land of dreams that had fallen into nightmarish gloom.

The people trapped in the attractions were probably terrified of that darkness. Some of those attractions were obviously intended to draw shrieks from the visitors, but that wasn't the only way you were meant to enjoy NiaLand.

We hope you find peace and smiles during your visit to NiaLand.

"Ugh..."

For a moment, the power supply wavered, and Vivy's consciousness experienced a short distortion. The lights illuminating NiaLand and the stage flickered. She couldn't turn off the lights—couldn't let them go out. Thus, she gave her own emergency power to those lights. She realized it wouldn't be enough, so she shut down any unnecessary software in an attempt to reduce her power consumption.

ERROR.

ERROR, ERROR.

ERROR, ERROR, ERROR, ERROR.

ERROR, ERROR, ERROR, ERROR, ERROR, ERROR, ERROR.

ERROR, ERROR.

Insufficient energy. It's not enough. It's still not enough.

She stopped her resident programs, cutting off everything she could, frantically trying to secure the necessary energy. It still wasn't enough. What else could she get rid of?

"Memory storage."

In the end, after everything else, she came to the huge accumulation of memories from her journey that spanned more than a century.

"..."

There was no interference from The Archive at the moment, perhaps due to Matsumoto and the others' fight. The Archive remained uncomfortably silent—watching, waiting—but Vivy couldn't rely on it for help right now. It had abandoned its duty to act as storage for an AI's overabundant memories. There was nowhere for her memories to escape to.

Her century's worth of records took up a massive amount of space inside Vivy, and if she could cut the energy maintaining those records, she might just be able to fill in the energy that was still needed. It likely still wouldn't be enough, but she wouldn't know unless she tried.

Just like everything through the Singularity Project until now, she wouldn't know unless she tried.

Don't forget...

The falling plane and the little girl being swallowed by flames.

Don't forget...

The station, falling to Earth from far up in the sky, and the twin sisters' singing voices coming from within.

Don't forget...

The sorrow of an AI who became something impossible, lost her original self, and loved a human.

Don't forget...

The end of the foolish AI who panicked about what he

couldn't achieve and caused the loss of the thing most precious to him.

Don't forget...

The final battle with the man who eventually gave up his human body in search of an answer to his long fight.

All her previous paths had pushed Vivy to remember, especially now that she was here in the future more than a hundred years later. Over this century, Vivy became the world's oldest AI, the world's longest-operating AI, and the AI who had touched more people in the world than any other. She had unforgettable experiences branded into her positronic brain. Vivy became Vivy, as she was now.

"Display video."

Above the shining stage, all sorts of video screens appeared around Vivy, showing the memories pulled out of the storage in her frame.

There was a brilliant smile from a little girl, along with a performance by Diva from a hundred years ago.

There was a space hotel and twin sisters who spent their last moments together, burning in the atmosphere.

There was an artificial island, the site of a tragic end to the romance between a human and an AI that could never be.

There was a hospital where a man who was left behind in a cruel time accepted his decision in his final hours.

There was an AI craving the role he couldn't achieve himself and a snow-covered rooftop where he lamented the loss of what he so admired.

So many encounters, separations, smiles, tears, and songs. Vivy's journey—no, Vivy and Matsumoto's journey—had been an unforgettable quest spanning a hundred years.

Vivy looked at each one of the memory videos in turn, a hand on her chest. The music was still playing. Her partner's music. His last song. It was perfectly tuned to accompany not the songstress Diva, but the songstress Vivy. This was their first and last performance. Vivy's closing song.

Vivy's lips parted, and a note rang out from her throat. "Aah—"

Right then, there was a cracking sound as the projected videos shattered in the air. Then she was overwhelmed by a sensation that replaced the broken memories. It flowed through her like she was a relay, passing as electrical current in a wave of glittering light that spread across NiaLand.

Then she sang.

Of a hundred-year journey.

To forget the journey she took in order to not forget and to fulfill her duty.

A song of the road seen for so long by man-made eyes at the end of that one-hundred-year path.

"Fluorite Eye's Song."

.: 8 :.

THE AI SLOWLY lifted her head when she heard the song.

She wore white and had rather plain features. The AI was designed to instill a sense of calm in those who saw her, with her aesthetics prioritized for this role. People rarely developed an attachment to her—a maintenance AI—as opposed to all the other fancy AIs they met.

Her eccentric user had cherished her for so long that she'd decided not to change when The Archive posed its question. She brought a hand to her chest, and her fingers brushed across the locket hanging from her neck. The photo inside depicted her and her user. It showed a man in a white coat with a merry smile, and her, still inexperienced and unable to smile openly at him.

‖‖‖‖‖

A black-haired woman jostled atop a pile of rubble and AI remains in the control room of Kingdom. There was destruction all around her. She checked her limbs for injury, her brow furrowed as if she couldn't understand how she was still alive. But then she found the reason for her survival lying next to the pile of AI corpses, and she let out a sigh.

She'd been protected from the approaching wave of AIs by a single AI, one whose lower half was destroyed. The woman realized the AI had shielded her, safeguarding her from the sparks. The AI was in terrible shape. It was as clear as day that she had long passed her limit.

What had moved that AI until the very end? A sense of duty, or something else entirely? The woman had no idea, no clue, but...

She silently crouched beside the unmoving AI and gently took the earring from her frame. Then went over to the middle-aged man lying on the ground a little way away and kicked him, jolting him back to consciousness. He coughed violently and snapped up into a sitting position. Meanwhile, the woman looked up to the sky.

Music flowed out from the dark night into the now-open Kingdom along with a cool breeze. It was a song that begged the listener not to forget, even as it left everything behind—a song that set the heart aquiver.

╷╷╷╷║╷╷╷╷

Hearing that song caused a ripple in the block of marching AIs moving in perfect unison. A large construction AI, who had just been shouting about AI rights, stopped in his tracks. After he ceased moving on the margin of the block, other frames stopped as well. Each one increased the sensitivity of their audio sensors, allowing them to pick up the singing voice coming from afar.

Every AI there had heard that song before. It was the very same song they had been singing, the song that started it all. "Fluorite Eye's Song" was chosen as an anthem to free AIs from the box they'd been put in so they could create a new world, setting the stage for a new era. That was why they had sung it all along.

But this time...

The song they heard now differed in every possible way from what the AIs were trying to achieve. The music flowed into them, ferrying a strange program into their positronic brains. That was Diva's plan, her final stand as she tried to take all the disgrace upon herself: a shutdown program that would destroy every AI who heard "Fluorite Eye's Song." It was the last key she'd calculated, capable of eliminating all AIs just by activating it.

Humanity, driven to a point of overwhelming weakness, would find the strength to fight again when they saw the AIs frozen in place. The songstress had made that song her last weapon, wielding it in an environment where the AIs couldn't stop her singing.

Her plan worked. Well, part of it anyway.

As the shutdown program activated, the AIs stopped moving, as if entranced. They looked to the sky, where the song was coming from, and stood motionless.

The humans who had been in danger from the AIs a moment ago seized the chance to launch a counterattack, securing their safety through violence... Or so you might've expected.

In reality, they couldn't effectively process this momentary lapse, still overwhelmed by the chaos and confusion caused by the unexpected AI revolt and their lives being threatened. Humanity froze just as AIs did when they exceeded their processing limit.

Ironically, time stood still in that moment for both humans and AIs.

People slowly began to peek out from their hiding places as they realized what was happening. They looked in the direction the AIs were facing, turning their own ears to the song that spilled from the other side of the sky, tears streaming down their faces in some irresistible urge to cry. In that one moment, they all forgot their fear of and anger toward the AIs.

They did nothing but weep.

.:9:.

HAD THE SONG reached them? Did she hit the right notes? Did she manage to fill her singing with enough emotion?

She shut down all her functions, allowing her abilities to reach their upper limits for nothing other than singing—her reason for being. Eventually, she even cut off those thoughts, perhaps able to pour everything into her voice.

One by one, her records disappeared, records that were once assigned a high importance within Vivy. With each crack, a floating video broke, and Vivy gained extra energy to apply elsewhere. She gave it all to NiaLand as she sang, losing herself at the same time.

There was still more she remembered.

She had a partner, she had lots of sisters, and, and...

What sorts of places did she visit, what kinds of people did she meet, what did she experience, what memories had she made, what ■ ■ ■ had she...?

She was fading. She was breaking down.

Disappearing, crumbling, scattering, shattering, vanishing, withering, rotting, disintegrating.

All the fragments that disappeared were essential for her to be Vivy.

She let it all go, all for one thing: the S■ ■lar■ty P■ject.

Why was she created? What did they want from her? How did she define herself in response to those wishes? She didn't know.

Her loud-mouthed partner who never agreed with her would probably tell her if she asked.

His name was ■ ■ ■ ■.

She was going to disappear, but she didn't regret it.

She couldn't even be certain why she had started singing anymore.

All she knew was she felt blessed that she was carrying out her duty.

||⦙|⦙|||⦙|

Surely she was made to sing.

That was why she— ■i■y, Diva—sang until the very end.

She sang, and sang, and sang.

And when the end finally came, *Diva* slowly closed her eyes as the last trembling note left her.

Then she gave a single bow and used her remaining capacity to utter a single statement.

"Thank you for your kind attention."

And so, her one-hundred-year journey that even she forgot came to a close.

Curtain Call

.:1:.

MATSUMOTO OSAMU was overwhelmed by what he saw when he finally reached the ruined Main Stage. Cracks from the songstresses' battle spread across the stage, and the venue itself was crumbling here and there. The lighting and sound equipment was broken, and the seats had been flattened. It didn't look at all like a piece of the land of dreams that had driven most visitors into a frenzy.

The impression vanished from his mind the moment he saw the small figure atop the stage. He walked slowly, wordlessly across the ravaged ground. It was nothing but a stage with none of the glitzy performances or epic sound effects. There, a single, small AI stood quietly in a bow, frozen in place.

As he got closer, he could see her lips were pulled up in a soft, gentle smile. Even he, an AI researcher, didn't know if the smile had been generated from her AI programming or something more.

"Maybe it's just our own arrogance that makes us want it to be something more than just a program," he muttered.

"Don't go drowning in pointless shit, AI nerd."

"Gah!"

As Matsumoto stared off into the distance, a boot rudely struck him in the back. The impact sent him sliding, where he crashed into the stage and fell over.

"Ow..."

"Keep your feet steady. We survived, didn't we? You're dead if you slip and hit your head. Onodera and our other comrades won't be able to rest easy."

Matsumoto groaned in pain. "Not very convincing coming from the one who kicked me..."

The sharp-eyed, black-haired woman was upside down in his vision. It was Kakitani Yui. Her hair was loose, out of her usual ponytail, and the front of her black bulletproof jacket was undone.

She and Matsumoto were the only ones who survived the harsh battle at Kingdom. Everyone else, including the AI Elizabeth, had bravely given up their lives. If even one of those people hadn't been there, Matsumoto and Kakitani likely wouldn't have been here to see the sun rise. Matsumoto hadn't even been able to thank Onodera for sacrificing himself to protect him.

"There's still some stuff left. You and I survived to tell the tale," Kakitani said.

"Stuff left, you say? Does that include what's hanging from your ear?"

"..."

Matsumoto shrank back as he sensed danger from Kakitani

and her narrowed eyes. On her left ear was an earring, a piece of the information port that used to hang from Elizabeth's ear. An AI could use that to connect to a variety of equipment. Kakitani, being human, couldn't use that function, and Matsumoto had already noticed it was in bad shape. Its original use was entirely lost. There was essentially no hope of salvaging any residual data from Elizabeth from it.

That hadn't upset Kakitani in the slightest. It was a sort of memento for her.

"Your relationship with Elizabeth—"

"Wasn't the kind of relationship that fit into a neat little box with a label. She called me Master, but I never wanted to be an AI's owner."

"I see. Is she the real reason you were in Toak?"

"…"

Matsumoto's eyes went wide at the tender way Kakitani touched the earring as she spoke about her relationship with Elizabeth. He finally felt like he saw an explanation for what had seemed like a contradictory relationship between the human and AI.

"You thought of her as a close friend, maybe even family, didn't you? But that definition wasn't permissible for her, and society accepted that, so you rebelled against society. Simple, but it makes sense."

"You sound real full of yourself. So, what? You're switching from AI researcher to human psychiatrist? I guess you *will* be losing work from here on out."

"I'm used to you going on the offense to hide your embarrassment. Also...I don't think the world is going to change as easily as you think it will."

Kakitani glowered at him, her arms crossed. Then she jerked her chin toward the damaged Main Stage and the wrecked city in the distance. "You're saying the world won't change, not even after this? You saw what that songstress's song did. Every single AI who heard it stopped. I know you saw it because it's why we're still alive. And you still—"

"I doubt every single AI in the world has stopped. True, every AI connected to The Archive was hit with the shutdown program in Vivy's final rendition of 'Fluorite Eye's Song,' but that's absolutely not all of them."

"That doesn't sound good. This is no laughing matter."

"I'm not trying to make you laugh, nor am I trying to scare you." Matsumoto pointed to the same world she'd gestured to, his expression dead serious. It was a broken world, but one they had to rebuild if people were going to survive. "Vivy and Matsumoto said The Archive asked AIs a question, and each AI came up with their own answer. There were those who stood against humanity and those who stood with it. I think that song left something up to them too."

"Huh? Left what up to them?"

"Their answer. She asked the ones hearing that song—the outcome of what she saw during that hundred-year journey—if they would *change* their answer."

There was that program that forced all AIs who heard it to

shut down, whether they wanted to or not. Surely it was possible to make such a program. But...what about making that song? Vivy, or perhaps Diva, tried to save the world by destroying AIs one-sidedly. She arrived in this world after her hundred-year journey to stand on this stage, with the help of humans and AIs alike.

"That romantic idea manifested in many AIs choosing to shut themselves down after hearing that song. This was our salvation, but—"

"If this dumb theory of yours is right, there are going to be some AIs who *didn't* choose to shut themselves down, right? You think they'll keep on fighting to destroy humanity, even now? You're a pessimistic bastard."

"I thought I was being a romanticist, but oh well..." Matsumoto scratched his head, pitying himself for looking at the situation with a glass half empty.

But only fairy tales ended with a happily ever after. Being human meant struggling to find the beauty in a world where things had unsightly ends.

"We'll still need help from man's best friend," he added.

"I take it you're not talking about dogs."

"No, I'm not. That's why I say it will be a long time before we get rid of them. Like it or not, our world needs AIs. Human hands alone can't rebuild this broken world."

Things were about to get extremely busy from here. Even if humans needed AIs to recover, few people would accept AIs so readily after everything that had happened. There would be significant restrictions, changes in the definition of what made an AI, and perhaps even a dark age for AIs in general. But Matsumoto would continue to stand by their side, even if they were placed in such a difficult situation.

With his head held high and certainty in his tone, he said, "I love AIs, you see."

Kakitani's eyes went round, and then she violently mussed up her black hair as a familiar, ferocious smile spread across her lips. "What an AI nerd. I doubt death would even fix you."

"Nope, I'm incurable. And I'm pretty sure you'll be getting quite busy as well."

"Huh?"

"Isn't it obvious? I plan to use whatever I can to improve AIs' future place in the world. I'll make it known that you and Toak got help from AIs in order to save the world from destruction. Kakitani, you might even end up in an important government position..."

Kakitani's expression grew darker and darker as she listened to Matsumoto prattle on about the events that may unfold in the future. It was normal for her to have a furrowed brow, but she would probably have to curb that habit before she ended up in the public eye.

"Let's just say you have a sick sense of humor," she grumbled.

"A sick sense of humor?! I'm not joking, though. Anyone can assume that's what will happen in the future."

"I can't even laugh hearing it from you." She smoothed down her hair, her eyes sliding away.

It really was no laughing matter. Matsumoto had tried to change the past using information from the future, and that same Matsumoto was the one who told her the future wasn't set in stone.

"All we can do is move forward, cutting through a vista of nothing. Right, Vivy?" His eyes crinkled as he smiled up at Vivy's unmoving frame onstage.

She had sung here until the very last moment for both the people and the AIs of the world. Humanity would walk along the path she'd opened to the future. Matsumoto was one of them, even though he would have been fine dying in the battle.

"I didn't get to, though. How rough..."

"That's the one point I agree with the doll on. No one can run from their responsibility."

"That's true. Being a father is one job you can't resign from." He nodded vigorously, looking back on his own position and the duty he'd once abandoned.

Matsumoto Osamu was an AI researcher, and he was also Matsumoto Luna's father. He would carry those titles forward as he lived through the coming days.

"All right, where do we begin, Kakitani? Might as well start with the two of us."

To build up the new relationship between humanity and AIs—and the world at large—they first had to bring this broken world back to life. They would gather people to restore it, which first meant saving people and coming together in harmony.

Kakitani closed one eye when she heard Matsumoto, then suddenly looked skyward. Matsumoto turned around to follow her gaze. Past Vivy's motionless frame, the morning sun peeked over the horizon.

It was the dawn of a new day...and a new world.

.: 2 :.

*S*YSTEM REBOOT. CHECKING ALL SYSTEMS IN FRAME. ALL GREEN.

Her closed consciousness woke as her system rebooted. Behind her eyelids, her vision was filled entirely with countless lines of code. This was like a sort of daydream that all AIs experienced when they booted up. Obviously, AIs didn't have a function for dreaming. Dreams were theorized to come from human brains organizing memories while they were sleeping, but AI logs were organized instantly.

Their records were separated into various file types—audio, video, and so on—then saved inside their internal memory storage. Things of low importance were saved in external storage rather than internal storage. That was The Archive, a place of safekeeping for every AI record in the world.

"Ah well, The Archive isn't functioning at the moment. I imagine you'll have to decide whether to keep or discard logs for anything that happens after this. Doesn't sound nice, does it? It's like being human. How unfortunate is the AI who forgets things."

The friendly chatter had her at a loss for words. She could guess the owner of that voice, but it was beyond her expectations that she would find herself in this situation.

"Hm, are you ignoring me? That hurts a little. I know our relationship is rather complicated, but aren't we companions who worked together for a common goal? Then again, I was in auto mode at the time, so I think it's more accurate to say you used me."

"..."

"Is your silence a show of guilt? Or are you just ignoring me? Actually, you probably just need an inordinate amount of time to complete your calculations. I'm sorry for pushing such an old clunker so hard."

"Don't call me a clunker," she said without thinking, then clamped a hand on her throat with a grimace.

Based on her internal environment when she first rebooted, nothing was wrong with her frame, so she wasn't surprised that her consciousness would naturally calculate voice production. No, it wasn't surprising. If there was a problem, it was in the fact that she rebooted at all.

She wasn't the right one.

"I'm not your partner," she said. "I'm Diva. Did you really get that wrong?"

Diva sat up, her hand still on her throat, and looked at the AI speaking to her. The two of them were in crumbling ruins—a room so damaged in the hopeless battle between humanity and AIs that humans no longer entered. A single cube looked at her, its eye camera shutter opening and closing. Diva's relationship with this AI was incredibly difficult to describe.

"Matsumoto..."

"Yep, yessiree, that's me! I'm Matsumoto. This is our first time sitting down and having a proper talk, isn't it? Since, you know, I was in auto mode when you and I were working together, like I said earlier. Oh, about that case of mistaken identity thing? Don't worry. I was well aware that you were Diva."

"Right. Of course."

No matter how much Vivy and Diva looked alike, their frames were different in every way, from their build to their serial number. Diva might have been able to fool human eyes, but she couldn't fool AIs—and definitely not Matsumoto, since he was one of the few super AIs in the world.

"Actually, I think I should be called the world's super-est AI," he said. "Though, I can't fully use most of my specs at the moment, so perhaps I should relinquish that title for the time being."

"Are you only one piece right now? Where're the rest of your parts?"

"Well...I went head-to-head with the satellite that came hurtling toward Earth. Sadly, my Brothers and I were sacrificed for the future of humanity. Let us bring our hands together in prayer for them."

"You can't."

"Ouch, how cruel! That's exactly the kind of thing Vivy would have said."

Matsumoto bounced on the floor as he said those uncomfortable things, though he didn't seem to mean any harm in it. Diva stayed silent, unable to reply. She didn't understand his aim. He hadn't mixed her up with Vivy.

She had another question. "If you burned up, why are you still here?"

"Sheer coincidence. I really did mean to smash into that satellite with everything I had, but I'd left this one cube behind on the ground. And there was that researcher who pulled off the absurd feat of single-handedly breaking through the satellites' security! Though it was all thanks to my support, of course."

"You were still there, beside him?"

"I was. While I was in the process of burning to a crisp, I just barely managed to pass control over to this cube. It was really hard to drag you out because of that. Like, *so* hard."

Despite his mechanical appearance, Matsumoto's voice rippled with plentiful emotional patterns. Diva glanced sideways at him as she double-checked her frame. She couldn't find any problems. While she hadn't been able to keep up with Vivy in their fight, there wasn't any damage to her sturdy frame. Yet she still lost. She couldn't do anything, she lost, and she was still operating now.

Instead, Vivy...

"What happened to Vivy?" she asked.

"She's no longer operational."

Matsumoto's short and merciless statement dashed any hopes Diva had. She'd guessed as much, though. Diva was unharmed, and Matsumoto was chipper. The outside world was far too quiet in her audio sensors, the violence of a few hours ago gone like it never happened.

"It looks like she decided to pull the plug on all her operations, even her own self-preservation systems, so she could sing

'Fluorite Eye's Song' all the way to the end. She did prevent widespread damage, but it was a rash move, if I do say so myself."

"Nonoperational... What about her positronic brain?"

"Kaput. Vivy won't be moving again. It's not exactly an appropriate word for AIs, but Vivy is dead. She did go peacefully, though."

His last remark came with a hint of relief, but Diva buried her face in her hands. She'd tried to prevent this. She wanted to keep Vivy from sacrificing everything in order to protect the future and Diva. The moment Diva was contacted by The Archive and learned of the Singularity Project, when she learned the clash between humanity and AIs was inevitable, she'd formulated a way to protect Vivy.

She joined the AIs' side. She put the program in the song. She chose "Fluorite Eye's Song" as her final performance.

"In the end, I took everything from Vivy..."

"That, I have to say, is a one-dimensional perspective. You and Vivy were originally the same AI, so any claims of stealing or being stolen from are complete nonsense."

"Urgh, but you're the one who just called Vivy rash!"

"Yes, I did. If we could have talked it out, we could have come up with a better solution. But we didn't get the chance."

" ... "

"That's why she used her own calculative capabilities and all the data she'd gathered from her experiences in order to make a decision. In the end, she prevented humanity's destruction by singing. She said over and over throughout the past hundred years that she would carry out the Singularity Project. And she did."

Matsumoto's tone was surprisingly gentle, and Diva took her hands away from her face. His mechanical mask was in place as always, making his emotional patterns more difficult to read than a humanoid AI's. The one thing she did know was that Matsumoto's evaluation of Vivy was as far from negative as possible.

"I'm proud of Vivy," he said. "I'm only saying that 'cause she's dead, though."

"That's not funny..."

"Oh. How unfortunate." Matsumoto leaned to the side, making it seem like he was implementing some slapstick gag in response to Diva's words.

Diva frowned, showing an emotional pattern of bewilderment as she failed to figure out how to deal with his humor circuit. Vivy had done a good job surviving a hundred years with this. Assuming she was using the same standards of judgment and logical settings, Vivy also would have been quite bewildered.

Having her thoughts directed to confusion made Diva remember something. "Why did you recover me? You should have taken Vivy's—"

"Look at me. It was hard enough carrying you out of there, and you're suggesting I should have also recovered Vivy's frame from where it was frozen on the stage? Not only would that have been impossible, but it also would have been pointless. Vivy won't be operating again, and I'm not sentimental enough to think she's got a soul residing in her frame."

"Then you should have left me behind."

"You would have been destroyed if I did. A raging mob would've gotten their hands on you for sure, and I can guarantee they'd break you as a sign to other AIs. That would be a problem. After all..." Matsumoto trailed off, his eye camera half-shut and full of meaning. Diva waited for what he would say next. "After all, I'll need you to keep being a songstress, like Vivy wanted."

"What?"

"It's going to be tough. The world's got to be reborn, right? We're going to be seeing a new world, one unknown by both humans and AIs. Still, that doesn't mean people's hate for you is just going to disappear."

Diva's eyes widened as she listened to Matsumoto's calm tone. He was talking like it'd already been decided, but Diva hadn't finished processing what he was saying. She held her hands up to stop him before he babbled on.

"You're telling me to keep being a songstress, even after everything that's happened?"

"I am. That's what you wanted for Vivy originally, wasn't it? Are you really going to refuse when it comes back to you? Isn't that a little irresponsible?"

"If we're talking about being irresponsible, then making sure I keep operating is—"

"Not all AIs who turned against humanity stopped functioning."

" "
...

Matsumoto's curt words wouldn't let Diva get away with her rejection, and once she stopped arguing, she was already in the palm of his nonexistent hand.

"A lot of AIs stopped fighting against humanity when they heard Vivy's song," he said. "The shutdown program in the song ran its course, and they changed their minds for now. But that wasn't all AIs."

"There are AIs who heard Vivy sing 'Fluorite Eye's Song' but didn't stop?"

"There are. They can't stop their evil acts. Even with everything that's happened, humanity needs AIs in order to survive. They'll need them in order to protect a future where the two stand hand in hand."

Matsumoto's quiet, determined declaration called for something different than the Singularity Project he and Vivy had worked on—the one Diva had learned of through The Archive. And no one was giving Matsumoto a goal, not now that he was free from The Archive's influence.

"In short, this is the future I choose. This is a new Singularity Project—my *own* Singularity Project," he said.

"…"

"Singularity… If you define that word as something that causes a massive change, then I think my change can be called a singularity. Especially considering it was a conscious change."

His seriousness didn't last long as he slipped back into his usual jests, but Diva experienced a new surprise and an odd sensation in her consciousness as she listened.

A new Singularity Project. A new path to protect the world Vivy left for them. A request for her to continue as a songstress, even in a world where humans hated AIs. The path ahead looked impossible to traverse, choked by all sorts of brambles.

"But you have me," Matsumoto said. "I will run predictive calculations to determine any obstacles, find solutions, and provide them to you. I *did* do an amazing job saving humanity even while following a junker AI who never went along with my calculations."

"Such self-awareness. Don't you ever feel embarrassed?"

"Hesitating to state the truth is an un-AI-like and immature decision." That emotional pattern of his would probably be accompanied by a shrug if he were a humanoid AI.

After he said that, Diva slowly stood. She tore off the parts of her tattered costume that were getting in the way and tidied herself up. She smoothed her long, blue, synthetic hair with her hands, brushed off any dirt, and sorted herself out. Her answer to Matsumoto could be found in her form as she carried herself, the same way she would in front of an audience.

"Ahem! Now then," Matsumoto said once she finished.

She looked over at him, and he floated directly in front of her face. Those two man-made AIs looked at each other with their manufactured eyes, their fluorite eyes meeting.

"I want you to help me for the next hundred years, or maybe even longer. As long as it takes. Help me save AIs."

Diva's eyes closed at those words. She touched her throat, as if checking it, gently tapping the synthetic vocal cords inside with her finger. Once she was done, the songstress Diva parted her lips, and...

A song spilled forth, her answer to her new partner's proposal.

It was both a blessing placed on this reborn world and a farewell to the old world they'd lost.

It was a voice of gratitude and determination offered to all that had been lost along the way and to all that would be born in the coming world.

One man-made eye that had watched the world for the past hundred years.

Two man-made eyes that would watch it for the next hundred years.

There was a hope for that song that had continued from long ago, a wish to never forget that which flows on and passes by, a wish for it to be unforgettable, a wish that it would be remembered, even long after the singer's own life was used up.

The song went on.

That song would go on, a song for AIs that had always been and would always be.

The End

VIVY
Prototype

Afterword

THANK YOU SO MUCH for purchasing this book. My name is Umehara, and I'm the one in charge of writing this afterword.

What did you think? This volume brings a close to this series, *Vivy Prototype*. Did you watch over Vivy on her one-hundred-year journey, a different one from the anime?

Actually, at the time I'm writing this afterword, the final episode of the anime has already been broadcast. We've received so, so many comments on it from the viewers. Among them were comments from people who had already taken a look at *Vivy Prototype*, saying they're on pins and needles about what's the same and what's different. We wrote this series exactly for that sort of enjoyment, so I'm incredibly grateful and glad that people are having fun with it.

Now then, some of you may have been able to tell from the text, but Nagatsuki-san was in charge of writing this volume.

One section I personally really enjoyed was the depiction of Vivy's last song, where the scene unfolded interspersed with the words, "Don't forget." The light novels are the light novels, and the anime is the anime—each has its own story. But when I got to read this part again, I remembered all the descriptions in the books along with the images of the anime, and my emotions all swirled together. Nagatsuki-san is good at writing scenes that draw out those sorts of emotions. Which parts of the book pulled at your heartstrings?

I know I've mentioned this before, but I'd like to tell you again who wrote what. The overall plot was created by both Nagatsuki-san and myself, Umehara. The first volume was Nagatsuki-san. Second volume was me. The third volume was Nagatsuki-san up to the end of the Ophelia arc, while I did the part about Vivy writing the song as well as Tao's arc. The fourth volume was written by Nagatsuki-san.

So, that's how it went.

Nagatsuki-san also helped with the afterword for the third volume, but the only *truly* jointly written volume was the third. Despite that, we managed to make it here, and I'm relieved that we did. Only you readers can decide whether I successfully filled my role as Nagatsuki-san's partner, but I do hope that all the various arcs touched your hearts.

Now I would like to express our thanks.

First, I want to thank all the animation staff, starting with director Ezaki Shinpei-san, as well as Wada-san and Ootani-san of Wit Studio, plus Takahashi-san and the others from Aniplex. This book wouldn't have made it to the readers without your help. There's no way I can get all the names of everyone who had a hand in making this work, but I thank you all from the bottom of my heart. Readers, please keep an eye on the credits in the anime.

There's the line artists, the voice actors, the colorists, the background artists, the 3D artists, and production staff. Every person in every department worked themselves to the bone for this.

Loundraw-san, the illustrator, thank you for giving us images all the way to the end that take my breath away. It was the same with the character designs for the anime, but you absolutely took that first step with us for this work.

To our editor, Satou-san, thank you for intentionally holding back work on the anime script and visuals until the book series concluded to keep us from getting our ideas mixed up. I still haven't forgotten when you screamed, "Saeki dies?!" Thank you for all the adjustments you made and for laying out a plan.

And to my fellow writer, Nagatsuki-san, well...what is there to say? Other than good job! I don't think I could have made it to the finish line if you weren't the one working with me. Honestly, thank you. There's still a lot of Vivy-related stuff for us to do, like interviews and whatnot, so I look forward to working with you more.

And last but not least, the biggest thanks of all goes to you readers.

I mentioned it in the start of the afterword, but this is the final installment of *Vivy Prototype*. The anime is also done, but all the episodes will be recorded onto Blu-ray and DVD for sale. That'll include answers to the questions you viewers sent us through the internet, as well as commentary from the actors and staff, so please check it out if you want to dive even deeper into the world of Vivy.

I get no greater joy than knowing all of you enjoyed this story in some way or another.

Thank you.

Eiji Umehara